Also Available From Jacy Morris

This Rotten World:

No More Heroes

By Jacy Morris

Table of Contents:

Prologue

Chad Mauer stood regarding the Bronson Farm. Down at the bottom of the hill, a tin shed where the tractors were kept rusted in the morning sun. He knew every tractor in that shed inside and out. He had driven them for the last five years. Off to the west of the hill, fields rolled, flush with row after row of crimson clover. Old Man Bronson's other fields were busy growing corn, potatoes, and watermelons, but the field next to the house was a sea of blood-red from atop the hill.

It was fitting Chad thought, all those blood-red leaves. He had worked for Bronson for five years, helping the man plant and harvest his crops. It was a hard life, but it paid the bills. But that's all it did. It paid the bills. It did nothing else for him. It didn't prevent Old Man Bronson from looking down his long, red nose at him. It didn't change Bronson's thoughts regarding the love that Chad and Bronson's daughter Desiree shared. It didn't give him enough money to move up in the world. All the job did was help Chad pay the bills.

He thought about his shitty trailer in the woods, where he had spent that very summer morning, glued to the TV as the sky lightened outside. Reed, his brother, paid for the satellite with his disability money; otherwise, Chad would have never been able to afford such a luxury. He still had trouble believing the news reports.

An image of a teenage boy in a letterman's jacket gnawing on the face of a firefighter kept popping into his head. He still struggled to accept those images as fact. *No. There was no fucking way that was real. No fucking way.* For a moment, Chad almost turned around and went right back home. He didn't have to go to work. No one would be working for the next few days until the world managed to sort itself out again. He would have left if it weren't for Dez. If this was all real, and not just some sort of huge joke, then he still had to worry about her.

Despite her father's general adeptness at taking care of anything that might pop up, Chad felt that Dez would be safer with him. Hell, her old man probably didn't even own a TV. That hardass son of a bitch only knew how to do two things: work and sleep. If what was going down was really going down, then Dez would be safer off with him. No doubt about it.

"Come on. Let's go get her." Chad picked his way down the hillside. Two seconds later he heard the shuffling footsteps of his brother Reed coming after him. His brother was twisted in the way that junkies often were. He had spent so much time high that reality seemed like a nightmare to the poor guy. His brain was fried, and he had spent months in and out of prisons and then subsequent mental institutions when they found out he was hardly capable of thinking for himself.

Chad was the only family Reed had left. His parents had disowned Reed after their truck went missing, only to be found by the police, crashed into a ditch with a zonked out of his mind Reed behind the wheel. If it had just been the truck, maybe his parents wouldn't have lost it on him. But in the middle of the night, he had managed to pawn several family heirlooms to his dealer in exchange for some meth. His mom never wanted to see Reed again, and that meant his dad, who had never seemed to care all that much for the two kids he had fathered, didn't really want to see him either.

Now, Chad was his caretaker. He tried to be at least. There was only so much you could do for a junkie. His brain was no longer the same. It was like something inside that skull of his had been severed. Despite all of this, there

2

was no one that Chad would rather have at his side. His parents might have bailed on him, but because of this, Reed had an undying devotion to his older brother.

Their footsteps kicked up dust as they strode through the clover, the red, flowery cones waving in the morning air. Despite his confidence, Chad felt nervous. This was not what he thought he would be doing this morning. He probably wouldn't be doing it if it weren't for Terry Ann across the way.

Chad only had a passing acquaintance with Terry Ann, but she had lived in the trailer park as long as Chad had. Reed knew her a little better, mostly because they had a lot of the same proclivities, namely drug-fueled bad decisions. There he had been, watching the red-faced man on Fox News, the only news that mattered, when all of a sudden Terry Ann had appeared at the screen door, banging on the ratty aluminum.

"Jesus, you scared me!" he said, his hands clutching the shotgun in his hands. After a half-hour of watching scenes of carnage on the TV, he had gone and fetched it from his room. Somehow, holding it made him feel better. You could never be too careful in a trailer park, and the news said that whatever was happening was happening everywhere.

Terry Ann said nothing; she just kept clumsily grasping at the screen door, as if she had no idea how to use it.

"Christ almighty! What the fuck do ya want?" He rose from his chair and approached Terry Ann, still holding the shotgun in his hands. She didn't respond.

From the back hallway, Reed appeared, his eyes puffy from too little sleep, scratching at the mop of curly black hair on his head. "What's that noise?"

"It's just Terry Ann, wasted out of her fucking mind again. Go back to bed, Reed."

"Does she want a piece?" Reed asked, jiggling his crotch with his hands. Chad didn't have time to respond to Reed, as Terry Ann finally figured out how to work the door.

"Whoa, whoa, whoa!" he yelled. "You can't just come in here, Terry Ann!"

She shouldered her way through the door, her arms held out to him like some sort of movie monster. That's when he saw the needle sticking out of her arm.

"You want us to run a train on you?" Reed joked.

Terry Ann turned toward the sound, her arms reaching for his brother. Chad knew there was no going back. He pulled the trigger, and buckshot ripped through Terry Ann's skull and sheered through the faux, wood-paneling that lined the trailer's walls. Morning sunlight shined through the holes in the wall.

Reed jumped backwards, his eyes going wide and his mouth opening and closing in an effort to string together the appropriate words to say. It was almost comical, if it weren't for the dead girl on the ground, leftover brains sliding out onto the floor. Reed never did get those words out, even when Chad squatted down and grabbed Terry Ann by the ankles and dragged her out of the trailer. Her body thumped down the rickety wooden porch, and he deposited her body underneath the pine trees that kept the residents of the trailer park from seeing the highway, or being seen by the judgmental drivers passing by on their way to the beach.

Other people began poking their heads out of their trailers, but he just waved at them and told them to get back inside. If they had called the cops, Chad didn't know, but by the time he and his brother had struck out for Old Man Bronson's farm, they had seen neither hide nor hair of the police.

In Chad's mind, either the world was actually going to shit, or he would wind up in prison for what he had done to Terry Ann. He had nothing to lose now, except for Reed and Dez. There was nothing that he couldn't do now. He had already broken the rule, the big one. Killing someone... that could get him the death penalty. He tried not to think about it as he walked across the field, his brother following closely behind him.

"Whatever happens, don't shoot unless I say so," Chad said.

Reed said nothing. Chad crossed his fingers and hoped that Reed had gotten the message.

Before they reached the edge of the field, the door to Bronson's house swung open, and the old man was there, his own shotgun in his hands. He raised it up over his head in a welcoming gesture, though his words were anything but. He stepped out onto the brown dust of his driveway and came to meet them.

"I see you there, Chad. You guys just turn around and go back where you came from. It ain't safe out here."

The old man had a knack for stating the obvious. "That's why we come out here. Wanna make sure you guys are alright."

The old man nodded. "We're doing just fine, but you guys probably want to hole up somewhere until this whole thing blows over."

Stubborn old bastard is gonna get himself killed. "You sure you don't want us to stick around? More guns is more safety."

"Nope. It's alright. We'll make do. Things ain't bad right now. Maybe come back tomorrow."

"I'm not sure I can do that," Chad said.

He saw the old man's jaw clench. It was a familiar foible of his. When Chad asked for a raise, the jaw clenched. When he asked for the day off, the jaw clenched. When he asked for Dez' hand in marriage, the jaw clenched.

5

Then something else clenched... Chad's finger. The old man flew backwards, a hole in his chest. In the dirt, blood splatter made dark spots around the man, and he lay on his back looking up at the sun, the gun far from his clenching hands. The old man coughed, and blood rose from his mouth for a moment, backlit by sunshine, before gravity took a hold of it and splashed it over the old man's face.

The screen door banged open with a screech, and the old man's wife came running out and down the steps. He saw Dez standing behind the screen, her eyes big and her hand to her mouth. What the hell had he done?

"You murderer!" Hannah Bronson yelled at him, tears streaming from her eyes. A cloud of dust kicked up as she squatted over her husband. How long had they been married? Thirty years? Forty?

"Man, that was badass," his brother said from his shoulder. Chad jumped as there was another bang. Then Hannah Bronson slumped over her dead husband, the side of her homespun blue dress stained with her own blood.

"You didn't have to kill her," Chad said.

"You didn't have to kill the old man," Reed said, "but you did."

His logic was infallible, and somewhere in Chad's brain he felt something happening to him. He felt power. For the first time in his life, he felt control, and he liked it. This whole dead rising from the grave thing... it might actually work in his favor. The sound of sobbing broke him from his rare moment of introspection.

"You want I should shoot her too?" Reed asked.

"No. I don't, you dumbass. That's gonna be my wife." Chad let his rifle drop to his side, and then he climbed the stairs of the old farmhouse. Dez still stood at the screen door, tears running from her eyes and snot running from her nose. Chad reached out slowly and pulled the door open, the wire spring creaking loudly. Dez stood there, in shock. She didn't acknowledge his presence.

Chad held his rifle out to Reed, who accepted it gingerly. With his hands free, he wrapped his arms around his soon-to-be wife. She shrunk from him at first, but then she gave in. They loved each other after all. Her fingers dug into his back as she grasped him tightly, her wet face pressing against his shirt.

He ran his hand over her hair, in an effort to calm her. "I'm sorry," he repeated over and over for what felt like an eternity. It was anybody's guess how long they would have stood there if Dez hadn't started screaming hysterically.

"Baby, it's alright. What is it?"

Dez could say nothing. Instead, she pointed, her eyes round like saucers. Chad and Reed turned to see what she was pointing at, and they watched as Old Man Bronson and his wife rose from the ground, stumbling across the gravel, blood dripping from their gunshot wounds.

Christ. It's all real. It's all really real. Reed held Chad's rifle out to him, and he grabbed it, his mind still trying to comprehend what was going on. They should be dead. They should still be dead. But they weren't. In his mind, he thought that maybe he had erred. Maybe he had committed some sort of sin against God, and the Bronsons wouldn't rest until they had their revenge.

Reed just giggled as he popped open his shotgun, pulled out the spent shells, tossed them to the ground, and plopped two more in. He closed the breach with a mechanical clunk and took aim at Hannah Bronson, the closer of the two dead folk. He pulled the trigger, and a flock of birds took off into the sky as blood blossomed across Hannah Bronson's chest. Still she came.

Chad screamed as he fired rounds from his own rifle into the woman and the man both, but still they pressed on, until Chad and Reed both had to reload their weapons. They were pressed against the wall of the farmhouse now, Hannah Bronson's boots scraping against the wooden porch as she climbed towards them.

"It's got to be the head," a voice said from the other side of the screen door.

Reed began to shriek as Hannah approached him. He dropped his shotgun and squatted against the wall, his hands over his head as the dead woman pawed at him. Chad struggled to keep his hands steady as he fed a round into his rifle. He rammed the bolt home and took aim at the old lady's head. He pulled the trigger just as she grabbed a handful of Reed's dirty hair.

Her brains painted the wooden siding of the house, and she fell atop Reed, who screamed. Chad had heard that scream before. It was Reed's irrational scream; it was the same scream he had made when they were kids and he snapped, attacking some poor son of a bitch on the playground. But this time, there was fear in it.

Chad turned and aimed at Old Man Bronson's skull. He pulled the bolt back on his rifle, and the spent shell hit the wooden porch, ringing faintly. He placed another round in the chamber, falling in love for the thousandth time with the sound of the bolt ramming another shell home. He thought of Roy Scheider in Jaws as he aimed at the oxygen tank sticking out of the behemoth's mouth. "Smile, you son of a bitch," he said, squeezing the trigger and ending Old Man Bronson's life for good.

When the echo of his gunshot faded away. He squatted down, trying to put together the rules of the new world in his mind. Part of him expected to hear sirens any second, but there were none. Then it dawned on him. There were no rules. He could do whatever the hell he wanted.

With this giddy realization still floating around in his mind, he pulled the body of Hannah Bronson off of his still screaming brother. It took him a moment to calm Reed down, but when he did, he told him to keep watch for the cops. Then he took Dez upstairs and made love to her. Later, they would bury the bodies and burn the house to the ground.

It's good to be the king, he thought as he watched the old farmhouse go up in flames.

Chapter 1: Into the Streets

Rudy gasped for air in the back of the army truck. He was surrounded by unfamiliar faces, hard faces that looked at him like he was a piece of shit. The rifles in their hands gleamed in the shadows. All eyes were on him, and he wished he had never woken up.

The sound of dead flesh clanging off the sides of the truck created a deafening racket. As the vehicle pressed through the dead masses, he could see their rotting faces through the back of the truck. The soldiers at the rear of the vehicle smashed at the dead with their rifles as they grasped onto the tailgate in a pathetic effort to reach the humans huddled inside. The butts of their rifles were covered in gore, and sweat soaked their filthy fatigues. Behind them, the Burnside Bridge disappeared in the distance, a thousand of the dead stumbling after the slow-moving truck.

Rudy was constantly jostled side to side as the truck rolled over the corpses underneath. His head ached and black spots swam in front of his eyes. They had come back for him, but he wished he had never woken up. Then Amanda squeezed his hand, and he looked at her to find her smiling; her face was harsher than he remembered, her cheeks less full than when they had first met in his apartment building when this whole crazy scenario had begun.

Rudy choked down a mouthful of water from a canteen proffered by a soldier, fighting to keep it down.

"How long was I out?" he asked, trying to take his mind off the roiling sensation in his guts.

"A week," Amanda said.

"We thought you were dead already," one of the soldier's said. The patch on his right shoulder had the name Epps printed in neat black letters.

The soldier next to him, his patch read Allen, said, "Yeah, well, he ain't out of the woods yet."

"You were just going to leave me there?" Rudy asked. "Just leave me to die in a tent."

Amanda looked away ashamed.

Epps, leaned forward, his forehead resting against the barrel of the rifle leaning between his feet, and said, "She fought like hell to get us to take you with, but the Sarge, he said we couldn't have you dying in the back of the truck and attacking us without warning. It's hard enough to deal with the ones that are right in front of our face without another sneaking up on our ass."

It made sense, but he was still mad. He was alive, that was the important thing. And Amanda had fought for him... maybe that was even more important. He didn't know how to say what he was feeling, and even if he had the words, he wouldn't be able to say them in front of the soldiers, so he just squeezed Amanda's hand to let her know it was ok. She turned to him with tears in her brown eyes, and she smiled at him. He smiled back.

Then he noticed that most everyone else was missing. Chloe, Lou, Blake, none of them were there, except for the kid from the movie theater who watched him with cold, dark eyes. "Where is everybody?" Rudy asked, afraid to find out the answer.

Amanda was silent for a second, and then she said, "They all left."

"Left?" Rudy repeated, trying to understand how that could happen. "Left to where?"

"They wanted out of the city," she said. He could tell that there was more to it, but he didn't press her on it.

"And why didn't you go?" he asked.

"I couldn't just leave you here all by yourself."

At that moment, there was a huge clang, followed by the sound of grinding gears. The truck slowed to a crawl, and the soldiers gripped their rifles tighter.

"Fuck. We didn't even get ten blocks," Allen said.

"Keep your shit together," Epps responded to him. Even as he said this, Rudy could see both soldiers tense up on the bench, their hands clutching rifles tighter. A window that divided the cab from the bed of the truck opened, and a red-faced man with a square head, square jaw, square everything peeked through.

The man spoke with an air of command as he yelled, "Be ready to abandon ship."

Adrenaline shot through Rudy as the fear of the dead settled on his shoulders once more. He knew he was back where he had always been. He was dead weight. There was less of him, but he was exhausted. He didn't know if he would be able to keep up with the soldiers around him as they moved through the city. They may have saved his life, but for how long? Even sitting up had been tiring him out.

"Epps, Allen, you two keep those civvies safe," the man in the cab yelled again.

Epps and Allen looked at Rudy, and he could see what was running through their minds. *Why me? Why did I get stuck with the worthless fat man who would probably collapse ten feet from the truck?*

"Stay between us," Epps said, "and everything will be alright."

"Your life is your own. If you value it, keep up," Allen added.

Rudy nodded his understanding. They would protect him as long as he could keep pace, but once he fell, he was on his own.

The truck yawed to the side, the rear of the vehicle bouncing over crushed bodies, the gears grinding one final time before it shuddered to a stop.

"Go! Go! Go!" the man in the cab yelled.

And with that, the vehicle came to a dead stop; everyone in the back of the truck jumped into action. They rose, their rifles slung over their shoulders, and they moved toward the eye-blinding brightness at the rear of the truck. Rudy was in the middle of them, Amanda at his side. He watched as the first two soldiers hopped over the lip of the truck, their heads disappearing below its height. Gunshots rang out, but they couldn't drown out the moans of the dead.

More soldiers hopped out to add their own rifles to the symphony, and Rudy made it to the edge of the truck. It was a long way down, but the adrenaline pumping through his body gave him the courage he needed to throw one meaty leg over the railing and then the other. He landed with a thud, falling to the ground and rolling over on his shoulder.

He had no time to see if he had hurt himself. The nightmare around him wouldn't allow such a luxury. All around him, the dead swarmed, a slowly closing vice that threatened to crush them between the wave of dead from the bridge and the wave of dead coming from the city.

He recognized the street as Burnside Street, a couple blocks west of where the bridge ended. The remains of a helicopter, the metal black and twisted, sat there looking as if it were the corpse of a thousand-year-old mechanical vulture. Rudy used his arms to push himself off of the hot asphalt. It was still summer, and the sun was high overhead.

The smell of the day cloyed its way up his nose.

"Come on," Amanda said. "We've gotta move." Then her arm was under his, and they propelled themselves down the street. Epps and Allen were at their sides, their rifles cracking now and then as they stopped to put down any of the dead that got too close. They headed west up Burnside. The street was wide enough to allow them to see in all directions. The gunfire and the noise of the truck breaking seemed to have attracted every shambling corpse within earshot. They poured from the side streets as if taking part in an obscene parade.

How long would this go on? How long could they survive against such ridiculous numbers? Rudy didn't give them much of a chance. Once the soldiers were out of bullets, they would all die. Despite this fact, he continued to move, his arms and legs struggling to move forward, buoyed by Amanda at his side.

At least he wouldn't die alone.

****

Sergeant Tejada cursed as he threw open the door of the transport, smashing an Annie square in the face. He didn't hesitate. He hopped out of the vehicle, pulled his sidearm, and executed the floored creature, its blood spraying across the pavement. He took stock of the situation around him and emptied his magazine into the closest threats to give his men room to breathe. Every target he aimed at fell to the ground, and Tejada reloaded his M17, slamming home another 14-round magazine.

"We have to move!" he yelled. Then he turned and began making his way up the street, scanning it for any sign of escape. He knew that they were in a trap, and he knew that time was slowly running out on him and his men. He never looked back to see if his men would follow. He knew they would, just like he knew that the clock was ticking on their lives.

The only way to move was forward. The side streets were teeming with Annies. They came pouring out of the streets by the hundreds, clogging the lanes. But Burnside was bigger than the side streets. It was four lanes across with a divider running down the middle. It would give them the room to move, and as a bonus, it was headed in the right direction.

The right direction. That's a laugh. He silently cursed himself for being so stubborn. He should have left when he had the chance, but something in him wouldn't allow him to simply give up entirely on the mission. That

15

the people that had commanded that mission were most likely in an Annie's stomach by now didn't matter. He was a career soldier, and breaking the habits of the soldier had been more difficult than he could have ever imagined.

He knew what he should have done. He should have abandoned the damn mission the day that they had let the other survivors leave. They could have been out of the city by now. But no, Will Tejada simply couldn't face the fact that this situation was one that he and his men couldn't handle. And some of his boys were going to die for that stupidity.

After the survivors had left, Tejada and his men had waited on the bridge, hoping that somehow there were even more survivors making their way through the city. But if there were, Tejada hadn't seen them. They had seen no one. It had begun to feel like they were the last people on Earth.

Even worse, he had sensed a change in his men. They were no longer joking, giving each other shit and arguing about who had banged more broads. Whiteside stopped swearing about everything. Allen stopped questioning the world. Epps stopped talking to his closest friends. They just sat on the bridge, killing any Annies that got too close and then lapsing into thoughtful silence. They were becoming cold, withdrawn, and that's when the suicide had happened. His name was Jason Carter. They found him in an old abandoned car, his brains still sliding down the vinyl upholstery.

The next day, Tejada ordered everyone to start packing their shit. As they had finished loading up the trucks, Izzy Allen, the poet of his motley crew, had called him over to the barricade. There, using a pair of binoculars, he saw the largest horde of Annies they had ever seen making their way down Burnside towards their position. They didn't have enough bullets to take on such a mass. It would rumble over this city leaving nothing but death in its wake, like a swarm of Biblical locusts.

He had spent a good part of their last day arguing with Amanda about the unconscious fat boy. But in the end, though he hated to do it, he had to err on the side of his men. He hadn't done enough of that since the end of the world had happened. His only goal in life was to help those boys survive. He thought that was what he had been doing from the moment the government had dissolved, but he had only been clinging to his rigid routines, his training, his inability to let a mission go by the wayside. They should have made their way out of the city on day one, but he was stubborn, and he was old. But he would try to learn this new trick; he would try to learn the trick of surviving.

He hated to admit it, but those damn survivors had been the catalyst for all of his own self-reflection. If they hadn't come along, he and his men would be dying on that bridge, fighting a last stand for the ages, though there was no one around to see it. But those survivors... without training, without half the weaponry Tejada's men had at their disposal, they had made it through the city. His men saw that, and as the numbers of the dead seemed to grow every day, he saw the following thought in their eyes: *We're not going to make it. We're all going to die here.*

Carter's death was the last straw, and he changed his mission. No longer would they fight the dead. Now their mission was to survive, no matter what. Tejada risked a glance behind him to see how his men were doing.

They were bunched up in the middle of the street, which was probably a wise decision. At the rear of their foot-bound convoy, the large man was being carried between Epps and Allen, the girl plodding along behind them. A knot of three soldiers, Whiteside, Beacham, and Gregg backpedaled behind them, shooting any of the Annies who got too close.

While the speed of the dead could mostly be described as a leisurely shamble, there were always about two out of a hundred that seemed to be able to form some sort of loping jog, like a drunk man with a beer belly running on his toes, letting his own weight carry him forward. These were the most dangerous ones, and with so many of the dead around them, there were quite a few of them.

"Save your bullets!" he yelled. "Only kill the ones that are close enough to be a threat! You don't want your rifle turning into a glorified baseball bat in the middle of a damn horde."

Whether his men heard him or not was inconsequential. That they knew he was still there and that there was still some sort of plan... that was the important thing. Now, the only problem he had was to come up with a damn plan. He lifted his hand and shot an Annie in the face. It slumped into a heap at his feet. *How the hell did these things manage to get so close?*

****

Andy Broussard stuck to the middle of the pack. On the bridge, Sergeant Tejada had taught him how to use a rifle a bit, but he had not yet "attained mastery" as the gruff soldier liked to say. For this reason, he had only been given a handgun for the escape. He was grateful for it. He was grateful for everything.

Most of all, he was thankful to be alive and away from the other group of survivors. He had watched them turn on their own. He had watched as one was accused of murder, which the woman had freely admitted to. He watched as they sentenced her to death. And he knew that he was on the outside looking in. If they could do that to someone that had been with them from the beginning, then they could do that to him without a second thought.

No, the situation with the army boys was much more palatable to him. They had discipline. They had routines. Most of all, they had someone in charge, and everyone knew where they stood and how things worked.

That was a comfort to Andy. He was used to structure. He was used to doing what was expected without thinking.

Sergeant Tejada was a good man. He was the type of person that could make a difference in this world, and Andy had already learned much from the man in the week he had been with him. He watched him and studied him. He saw the way Tejada delivered his instructions and orders without emotion, without anger or panic. He was a calming presence. He knew how things could go. Hell, even the way he walked was cool as fuck.

Though the Sergeant wasn't the tallest man or the strongest, everyone seemed to gravitate to him. Was it just soldiers following orders, or was there something else at play? Andy didn't know. But he knew he wanted to be like the man everyone called Sarge.

He watched the man walk down the street, his handgun held at the ready. Sarge looked like a pitbull. He had forearms like Popeye, and his legs were like tree trunks. How much weightlifting had the man done to build a body like that? Andy suspected that they wouldn't be finding a weight room any time soon, but when they did, he would work to build his body like that.

Even Sarge's haircut meant business. Every morning, he sat looking into a tiny mirror, a pair of small scissors on his fingers, snipping away any hair that looked like it was getting too long. Sarge's black hair stood out like a million tiny needles pushed through his skull from the inside. Around his temples, those hairs were silver. *How old was the man? 40?* Maybe he was a little younger, but not much. Would Andy even live long enough to be half the man's age? The odds seemed stacked against it, but if he kept following Sergeant Tejada and learned from him, he thought that maybe he could get there. It was only eight months until his birthday... but eight months seemed a whole lot longer than it used to.

From the right side of the street, the Annies began to get a little closer. Andy raised his gun without thinking to shoot them. Just as he was about to pull the trigger, a soldier stepped in front of him, causing the soldier behind Andy to grab his arm and force it to the ground where a bullet ricocheted off the asphalt.

"Whoa! Whoa! Whoa!" the soldier said. "Watch what the fuck you're doing! You almost killed Masterson." Even over the noise of the dead, the Sergeant was aware of what was going on.

"Take his gun, Kazinsky!" Tejada yelled.

Kazinsky grabbed the handgun from Andy, and shoved it in his waistband. "You gotta watch where everyone is, man. Can't be shooting these things off without knowing where the man next to you is and what he's going to do next."

Andy shook his head to indicate that he understood, but he could feel his face reddening. Kazinsky had to be the same age as he was, but the man looked at him like one might look at a five-year-old who had gotten caught with their hand in the cookie jar. He tried to look anywhere but at Kazinsky. He tried to think of something cool to say, some way to play it off like the rebuke meant nothing to him. But he couldn't think of anything like that. So he just had to take it.

Even worse, when he looked over his shoulder the fat man and the murderess were looking at him. At least the soldiers had the common decency to keep their eyes trained on the Annies. Andy's hands clenched open and closed. He was now as worthless as those two were. He was dead weight, and everyone knew it. How could he have been so stupid?

If Burnside Street hadn't been teeming with hordes of the dead, he would have run off to avoid the shame. He felt hot tears welling in his eyes, but he choked them down. He let his embarrassment turn to anger, and then he channeled it towards the only people he knew he could get away with directing it at, the fat boy and the murderess. He wanted to walk to the back of the line and punch them in the face, but he didn't. Instead, he focused on the soldiers' targets, watching how they moved and trying to predict which targets warranted a bullet.

He watched as the dead shambled their way towards the soldiers, focusing his attention on the nearest. He waited for the gunshots so that he could see the Annies die, their brains splattered all over the ground, their foreheads caved in by bullets. It was satisfying to him, and eventually he stopped imagining the fat boy and the murderess' face on the Annies, and he just soaked in the sight of the dead falling to the ground, restoring the natural order of things.

As he faced forward again, he saw that trouble was heading their way. Up the street, there was a traffic jam. Well, it wasn't so much a traffic jam as it was a complete traffic clusterfuck. City buses were stacked in a pile, the paint blistered off of their twisted metal carcasses from a fire that had come and gone. Inside, he could see the dead moving around, their charred carcasses trapped in the jumbled wreckage, blackened arms clawing at the air. Cars were scattered about the perimeter, and the dead, combined with the wreckage, effectively cut off their planned escape route.

Tejada had seen the snarl before him, and, as their window of opportunity began to rapidly shrink, he led them to the only place that he could, the giant pink building. It had held the title of tallest building in the city for a grand total of 24 hours after the original title-holder had burned to the ground. Then a helicopter had ripped through the thirty-fifth floor, killing the man that was supposed to be in charge of martial law in Portland. Now it was just a smoldering ruin from the twentieth floor up, but they had no other choice. The building used to be called Big Pink, but now it was more like a cigar stub, noxious smoke pouring out of the collapsed upper floors. How the fire hadn't spread to the bottom floors was anybody's guess, but it offered them their only means of escape, so he wasn't going to look in that horse's mouth for too long.

Tejada waved his men into the lobby as the noose of Annies closed tight around them. The soldiers moved quickly. The ones at the rear shoved their hands under the flabby arms of Rudy and ushered him forward, his toes barely striking the pavement. Amanda came bouncing along after him, and Andy couldn't help but be disgusted by her.

Andy followed along as well, wondering if the sweat-soaked Rudy was going to have a heart attack. He could only be so lucky.

Chapter 2: Big Pink

The lobby of the building was a nightmare. Bodies lay along the polished marble floors. Dried streaks of blood were only slightly concealed by the literal ton of shattered glass that covered the floor.

Bill Epps imagined that the building must have been pretty impressive before this had all happened. The lobby was huge, open, and before the world had died, it had been plastered with a thousand different panels of glass. But those had all been shattered. Fallen soldiers, their bodies decaying, lay in puddles of dried gore all around, and flies buzzed in the air. The smell was nauseating, and he fought back the urge to vomit. Allen, his partner in the odious task of carrying the fat civvy, was not so lucky, depositing his canned-food breakfast on the marble floor.

On the other side of Epps, Allen simultaneously dry-heaved and continued to drag Rudy along. Epps stepped on spent brass with his boots and kicked shards of glass to the side. The man between them was covered in sweat, and he could barely put one foot in front of the other. This was the fat man's boot camp.

"Up the stairs!" Tejada commanded, his voice ringing out like a gunshot.

Epps didn't want to, but he looked up anyway, dreading the chore of dragging the boy's dead weight up the stairs. Rudy looked on the verge of passing out. If he did that, he was a dead man.

"Don't pass out, man. Or we're going to leave your ass here," he said. He didn't say it to be mean. He just didn't want the man's death on his conscience if he did wind up slipping into the big black.

The man was gasping, his chin fluttering as he tried to suck in breath. "In-in..."

"What the hell is he trying to say?" Allen asked.

Epps had no idea, but then the man's friend showed up with a canister in her hand. "He needs his inhaler," Amanda said. They stopped for a second as she held the inhaler up to the man's mouth, losing precious ground to the nonstop parade of the dead. Rudy took a deep breath, and she slipped the inhaler into the front pocket of his pants.

Behind them, they could hear the dead shuffling their way through the broken glass and bullet casings. Most of the men had reached the top of the stairs by now, and they were lagging behind.

"Come on, you two! We haven't got all day! Get your asses up here!" Tejada yelled. Epps and Allen dragged the man up the stairs, as the other soldiers arrayed themselves on a catwalk that overlooked the whole lobby. The first shot made him jump, and though he thought he had used up all of his adrenaline, another round of the neurotransmitter dumped into his body.

The sound of gunfire reverberated like thunder in the lobby of the building, but even though the sound was resounding, he could still make out the groans of the dead.

"Move your asses!" Tejada yelled, and they did, as fast as they could drag the big man. Thoughts of boot camp again filled Epps' mind. He recalled sweating in the summer as the drill sergeant busted his balls for doing everything too slow. Only, if he fucked up here, he didn't do more push-ups; he died.

"I can't make it," the fat man wheezed.

"No one truly ever makes it," Allen said.

"Stow the philosophy, Allen." To Rudy, Epps said, "I didn't carry your ass all this way just so you could die on me. One foot in front of the other; that's all it is. One foot in front of the other."

The man seemed to listen to him, so Epps repeated the phrase over and over until they reached the top of the stairs. As soon as they set foot on the catwalk, they stopped to catch their breath. The men around them continued to fire on the dead.

"Epps, Allen. Nice work. Brown, Ramirez, take over."

Epps leaned the fat man against the railing and then bent over, his hands on his knees, sucking up as much air as he could.

"No one wants to see your ass, Epps; get your finger on the trigger." Tejada pointed towards the offices on the opposite side of the catwalk. "Let's get somewhere," he said moving toward the offices.

Epps watched as Brown and Ramirez both swooped under the flabby arms of the civilian, dragging him off after the other men. He knew the look on their face. Every man in the military wore that look at one time or another. It was a look that said, "Why me?"

Bill Epps didn't particularly care at the moment. The smell coming from the guy would have been enough to make his eyes water if the world hadn't been filled with so many other smells, chief among them the rotting flesh all around. He figured he should have gotten used to the smell by now, but it was impossible to get used to. There was something almost evolutionary in that. His body was hardwired to be disgusted by the death around him. Maybe it had something to do with the diseases that dead bodies spread. Maybe it had to do with old memories of dead animals in the forests of Georgia that he had roamed as a child with his brothers. Maybe, when it all came down to it, they just smelled worse than anything he had ever smelled before.

He brought up the rear with Allen, and they moved backwards, their feet sliding through more shattered glass. The railings of the catwalk used to be covered in glass, but all of the panels had been shot out. How long ago now? How long had it been since the world had gone to hell?

Memories were painful these days. He tried not to think of all the men and women he had seen die in the last two months, but it was impossible not to think of them from time to time. That the military had failed so utterly still gnawed at him. For three years, he had felt invincible as a cog in the biggest, greatest machine that had ever been assembled, and then it was gone almost overnight.

When the order had come down, and they realized that the military was no longer a thing, he had sat on an empty ammo crate and watched as Uncle Sam's big green machine splintered apart. Some men followed General McCutcheon to Colorado. Some just bugged out completely. One of his buddies had asked him to hop on a chopper, but when he asked where they were going, they had no idea. He didn't want to sign up for something like that. He needed a purpose. He needed someone to tell him what to do.

In Georgia, left to his own devices, he had gotten up to so much trouble that the army had become the only option left to him. He was a bad man when left on his own. Dangerous some would say. But with the right guidance, he could be a good person. That's what the army had taught him, and yeah, he had killed a few people overseas, but they were people that deserved it. Without the army, it was as if he had been stripped naked and left to rot in the sun.

He would probably still be sitting on that ammo crate or walking around as one of the dead if it weren't for Sergeant Tejada. He had been sitting almost comatose on that ammo crate for two hours when Tejada, in the process of leading a group of soldiers somewhere, the men he now counted as friends, had happened to walk by.

"What'r ya doin'?" Sarge had asked.

All he could do was shrug his shoulders as the other men looked on.

"That's it? Just a shoulder shrug?" The Sarge looked at his other men, and Epps saw something on his face that he'd never forget. It was pure, unadulterated concern. Epps had always been a tough guy to love. He was, for lack of a better description, kind of an asshole. The only other people that had ever looked at him like that had been his parents and his grandparents. Even his brothers had never cared that much for him.

"You just gonna sit there and die?" Sarge had asked him, confusion in his voice.

"I was thinkin' about it," Epps had said.

"That's a load of bullshit. Stop that fucking moping, grab your gear, and follow us."

"Why?" Epps had asked, knowing in his heart that any answer would have been good enough for him. Sarge could have said, "Because we're going to go hang ourselves by our dicks from a tree," and Epps would have gone along.

But he didn't say that. All the square-headed man had said was, "Because we got some killing to do."

That had been good enough for him, and right now, he was neck-deep in killing. His rifle boomed in the lobby of the skyscraper. More blood splattered against the walls. Another shell clanged as it ricocheted off the marble floor.

"Fall back into the offices," Tejada yelled between rifle shots.

Epps didn't bother looking behind him. There were a bunch of soldiers with well-honed trigger fingers back there. He concentrated on what was in front of him... a wall of the dead, clawing their way up the stairs, knocking each other over in their hurry to get at the soldiers above them.

"Wish we had some grenades to blow this catwalk," Allen said from his right.

"Just keep shooting," he replied, as the dead tumbled off the stairwell to the ground below.

Behind them, they heard more gunshots, small arms fire. Still loud, but not like the thunder he and Allen were playing.

"Get in here!" Tejada yelled.

Epps took one more shot, smiled as it blew through the skull of a Latino dude with one eye, and then he turned and ran. Ahead, he saw Tejada waving him on. He moved as quickly as he dared amid the broken glass shards and spent shells, leaping over dead bodies still spilling their brains onto the catwalk. He had to turn sideways to slide into the opening that Tejada had left him. Once he was through, Tejada slammed it shut behind him.

"Three blocks down," Epps crowed. "How many more we got left Sarge?"

"Aw, hell, Epps. I didn't know you could count to three. You learn something new every day."

The men all smiled at Tejada's joke, with the exception of the civvies who were sitting on the floor and gasping for breath. *Man, they are out of shape. Homeboy over there is like a pile of Jell-o with bones in the middle.* But he was alive. That was impressive. If he had lived this long, maybe he would have a chance.

****

Amanda felt better with the door blocked off. She had tried to help the soldiers block the door, but the men had just told her to stay out of the way. Rudy sagged against the wall of the office, still trying to catch his breath.

In the corner, Tejada and a couple of his men were pouring over a map of Portland. Amanda was grateful for the respite, though not so much for herself as for Rudy. As he prepared to doze off, Amanda forced a bottle of water into his hands.

"You need to drink this," she said.

He grabbed the water bottle from her and dutifully began slugging it down.

"Not so fast. Small sips. You don't want to make yourself sick." He nodded his head, the skin underneath his chin waggling up and down in response. "You alright?" she asked. He said nothing. He was too tired to talk. "Finish that water, and then see if you can't catch some sleep."

"I feel like I've slept long enough," Rudy said.

"You need to rest."

Rudy lapsed into silence, too exhausted to argue the point.

Andy sat away from everyone in his own little world. Amanda watched as he listened to the soldiers' conversations intently. He was as transparent as the row of windows that lined the wall. He wanted to be one of them so badly. He wanted to be a badass. He wanted to be in control. He was going to get himself killed, or worse, someone else. It wouldn't be so bad if he got himself killed. That was Darwinism, right?

She smirked in her mind. The concept of Darwinism seemed so ridiculous to her now, like saying the sky was green, and the earth was flat. She looked around at the room, and what she saw spat in the face of everything that Darwin had ever written. The strong were not surviving. They had dropped like flies. They had gone the way of the dinosaur. What was left now were the pathetic, those that were good at playing hide and seek, the cockroaches of humanity, sprinting about an apartment looking for crumbs while the apartment's owners were away. Rudy... according to Darwinism, he shouldn't be here. There was nothing special about him, nothing special at all. He had almost died a dozen times since this whole thing had begun. Yet, he was still here, though he wasn't the fittest, he wasn't the smartest, hell, he wasn't even the most likeable person out of the group. Somehow, he was still kicking.

Darwin... what would he write after an event like this one, one that had taken over the whole world? Would he continue to trumpet the virtues of "survival of the fittest," or would he massage his hypothesis to account for people like Rudy... someone who clearly didn't fit the profile of the "fittest?"

Perhaps Darwin had it wrong. Perhaps it wasn't the fittest that survived, but the luckiest. She looked around the room and had to hide a scoffing laugh. If they were the luckiest, she would hate to see the unluckiest. But wasn't that what had happened? Wasn't it just luck that had led her to find Rudy and Chloe? Wasn't it just luck that had brought them to the Memorial Coliseum when the rest of the world had been dying around them? And what about meeting Zeke and the other survivors? How had she known to check on Rudy when Chloe had been about to smother him to death?

She supposed she was lucky. They all were. She just hoped that the luck held out. You might flip a coin ten times in a row and get heads every time, but sooner or later, that motherfucker was going to come up tails. Perhaps that was when Darwinism kicked in. Maybe she hadn't even been tested yet.

Amanda regarded the lumpen form of Rudy and pondered his own survivability index. Overweight, just woke from a coma, asthma. He was marked for death.

She wished she had never been forced to study anthropology and biology in college, two fields whose relevance had become extinct within the last couple of months. When her time came, and she knew it would come, she just hoped that she wouldn't choke.

She peeled the wrapper off of an energy bar and bit into its sweetness. Never had an energy bar tasted so good.

****

Israel Allen sat on the floor of the office, running his hand across the carpet. He only half-listened to the Sarge trying to plan his way out of the situation because he already knew what would happen in the end. They would be rappelling out the damn windows. It was the only way to get out. They didn't have enough ammo to blast their way out through the lobby, and that left two options... suicide or leaving through the windows, and no one was ready to die just yet.

He leaned his head against the cool wall. It was still August. Still hotter than a bare inner thigh. *Yeah, that's a good one.* Izzy, or Allen as the other men called him, fancied himself a writer. He had joined the army to get some life experience, a move that seemed naive at this particular point in time.

All the best writers had served. Tolkien, Hemingway, Cummings Whitman, Orwell, and dozens of other without the cachet of the ones he could name. What a plan... what a gloriously stupid plan.

Allen was almost embarrassed by what he had done. Where would he be if he hadn't joined the army? He'd probably be dead, but if by some stroke of God's mercy he had managed to survive, he would most likely be in his parents' farmhouse, drinking moonshine with his father as they sat on the roof with rifles in their hands. He wasn't the best shot, certainly not good enough to get accepted into sniper school, which was fine by him. As he understood it, there was a lot of downtime for a sniper. The urge to pull out his notebook and scribble down a line or two would have been too great. It probably would have gotten him killed.

He could picture his father on top of their Missouri farmhouse, sitting in the tangerine-orange sunlight as it sloped its way across the horizon, the Annies shuffling like a child on its way to an unwanted rendezvous with their bed. He could picture the mist that erupted from their heads, making the Annies look like land-bound whales trundling across the plowed earth as his father gunned them down.

His old man, now there had been a sniper. Once the fields were worked and dinner was eaten, he and his old man had sat on the roof as it cooled to a temperature that didn't threaten to sear their skin off. His old man would balance an ice-cold bottle of MGD between his legs, stare down the sight like a priest seeing God for the first time, and kill whatever dared to mess with his crops. There was no need for a scarecrow at the Allen farm; his dad took care of that.

Allen's mother would be downstairs washing the dishes by hand and setting them on the tacky drying rack that had been a staple of the kitchen since before he was born. He could picture her skinny hands now. He imagined the tendons in those hands flexing, popping out as she worked, threatening to lift out of her skin to reveal that she was just a puppet being worked by an unseen force in the heavens. Her wedding ring would be gleaming on her finger, draped in suds that sparkled only half as much as the diamonds set into the golden metal.

Somewhere, there would be an apple pie, sticky goo dripping out from the latticework of crust layered on top, like a trellis knocked over on its side. He would be there too, secure in the fact that he was with his family while the world was ending. To die fifteen-hundred miles away from his parents was enough to make a man want to howl. But he couldn't do that, not here, not in this tiny office with the men covered in sweat and fear, like those god-awful body sprays that the younger men wore when they were given leave. The smell so strong and so thick, that even after they left, leaving you in the barracks alone, you could still taste them in the back of your throat like the first signs of sickness.

In his mind, an image of those little, green, plastic army men blossomed, only this time the shapes were different. Instead of sitting on one knee with a bazooka on their shoulders or talking into a radio, they were fleeing, their green faces turned to look over their shoulders, their mouths open in a scream that would last for all-time or at least until the sun blew up.

He opened his eyes and looked around the room. It was a monument to the old way of the world, before the Annies, before the dead refused to be a part of the cycle of life. There were desks, bits of flair spread upon them, camouflage to prevent the worker from seeing how pointless their lives really were, blinders in the form of happy calendars, Post-It notes scrawled with in-jokes, reams of files that would never be opened again. There was a cardboard cutout of a movie star standing in the corner. Allen could only imagine the hi-jinks that it had gotten up to.

"Who is that?" Allen asked Epps.

"You don't know who that is?" Epps asked. He was continually amazed at Allen's complete lack of pop culture knowledge. "That's the Dancing Dude."

Allen just shook his head, not understanding what Epps was referring to.

"He was in Step Up, White House Down, 21 Jump Street, any of these ringing a bell?"

Allen just shook his head.

"Magic Mike?" Epps asked.

"Yeah, you would mention Magic Mike, Epps. That movie get you hot?" It was Brown, flipping Epps shit. Epps just gave him the finger.

"My favorite was This Is the End," the wormy little kid with the Southern accent chimed in.

Allen knew none of these things. "Yeah, well his head looks like a big toe."

"I'll give you that one," Epps said before going back to cleaning his gun.

The air in the office smelled like a cross between a honey bucket baking in the summer sun and rancid meat coated in garlic. He was surprised he could smell anything. When was the last time he had taken a shower? Back when

33

the world still made sense he guessed. He closed his eyes and spared a moment to think about his parents. His old man would keep his mom safe, at least until the ammo ran out. After that, they would need all the help they could get.

He reached up and scratched his scalp. He looked at his fingernails when he was done. A crescent of black grit greeted him, and he began to wonder how long a human body could go without washing before disease set in.

"I got good news, and I got bad news," Sarge began. "Since you're all badass motherfuckers, I'm gonna give you the bad news first cuz you can handle it. In the morning, we're going out that goddamn window. We're going to do it quick, and we're going to do it fast."

Ramirez, the loudmouth of the group, asked, "Why don't we just go now? The sooner we get out of this city the better."

"You looked out that window, Ramirez? It's like the goddamn Macy's Thanksgiving Day parade down there. By the time your slow ass got halfway down the rope, there'd be thirty Annies ready to tie your shoes for you."

"What's the good news, sir?" Whiteside asked.

The conversation was so cliché, so droll. Allen could barely stand it. Good news, bad news... how could conversations like this improve his writing?

"Don't call me sir anymore. I thought we went over that." Sarge straightened his shirt and then picked up a garbage can. "The good news is we have a toilet, so we don't have to shit on the floor like animals." He tossed the garbage can on the ground where it clanged off the floor. "No lights tonight. Clean your guns two at a time. I don't want everyone doin' it at once just in case those things find a way through."

The banging on the door had never ceased. Like a negligent mother with a screaming baby in the supermarket, they had all sort of drowned it out with their own thoughts. But sooner or later, they would have to deal with it. Epps picked the garbage can up off the floor and carried it behind one of the cubicle walls.

Izzy Allen closed his eyes and began to use similes to describe the sounds that he heard. Perhaps one day, when the world had righted itself, as he knew it would, there would be people to read the poems he wrote. But the only words that came to mind that night were of the four-letter variety, and they were most definitely not the stuff of literary legend.

****

The night passed, cool and slow. Sergeant Tejada enjoyed every breath. His men, all 11 of them, slumbered on the floor along with the three civvies. He tried to catch as much sleep as he could, but it was damn near impossible knowing that there were so many Annies clumped up all around them. At one point, he stood up and edged over to the floor-to-ceiling windows that looked down on the street. He stood for a while, trying to peer through the gloom that dominated the valley between Big Pink and the next building over. It was no use; it was too dark.

He closed his eyes and tried to feel them looking up at him, but that was no good either. He knew they were down there though. The Annies never gave up once they had prey in their sights. The only option was retreat. And when they ran out of places to retreat to, then it would be the long sleep for all of them. He wouldn't let any of his men turn into those things if he could help it.

Tejada ran his hand over the cold metal in his pocket. It weighed as much as a can of beans, but it was smaller. In daylight, it was that same olive green that had dominated every waking moment of his daily life for the last twenty years. The thing about seeing that green every day... it had a way of freezing time. The last twenty years seemed like nothing more than the blink of an eye. He had gone from a young pup full of fight to a grizzled old bastard in no time at all.

35

The fact was, it was all he really knew. Somewhere back there in his gray matter, there were memories of a life before the army, but they were like a dream, things half-imagined when lying on a rough cot. He looked around at the men on the floor and shook his head. They were the only real family he had.

He would never tell them that of course. It was unfitting for a leader to do so, and even though he was technically not their leader anymore, they were all still looking to him. The last thing he needed was a communication breakdown in a tense moment. He didn't need anyone's trigger finger tensing up because they were questioning the order of things. That's why he had tried to shed himself of his status in the first place.

If you put a leash on a dog that was scared, they would dig in their heels. If you let them know that they had nothing to worry about, well, you had a friend for life, and they would go wherever you wanted them to... until you got them hurt or killed. He was trying not to do that.

No, his men knew who he was. None of them had to say it.

He felt them now. He felt the withered eyes of the Annies trained upon him from the dark streets below. They couldn't see him, not in the dark, not with the mirrored glass of the skyscraper between him and them, but they knew he was up there just the same.

He ran his hand over the smooth steel of the grenade in his pocket. *Would I die for them?* He didn't have to anymore. They were freed of debt to him, and he of debt to them, as it should be. But would he die?

He looked over their sleeping bodies on the floor, shadows upon shadows, their position only given away by their soft snores. They were all he had. *Yeah. I'd die for them.* He placed his palm over the hand grenade in his pocket, gave it a reassuring squeeze, and then moved to his own spot on the ground. He stepped gingerly over a body, lest he step on the poor sleeping bastard.

Out of the corner of his eye, he caught the glimmer of an open eye, and he knew that the boy was watching him. The boy thought he was a man, but he had never had the opportunity to learn such things. That much was obvious, like teenagers falling in love for the first time... so obvious, yet so tragic at the same time. Andy he said his name was.

Tejada felt something for the boy. He was not unlike any raw recruit he had ever come across. He was green. He was stupid. He had a lust for the world's treasures that would get his ass killed. Given enough time, he could break the boy of his youth, but they didn't have enough time. He was a problem, and yet, he found he couldn't just give up on the kid.

Tomorrow, he would give the kid his gun back, along with a stern warning to not get anyone killed. If he learned, he learned. If he didn't, well, that would be it for guns. He would give him a nice knife or something.

He laid back down, trying to put the slit-eyed regard of Andy out of his mind, but he found himself wondering why he cared. Why did he give two shits about some civilian asshole who didn't know the barrel of a handgun from its grip?

I just do. God help me, I just do.
****

Andy watched Sergeant Tejada lay back down. He sensed something in him, something that he didn't care for. There was a weakness there. Perhaps the old soldier wasn't as perfect as he had thought. He hoped he didn't get killed because of his weakness.

That he had ordered the men to take away his gun was the most embarrassing moment of his life, and he had experienced plenty of them. All evening long, he had sensed the disapproving looks of the other soldiers. They didn't look at him as one of them. They looked at him like he was Rudy or Amanda, helpless, useless. In their eyes, he might as well be a baby in a shit-stained diaper, and Tejada had only solidified that image.

But it wasn't his fault! *That dumb motherfucker moved right in front of me. He should have known better!* The argument rang hollow in his brain, but he couldn't escape the feelings that came with it.

Embarrassment, rage, anger... these emotions warred within him, but anger was always the most dominant. He tried to stuff the emotions down inside as Sergeant Tejada began snoring. *I'll show them. I'll show them all. I'm just as good as they are, if not better.* Tomorrow he would show them all.

He lay down to sleep, his dreams filled with the faces of the dead, parents thousands of miles away, and his own voice screaming in his ears. In his dreams, he cried, tears running down his face as he was left behind, alone and trapped by the dead. When he awoke, he felt the wetness on his cheeks as the other men around him avoided looking in his direction.

Chapter 3: Exfil

The sun came up orange, filtered through the smoke of a hundred smoldering fires in the city. The sunlight filtered in through the windows of Big Pink, stained, rotten. It shone on the faces of the survivors, playing across their faces like the light of hell. The sky, had it not been obscured by smoke, would have shined a clear blue. But instead, it was obscured by haze.

Sergeant Tejada rose, his body complaining for the hundredth time about sleeping on a cushion-less floor. Today was the day they left the city behind. This he vowed. He rose and stretched, his back sounding like a burst of automatic gunfire. Others were awake, but silent, allowing the others in the company to get as much sleep as they could. Who knew when they would have another such opportunity?

Tejada could feel the dread in the air. He could taste it like ashes in his mouth. Tejada moved slowly to the windows and looked down. They were still there, spread out, but that wouldn't last for long once they busted open those windows. Timing would be key.

Tie the ropes off. Bust the windows. Get everyone out and down. How long would that take? The civilians were the x-factor. If one of those civvies clammed up at the edge of the window, things could get hairy real fast. They didn't have the ammo to shoot their way out of a real horde. 5 minutes... that's all the time he estimated they had from the first broken window to the last man hitting the ground. After that, they would be surrounded, and they would be overrun by the sheer numbers of the dead.

He looked over the men, calculating, deciding the order. Rudy was the riskiest proposition. Lying in a coma for a week, already grossly overweight, how well could he manage this part of their journey?

Rudy sat in discussion with Amanda. He had no qualms about Amanda. She would do what she needed to do. He had seen that on the bridge when the Chloe situation had been thrust upon them. She was a survivor. Rudy? He was a wild card.

Tejada stalked over to the pair and squatted down next to them. He felt the boy's eyes on him the entire way.

"Good morning," he said, smiling a grin that he knew was toothy and filled with bright square teeth. He had been described as bullfroggish as a youth, but people still responded to his smile despite that fact.

"Good morning," Amanda said.

"Good morning," Rudy began, his awkwardness like nails on a chalkboard to Tejada. "I'd like to thank you for coming back for me," he stammered.

Tejada waved him off as if it weren't a big deal, even though the delay in retrieving the unconscious man on the bridge had most likely fouled up their plans to begin with. The dead wouldn't have been quite as dense, quite as bunched up, if they hadn't had to double back and grab the man. But he had ordered it. The way Tejada saw it, there just weren't enough lives left in the world to be throwing them away in the name of expediency.

"It was nothing," he said. "Hopefully, you would do the same for me or any of my men."

The kid nodded, his chin disappearing as the fat of his neck billowed around it.

"Good, good." Tejada hesitated as he tried to word his next statement in a way that would not hurt or embarrass the kid. "Listen, I uhh... I wanted to talk about today." Amanda and Rudy were all ears. "You know that we're going to be going out those windows, and I just wanted to make sure that when the time comes, you're not going to hesitate."

"What do you mean?" Amanda asked, her hand going protectively to Rudy's arm.

Tejada sighed. This would be so much easier if they were military people. He had never been known for his tact. "I mean, in a few minutes, we're going out those windows. Below us, are a hundred of those damned things. Any sort of hesitation, and we're going to find ourselves surrounded. We are going to die. So I'm just wondering if you're up to it, kid? Can you do this?"

Rudy laughed. "You don't have to worry about me, sir. I have experience jumping out windows. This time I have a rope. That's going to be good enough for me."

Tejada smiled, still not sure if he could trust Rudy. But he liked the confidence he saw in the man's face. "Well, that's all there is. So, if you guys are ready, we ought to get this show on the road."

Rudy nodded at Tejada, his eyes free from fear. *He has the confidence at least. That's something.* "Masterson!" Tejada yelled. "Get over here and show these people how to rappel down a wall."

"Yes, sir!" Masterson quipped. Tejada winced again. That damn word. Would they ever stop calling him "sir?" He let it go for the time being, as there simply wasn't enough time to bother arguing about it. Plus, it showed that his men were still in a military mindset. And that was just fine with Tejada for the moment.

****

Rudy watched closely as Masterson showed him how to wind the rope around himself in order to control his descent and not end up as a puddle on the street. It seemed simple enough. He certainly felt better about this than he had about jumping out of an office building onto the back of a semi-truck.

"You got it?" Masterson asked.

"Yeah, I think so," he said.

"Don't think. Know. Do you got it?"

"Yes, sir," he said. He felt the rebuke in the man's words, and the word "sir" just came out of him unbidden.

"I'm not your sir," the man said before he headed over to Andy, the boy from the theater, and began repeating his explanation for how to rappel down the wall.

Rudy watched the men gather their belongings, tying their equipment down so that nothing shifted or hung loose. The smell in the office was awful, their makeshift bathroom was full, and Rudy was looking forward to escaping the claustrophobic confines of the office building. Rudy and Amanda watched as Masterson explained to Andy what to do. It wouldn't hurt to pay attention to the instructions one more time.

Sergeant Tejada, sensing that preparations were just about over, yelled out orders. "Alright, Masterson, Brown, Allen. I want you three going first. Get down there as fast as you can. Establish a perimeter. Whiteside, Quigley, and Day, you three are next. Then I want Kazinsky, Beacham and Gregg out. The three civvies will come next, while myself, Epps, and Ramirez cover them from up here. Once they're on the ground, Ramirez and Gregg are out the door. I'll cut these ropes, then I'll join you all at the bottom in time for a cup of tea."

Everyone nodded. And with that, there was nothing left to say. Rudy, who had never been religious, began to chant a mantra in his mind. "Lord let us live. Lord let us live." He repeated the phrase over and over. For good measure, he took a puff off of his inhaler, and he readied himself for the part that was to come next.

He flinched when the soldiers blew out the glass windows with a handful of shots from their rifles. The soldiers tossed the ropes out the window, and Masterson, Brown and Allen quickly snaked the ropes around their bodies. Without hesitation, they stepped out into the smoky day and disappeared from sight.

"Cover 'em!" Tejada snapped. The next soldiers up stepped to the edge of the windows and began picking off the dead.

Rudy felt his body infused with adrenaline. Amanda laced the fingers on her left hand through his fingers, and he turned to her and smiled. She smiled back. It was beautiful. It melted away the soreness in his body from the previous day's exertion. He knew he was ready.

"They're down!" one of the soldiers yelled.

"Go!" Tejada yelled, and three more soldiers coiled the ropes around themselves and disappeared from sight.

It seemed like only a matter of moments, and then three more soldiers disappeared.

"You three are up next," Tejada said. Rudy, Amanda, and Andy inched their way to the edge of the building. Rudy leaned out over the edge and looked down. His head began to swim immediately, and he had to lean backwards and take a deep breath to make the rocking in his head stop.

"You can do this," Amanda said, and he knew he could, because she believed in him, and that meant he couldn't let her down.

"They're down," Andy said, and then the three survivors sprang into work, coiling the ropes around their legs, around their waists, and over their arms. Andy, as if he had done this a thousand times, stepped out into the air first, then Amanda.

Rudy inched to the edge, and his head began to rock again. He hesitated.

Tejada had no time for his bullshit. "Get out there, Rudy! Now, motherfucker!"

Rudy stepped out over the edge, dropping immediately and banging against the side of the building. He hit hard, and it knocked the breath out of him. The wind swirled around him, and he had to will himself to loosen his grip on the rope. The rope snaked across his body as he began to descend. He squeezed his eyes shut.

"You gotta go faster than that!" Tejada yelled from above.

Rudy opened his eyes and looked upward, his teeth locked in a death grin. Tejada was looking down at him; his square head seemed bloated and angry, the skin on his face had turned an angry red, and Rudy released his grip on the rope to get away from it.

The windows slid by, and he coughed on the smoke in the air. As he passed one set of windows, he screamed as a shirtless dead woman banged against the window, what remained of her once ample breasts flattening against the glass. He slid further down, the rope zipping across his pants and his shirt and his forearm, stripping some of the skin off the latter.

He chanced a look down and saw hell below him. In a circle, the nine soldiers stood, their rifles at the ready as they fired into a ring of the dead that seemed to inch closer and closer with every second that went by. How long could the soldiers' circle stand and not break? From his vantage point, he saw the dead spread out along the streets, moving so slow that at first it seemed like they were standing still, but they weren't. They were coming.

The city around him was beautiful. The buildings stood broken and empty. Car wrecks were spread out in the streets like smashed bugs, their fenders and tires dotting the concrete like appendages ripped off by the dark kid who sat at the back of class and laughed whenever someone hurt themselves.

He could see the top of Amanda's head fifteen feet below him. She would reach the ground before he did, and this is what caused him to speed his descent. He didn't want her standing down there by herself. She needed him to watch her back, and he owed it to her. Amid the sound of gunshots and the plaintive groans of the dead, the rope stripped the flesh from the palm of his hand, and then he landed on the ground with a thump, his knees buckling under him.

He stood, ignoring the sting of his hand as he reached up to help disconnect Amanda from her rope.

"Untie yourself!" Masterson yelled at Rudy. "You're wasting time! She can take care of herself. The soldier took aim at another of the dead and turned his brains into a red mist that exited out the back of his skull.

With blood pouring from his hand, he untangled himself from the rope and then walked over to Amanda to help her.

"I'm fine," she said. And she was. As soon as they were free, the ropes began to dance. Rudy looked upward to see Epps and Ramirez stepping into space, literally running down the side of the building like the overpaid actors of an action movie.

"Holy shit!" Rudy said, pointing up at them so Amanda could see.

When they got close to the ground, they pushed away from the building, spinning about so that they would land on their feet instead of their face. As soon as they touched the ground, the rope that Rudy had used to descend fell to the ground, severed at the other end by Tejada. Andy began coiling the rope, as Rudy and Amanda clung to each other.

The dead did not seem so distant from this vantage point. In fact, they were closer than ever. The soldiers had begun to inch backwards, their circle tightening as the dead closed in. There were simply too many of them and not enough bullets to go around. Even if they had all the bullets in the world, there was no way that a handful of soldiers could bring down all of the dead before they were eventually overwhelmed.

"Heads up!" Andy yelled as another rope tumbled to the ground. Then the last remaining rope began to jerk around like a living thing. Rudy looked up and watched as Tejada came sprinting down the side of the building, the rope laced around his body like a harness. He didn't even bother to hold the rope with two hands as everyone else had. In his left hand, he held a handgun, and he fired down into the mass of the dead.

Rudy could smell the dead now. He could see their tattered bodies and ruined clothing up close, and panic began to take hold. He looked around for a weapon, anything that he could use, but there was nothing. He had never felt so helpless in his life.

Tejada landed on the ground with a thump. He pulled a knife from his belt and handed it to Rudy. "If they get close, stick 'em in the eye. You miss, you're dead."

Rudy took the knife with gratitude, and then Tejada handed Andy a handgun. "You fuck up this time, and I'm never giving you a gun again," Tejada said.

Andy nodded his head, a slow grin spreading across his face as he accepted the weapon. "We gotta move people!" Tejada yelled.

And they did. They ran down the west side of Big Pink towards Burnside Street, circumventing the pile-up that had initially ruined their escape. They picked off the closest of the dead as they moved. The soldiers were good; Rudy had to admit that. Their aim wasn't perfect, but it was certainly good enough to keep them from getting swarmed for the time being.

They angled their way onto Burnside Street, and then they looked west, where the road rose to meet the hills that separated Portland from the suburbs to the west. Cars smoldered in the road, but for the most part it was clear, you know... if you didn't include the hundreds of dead bodies heading their way. There was no way they would be able to make it through the wall of dead in front of them. They were staring death in the face... only it didn't have one face anymore, it had hundreds.

The guns around him fired nonstop. The noise was deafening. It was understandable that Rudy didn't hear Tejada's order to get down. One minute he was standing there, clutching Tejada's knife in his hand, and the next, Amanda was inexplicably pulling Rudy to the ground.

"What's going—" he had time to say before the world erupted. Ahead of them, the bodies of the dead exploded in a shower of blood. Limbs flew through the air, and Rudy saw it all as if in slow-motion. The blood geysering upwards as if Old Faithful had suddenly vented underneath the dead. Arms and legs and unrecognizable chunks of meat arced outward and then splattered the dusty pavement. He was amazed and horrified at the same time.

Then Amanda was on her feet, pulling Rudy upwards as the soldiers picked themselves up. All except for the one they called Kazinsky. He tottered on his feet, wobbling back and forth like a drunk. He hadn't heard the order to get down either. He turned then, his scruffy mouth opening and closing as if he couldn't find the words to explain the shaft of bone that stuck out of his chest. "Sarge?" Kazinsky said, blood bubbling out of his mouth. Then the soldier fell to his knees.

"We don't got time for this. Get through that breach!" Tejada yelled.

Then they were running through the hole that Tejada had blown wide for them. Rudy flinched as Tejada executed Kazinsky on the spot, his handgun somehow sounding louder than all of the shots that had already been fired that day.

"Watch your fucking ankles!" Epps yelled, and then Rudy saw why. The dead, though they had been blown apart, were still active. Heads attached to armless torsos gnashed at the soldiers' ankles as they picked their way through the mess.

He watched as Brown kicked one in the teeth with his boot and sent the head spinning away across the pavement. Then it was his turn to pick his way among the dead. The pavement was slick, the way it gets when it rains for the first time in a couple of weeks. It made him recall one of his persistent nightmares from when he was a kid, the one where he was trying to flee a faceless human and no matter how fast he ran, he couldn't get any traction.

But in the real world, he moved, kicking arms and legs aside and swearing under his breath. The gap that Tejada had created began to tighten as the still functional dead pursued them, and in a minute, maybe less, their route to freedom would be gone completely if they didn't get to the other side. The dead were not deterred by seeing their mates die. The dead did not stop to honor the fallen. They only had one thought, one wish... to feed.

Ahead of him, one of the soldiers slipped in the mess. He fell flat on his back within arms' reach of the severed torso of a priest. As the clutching limbs of the maimed priest began to squeeze at his arms, he screamed a scream that sounded like it was being pushed out of him. Rudy heard his arm crack, and then the other soldiers were there, firing into the heads around him, sending up shards of pavement and bone. They lifted him to his feet, and his arm flopped around like it was made of rubber. The sight of the man's arm, flopping like a rubber chicken, sent chills up Rudy's spine.

"Beacham's broken his arm!" Brown yelled.

It didn't seem to bother Tejada. "Then give him his handgun. He can still shoot with one arm."

Rudy's blood ran cold at the thought. There had been many times over the last month when the reality of this world had caught him by surprise, but the coldness of Tejada's words hit him hard. He had no time to dwell upon this as he focused on not slipping to the ground so that he might avoid the grasping arms and gnashing teeth on the street. He stifled a laugh as the thought crossed his mind that America had finally become a true melting pot, for on the pavement lay people of all races, creeds, and religions. Humanity was finally coming together... by being torn apart.

When his feet hit dry pavement, he let out a breath that he didn't even know he had been holding. The voices of the dead sounded like a dry wind whistling through the night air, only louder and more persistent. It wormed its way into his ears, until he actively had to think about something else.

He focused on Beacham, the soldier with the broken arm. It dangled at his side, swaying with each step. Beacham let loose a solid stream of swear words, unbroken and blistering, as he moved down the street. Swearing didn't matter anymore. No one looked twice at Beacham as the vilest string of profanity that Rudy had ever heard kept pouring from his mouth. He heard word combinations that would have made him laugh out loud just a couple of months ago, but now they were just something to file away for later use. Beacham, despite his broken arm, moved forward, keeping pace with the others. It was as if he were a steamboat, and his profanity was the coal that he used to heat up the engine.

There were still sporadic dead ahead of them, and who knew how many more in the buildings around them, but they had busted through the heart of the city. He was still alive and so was Amanda. To Rudy, that was the most important thing.

Rudy tossed a glance over his shoulder to see a mass as wide as the street advancing upon them from behind. At the feet of this mass, he caught a glimpse of several torsos dragging themselves along the road, their fingernails tearing off as they scrabbled at the unforgiving pavement.

He focused on Beacham's swears... at least they came from something alive.

Chapter 4: Burnside

The gun in Andy's hand felt cold. It smelled of cordite and oil. But he loved it. He loved it the way a boy loves the first girl they ever kiss. He had pulled the trigger, oh, how he had pulled the trigger. He hadn't even flinched as the slide ratcheted back, quick as lightning, to eject a shell with each purposeful squeeze. He didn't flinch as fire erupted from the barrel of the gun.

He couldn't afford to. He wanted to see it. He wanted to see them die. And while he had missed more times than he had hit, for a beginner, he thought he had done fairly well. He hadn't gotten impaled by bone shrapnel or broken his arm. That was something the soldiers couldn't say.

Understanding, that's what had been missing. He understood now. He understood how this group worked. This group wasn't about friendships and relationships. It was about function. They did what they had to do to accomplish their goals. Just as he had done what he had to do to escape his home and the daily beatings the other boys in town had given him. It was no different. Leave town. Get a job. Become a man. He didn't do this because he wanted to, but because it's what he had to do.

The men around him had done the same, all except for Rudy and Amanda. Amanda was a woman. Rudy, well, he wasn't exactly what one would call a man. They were more like lost little dogs he decided, pathetic, pitiable but expendable. If they died, there might be some tears, but in the end what did they actually lose? A couple of mouths to feed? Some dead weight?

No, he was *becoming*. That was the only word he could think of to describe his newfound badassness. He was *becoming*. Becoming the man that the bullies back home would never let him be. Becoming self-sufficient, the way his father had never allowed. He was one of them. Maybe not entirely, but it was only a matter of time.

If more of them died, that time would come even sooner. He felt bad for thinking like that, but the truth was the truth. A machine didn't lie. When a gear was stripped of its teeth, the machine stopped running. There was no crying about it. You just pulled the old gear out and put in a new one. He was the new gear. Shiny, new, capable. That's what he decided he was. When Tejada had put the gun to Kazinsky's head, it had crystallized this idea in his own head.

As a boy in high school, he had read Jack Kerouac novels and fantasized about how one would develop the ability to think the way that the author did. How did one see through all the bullshit and come to realize the reality of things without judging? It was experience. Experience made the man, and for the first time in his life he was getting it.

He didn't mind the screaming of Beacham. He didn't mind the fact that they were running out of bullets. He didn't mind the hundreds of dead that were following behind them, no more than an engine minds what car it has been put into.

They passed by Powell's Books, and he remembered the world as it was, dirty... teeming with humans who were little more than wastes of time and space. He had been a fan of books, devouring cheap paperbacks hoping to find the secrets of life contained within. He had seen them, but he had somehow failed to notice the truths within. Hunter S. Thompson told him to live. Kerouac had told him to get out there. But had he listened? No, he had stared at the brush strokes but never succeeded in seeing the big picture. It was embarrassing, but better late than never he supposed. But he was getting it now.

He remembered this bookstore. He remembered the promise held within. Powell's was the first place he had applied for a job. Living under a bridge, with a cell phone as his only proof of existence, he had waited a day for the bookstore to call him. They never did. Now they were all dead. He would like to think of it as karma, and he could almost trick himself into doing so if it weren't for the fact that everyone who worked at the place that had eventually hired him was dead as well. But fuck them too. None of them had even bothered to call the theater to see how things were going when the world started to fall apart. He couldn't blame them. It was a shit job, and he had only worked there for a couple of weeks. He hadn't even gotten his first paycheck yet. But still, there was a tiny part of him that hoped they all got what they deserved.

You're being petty, Andy. It was the voice of his mother, the great socialite. He never could find the right balance of manners and machismo to please the woman. Neither could his father, which was why his dad had spent most of his waking hours out on the golf course or at work. But if she could see him now, a gun in his hand, trekking the earth while the majority of the world lay dead or dead-ish... what would she say? Maybe, for once, she would be proud of him. Maybe she would overlook the fact that he had had his ass kicked daily for a year by the sons of her other socialite friends. The nerve of him, showing up at one of her parties with a black eye.

They passed by the book store, and he wondered if anyone would ever read a Kerouac book again? He certainly wouldn't. There was a crash from one of the buildings behind them, and a handful of the dead tumbled to the street.

"They're falling out the windows!" Epps announced.

"All the more reason to get the fuck out of this city," Tejada said, cool and calm. Andy filed away Tejada's tone and inflection in his brain as he maneuvered around a car with several flat tires and busted windows. Had the dead destroyed the car or had looters?

They pushed forward, the road rising slightly. A small amount of smoky haze obscured the hills in the distance. They moved at a pace slightly quicker than a walk, and already Andy could see Rudy struggling to keep up. For his part, he did seem to be in better shape than he had been yesterday. The murderess, Amanda, held tightly to his arm. He wondered if they had fucked yet. He doubted it. He just couldn't picture that great ball of flab spreading that little girl's legs. The thought made him ill.

What would happen to her if Rudy were gone? That would be an interesting predicament. Would she glob onto the next nearest man? Would she fall for him? He scoffed at himself. If there was one thing he knew, it was that no woman found him attractive. He had the stink of loser about him. Maybe that's why he liked Tejada so much. He was pure winner. Pure alpha male. Tejada, back when the world was still a thing, could probably pull a different girl every night if he wanted to.

Andy felt himself getting angry again, his temper rose within his chest, and he raised his gun at the nearest dead thing. He pulled the trigger, but the handgun just clicked.

"You gotta have bullets to make it work," Epps said.

Why did everyone in this world talk to him like he was the village idiot? Andy just nodded and ignored the tiny knot of hate that had been planted in his brain. The knot was for Epps. If Epps was good, it wouldn't grow. It would just be a small dot in his brain. But if Epps ever said anything like that to him again, it would grow. And that would be dangerous for Epps.

Tejada slammed a fist into Andy's chest. "Here. Load it up. Never know when you're going to need it."

Andy cupped his hands under Tejada's fist, and a handful of 9mm rounds clinked into his hands. He ejected the handgun's magazine, relishing the sound of metal sliding against metal, and then he fed the bullets into the magazine one by one. When the magazine was full, he slammed it home. He felt like James Bond, one of those alpha male assholes, and he liked it. Ahead and to his right, he saw a man that looked a lot like Rudy, tougher, more tattooed, but still doughy and pathetic looking. He was dead of course, but he still moved.

Andy took aim with the handgun, squeezed the trigger, and smiled as the fat dead guy crumpled to the ground.

"Nice shot," Tejada said.

Andy tried to fight off the blushing, but it happened anyway. The other soldiers saw, and that only made him blush even more. Normally, he would berate himself for being weak, but it didn't matter now. They would all know how great he was sooner or later. He was betting on sooner. He was *becoming*.

Buildings rose around them, and the noise of the dead trailing behind them echoed off the walls. The street was narrow, and the buildings were tall. He could see the dead at the windows now, looking down upon them like Greek gods from the top of Mount Olympus. They pressed against the glass, their hands banging upon the panes. The pounding combined with the moans of the dead behind them, and then a new sound began. It was the sound of breaking glass.

"Get away from those buildings!" Tejada yelled. The survivors scrambled over the hoods of cars and around twisted and burned vehicles as the bodies tumbled to the ground, only to rise again with broken bones and smashed faces. In the middle of the road, they were safe from the plummeting dead.

"Pick it up!" the soldiers yelled to each other, urging each other onward. The dead shambled after them, struggling to match the soldiers' speed. The soldiers executed the ones that were close enough, and onward they marched until they came to an overpass. Cars, trucks, and vans were parked bumper to bumper, and they had to split up to make their way through the maze of automobiles.

Andy stifled a scream as a decayed arm shot out of one of the windows and clutched at his clothing. The stench was strong here, and there were several of the dead trapped within the cars, held in place by seatbelts that they had lost the wherewithal to remove. Andy bashed at the arm that held him with the handle of his pistol. The arm broke, and he was free to move forward once more. More hands waved at the survivors, but the dead were not smart enough to wait until the soldiers passed by. They just stuck their hands out and waved them around in the hopes that someone would walk right into them. They were easy to avoid except for a couple of bottlenecks.

As they crossed an overpass, they were offered a stunning view of the highway below them. It was nothing but twisted metal, bodies, and the dead as far as the eye could see. Then they were across. They strode across the bridge without giving a second thought to the vision of hell that they had just seen. There was nothing to think about. There was only one way to go now... straight ahead. They either kept moving or they died.

The buildings around them were older now, their fronts lined with glass windows. These were not office buildings anymore. They were storefronts with apartments above, and they offered about as much shelter as a wet cardboard box. There was more banging as the dead tried to reach them, and up and up they went, up Burnside Street, one foot forward, a step to the side, a bullet here and there. How long could they go on like this? How long until the noose tightened?

He didn't know, but he supposed they would find out.

****

Rudy was feeling the march more than anyone. His mouth was so dry that his tongue stuck to the roof of his mouth. It felt like he was breathing glass. His calves and thighs burned with pain. And ahead of him, there was only the promise of more. But he pressed on, knowing that to stop was to die. He hadn't come this far just to give up now. It was cliché; he knew it, but it was the truth.

When the dead poured out of the windows above them, he gripped Tejada's knife tighter, wishing that he still had his sword with him. He had lost it in the fall that had put him in a coma. That had been over a week ago, but for him, it seemed like only a day.

The period when he had been unconscious was a mystery to him. There were no dreams, no nothing. It was as if for an entire week he had stopped existing completely. If that was what death was, maybe it wouldn't be so bad, but he suspected death was something else entirely. Certainly, the deaths of the creatures around him were drastically different from the typical ideas about death that he harbored just a couple of months ago. Either way, he was in no hurry to experience it again.

He was in a hurry to stop this march though. A vehicle, hell a motorized scooter, anything would be welcome right about now. His shoes, which had once been snug and comfortable, seemed like they had been molded to the feet of someone entirely different. He had lost a lot of weight when he had been unconscious, hell, since this whole thing had begun. He had never been a big fan of stepping on scales, but the clothing he wore hung off his frame, billowing around him. His shirt, which had once been tight against his belly, now hung like a muumuu. The

56

knotted shoestring belt around his waist kept his pants in place, but he felt like he was swimming in those as well.

He suspected much of the weight-loss was muscle. He was exhausted already, and they had only been walking for fifteen minutes. Granted, it was some of the most harrowing fifteen minutes of his life, but he began to suspect that even though his will to survive was a strong as ever, his body may not be able to match it. But he didn't complain. He didn't want to give anyone an excuse to leave him behind.

Which brought him back to the question that had been on his mind for most of the previous evening, but which he couldn't bring himself to ask of Amanda. *Just what had happened while he had been asleep?* Amanda, who had always been bright and cheery seemed different now. One minute, she had been this bright, happy-go-lucky girl, then, upon waking, he found her much the same but changed in some critical manner that he couldn't quite put his finger on. Something had happened to her, something which had hardened her in some way.

"Help!"

The scream came from above, and the veil of Rudy's thoughts fluttered away like a plastic bag in the wind. He looked upward to see a woman, covered in grime, leaning out of the fourth-story window of an apartment building. Her hair was long, gray, and wavy. It blew in the wind, and the hope on her face pulled at his heart.

The soldiers had heard the scream as well, and they all looked to Tejada.

"Keep walking," he said.

Rudy knew it was the right thing to do, but he knew it was wrong as well. That's how this world was now. Everything that was right was somehow wrong. The woman, tears gleaming in her eyes, yelled again, as if they hadn't heard her the first time. Everyone stopped looking at her, but they couldn't avoid hearing her pleas for help as they became frantic, almost sobbing, in nature.

"We can't just leave her," Amanda said.

No one said anything. Rudy looked at Amanda and wrapped his hand around her own. He squeezed it, but he knew the gesture meant little to her.

"No!" Amanda yelled, stopping in the middle of the street. "We can't just leave her!"

The soldiers turned and looked at her, and the look on their faces was one of resignation. They all knew they should help the lady, but there was no denying this simple fact: if they tried to help her, more of them would die in the process.

"Amanda," Tejada began.

"No! I know what you're going to say, and it isn't right!"

Rudy looked at Tejada, and he saw something there that he hadn't expected. He saw compassion etched on that granite face. He saw how much it hurt to leave that woman screaming in the window.

"We'll all die," Tejada said.

And there it was, as plain as day. He had said it, the one thing that couldn't be argued. To do the right thing would be to throw their lives away. So, it was the wrong thing that they did. Tejada turned and started walking, and as he did, so did the soldiers that followed him, their heads held a little lower.

Rudy walked back to Amanda and grabbed her hand. "Come on."

She came, shuffling forward like one of the dead that they were fleeing from. Behind them, the woman's screams echoed off the buildings. Her scream was the sound of hope dying, a haunting sound, the type of sound that found its way into your dreams, the type of dreams that brought you awake with tears in your eyes and a racing

58

heart. Her screams were the screams of one who knows they are going to die.

Rudy looked over his shoulder once, and he saw something that he would never forget. Below the woman's apartment building, the dead walked side by side, filling the street from one side to the other. Above, the woman leaned out of her window, her hand outstretched to him, her gray, wavy hair blowing in the wind. Her face was one of pure pain and torture. Slowly her arm fell, and then she too was falling. Rudy turned his back before he could see her hit the ground, but his mind went ahead and did him the dubious favor of filling in the blanks.

They continued onward.

They came to a stretch of road, where cars were piled up on top of each other, cars of all shapes and sizes, some looking like they were brand new except for a layer of ash and soot that had settled on their surfaces. Other cars had seen better days, their windows busted out, their upholstery covered in blood. The way the cars were situated, it was obvious that someone had built themselves a barricade.

The barricade was a seven-foot-tall snarl of rubber and metal. On the other side, the yellow-orange struts of a crane rose into the air, its giant claw swaying lightly in the wind.

"Get up there," Tejada yelled to Quigley and Day. Rudy remembered Quigley. He was the one with the blonde beard. Remembering all of the soldiers' names had become a test of his memory. The soldiers had distinct faces and names, but personality-wise, he was still trying to figure out who was who. Epps he knew. He had looked at the patch on his uniform multiple times until he had remembered his face. He was one of three African American soldiers. Everyone else was white except for Tejada and Ramirez who both seemed to be Latino as far as he could tell.

Quigley had a soft face surrounded by a startlingly yellow beard. It almost looked unnatural to Rudy, like that douche that was always stopping in at diners on The Food Network. But for Quigley, it worked. His hair, which was long enough to cover his ears, was also startlingly blonde. The other soldiers referred to him as "Quigs" for short. Amanda and Rudy stood close to each other, breathing in each other's scent. They oscillated between looking behind them at the approaching horde and keeping an eye on Quigs as he made his way up the barricade. It was a harder task than it looked, as the cars had been stacked in a reverse pyramid formation. The cars at the top overhung the cars at the bottom.

Luckily, for Quigs, there were enough handholds to allow him to reach the top, but Rudy bet that the dead wouldn't be able to scale such a creation. Although, he had once bet that the dead wouldn't be able to bring down the Memorial Coliseum as well. As Quigs reached the top, Rudy looked over his shoulder to check and see that none of the dead had appeared out of thin air right behind him. He was in luck, they were still a block away, but time was running short.

He turned his attention back to Quigs as he crested the top of the barricade.

"Stay low," Tejada hissed at the man, just before Quigs disappeared from sight.

Rudy eyed the barricade dubiously, and that sand through the hourglass feeling started to come over him. Time seemed to slip by faster and faster with every step that the dead took in their direction. Would he be able to climb the barricade when the time came... and what if what was on the other side was even worse than what was on this side? Maybe they could lift a manhole cover and disappear that way if worse came to worse.

Suddenly, Quigs appeared, hanging over the roof of a Rav 4. "Hey, it looks good on the other side here. I think we can get out."

"Alright, everybody get up and over those cars," Tejada said. "You two, get a rope around Beacham." Epps and Allen began to tie a rope around Beacham's waist. Rudy had time to look at the big man's ashen-brown face before he began to try and climb up the barricade on his own. He surveyed the stack of cars before he chose a suitable place for his ascent. The real trouble wouldn't be the climb, it would be when the wall of vehicles doubled back on itself overhanging the pavement.

If he fell from that height, he probably wouldn't hurt himself, other than his pride, but he would waste valuable time, during which the dead would steadily be closing the gap. Up he went, grasping onto the rearview mirror of a tan pickup truck. He pulled himself upward, feeling the strain in his arms. He was still weak, and that first move upward had proved just how weak he was.

He managed to climb a few feet further, but then he stalled, clinging to the tire and the undercarriage of an overturned truck. He looked upward, his free hand searching for a handhold that wasn't there. This was a bad idea. He saw a handhold that would stretch him to his limit, but if he was able to reach it, he might be able to make his way to the top of the pile without too much trouble. He should have stood next to Beacham while they were roping him up, let them pull him up like a helpless baby, but his pride had gotten in the way. Damn him and his stupid pride.

He decided to go for it. The worst that could happen would be that he fell a few feet, but maybe, if he could pull it off, he could save some face and not come off like a total pathetic loser. He readied himself, took a deep breath, and then swung outwards, his hand poised to grip the steering wheel of a truck through an open window.

He came up just short, the tips of his fingers curling around the steering wheel for a brief second, and then the momentum of his own body weight shifted backwards, and his fingers lost their grip. The sudden loss of pressure caused him to lose his balance, and then he lost his grip with his other hand. He tumbled awkwardly to the ground, landing with a great smack of flesh on the pavement. It sounded like a man doing a belly flop onto the calm surface of a pool.

The breath left him, and he thought he had broken everything in his body. He rolled on the pavement, aware that Amanda was calling his name along with the others, wondering what the fuck was going on down there, as they couldn't see over the lip of the barricade. At least they couldn't see his embarrassment. He rolled from side to side, wondering when he was going to die, and then the pain finally came to a point where he realized he was going to be alright... embarrassed but alright.

"You ok?" Tejada yelled down at him. He didn't have the breath to answer back. "Get a rope down there," Tejada called out to someone else. With Rudy still in pain, Epps dropped down to the ground and began tying a rope around him. He stood there like a baby as the soldier looped the rope around his waist and through his legs to make a makeshift harness.

"This ain't gonna feel good, but it's certainly better than the alternative," Epps said.

Rudy said nothing. He was too busy being embarrassed.

"Hurry up down there! The parade is almost here."

The dead were only five feet away when they began to hoist him up. A thousand rotten faces with their arms outstretched looked at him rising up off the ground, and for a brief moment, he felt like a piñata. And to the dead, he supposed he was, a piñata filled with treats, great, curvy twisty treats. He imagined his intestines pulled out, displayed like the ribbons of a maypole. Then he was at the top, the soldiers squatting down and yanking him up and over the lip of the barricade.

"Thank you," he said over and over again. He was truly appreciative of their help. They looked embarrassed by his gratitude and mumbled phrases like "It was nothing" and "No problem." But Rudy knew that if it wasn't for these men, he would be dead several times over already.

As he turned to check on Amanda, Rudy spied a look of pure hatred on the face of Andy, the guy from the movie theater. He had been distant, almost nonexistent as far as Rudy could tell, but to see such a look of pure hatred on his face caused Rudy's heart to skip a beat for a second. Then the look was gone, and Rudy began to question whether it had ever been there to begin with.

"Are you ok?" Amanda asked.

"Yeah. You?"

Amanda nodded, and then they turned to survey the other side of the barricade. Side streets had been blocked off and body after body lay rotting on the ground. It looked like a great battle had been fought here. Someone had survived here for a while in this intersection, using the crane to block off all the streets. However, the barricade to the west lay open now, and black scorch marks and twisted pieces of shrapnel gave some clue as to what had happened. Someone had found this barricade and tore right through it.

"Must have been one hell of a battle," Epps said.

"I doubt it. It was probably over in five minutes. I don't see a lot of brass on the ground," Allen said.

Whether it was over in five minutes or it lasted longer, they would never know. The world was full of mysteries like this now. Tableaus of carnage left like paintings. Only these paintings were like if you were looking at The Last Supper and Jesus had been removed. You had to fill in the blanks yourself, and sometimes, as in the case of the destroyed barricade, that was impossible.

They climbed down the barricade easily, as it was designed to keep people out, not in. On the ground, they stepped over bodies rotting in the hazy morning. They put their hands to their faces to try and mask the smell. Rudy tried not to see the white shapes crawling over the faces of the dead.

"Ooo-wee! Smells like when grandpa used to empty out the RV's shitter!" It was Quigs, smiling despite all of the nastiness on display.

Epps, not in the mood for levity, said, "Stay on point, Quigs."

As a group, with Quigs in the front next to Whiteside, they pushed through the busted barricade, each of them hoping that it wasn't an omen for what was about to happen to them. To the west, Burnside Street rose before them, and to their surprise it was clear except for a smashed bus and a few other random cars. Most of the wrecks must have been used in the making of the barricade. As an added bonus, the dead were staggered as well.

"Smooth sailing," Epps said. Rudy, having survived several worst-case scenarios, thought that Epps might have spoken too soon. But for the next mile, Epps was right.

Chapter 5: The Last Run

At the crest of Burnside Avenue, there was a tunnel. Cars choked off both sides of the tunnel, but inside, it was clear of both the dead and the living. Izzy Allen stared at the walls with the rest of the survivors. One message read, "WE MADE IT OUT. HEADED TO HILLSBORO - JAMES KING." Allen wondered who "we" referred to. Was it a family? Or was it another hodgepodge of survivors like Allen and the others?

Another message on the opposite wall, this one done in hard-to-read gold spray paint read: "DON'T GO INTO PORTLAND. ALL DEAD." How long ago had that one been written? A week? Two weeks? It seemed like Portland had died in no time at all. These things... these dead things had smothered the life out of an entire city as if it had been nothing more than a toddler in a crib.

But the message that really spoke to him was the one that said, "ALL ANGELS NOW." Allen couldn't stop thinking about it. All angels now... the vagueness fascinated him. It was poetry. That much was for sure, but how to interpret it? Was this message meant for the living? Was it meant to point out the fact that pretty much everyone was dead?

Allen certainly felt like no angel. Hell, he didn't feel like anything. He eyed the words, staring at them until the edges blurred, and they made no sense.

"Izzy! Come on!" Epps yelled from the edge of the tunnel.

Allen snapped out of his trance. "I'll be there in a second." He nudged the spray cans on the ground out of the way with his foot, and when he found one that seemed to still have some juice, he bent down and picked it up, looking left and right just in case one of the dead had managed to climb its way over the barricade of vehicles at either end of the tunnel. Seeing none, he stood up and shook the spray paint can, reveling in the sound that the widget made within as it mixed what was left of the paint.

He stepped up to the wall, hesitated a moment and then began to paint. The spray paint fumes smelled like hot junkie candy, wafting around his head as his arm moved methodically up, down, and around.

He stepped back and admired his work. Underneath the line, he had written: TRAPPED IN DEATH'S EMBRACE."

He let the empty spray can fall from his hand, and it tumbled to the ground with a hollow clunk. He ran to catch up to everyone else, and as he climbed over the barricade of cars at the end of the tunnel, he pondered how long the tunnel would last without constant maintenance. How long until there was no way into Portland from the west?

Ahead of him, the trees on the side of the road gave way to blue sky. It seemed like ages since he had seen such a thing. The smell of smoke was still in the air, and a few scattered plumes of smoke still swirled into the sky like upraised cat tails, but there was that blue sky, the same as when this whole shitty situation had begun.

He fell in line next to Epps, who shot him a look that said he was an idiot. They were moving slowly. Rudy, God bless him, had actually made it up the hill. It was afternoon now, and they were all feeling the march and suffering the aftereffects of prolonged adrenaline exposure. Their pace had been slowed by Rudy, who gasped the whole way up Burnside. It was a steep hill and not an easy climb, but Rudy had toughed it out. It helped that they had never been in any real imminent danger. The dead were still present as they climbed, but they were in such small numbers that they could afford take a break every now and then when Rudy needed to pause.

In the tunnel, they had paused even longer, everyone stopping to take in some fluids or piss against the tunnel walls. Allen's calves had been burning by that point. He silently cursed at how out of shape he had let himself become on the bridge. Just because it was the end of the world doesn't mean that you can't keep in shape.

Birds chirped in the air, and Allen actually couldn't remember the last time he had actually heard a bird singing. As he caught up to the others, he found himself walking through a cemetery. The group fell into a solemn silence, and Allen admired the rolling hills. The lawn, which had once been well-maintained, had grown to knee-length, obscuring many of the grave markers. The taller tombstones jutted out of the grass, looking lost and forlorn. On the crest of the hill, a shuffling zombie walked towards them, head cocked to the side and an ill-fitting suit hanging from its wasted body. Its arm reached out to them, and Allen had the impression that it was asking for help. It was the first zombie they had seen since climbing the hill. He wondered if the dead were like water, collecting at the lowest point possible. Perhaps the mountains would be free of the dead if that were the case. He trained his eyes to the west. That was where they were headed, and he saw the hills rising as purple shadows in the distance.

They were far away. They held such promise, room to breathe, a place to live and survive. He wanted to be there now. If only they had a helicopter, their struggle would be over in a few hours. He thought again about his decision to stick with Sergeant Tejada. Perhaps it had been a fool's choice.

When the message had come down from the President, a feeling of woe had swept through his fellow soldiers. *How could he do this? How could the President just give up? If the President is giving up, all is lost.* These were the prevailing sentiments of the day. Izzy Allen had not been immune from them. The next day had seen many deaths. Some soldiers just stole off into the day without weapons or supplies, their minds seemingly robbed of any common sense. General McCutcheon had relieved them of all their obligations and declared that he was going to Colorado. Izzy could have gone with him. He wanted to. Colorado was certainly closer to Alabama than Portland was, but something had held him back.

Then Tejada had talked to him, and everything had changed from there. Izzy was 22. There wasn't much waiting for him back at home. There was a girl, maybe. There was his family. But he couldn't bring himself to find out what had become of them. To find them dead would be too much for his soul. He knew this without a doubt. He knew that to see his parents rotting and dead would render this world pointless. Even worse would be finding that he couldn't find them. If he showed up at the old family homestead and couldn't find his sister, his parents, or any of his family, he would be left in a state of limbo, an unresolved morass of emotions that would lead to his eventual death as he hunted through the city and the Alabaman countryside looking for some sign of their survival or death. That would be a long haul, a long draining haul, and he knew he would wind up walking with the dead at the end of it.

No, it was better to cut the past off, sever it like a gangrenous limb and move forward. The past was nothing anymore. That was an entirely different world, a place where someone could sit on their back porch and sip some iced tea while listening to a ball game on the radio. There was no radio now. There were no ball games, and the amount of effort required to produce an ice cube wasn't worth it anymore. You would have to find a generator, find some potable water, hook a refrigerator up to it, and wait with your firearm in your hands for the Annies that would show up, drawn to the sound of a generator's chugging motor. Allen didn't expect to have iced tea any time soon.

They wound down the road, the overgrown cemetery sliding by. The other soldiers kept to themselves.

The only real sound came from Beacham who was breathing hard, holding his broken arm to his chest. His face was ashen and covered in sweat. Allen couldn't help but feel that Beacham would be dead sooner or later. It was a harsh thought, but not improbable. That arm would never heal fast enough. He could almost see the halo of fear that surrounded the man.

Beacham was big and simple, a real teddy bear. His impending doom was not being taken well, as the big man seemed like he was on the verge of tears. His head swung from side to side, more so than the other survivors, as if he expected an Annie to pop up behind him at any moment. Allen felt for the man; he felt for all of his fellow soldiers.

The dread of being stuck in a dying world had been too much for many of them. He remembered walking into a bathroom on the base soon after the announcement of their release. He found them hanging from the pipes in a shower room that dockworkers had used after work. Soldiers of all different sizes and races, their hands and feet twitching, ropes wrapped around their necks, the other ends of the rope secured to the pipes above.

Allen stood, watching them, lines from Abel Meeropol's *Strange Fruit* running through his mind. He tried not to look at their faces, but he did. He knew those faces. He had gone through basic with one of them. Others he had had beers with, conversed with, and shared smokes with. His heart felt like it was going to split, and he dropped to his knees, two dozen dead eyes following his every movement.

That's when Tejada had found him. He had jumped as Tejada had placed a comforting hand on his shoulder. "You're not thinking about joining them, are you?"

Allen had no answer. He had, in fact, been thinking about killing himself, finding some rope and tying it around one of those sterling silver pipes. It would have been easier that way. The dread would be gone. The doubt would be gone. He wouldn't have to see his friends die.

"Come on. Let's finish this," Tejada said. He pulled Allen to his feet and reached across his body to draw Allen's sidearm from his holster. "Let's send these boys home." He held the pistol out to Allen, and Allen just stared at it. He nodded as he took it from Tejada, tears streaming from his eyes. Then, one by one, they sent the boys home, putting them to rest forever.

"Should we cut them down?" he had asked when all the bodies were still.

"Leave them hanging. We've given them all the mercy they deserve. Come on."

Allen had followed. Tejada had never asked him to come along on their little journey, and Allen had never asked where they were going or what they were doing. He just accepted it. Tejada had saved his life. His life belonged to Tejada now, and he was fine with that. He spotted a small cat bounding through the grass in front of an apartment complex, and he thought, *That's the most beautiful thing I've seen today... until I see the next.*

****

Andy could feel adrenaline rushing through his body yet again. They were in a residential area. Apartment complexes rose to their right and left. Along with the apartments came the dead. Gone was the quiet of the cemetery, replaced by the scrape of shoes and bare bones on the pavement.

He didn't mind the sound of the shoes so much, but the sound of bone scraping on the pavement made Andy grit his teeth. The rhythmic scraping of the dead woman in front of him was driving him nuts. He had to forcibly keep his finger off the trigger. He was *becoming*, and to give in to his urge to stop that incessant scraping would only make the others look down on him again. He needed their trust, but more than that, he needed their respect. He wouldn't get either if he ended the noise. He walked around the dead woman, and she turned and followed him, her teeth locked in a horrible smile due to her missing lips. Dried blood covered her scalp where her hair had been, and she walked with an uneven gait, as she had lost one of her shoes. As she turned, the bones of her exposed toes, the flesh worn away, scraped across the gray street one more time, sending a shiver up his spine all the way to his teeth.

He walked past the dead thing, though the sound of her shuffling followed them. Down they went, Andy trying not to look at Rudy. The bastard had made it. Against all odds, Rudy was still alive and kicking. His entire body was covered in sweat. His pants, which were held up with shoestrings that had been knotted together, kept sagging. His shirt, a red polo that floated on his body, was covered in his sweat, and his red hair, which had begun curling in the strangest of spots was slicked down to his head despite his many cowlicks. He walked with his head down, his legs flopping forward as if they weren't being controlled by Rudy at all. He reminded Andy of a child at the end of a long shopping trip forcing themselves to make it to the car. Amanda stuck close to him.

He didn't trust her, but no one else seemed to mind her presence. But that was ok. She would get hers. The universe had a way of making people pay for being shitty people. The universe would bide its time, and she would pay. Rudy would as well. Though the man had done nothing to him, Andy couldn't stand looking at him. His freckly face, his billowing neck, the sheer size of him. Even when he talked, he sounded like a whiny little bitch.

The scraping continued behind him as the road curved to the right. For his part, Andy felt just as tired as Rudy looked, but he was able to put on a show of not looking as tired as he was. The soldiers seemed fine, with the exception of the man with the broken arm. Andy shook his head. *Tough break, literally.* He smirked a little bit at his joke, but then wiped it off his face as Tejada turned to survey his people.

"Keep your eyes out for some place to hole up. It's been a long day."

They all agreed, and he could see the other soldiers perk up at the prospect of resting somewhere, and as they rounded the bend in the road, their wishes were answered.

Ahead of them was a supermarket, its front windows smashed. Bodies lay in the parking lot amid cars with their windows bashed in and overturned shopping carts.

"What do you think about that?" Quigs asked Tejada.

"I think it has some promise. Beacham, I want you to stay outside with the civvies. Everyone else, let's sweep and clear that place. No guns. You see an Annie, you bash its head in. Let's keep it quiet; I want to be able to sleep tonight without any damn banging on the walls."

"Can I go?" Andy asked. Tejada looked at him sideways, and he turned away from Andy.

"Walk with me, Andy," Tejada said.

Andy trotted to keep up with the Sergeant as they made their way closer to the supermarket.

"What is going on with you?"

"What do you mean?"

"Do you have some sort of death wish? Are you trying to get yourself killed?"

"No... I just..."

"Spit it out."

"I just want to be useful. I want to be capable."

Tejada nodded, and patted Andy on the shoulder, and Andy knew he wasn't going in the store with the others. "You said you want to be capable, and that, to me, means that you, down in that great big heart of yours, know that you're not capable. And until you are capable, I can't take the risk. So please, stay outside and help protect the others."

Andy nodded, though he was screaming in his head. He had been dismissed again. As he stood in the parking lot, he watched Tejada and the others step inside the supermarket through its smashed front windows. The interior was black, and despite the fact that he wanted to go with them, he waited with Beacham, Amanda, and Rudy. The latter sat on the ground wheezing.

He flinched as he heard bone scraping against the pavement.

****

Quigs halted at the threshold of the store. He reached into the pocket of his pants and pulled out a flashlight. He fastened it to his rifle and turned it on. The others did the same, tiny pools of blue-white light illuminating the darkness of the grocery store. They spread out wide over the front of the store, and they pushed forward through the cash registers towards the aisles.

Quigs couldn't help but lick his lips as package after package caught his eye. Though much of the shelf space was empty, there was still plenty of food left over. This fact alone was a testament to how fast the Annies had overrun the world because there shouldn't have been a scrap of grub left.

He walked softly, heel to toe, but the glass still crunched under his boot heel. They moved through the line of cash registers, pressing forward as a group, and he had to resist the urge to reach out and grab a candy bar off the rack. There would be plenty of time for that later.

From somewhere in the darkness, he heard one of their calls, a soft little moan like that of a child being woken up when all they really want to do is sleep. The hair on the back of his neck stood up. He flipped the safety of his rifle to the on position. The last thing he wanted to do was accidentally shoot himself while taking a swing at an Annie... not when he was this close to scoring some tasty food. God he was hungry.

The moan came again, and he shined his flashlight down the aisle in front of him. He was in the baked goods aisle. Tin baking pans and rolls of wax paper sat untouched, along with a rack full of flour and sugar. He stepped forward and lost sight of the other soldiers in his area. He pushed dislodged packages of cupcake wrappers out of the way with his boot and slid forward, despite the fact that he wanted to turn around right then and there. There was something unnatural about this whole situation. They should just keep running, but Tejada wanted to stop, and Beacham and Rudy needed a rest. But still... that groan. It came again, closer this time.

He was in the middle of the aisle when he heard a thump against the rack to his right. "Shit," he said a little too loudly.

From the aisle to his right, he heard Ramirez shout, "I got one!" Then he heard the sounds of struggle. The next thing he knew, the rack next to him was falling over and he was buried underneath bags of flour and sugar. They might as well have been bags of cement.

The tumbling rack was unbearably loud, and then he heard voices screaming left and right. He was trapped, the weight of the rack combined with the weight of the sugar and flour to prevent him from moving.

"This place is fucked!" Epps yelled in the distance.

"Keep cool!" Tejada yelled. "Fall back! We'll get them outside!"

Quigs could hear Ramirez swearing in Spanish as he struggled with one of the dead. He heard the crinkling of plastic as they fought among the groceries, and then he heard the sound of broken glass. Then Quigs heard something else, something that made him stop breathing. It was a groan, the one that he had heard before.

He was trapped on his back with only his head sticking out of the pile. He had to tilt his head backwards to see where the source of the sound was coming from. But he couldn't see anything. He could only sense someone approaching. Then he heard a pop and a crunch as someone or something crushed something on the ground in front of him.

That was enough for Quigs. He wasn't going to go out like this.

"Help! Help! I'm trapped underneath this goddamn thing!"

He heard their voices then, his fellow soldiers, his fellow survivors.

"Where are you?"

"It's Quigs!"

"Where the fuck is he?"

"We gotta get Quigs!"

But these words were not comforting, as all of the voices were too far away.

"Over here!" Ramirez yelled, and Quigs remained quiet. The shuffling was closer, and he could smell the death coming from the Annie in the aisle. It was old rot. Quigs saw flashlight beams shining through the darkness, and in his brain, he screamed. He tried to breathe as quietly as he could, and then he felt something bump into his head... it felt like the toe of a shoe.

He heard someone sniffing around, and then a drop of something cold fell and splattered on his face. Quigs squeezed his eyes shut as he felt the first caress of the Annie's dried digits. *Not my eyes, please, God not my eyes.*

There was a loud bang, and cold liquid splattered his face.

"I told you not to shoot Goddammit!" Tejada yelled.

"He was going after Quigs!" It was Brown; he could have kissed the guy.

"Get him out of there," Tejada yelled.

75

Quigs thought he was going to explode from sheer joy as the others began kicking groceries to the side and pulling the shelf off of him. He felt the pressure loosen, and it was like being born again.

"Someone go get Beacham and the others. That shot will bring more Annies. You can bet your nuts on it. Hey, where the fuck is Ramirez?"

"I haven't seen 'im," Epps said. "Anyone else seen him?"

Everyone looked around, but Ramirez wasn't present. "I heard him fighting with an Annie. He was right over here." Quigs walked through a crack in the displaced shelf, unslinging his rifle as he went. It seemed no worse for wear despite his tumble. He shined his flashlight around and spied a puddle of blood next to an Annie with its forehead bashed in. The blood was fresh and not dark like the blood that came from the dead.

"I got something," Quigs said.

"Alright, Brown, Whiteside, get out there and bring Beacham in here."

"And the civvies?" Brown asked.

"Yeah, them too."

Brown and Whiteside turned and moved back towards the front of the store, purpose in their steps.

"Lead on," Tejada said.

Without having to be told, everyone went into operational mode, and they began to follow the trail of blood. It led through the store, heading deeper into the darkness. Quigs knew what they would find at the end of that trail. It could only be one of two things. It was either going to be a dead Ramirez or a living Ramirez scared out of his mind at the prospect of death. But he was one of their own. They would help him, no matter the situation.

Quigs inched forward, and his friends fanned out beside him as they approached two green double-doors. Two circular windows were set into the swinging doors.

The windows shone black, and the blaze of their flashlights reflected back at them. There was a bloody handprint on the left door. A drip of red ran down the green paint.

"No more gunshots," Tejada hissed.

Quigs hated this whole situation. He felt like he was hunting his friend. Ramirez had always been a good dude, a little too religious for Quigs' liking, but that was alright. At least he had something to believe in. What did Quigs believe in? Sleeping in and football? Wasn't much of either going around these days.

He stepped through the left double-door, and Day pushed through on the right. They pressed the doors to the wall, holding them there and waving their flashlights around the dark interior of the grocery store's storage area. He could hear the buzz of flies. Fruit, long gone bad, sat molding and rotting in wooden crates piled high with the stuff. The smell was sickeningly sweet. He saw nothing, no movement. Then he spied some blood on a wooden crate. He highlighted it with his flashlight, and Day tapped him on the shoulder to let him know he saw it as well.

The other soldiers moved into the space, and more beams of light lit the interior. There was a bang from somewhere, like the sound of a boot hitting metal. Then there was a rattling as a sliding metal door was lifted upwards. Blinding daylight filled the space, and they all saw Ramirez roll under the door and into the sunshine. Then he disappeared as the door crashed closed behind him.

The soldiers rushed forward, Day and Quigs flinging the door upwards, blinding light pouring into the storage area. As the door rumbled open, they saw the back of Ramirez in full flight, his dripping blood dotting the back alley of the grocery store.

"Want me to?" Allen asked Tejada, raising his rifle and sighting down its length.

"No, he made his choice," Tejada said. "He wants to walk with the dead, we'll let him. He's not ready yet."

Quigs wondered what had come over Ramirez, but then he saw something that shook him more than it should have. On the ground there was a small bible. Something stuffed inside glinted in the daylight. After they lowered the door, Quigs went over to the bible and picked it up. Inside was Ramirez's crucifix still attached to the gold chain.

"Fuck," Quigs murmured.

Tejada, all business, as if nothing had happened, said, "Alright, lets grab some food, and get back here on the double. I got a feeling more of the dead are coming our way. I want to get some food, get those civvies in here, and barricade the shit out of this place. We get trapped, we got a nice back door here."

No one moved. "Come on! Make it happen, people," Tejada exhorted. The soldiers, knowing that food was at a premium, moved into the grocery store dutifully, grabbing whatever caught their fancy. Instinctively, they stayed away from the meat and dairy part of the store. No one wanted to see or smell what happened to hundreds of pounds of spoiled dairy and meat.

When they were done, they bundled up their wares and returned to the back of the store. They began piling box after box of canned food in front of the double doors, but none of the dead were coming. They all knew that.

Beacham had already related the tale of Ramirez running past them like his ass was on fire. The wounded soldier had sprinted past Beacham and the others without saying a word, a haunted look on his face. The dead, already converging on the grocery store due to the gunfire, locked in on Ramirez as he streaked past them. Beacham, Rudy, Amanda, and Andy had taken the opportunity to get into the shadows of the grocery store. They watched silently as the crowd of gathering Annies turned to follow Ramirez.

Quigs liked to think that Ramirez had planned the whole thing. He liked to think that he was giving them a better chance at surviving by drawing off the Annies, so they wouldn't have to fight their way out of the grocery store. But another part of Quigs thought that maybe Ramirez's mind had just snapped. Maybe he had gotten bitten, and the only thing he could do was run, foolishly thinking that maybe he could outrun the virus that was coursing through his veins.

With a pack of batteries at his feet, Quigs ripped open a Whatchamacallit candy bar. It was sweet and chewy... but he wasn't in the mood. He choked it down, his mind elsewhere. Periodically, Quigs' hand would go to the small bible tucked away in his shirt pocket. Maybe he had meant to draw them away. Nah.

****

Private Sergio Ramirez had always been a fan of running. On base, you could find him jogging the perimeter in his spare hours. He loved the feeling that came with getting into a solid stride, that moment of unconscious effort where his legs just seemed to move on their own, and his mind went elsewhere. Even in the desert, with the heat hitting dangerous levels, he would make time to get into that zone. His life, once he had been deployed overseas, had been one of constant fear. His first month there, any time he heard a noise, he would duck and cover his head.

The other soldiers ribbed him constantly because of this, but he knew that they had all gone through the same thing. Still, walking around the base, Sergio had the constant fear that at any moment he could just end. Before he even heard the sound, his head could be turned into hamburger by a random sniper round. It had happened before to other unlucky soldiers, rarely, but it had happened.

Jogging had been his escape from the threat of death. He would change into a raggedy old T-shirt and some army shorts that were a little too short to go without remark from his fellow soldiers, but he didn't care. He would start out at a gentle lope just to work the kinks out. Around and around he would go with the sun beating down on him. He would chew up mile after mile in his jogging shoes, stepping lightly over the sandy sections and picking his way through the rocky areas. He would do this until his mind went away, until it disappeared completely and he stopped existing. Running allowed him to escape.

In the grocery store, an Annie had popped around the corner, and he had swung at it with his rifle. He missed its head and was forced to retreat backwards, struggling to keep his flashlight trained on its gruesome face, only to trip over cans of food spilled haphazardly on the ground.

He had gone down to the ground, a prayer on his lips. He was able to get to his knees when the Annie pounced on him. With no room to swing his rifle, he fought with every ounce of his strength to push the creature off of him, using the rifle for leverage. The smell of the dead thing made his eyes water, and his breath quickly became ragged as he started to panic. Ramirez and the Annie danced in the aisle, and he had barely enough strength to call for help. The Annie shoved him backwards, pinning him between the shelf on his left, his rifle stuck uselessly between his body and his assailant.

He could see nothing. The flashlight was shining downwards, and in his mind, he imagined the dead thing's face taking a bite out of his throat. The Annie pushed him further backwards, and the shelf tipped, falling over with a loud crash.

On the other side of the shelf, he heard someone scream, but he couldn't place the voice. Was that Quigs? Or was it him, screaming his own death knell? He slid downwards, pushing the Annie off of him trying to feel for its shoulders so that he didn't wind up placing his fingers in the damned thing's mouth.

The cold skin of its stomach pressed against his face, and then it dropped to the ground with him. Its teeth clacked together in an effort to bite him. Ramirez tried to roll out from underneath it, and it lost its grip momentarily. As he rose upwards, visions of escape danced in his head. He would just sprint over to the nearest beam of light, and everything would be alright.

But as he rose from a sitting to a standing position, he met resistance, right at the moment he was halfway between sitting and standing. The Annie had a hold of the strap of his rifle, and he fell backwards. He involuntarily put his hand out to break his fall, but it didn't touch the floor. It touched something cold and hard, and then there was pain. He pulled with all his might, but he couldn't free his fingers... and then they were free... no, they weren't free. They were gone. With his elbow, he bashed repeatedly on the Annie's skull. Hot blood splashed from his missing fingers onto his face, and he bit his lower lip to prevent himself from screaming.

He was a dead man now. He might as well be an Annie as far as the others were concerned. He had seen how this all went down. When the Annie stopped moving, he picked up his rifle and headed for the back of the building, hoping that there was some means of escape.

He staggered up the aisle, kicking food out of the way. None of it was any good to him now. Death was here, and it was coursing through his veins. He tried to pray, but the words wouldn't come. They were locked away, blocked off by the devil's virus. He would be one of them. No one else had survived a bite, and he knew that he wasn't anything special.

Double-doors loomed ahead of him, and he pushed through, shining his flashlight left and right, swatting the buzzing flies and the stink of rotted fruit away from his face with his good hand. At the far end of the storage area, he saw the rolling metal doors of the loading dock. That was his way out. Behind him, he could hear people shouting. A gunshot boomed through the grocery store, and he knew they would come looking for him. He also knew that they would put a bullet in him.

The one he feared the most was Tejada. He was the most practical son of a bitch that he had ever met. He was the type of dude that would cut a kid's dog in half so they would stop arguing over it. In this case, he was the dog.

Though he feared the man, he loved him as well. Tejada had kept them safe, all of them, over the preceding weeks. He had prevented them from doing stupid things; he had given them a sense of order, but he couldn't let the man kill him. It would weigh on him. No, he owed Tejada more than the occasional nightmare of his death. He owed every one of those men in there more than that.

They weren't going to see him die. They weren't going to see none of that bullshit. He would go out doing something he loved... running. And if he helped his friends in the process, well, that was even better. Besides, waiting for the bullet, that might be considered suicide in God's book. If there was a heaven, he planned on being there. If this was God's plan for him, then so be it. He would see it through to the end. He pulled his rifle over his head, then his crucifix. He reached into his shirt pocket and pulled out a small, dog-eared bible. In this, he stuffed his necklace, in the hopes that someone would pick it up and carry it with them, and maybe, just maybe, save themselves.

He squatted down and lifted the rolling door just as he saw beams of light shining around the storage area. He lifted the door, ignoring the pain in the severed fingers of his left hand. Once he had lifted it high enough, he rolled into the daylight, dropped off the edge of the loading dock, and hit the ground running. His feet felt heavy, and the blood from his hand jetted out as he ran.

The sun had never been so beautiful. It splashed off the dusty pavement, and he let loose with his stride, not bothering to wait until he was warmed up. He ran with crossed fingers on his good hand. He heard them yell, but he didn't stop, and there was no gunshot. He rounded the corner, juking to the side, out of the arms of a random Annie. He sprinted up the side of the building, noticing nothing but the freedom of his pumping legs and the beauty of the day.

At the front of the grocery store, he zipped past Beacham and the others. He felt them turn and watch him. Already, the dead were gathering around the grocery store.

"Come on, you fuckers! Come and get some!" he yelled. He almost laughed as they turned and looked at him like a drunk affronted in a bar. They would follow. He had gotten their attention. He waved his bloody hand in the air so that the dead could see he was alive and well, and then he ran in earnest.

The wind rushed through his hair, and it was as if this was his first run ever. He had forgotten what it felt like to have your hair blowing behind you as you ran. Overseas, he had always kept it short, spiky. But it had grown some over the last few weeks. Some of the men kept their shit neat with scissors, but Ramirez had let his grow unchecked. He was glad now.

As his feet pounded the pavement, he disappeared into his mind, freed from the stress of knowing he was going to die. All that existed was the road. He weaved in and out of the dead and back towards the city. It was an uphill climb, but he didn't care. Sweat dripped from his head, and he ripped his shirt off as he ran, letting the sun kiss him one last time.

He let loose with a primal yell, and his lungs, though they burned, fed him with great bursts of oxygen that flooded his body. He felt high. He felt good. He could run like that forever, and that's just what he intended to do. He thanked God for his time on the earth, and he pressed forward, digging into his run, ignoring the ache in his quads from pushing up the hill. It was a great day for a run.

Chapter 6: Old Friends

The road before them was blocked off completely. As Highway 26 veered off and up, it disappeared around a bend. On the left side of the highway, there was a sheer drop off. To the right, the scar of a mountain sat. The scar had been made when the road had been blasted through the side of the mountain, exposing red clay and spurs of rock older than anything man knew. On the road itself, the smoke-stained ruins of a semi-truck sat sideways, blocking off any chance of making it through to the other side.

The survivors sat looking at the ruined truck, cursing the dumb soul that was responsible for causing the roadblock. They had been forced to hike a mile up the damn hill once they had run into the traffic snarl.

They had hoofed it past row after row of abandoned cars, their packs heavy on their backs. In some vehicles, the dead rotted, their cars and trucks turned into their tombs. Mort walked faster past these, lest one of the dead punch through a car window and escape, only to appear behind him when he least expected it. The others felt much the same way. Whenever they passed one of these tombs, he could see them pick up the pace as well. It was illogical he supposed. If they could have escaped, they probably would have done so by now.

Others had been this way. They were sure of that. At the beginning of the traffic snarl, they had seen cars with little to no dust on the windows, the keys still sitting in the ignition, the insides stripped bare of anything that they could use to survive. But whoever those mythical survivors were, there was no sign of them now. They were gone, and Mort, Claire, Joan, Lou, and Katie were the only living people in the entire world as far as they could see.

How long that would remain was anybody's guess, but Mort still hoped to live for a couple of months at least. Anything longer would be setting himself up for failure.

"Looks like the only way through is over that tanker," Lou said.

Mort didn't like it, but there really was no other choice. The semi-truck had clearly been heading west when it had jackknifed. The rear wheels hung precariously over the edge of the drop-off, the guard rail turned into a dusty blue, metal ribbon that floated in mid-air. Underneath the tanker, a line of cars sat smashed. The driver had lost control of his truck, and the trailer had swerved into the oncoming lane, crushing the tops of a line of cars.

At some point, a fire had begun. The tires on the semi-had exploded from the heat, and now the whole damn mess sat low to the ground. They had already tried the doors to the cab, but they were fused shut from the fire, and the front of the semi had been buried underneath a jagged rockslide. Whether the rockslide was a result of the exploding tanker or simply an occurrence of nature, none of them knew, but Lou was right. Up and over was their only option.

The cab would be infinitely easier to climb over than the jagged metal of the exploded tanker. Lou went first, scrambling up over the top. They waited patiently as he lay low on the roof of the semi to look at the road before them. Mort found his patience waning as he stared at the bottom of Lou's well-worn boots. Then Lou spun around, his eyes large, and he put his finger to his lips.

Whatever it was that he saw, it had him spooked... and wanting them to be quiet. Mort knew what that meant. More dead, more fighting. He nodded at Lou, and then shared his own wide-eyed looks with the others. Lou turned around and helped the women up, one by one. It was an awkward climb with everything they owned on their backs, not to mention the rifles that they had scavenged. No one was in the mood to lay down their gear. It was too great a risk. Situations changed so quickly in the new world that it was only prudent to lay down your stuff when you were sure that you were safe, and out in the open, they were never safe.

He had grown to hate his own rifle. The skin at his neck was sore from where the strap constantly rubbed against it, but he would take that chafing if it meant that he wouldn't be eaten alive. He reached up and scratched his itchy beard. It had been bothering him for the last week, but scissors had been low on their priorities. The damn thing itched, and it itched bad. A beard was a great thing in winter, but it was still the tail end of summer. The heat was still there, and he found his beard wet and itchy for most of the days, except when they had ridden in the car, the cool A.C. blasting over them. That had been heaven.

But they knew there was more heaven on the way, something even better than air conditioning. There was a place out there where they could put their backs to the wall and live how they wanted to, without fear of being overrun by the dead in the middle of the night. With each mile there were less of them, and that was a good thing. It was getting so that maybe one day he could just sit back and relax. Maybe he will have found some scissors by then.

Before he knew it, it was his turn to climb the semi. The cab was blue and plain. The words on the side were only half visible, the other half buried in rock and dirt from the rockslide. He reached up and grabbed Lou's hand, and as he pulled himself up, feeling that damn rifle strap dig into his neck again, he knew why Lou had wanted him to keep quiet.

The others had slowly maneuvered their way onto the top of the rockslide. They were silent as a spider in the corner of a bedroom. There was noise now that the wreckage of the big rig was no longer blocking the sound, but it wasn't coming from them. It was a scraping noise, the scrape of boots on pavement.

The dead were there, on the other side, lined up between the cars like impatient drivers looking to see what was going on ahead. There were dozens of vehicles. In their desperation, some drivers had attempted to drive through the parked cars. Snarled bits of metal and broken taillights littered the ground. But this was all insignificant next to the hundreds of dead that wandered the road. They shuffled slowly, not seeming to go anywhere in particular. As he watched, an eagle swooped down and picked at the shredded flesh of one of the dead. It reached up to grab the bird, but it was off and away before the dead man could seize it. It looked into the sky, reaching to the heavens, and a lone feather helicoptered to the ground.

"How the fuck are we going to get by that?" Mort asked.

"I don't think we can," Lou said.

"So what? We just go back?" Katie hissed.

Lou shook his head, and Mort waited expectantly. Lou was good with plans, certainly better than Mort was. He could swing a hammer and run all day, but when it came to clever things, Mort was more a doer than a thinker.

"We can't go back," Joan said, and Mort knew without looking that Clara would be nodding right along with her. Sometimes it seemed as if they were of one mind these days.

"Let's climb down," Lou said. "I don't want these things to see us and get agitated. If what I have in mind works, we may be able to go around these things."

Silently, they descended the semi-truck's cab, steadying each other as they dropped to the pavement. Mort tried not to look at the dead mother in the red jeep nearest them, her seatbelt locked tight against the rotting fabric of her shirt, the shadow of a child safety seat in the back. How long until all these things would be naked, until the clothes they had been wearing when they died rotted right off them? Somehow, that idea was even more horrifying. He hoped he wasn't around for that day.

"So what's this plan?" Katie asked.

"We're gonna go under," Lou said.

"Under?" Clara and Joan questioned in unison.

"Hear me out," Lou said, holding his hands up as if fending off coming blows. "When we were up there, I got a good look at that road. Now, if we just hop down off that cab on the other side, I figure we got a good chance of getting ourselves killed."

"We can take 'em," Katie said, her eyes fierce and cold at the same time.

"No, we can't," Clara said, and Mort could feel the tension between the two. There was something unspoken there, but Mort didn't know enough about women to be able to figure out what it was. "That road goes straight up. Once the dead see us, they're going to bunch right up, and we don't have enough ammo to put all of those things down."

Mort nodded. Clara made sense.

"We can run over the top of the cars," Katie responded.

"Straight up hill?"

"Listen, we don't have to do any of that." Lou stalked over to the end of the semi-truck. "On the left side of the road, there's this drop-off, right?" Mort nodded as he began to follow Lou's thinking. "But between the drop-off and the road, there's this railing. If we hang down and stay on the railing side, we should be able to sneak right by those things."

"Uh-uh. No way," Joan said. "There's no way we can just drag ourselves up the side of the road. Our arms will give out."

"You don't have to go the whole way," Lou said, "just part. I'll climb on top of the truck, and draw them all over here. While they're distracted, you guys climb along that railing until you're clear of the dead. Leave me with that rifle, and I'll pick off any of 'em that get too close."

"You're a shit shot," Joan said. "I'll stay."

Mort knew she was right. Joan had practiced enough with the rifle. The rest of them were amateurs compared to her, and she wasn't even that great. "I agree with Joan," Mort said, drawing a dark look from Lou. "She's the best shot, man. If I'm gonna dangle off the side of this canyon, I wanna make sure ain't no one bitin' my fingers off while I'm doin' it."

"If Joan stays, I stay too," Clara said.

Katie looked up at the sky as if to say, "How stupid can these people be?"

"You can't stay; that sort of defeats the purpose of one of us hanging back," Joan said

Clara didn't like the idea. "But what if something goes wrong?"

"Nothing is going to go wrong," Joan said, channeling the remains of the reassuring doctor that had once lived inside of her.

"If you die because of this I'm going to kill you," Clara said.

"I would do the same for you."

Clara nodded and that was it. No goodbyes. No tears. Silently, they waited as Joan climbed the side of the semi-truck. Her ascent was quick and easy. They watched as she stood on top of the cab of the semi like a Greek goddess ready to rain fire down on Athens, and then she began to holler.

"Here I am you dead fucks! Come and get me!" She stomped on the roof of the truck, producing a hollow clang that seemed as if it would carry for miles. She looked over her shoulder and tossed them a smile. "It's working." Then she turned back to the task at hand.

Mort turned his back and made sure that everything he had was tight on his body. The rifle was tight. He cinched the straps on his backpack; the food and water within could be the difference between life and death. Then he bent down to tie his shoes, pulling the laces tight and double-knotting them. He would have to undo them later, or else he would strangle the circulation to his feet, but he wanted to make sure that he didn't lose a boot over the side of the canyon. There would be no getting it back. A good pair of shoes was as important as water or food in this world. But as a homeless man, that had always been true. Your shirt could have holes in it. Your pants could have holes too. But if you didn't have a good pair of shoes, there wasn't much you could do about it. He had seen men fight over shoes like rabid dogs, homeless men who cared little for the world. A man could lose a few teeth just for staring at another man's boots for too long.

     He stood up. He was ready. He crept over to the edge of the pavement. His head swam from side to side as he peered over the edge of the road. He saw red clay, billowing outward at a steep angle. It wasn't the fall that would kill you, it was the rocks that jutted from the side of the hill. Once a person got falling fast enough, those jagged edges would cut skin open like a filet knife, and their guts would be spilled on the side of the mountain until the vultures got to them.

     He inched over to the area where the railing hung suspended in the air. The end of the semi-jutted into space. The only way to get around it was to go under. He looked back at the others. They stared back at him, anxiety etched onto their faces.

     "Go!" Joan yelled at them.

     With that, Mort crouched down and reached underneath the trailer of the semi-truck. He wrapped his hand around a mud-encrusted pipe, and slowly, he inched his way under the truck. As he reached the edge of the overhanging trailer, he became aware that he was going to have to go quite a way without the benefit of the guard rail. He pressed his body against the slope of the canyon, his hands above his head, gripping the edge of the road. He felt as if he were one wrong move from plummeting down the side of the ravine. If he had tried to stand straight up, he would have tumbled all the way to the bottom.

He pressed his chest into the rough earth and inched sideways, never able to shake the feeling that he was going to tumble backwards. His fingers were suspended above him, gripping the edge of the warm pavement. He could feel the strain in his fingers, and at any moment, he expected one of the dead to see his fingers slowly shuffling along the edge of the road.

He could hear the dead above him, pressing into the wreck of the semi-truck in an effort to get at Joan. Mort imagined one of the dead, walking slowly over to him and dropping to its knees. Achingly slow, it would lean toward his hands and take a slow bite of his fingers, sending him tumbling to his death.

As a rifle shot rang out, the image in his mind solidified. He began to move faster.

****

Joan racked the bolt on her rifle, swearing quietly under her breath. She heard the click of the bolt and the clang of the shell on the roof of the semi. She drove another round into the chamber and aimed at the dead thing again.

Most of the main body of the horde were there at her feet, pressing mindlessly into the wreckage of the semi-truck. For some reason that Joan couldn't figure out, there were a few inquisitive types that were drawn to the area where the others were trying to sneak by. *How did they know they were there?* The noise she was making should have been able to cover any sort of sound they were making as they inched their way along. The tips of their fingers were the only parts of their bodies that could be seen, and even she could barely make them out from this distance. Maybe those would draw one or two of the dead, but most of them should be paying attention to her. As she sighted down her rifle, the head of another one bobbed into sight, just a few feet from the guard rail.

"What the fuck?"

They knew they were there. Somehow, the dead knew they were there. She squeezed the trigger, slowly. This was how she had learned to shoot. Aiming at signs from the side of their vehicle, she had learned to slowly depress the trigger as opposed to jerking on it, which would throw her aim off by the smallest of amounts. But when dealing with hundreds of feet-per-second, that small variation added up quickly. In order to pull off headshots, she had to be slow, deliberate, like a person with tweezers pulling a splinter out of the palm of their hand. A puff of red mist let her know that her aim had been true.

The dead man fell to the ground, and Joan began to stomp harder on the roof of the semi as she lined up another shot.

"I'm over here, you bastards!"

Her cries were heard; the dead turned towards her, their arms held out to her as if she were their savior. She tried not to see them, not to see the humanity on those rotten and scarred faces, but it was impossible. There were children in the crowd, women, the elderly, men who looked like they were as strong as an ox in real life... and yet, here they all were, dead. They pressed against the wreckage of the tanker, splitting their skin wide open on the sharp metal, but they didn't care. They still wanted her.

She squeezed the trigger again, and her rifle tore through the shoulder of a balding old man who approached the area where the others were inching along. He could have been a professor in his past life. Though the bullet wound was large enough to fell a normal human, it did absolutely nothing to the dead man. He continued to shamble forward, his arm hanging at an impossible angle, until he reached the guard rail. He bent over and began pawing at something below, hiding his bald pate behind the

93

trunk of his body. She didn't have a shot, unless she could shoot through his body and hope that the bullet found its way into the creature's brain.

****

The first shot almost did Lou in, not because it had almost hit him, but because he hadn't been ready for it. Inching along, holding onto the road above, he had almost released his grip out of pure shock as the shot echoed across the ravine. It scared him bad enough that he lost his grip on the road with his left hand. While all of his weight was held up by the four fingers of his right hand, his left arm pin-wheeled in the air, until his brain registered that if he didn't get his hand back up on the road, he was going to die. With a grunt, he reached upward, panic flushing his body with fear. Sweat covered his head.

The creature fell to the ground above him with a thump, and black blood infused with the smell of rot began to drip over the side of the road like syrup off the side of a stack of pancakes. *Chalk another one up for Joan.* He continued sliding to his left, towards the area where the guard rail was still intact. Life would be much easier once he could grab a hold of it. Until then, he was going to have to fight the exhaustion that was steadily working its way into his arms, like a worm boring its way into an apple.

He could see the strain of Katie and Clara, who had climbed out ahead of him. He hoped they were holding up better than him. His brief moment of dangling had sapped whatever reserves he had. Sweat poured down his face, and he grunted with each shift.

Another shot rang out, and he heard footsteps above him. They were close. He heard the soft patter of blood on the ground. And then he heard a thump as one of the creatures dropped to the pavement above him. It grumbled and groaned, releasing a soggy moan. Lou slid to his left some more, taking the room that was available to him.

"Hurry up," he whispered. The dead thing above him reached out for his hand, and Lou knew he could either take his chances dropping to the ravine floor or getting bit by the leering face of the dead thing above. "Shit, shit, shit."

"Hold on, Lou," Clara said.

He could see the top of the creature's head above him. Its eyes, oddly wet for having been dead for such a long time, still looked human, which made the whole situation worse. It didn't look at Lou. It was fixated on his fingers. As it leaned in to take a bite of one of his fingers, Lou slid left once more, far enough to avoid the ghoul's bite. Its teeth clicked off the pavement above, and Lou could sense the quiet desperation of the people to his left, who knew exactly the danger he was in.

There was another shot, and blood sprayed the air. But the dead man was still active, still hungry, and still eyeing Lou's fingers like a side of breakfast sausage.

The group was halfway across now, and, if Lou was hearing it right, the commotion had drawn several more of the creatures. All he could do was scream in his mind, and that was the most horrible thing. If only he could scream and let loose all the swears that were flowing through his mind, he would be alright. He was sure of that. There was another gunshot, and the bald man's head blew up, spraying Lou's hands with cold blood.

****

Joan smiled with satisfaction as she ejected the spent shell. She had gotten him. She only hoped she had gotten him in time. With her adrenaline pumping, she took shot after shot, thinning out the small pack that had broken off to investigate what was going on at the edge of the road.

They went down, one by one. There was a part of her that felt bad for what she was doing. These were people once, just like her. When the virus had first broken out, she

95

had dreamed of a cure, even dreamed of being the first to find it. But there would be no cure. These people could not be saved.

The world had fallen apart way too quickly. It had been built like that old game with the wooden blocks, the one where you would pull one out and hope that the tower of blocks would keep standing. Only, this time, as the dead had risen, it had been like pulling out five blocks at a time. The world's collapse had been sudden, startling, and absolutely complete. Joan couldn't fool herself into believing that even the largest, most secure labs in the United States had been able to withstand this onslaught. Power was gone; the military was no more. Hell, even the United States was gone.

She squeezed the trigger again, sending a waitress in a pink dress tumbling to the ground. The road was as good a grave as any she supposed. As her thoughts drifted, she found herself locked into a rhythm of fire that seemed almost holy. She acted on instinct, firing, chambering another round, and then sighting, until one moment she blinked, and she saw that there were a dozen bodies on the road. She reached into her pocket to find that she only had a handful of shells left.

The dead were still breaking off in bunches, but the angle they were taking told her that Clara and the others were farther along now. But she still needed to give them more time. Without more ammunition, she needed to think of something else to do.

She looked down at the creatures below her, and she knew that she needed to present a more attainable target. She sat on the edge of the semi's cab and waved her feet around, just out of range of the horde's grasping hands. This excited them; they emitted bubbly moans of hunger with an almost fervent desire.

Joan tilted her head back and screamed the way the girls in the horror movies used to scream, shrill and terrified. She didn't feel the terror, but the dead responded to it anyway. It drove them into a frenzy. Their arms waved about faster, and they pressed in tighter to the wreck of the semi-truck, crushing each other until they were nothing but an indistinguishable mass of waving arms and hungry faces.

In the distance, the ones that had broken off from the main pack turned around and began shambling back in her direction. Joan screamed some more.

****

"Oh, God, they're killing her!" Clara said.

"Just keep moving," Katie spat back. There was nothing they could do about Joan's screaming now. Her arms were weak and she was hyper aware of the small bulge of her pregnant belly pressing against the face of the ravine. She couldn't get off the side of this damn hill fast enough, and then, just like that, she was there. The guard rail was back, and with it, they now had something to grab onto. With the last of her strength, she pulled herself up, and grabbed the steel guardrail supports, her fingers curling around them.

They still had to inch across, but it was easier now. Instead of relying on their fingertips, they could now slide along at an angle, grasping the supports of the guardrail. They continued like this for what seemed an eternity. Joan continued to scream in the distance, and Katie assumed that meant that she was alright because if she had been bitten, she would be dead by now.

Katie inched along at a reasonable pace. Soon the sound of the dead was nothing but a buzz in the back of their minds, and she risked a peek over the guardrail. She saw a line of cars, abandoned with their doors thrown open, but little else.

"I think we can go up now," Katie said.

"You sure?" Lou asked her.

"Take a look for yourself." Katie watched Lou hoist himself up with a small grunt, and then he went up and over the guardrail. Katie and the others did the same. They all leaned against the side of a copper Cutlass Supreme, an ancient vehicle covered in dust. Their arms hung at their sides, useless and rubbery.

"Hey? You hear that?" Mort asked in halting syllables as he caught his breath.

"What?" Katie asked.

"There's no more screaming."

****

Joan dropped off the top of the semi-truck. She had seen her friends climb over the guardrail a hundred yards up. They looked exhausted, and Joan wasn't looking forward to what she had to do next. She was alone. For the first time since this had all begun, she was actually alone.

It was an odd sensation for her. She had always been a loner, prone to long bouts of existing by herself. Human contact had never been something that she valued. It had always seemed like there was something else to work for, something else to strive for that prevented her from spending time with other people. Now there was nothing to strive for. There was only one goal and that was survival, making it to the next day so you could make it to the next one and so on.

Now, she spent every moment of every day huddled with the others for protection, to assuage her own fears and for friendship... being apart from the others felt like being naked. She felt as if the entire world were made of eyes, and each pair of eyes out there belonged to a hungry, dead monster that wanted nothing more than to kill her and make her one of its own.

She sprinted along the length of the wreck and flung her rifle's strap over her shoulder. She dropped underneath the tail of the semi-truck and began the arduous process of

98

climbing along the edge of the road. She never looked down, but she sensed how far the drop was. It would break every bone in her body if she faltered.

But she did it because she had a goal. She had to get back to her people. She had to get back to safety. If Joan were going to die, she wanted it to be in the arms of the people she had survived with. The feeling of loneliness so infused her heart that she couldn't think about anything else... until she heard the shuffling feet of the dead headed in her direction.

****

Clara poked her head up over the hood of the Cutlass Supreme. Joan was nowhere to be seen.

"I think she's climbing across," Clara said.

"Do you see her?" Lou asked from the shadows behind the body of the car.

"No. There's nothing."

Clara strained her eyes for any sort of sign of Joan. She eyed the length of the guardrail, trying to spot her hands somewhere, anywhere, but again, nothing. Then she had to retreat. The dead were turning. They had lost interest in pawing at the side of the semi-truck.

"The dead are coming," she said as she sat back down.

"Did you see Joan?" Lou asked.

Clara shook her head.

"Well, how long do we wait?" Katie asked.

Katie just looked at her. *Why would she even ask that question?* "As long as we have to." Katie, for once, let it be. That woman had a way of getting under Clara's skin unlike anyone she had ever met before. And once again, she pondered if Katie were actually worth bringing along. At what point does a person become not worth it in the apocalypse? On one hand, they could be the only five living people in the world. On the other hand, one of them was a raging bitch sometimes.

"I'm going to take another look," Clara said. They nodded at her. There was enough room between them and the dead that, even if the dead saw Clara, they would have enough time to react. She rose up over the hood once again, her hands perched on the warm metal. The heat felt good. Seeing a pack of dead shambling towards the guard rail did not.

"We've got trouble," she said.

"What kind of trouble?" Lou asked.

"There's a pack of 'em breaking off to check out the guard rail."

"Should we shoot 'em?" Mort asked.

"I don't think we have any other choice."

"Alright, you do it. You're better than me anyway," Lou said.

Clara just nodded, though being better than the others wasn't saying much. None of them were particularly great at shooting, and the dead were farther away than she felt comfortable with. Clara unslung her rifle and took aim at the dead thing nearest to the guardrail, where she hoped Joan was. It was a big one, flabby pale skin flopped with each step, and its huge breasts were contained under a forest green sweatshirt. Raggedy strands of black hair hid its face as it shuffled forward. She took aim, lining up the sight with the thing's head and pulled the trigger. Nothing happened.

"Damn safety," she hissed. She clicked the safety off and then took aim again. To her, the shot sounded like an atom bomb exploding. It echoed across the mountains, and immediately, a hundred eyes turned in her direction. Her first shot had done nothing.

"That got their attention."

She aimed again and took another shot. It was a hell of a shot, the type of thing that couldn't be reproduced if she had tried a hundred times. First, the bullet ripped through the jaw of the large woman, changing direction to then rip through the side of a large red pickup truck nearby. The bullet then penetrated the gas tank while simultaneously creating a spark.

The truck had once belonged to the very same woman that Clara was shooting at, though she had no way of knowing this. She had sat in that truck for hours, hoping that someone would come along and clear the road so that she might make it into Hillsboro to find her daughter and her granddaughters. She had sat for hours, until the gas gauge had read empty. Then she had turned her truck off. When the dead came, there were nothing but fumes in the gas tank.

The bullet shot through the gas tank, and then, its momentum dulled by jaw, truck, and gas tank, it struck the other side, creating the tiniest of sparks. Though the spark was tiny, it created enough energy to ignite the fumes in the truck. The truck exploded, lifting off the ground for a split second before slamming down and rocking on its wheels.

From behind the truck, on the other side of the guard rail, Clara heard a scream. It started out loud, and then it became softer, as if the person that owned the voice were moving further away each second. Then it stopped suddenly.

"Did you get it?" Mort asked.

Clara didn't have the words to say.

****

Reed Mauer watched the woman tumble off the side of the cliff. *Like an angel*, he thought. She screamed with the fear of someone that knows they are going to die, and Reed couldn't tear his eyes away as she descended. Such a beautiful thing, a scream. Like a kiss for the ears. He had always enjoyed hearing the screaming, and the new world... that's what Chad called it... the new world created a

101

symphony of the things. *A shame*, he thought as the woman tumbled to the ground.

The voice on this woman was something amazing. He wanted to kiss her for her performance, even if she would be all sticky and gross by the time she reached the bottom of the hill. He shrugged his shoulders and walked to the place where he supposed her body would be. He would just kiss her, that's all. Chad couldn't get mad about that.

****

The climb down to the bottom of the ravine was harrowing, but they had all managed, though their hands were cut and scraped to ribbons. They had argued for a few minutes before Clara had decided that she was done listening to Katie try and talk them out of going to find Joan. When she had set off to climb down the side of the ravine, they had all followed, even Katie. Even if they hadn't, Clara would have gone on alone to find Joan. If Joan had died, she would have turned by now. That's just the way life was. Death meant a second life, one that no one wanted. Clara couldn't let that stand. Friends didn't let friends turn.

So, now here they were, sweeping the bottom of the ravine for Joan. Clara couldn't leave her. This entire situation had been her fault, but Joan was nowhere to be seen. She cursed herself again for the shot she had taken. The bottom of the ravine was covered in more vegetation than she had expected, but they should have found her by now if she still lived. If she was dead, it would only be a matter of time before Joan's corpse found them.

As she pushed through the brambles and vines that clogged the ground between giant evergreens, she flinched at the sound of another of the dead tumbling down the side of the ravine. They were following, one by one. Mort and Lou stood at the bottom of the ravine, scanning the side of the rocky slope, waiting for any of the dead that tumbled down the side. When they came down, they made a hell of a racket as they fell, dislodging rocks and breaking their bones in the process. Before they could even get up, Lou and Mort would skullcrack the bastards with either Mort's hammer or Lou's crowbar.

Katie walked ten feet to Clara's right, kicking through the dense vegetation and mumbling under her breath. She was definitely not happy about this whole situation.

"I've got something!" Katie yelled.

Before she could even finish her sentence, Clara was bounding through the trees, tumbling once, but getting up so fast that she didn't even know if she had actually fallen or not. She skidded to a stop next to Katie. On the ground was Joan's rifle, bent and twisted. It was useless, but Joan was nowhere to be seen.

"Shit, where is she?" Clara tried to peer through the trees to see Joan, but there was nothing. Katie tapped her on the arm. She was pointing at something. Clara turned to look and she saw it, a path had been made by someone or something. The vines were disturbed, as were the leaves and piles of pine needles on the ground. Something had come through here, or else Joan had dragged herself through the woods.

"Let's go get the others," Clara said as another dead thing tumbled down the side of the ravine.

Chapter 7: Did You See That Elephant?

As the sun went down, they sat in the backroom of the grocery store, silent among the buzz of fruit flies. Allen had become accustomed to the smell of the rotten fruit, and the can of Chef Boyardee's Beefaroni he was eating was mostly flavorless. It should have been a treat. They should have been having a joyous feast, the likes of which hadn't been seen since the first Thanksgiving, but they were not.

Instead, they sat in the darkness with only candles to see by, the ghosts of their fallen friends flitting by in the gloom. They covered up the tiny, porthole-like windows of the swinging doors, barricading themselves into the loading docks area. They piled box after box against the swinging doors. So far, they had enjoyed glorious silence, and none of the dead had yet to disturb them, except for memories of their own dead.

The loss of Ramirez and Kazinsky had hit them all hard. Beacham groaned in pain in the corner, his back against the wall. Tejada gave him a small bottle of wine to drink and some Advil, but other than that, Beacham was going to have to suffer through the pain of his broken arm. He dozed fitfully, stirring periodically as his nightmares caused him to jerk awake every ten minutes or so, whereupon he would clutch at his broken arm. They had set it as best they could and outfitted him with a sling to help keep his arm stable, but that was the best they could do.

Allen sat in a small circle with some of the other soldiers. Day and Gregg sat across from him, two plain old soldiers without an ounce of poetry in their souls. But that was alright; Allen kind of wanted it that way today. Their ability to not think so much about the day's events seemed like a blessing right now. They took turns cleaning their weapons by candlelight, one by one, so they weren't caught off guard. They didn't need to be told this anymore, but

Tejada always made sure they knew that this was the way he expected things to run.

No one blamed Tejada for what had happened. As far as they were all concerned, they were all living on borrowed time anyway, borrowed time that Tejada had loaned them. That they were still alive appeared to be something of a small miracle, and Allen didn't want to look too much deeper into.

Tejada snored fitfully in the corner. After trimming his hair and shaving his face with some honest to goodness shaving cream, he had made a bed out of cardboard, pulled his hat low over his face and dozed right off, as if they had all come back from a standard-issue march. Allen expected nothing less from their fearless leader.

Quigs sat in the corner, reading a small bible by candlelight, a small gold crucifix dangling from between his fingers. Quigs had been silent for quite some time.

"It's like a damn funeral in here," Day said. He had always had a way with words... a poor way.

"It kind of is, you know?" Allen said.

"Enough of that sad business," Gregg said. "We don't have the time to sit around mourning."

Day looked down the barrel of his rifle with one of his squinty eyes. He was one of the least attractive people Allen had ever seen. His hair curled around the edges of his hat, his drab brown hair framing his rodent-ish features. All you had to do was add a couple of whiskers and he would be a rat personified. Squinty eyes, almost always red from allergies, buckteeth, a bulbous nose that jutted out too far, Day was the kind of guy that you looked at sideways when you talked to him because it would be too hard to hide your revulsion if you looked him dead in the eye. "Don't you think we ought to be sad?" Day said.

"Do you feel sad, or are you thinking, 'I'm glad it wasn't me?' Shit, man, as much as I feel like I ought to be sad, I can't shake this feeling that I'm lucky and that

105

Ramirez and Kazinsky died for something. They died for us," Gregg said while munching on a bag of Funyuns he had scrounged up.

Allen was shocked. "You believe that? You really believe that? You believe we're the lucky ones? Look how many of us there are, man. We're almost extinct. Each loss is something gone from the world forever. Hell, back when there were billions of people on the earth, maybe losing someone wasn't a big deal. Maybe then you could afford to just say, 'Better them than me.' But that's not how it is anymore."

Day just shook his head. "Man, you want me to curl up into a ball and start cryin', but them days are done."

"I don't want you to cry, Day. I want you to admit that you feel it. I want you to admit that you understand that no matter what happens, something special is gone from this earth. In Ramirez there was a code, a code that has taken thousands of years to form. It's comprised of bits of DNA from as far back as the beginning of time. It's unique, it's evolved, and now, it's out there walking around, rotting on the bone."

"Why the hell do I even talk to you, Izzy?" Gregg asked.

Allen actually smiled at that. He looked around the room for emphasis and said, "What choice do you got?"

Gregg shrugged his shoulders. "I got plenty of choice. I'm going to go hang with Epps. At least he knows how to have a good time." Gregg grabbed his rifle and headed over to the pool of light where Epps sat with Whiteside and Brown, gambling over peanuts with a deck of cards, smiles on their faces, as if this were just a normal day in the barracks with nothing else to do.

Allen wished he could turn it off like that. He wished he could just pretend that two people had not just lost their lives, ending an unbroken line that went back as far as the beginning of man itself. Maybe Gregg was right. Maybe he thought too much.

"You gotta relax, man," Day said.

"Why?"

Day blew down the barrel of his disassembled rifle. "People feel things in different ways. You think that because Gregg isn't sitting here moping that he doesn't feel their loss? He feels it. He just feels it differently."

Allen thought that Day was probably right, but that didn't make him feel any better. He shoveled another mouthful of Beefaroni into his mouth. It was cold, but that didn't bother him none. They lapsed into silence, Day cleaning his gun and Allen finishing off his meal.

****

Amanda and Rudy lay on a flattened cardboard box away from the others. They inherently felt the difference between themselves and the others. The group was not one cohesive unit. If anything, Amanda and Rudy were nothing more than baggage. They were something to be lugged and protected, but when it came to downtime, the soldiers had largely retreated to their own company.

Rudy lay on his side, staring at Amanda. She slept quietly, and Rudy watched and listened as she breathed in and out. He lifted his arm slightly, as if to touch her, but then he let it drop. He had no experience in the ways of men and women. He was content to just watch her by the candlelight for the time being.

He fantasized about running his hands through her hair, then kissing her. He imagined her with her clothes off, and then felt like a jerk because of it. Did she like him as more than just a friend? *God, isn't that what middle school kids asked?* He was so pathetic. He was nothing more to her than just a friend. He knew that without a doubt. He knew what he looked like, and he knew that there were plenty of other men around, some of them not much older than either of them, and all of them, with the exception of Day, would be considered better looking than himself. Even with Day it was a toss-up. The odds that she would fall for him over one of the soldiers must have been astronomical, but at least he wasn't the ugliest person in the world yet.

Amanda stirred, her head snapping up as she looked around, her eyes wide, fear on her face.

"It's alright. Everything is fine," Rudy said.

She saw him then, and she smiled. She rolled over, hiding her face from him, and then she slid her body closer to his. Without looking, she grabbed one of his arms and threw it over her body like a blanket, snuggling in tight.

Rudy's heart was thumping in his chest. This was as close to a woman as he had ever been. He felt her softness underneath his arm, and blood flooded his face and other areas of his body. It was going to be a long evening, but he wouldn't trade it for the world.

****

Pocket threes, a sucker's hand. Seems like that was all Epps had been dealt since the entire world died, but if pocket threes were what he had, he was going to play 'em. He tossed another handful of nuts onto the pile and called.

"Read 'em and weep," Whiteside said in his Southern drawl. Shit. A pair of fours. What were the odds of that. Epps threw his cards in face up. "Holy moly, you're comin' at me with a pair of threes? Get a load of this guy Brown. Epps is the type of guy that would run into a knife fight with his dick in his hands."

"Yeah, well, I'd still come out on top."

"I highly doubt it," Brown said. "You look like a bottom to me." Epps liked Brown. Along with Beacham, he was the only other brother in the entire group besides Beacham. That meant something to him, even though race was quickly becoming a moot point in the world.

"Top, bottom, I'm still gettin' mine." Whiteside shook his head, and Brown just laughed.

Whiteside picked up the cards and shuffled, bridging like a pro. He did this a few more cycles while Brown and Epps threw their peanuts into the middle of the piece of cardboard they were all sitting on. Whiteside dealt the cards with ease, and Epps pulled his hand to him. A four and an eight, boy, Lady Luck loved him tonight. Whiteside dealt three cards face-up in the middle of the cardboard. Nothing there excited him, but no one else seemed to have anything so they all called. It was the same for the turn.

Gregg joined their group, settling down into a cross-legged position with practiced ease. "Deal me in," he said.

"You can't just join in the middle of a hand," Brown said. "You gotta wait."

"Aw, come on. What's it matter?" Gregg asked.

"It's the principle, Gregg. There are rules. If you don't follow the rules you might as well be playin' Go Fish with your granny."

Gregg shook his head. He wasn't buying it, but Gregg never did. He was an ass of the highest order, but he was an alright guy. He was the type of guy that would be there when things went south, but if you wanted stellar conversation or deep philosophical shit, you were out of luck.

The next card Whiteside dealt put a gleam in Brown's eye, so Epps folded immediately, which was easy to do when all you were playing for was peanuts. He got a look at Gregg's face and asked, "What's wrong with you."

"Nothing."

Epps just nodded. He knew what was wrong. It was the same thing that was wrong with all of them. The world was dying, and so were they. "It'll get better," Epps said.

"When?" Gregg asked.

"When we down by that beach, boy!" Brown said.

Epps nodded in agreement.

"All mai tais and bikinis. You just wait and see," Brown continued.

Gregg shook his head. "I don't know, boys. I got a bad feeling I'm not gonna be around to see any of it."

Epps knew that feeling. He knew it well. "Nonsense. We're gonna wake up in the morning and get our asses out of here, and that's the truth. I'd bet my left nut on it."

Gregg just laughed along with the others. Existential crisis averted.

****

Andy listened to them all. No one spoke to him, not the soldiers, not Rudy and Amanda. He was all alone, even with people all around him. He had made it through like the rest of them! He had even killed several Annies! Yet, he was nothing but an afterthought to these people.

He just wanted to close his eyes and drift off into oblivion. Despite all of the day's hardships and the relative peace they were enjoying, Andy still found it hard to sleep.

Something was wrong. He didn't know what. It was that same something that had made his life a living hell back home. He had it again. The depression. It was coming back, but he was powerless to stop it. This was supposed to be his new beginning, here on the other side of the country where no one knew about the things he had done to himself. This was supposed to be his fresh start. The end of the world was perfect for that.

Yet, the old problems were still there. He didn't know what it was about himself that turned people off, but he knew that there was something. He might as well have a sign tattooed on his head that said "loser." It was as if he gave off some sort of pheromone that made people reject him. They never rejected him outright. They just sort of... moved beyond him, in conversations and even distance.

110

Even now, he was so physically far away from anyone else that he doubted any of them even remembered he was there. He was a ghost among these men. It was so unfair. Oh, if his father could hear him now, whining about fairness like a giant child. He would just have to show them. If they weren't going to like him for who he was, then he would become someone else entirely. He would become the biggest badass in the group.

He was already on his way. He felt stronger, more capable, every day. If only they could see that. His bitterness crawled over him like ants, and he curled into a ball, resisting the urge to scratch at his skin. Even the fat guy had someone that liked him. What did he have? Nothing, that's what. Tears rolled down the side of his face, but he dared not sob. He didn't want the others to see, especially not Tejada.

He would fall asleep soon. Any minute now. At least, that's what he thought. But the night rolled away, taking him along with it. He thought he might have slept a few times, but he couldn't be sure. Andy woke before everyone else. He sat up and rubbed at his red eyes, readying himself for the day, the weight of exhaustion still upon him. When he had eaten and packed, he laid back down and closed his eyes, waiting for the day to begin.

Tejada was the first to awaken. Andy knew he was awake when he lit the stub of a candle. The light cut through the darkness of the store room, and he opened his eyes to see the offending source. Tejada was sitting up, his back against the wall. He twirled the remains of a cigar in his hands, looking thoughtful. He looked like a goddamned classical painting, swathed in shadows, his temples flexing, the veins on his forearm popping out as he flexed his left arm. He looked tired. This painting should be titled "The Weight of the World" because that's what Tejada looked like he was carrying at that moment.

111

From around the store room, there was more movement as the others began to rise. Andy rose as soon as someone else moved. In the future, he would be the first to rise, for that was a small battle from which he could win respect.

****

Tejada's night had been long, his sleep fitful. He felt guilty that he had fallen asleep so quickly. But that was how it always was when he lost a soldier. The death of a squadmate took something out of him every time. Yesterday, they had lost two people, and when everything had been secure, he had gone down like a sack of turnips.

Kazinsky, Ramirez... they were getting light on people. They would be missed. He wanted the time to mourn them properly. He wanted to see them buried and given the respect that they deserved, the old flag on the coffin, bawling mother and father, maybe even a wife, guns firing in the air. They deserved the works. Instead, all they got was a spot on the concrete where the vultures could peck at their eyes.

What a failure he had been. He was as ill-prepared for this world as everyone else. The only difference was he had to pretend like he wasn't. That was his cross to bear. His dreams were now a play-by-play of the people he had lost. He hadn't seen Kazinsky and Ramirez in his dreams that night, they were too fresh, their loss too new. It wouldn't be for a while that those losses would turn into deep scars, and those scars would become visible every night that he closed his eyes.

He was fighting a war of attrition. They had a goal, but each step forward cost them another life it seemed, and there simply weren't enough of them for that to be a winning war.

But sitting around eating potted meat and crackers wasn't going to get them there. It was time to move. He gave the order to pack up, and everyone hopped into action. He paid them little attention, ignored their conversations. He didn't need to put his fingers on their necks to know their pulse. They were cold. They were dejected. They needed a win or morale would slip even more. And when morale slipped, bad things happened. Soldiers became locked in their own heads, feeding their energy into the flames of their own thoughts. In this way, they became lazy, and when they became lazy, death inevitably followed.

They needed a big win.

They lined up at the sliding metal door of the loading docks. Day and Quigs lifted it up, and it rattled on its tracks, sending a shiver up Tejada's spine.

"Shit," Beacham said, backing away from the door.

Ramirez stood there, his arm gone, his skin almost blue from the loss of blood. Yet he still shuffled back and forth, only his head visible above the smooth concrete of the loading docks.

"I got this," Gregg said, reversing his rifle for the purpose of smashing Ramirez's head in.

"Use a bullet," Tejada said. "He's worth it." And there it was, the ultimate measure of respect for death. Ramirez was worth a bullet. Putting Ramirez to rest was worth giving away their position to the Annies.

Gregg took aim, making sure to get it just right. He pulled the trigger, and Ramirez sank onto the concrete below the loading docks.

"Let's move out," Tejada said. In his mind, Tejada could already picture them, the dead moving, walking slowly towards the gunshot in the distance. They were like the ripples of a pond going in reverse, the circles getting smaller and smaller, the gunshot acting as the stone in the water.

They each hopped down from the loading dock, except for Rudy who lay on his prominent belly and slid his legs over. As they passed Ramirez's body, most of the soldiers avoided looking at him. Tejada didn't. He gave that brave bastard a full glare, and in his head, he silently thanked the man for his service.

****

They continued down Burnside Street, which at some unspoken point turned into Barnes Road, and despite the dead that lingered in the streets, Amanda was glad to be out of the grocery store. It was a fine place, defensible, with plenty of food, and several escape routes, but she had spent enough time in dark places with no windows, huddling in the shadows, and waiting for the dead to find them.

She was much happier out in the open, looking the dead right in their eyes. Even this curly-haired mom, in the ridiculous cat sweater that was stumbling up to her now... even she was superior to the imagined dead that Amanda dreamed up in her mind whenever she was stuck inside.

She turned sideways, brushing past the curly-haired mom, just out of arm's reach. When she was past, Amanda spun around, keeping her eye on the dead thing. You never knew when one of the dead would find a sudden burst of energy. She had seen it happen multiple times before.

They were in the middle of the street, flowing around cars the way water flowed around rocks in a stream, when they heard something that made all of them stop in their tracks.

"Was that an elephant?" Rudy asked.

"I don't know what else makes that noise," Epps said.

They waited silently, hoping that the creature that had made the noise would erupt from the side of the road at any moment. They couldn't have said why it was important to them, but to a man and to a woman, it seemed like the most important thing in the world at that time. In their heads, they willed it as much as they had willed the world to return to normal when they lay down at night. They filled their hearts with the hope that something majestic still lived in the world, something other than the wandering dead and the wild dogs that now roamed the street.

But it did not come...

"Maybe it's hiding," Quigs said.

Then there was a flurry of noise as a giant form came thundering out of the trees. It was a hundred yards ahead of them in the middle of the road. But even then, they could see the blood gleaming red on the creature's tusks. As it pounded up an unobstructed stretch of road, it lowered its head at one of the dead, pitch-forked it through the middle and flung it up into the air. It landed on its face, and the giant grey beast brought one thick foreleg down on the creature's skull crushing it and spraying brains all over the road like a kid hopping on a milk carton during recess. This brought a cheer from the soldiers and even Andy. Then, the elephant was gone, as if it had never existed.

When it had disappeared into the woods, Amanda found that she was holding hands with Rudy, and when she looked at him, she felt something weird in the pit of her stomach.

"It was beautiful, wasn't it?"

Yeah," Rudy answered back, but Amanda didn't think he was talking about the elephant.

Chapter 8: The Compound in the Woods

When Joan awoke, pain shocked her mind. She didn't know where she was, when she was, or even who she was. She tried to sit up, but it wasn't happening. The thought that she was paralyzed shot through her mind, and then she remembered why being paralyzed would be a bad thing, and then she began to thrash in her bedding only to find that the reason she couldn't move wasn't that she was paralyzed; it was that she was tied down.

Ropes strangled her wrists and ankles, and she moved her head from side to side, struggling to escape. At any moment, one of the dead could come in here, but where was here?

She remembered hanging on the side of the mountain. She remembered hearing the gunshot. Then there was an explosion, and she had been falling. She had stuck her hands out against the coarse clay and rock on the side of the ravine in the hopes that this would slow her fall, but all this had done was take the skin off her fingers and the palms of her hands. Then her boot hit an outcropping of rock, and she went tumbling head over heels. Her world had become a blur of blue sky and red clay. Then her head hit the side of the ravine, and that was the last thing that she remembered.

Around her, she saw faux-wood paneling. There was a window to her left; a yellowed-curtain let in dozy sunlight. The bed she lay upon took up most of the room, and the interior felt cheap and sparse. It definitely had the feel of a trailer. She remembered that feel from when she had been little and her parents had gone to visit their "family friend." Joan had stayed in the living room while they had disappeared to the back part of the trailer. Soon after, coughing was followed by a funny smell that Joan would recognize years later at her one and only high school party.

She doubted Clara would have let them tie her up like this, unless... Joan strained to see her body, to see if she had been bitten while unconscious. Her hands were bandaged. Was that because she had scraped the skin off them? She tried to wiggle her fingers. They all moved. She lifted her head up to look at her feet, but they were covered by a blanket. She could feel the ropes around her ankles. Her back burned with fire as she squirmed.

Outside, she heard voices. They echoed through the thin walls of the trailer, and then she heard a rickety door squeal open. It slammed shut like an airplane lavatory door. A man entered the room and stood there. He smiled at her, the way few men had ever smiled at her before.

"You're awake."

Joan felt like a deer frozen in headlights. She didn't know what to do. Fight or flight, both options had been stolen from her by those damnable ropes. Now all she could do was nature's third most successful tactic, sit completely still and hope that the predator overlooked the prey.

"Are you going to talk?"

Should she? What did this gain her? If she was in trouble, being silent might just bring her more trouble. "Why am I tied up?"

The man had a thick brown beard on his face. It was wild, hair sticking up from the sides and all over the place. "I thought you might ask that." He smiled reassuringly, as if her being tied up was nothing out of the ordinary. "We found you at the bottom of the ravine. Didn't know if you were alive or dead, and, just in case you died, we wanted to be safe. Can't have you walking around eating on my friends and family." He laughed then, and Joan sensed his falseness. Working in an E.R. had finely honed her ability to detect bullshit. The smile the man wore now was like the smile she would see on the faces of abused spouses. "Oh, I fell down the stairs," they would say, sporting the same grin that the man in front of her wore now.

"My brother says he saw you fall down the ravine. You're lucky to be alive."

Weren't they all?

"He thinks you shouldn't be alive. But here you are, a miracle of sorts."

The conversation stalled, and the man with the brown beard sat there smiling at her. "Can you untie me now?" Joan asked.

"Oh, of course, of course." The man came to her and leaned over her, his hands sliding up the length of her arms in a familiar manner. He smelled... clean. She was surprised how long it had taken her to name the smell. She had become so used to the specific scents of her friends on the road, that the scent of clean simply hadn't registered. It wasn't a lack of scent, but a different scent, and a wave of nostalgia for her shower washed over her.

The man finished untying her wrists, and she brought her arms to her side. They were numb, and her shoulders ached from sleeping with her arms over her head for so long. She tried to massage some blood back into her hands, but the bandages on her fingers got in the way, and now that the blood was beginning to return, so was the pain of her fall.

She tried to sit up, but it was impossible. Her abdomen was on fire, and she knew that she had likely bruised her ribs. The bearded man pulled the blanket back, and she saw the horror of her leg. It was bruised and swollen looking like a dark, marbled blue cheese. It had quite obviously been broken. A makeshift splint was secured with strips of cloth, and Joan began to understand just how bad of a situation she was in. She was immobilized in the world of the dead and stuck with a group of people that she knew nothing about.

118

"What's your name?" she asked the bearded man as he untied her feet, not that she would be going anywhere with a broken leg.

"Name's Chad," he said.

Joan just nodded her head, noticing that for the first time her head felt swimmy. "And you?" he asked.

"Joan," she said. It was nice to be able to introduce herself to someone new. She didn't know how many more opportunities she would get to do that.

"Joan," the man repeated. "What were you doing out there, Joan?"

"We were trying to get to the coast."

"We?"

Shit. "Yeah, I was traveling with some others, but they probably left me for dead. I would have."

Chad just nodded. But Joan sensed something not quite right with him.

"Alright," he said. "I'm just going to leave you to rest. I'll have someone bring you some food. You're probably starving."

"That would be awesome."

"Very well then." Chad nodded at her and then exited the trailer. She heard the clank of metal on metal after the door closed behind him. She was locked in, not that she could go anywhere with her leg busted up. She lay back on her bed, trying to figure out just how much trouble she was in.

****

They had tracked Joan for miles. At first, it had been somewhat difficult, but then they saw the blood. Joan was being dragged. Of that, they were certain. They found bits of her hair caught on downed tree limbs. When the blood had showed up, they had picked up their pace, and now they squatted in the trees, examining the compound before them.

It was a ramshackle thing. The outside wall appeared to be made of double-wide trailers, the spaces between reinforced with wooden barricades. They didn't look like they had been made with any sort of craftsmanship, but they looked like they would keep the dead out. The spaces underneath the trailers had been packed in with dirt so that nothing could crawl underneath.

In the middle of the circle of trailers, an old house rose up. It was wooden and dilapidated. Part of the roof had caved in at one point. A blue tarp covered the opening, held in place by river rocks. It was a two-story affair. Its wood was gray and had seen better days.

At the front of the compound was a gate, a rickety length of chain-link fence covered by a tarp. Above the gate were two wooden platforms that served as watchtowers, and two armed men sat talking, their voices inaudible to the survivors.

"Look at that," Mort said. "Looks like a pretty nice set-up."

Lou didn't say anything.

They sat in silence, their thoughts rattling around in their brains. It was as if they were waiting for something, some sort of sign to give them some clue as to what their next move should be.

"We should just shoot them all," Katie said finally. She was tired of waiting. She was also exhausted. The pregnancy was progressing, and it was taking a toll on her stamina. She just wanted this whole thing to be over. Katie couldn't wait for the baby to get out of her. At night, while trying to sleep, she sometimes fantasized about carving it out with a knife.

"We can't just shoot them all. We don't even know where Joan is. Hell, we don't even know if she's alive," Lou said.

"What if she's dead?" Mort asked.

120

Lou thought about it and said, "Then we go around. No reason to get caught up in something that's likely to get us killed."

The men on the guard towers laughed. Clearly, life was easy for them. They didn't look like killers, but to survive this long, they had to be.

"Can we just wait until night? Sneak in and take a peek around?" Clara asked.

Lou just shrugged. It wasn't a terrible idea, but the thought of sitting in the woods until it was dark enough gave him the creeps. It would be hard to see, and you never knew when one of the dead was going to pop up. They had heard quite a few tumble down the side of the canyon after they had left it behind. He bet more would follow. "I don't like the idea of sitting out in the dark, but if that's the best way, then that's what we have to do."

Atop the watchtowers, there was a commotion. The men on top suddenly had their rifles in their hands, and they began scanning the forest around them.

Lou waved the others back, and they hid among the trees. There was a rattling as the chain-link gate slid along a track in the dirt. Lou poked his head out from behind a tree.

A plain looking man with a brown beard stepped into the clearing in front of the gate. He scanned the forest, looking into the shadows. Lou didn't like the man. There was something smug about him. He reminded Lou of the drug dealers that had ruled his neighborhood as a kid. He had that old drug dealer swagger, the sort of walk that said, "I'm intoxicated by the small amount of power I have, and I'm loving every minute of it." Those were the most dangerous of men because they believed themselves to be gods... and they wanted to be treated accordingly, and when you didn't bow down to them, they would fuck you up.

"If you're out there, we've got your friend," he called. His voice was inviting. It spoke of safety and welcome. He paused, looking this way and that, waiting to see if there was going to be a response. "Come on out. We've got plenty of food and space. I'm sure Joan would love to see you. She's busted up pretty bad."

Upon hearing Joan's name, Clara began to stand. Lou, without looking, placed a hand on Clara's shoulder. She paused halfway to standing, and then she settled down. Lou knew she would do anything for her friend, but Lou also knew that the man at the gate was dangerous.

The bearded man smiled at the trees, rocking back on his heels and looking at the sky as if he were the most put-upon man in the universe. "What can you do?" that look said. He looked like an old man stuck giving sage advice to someone who wasn't willing to listen, no matter how much sense his advice made. "Alright. If you change your minds, all you have to do is one thing. Just knock." The bearded man smiled again, and then he turned and walked inside. "Close it up," they heard him say, and the chain-link gate rattled closed.

Lou wiped the sweat from his brow and took a deep steadying breath. He felt it again, the mantle of leadership settling on his shoulders like a pair of shoulder pads fashioned out of responsibility. He leaned his head back against the rough bark of the tree.

"Should we go introduce ourselves?" Mort asked.

Lou just shook his head. "I don't like it."

"They've got Joan. They said her name. That means she's alive!" Clara said.

A pang of guilt washed over Lou as he wished that Joan had not survived the fall. But she had, and she was one of them. They couldn't leave her behind, even though it would be easier for all involved. Zeke had come back for him in the police station. He wouldn't abandon Joan. But he wasn't going to walk into a trap either. "We stick to the plan. We wait until night, check it out. This man seems a little too inviting to me."

"Me too," Katie said.

Clara shook her head in frustration. "But what if we're all making this more difficult than it has to be? What if we're creating the problem?"

"You wanna take that chance? What if I'm right? We all die." *Or worse,* he thought. "We'll wait until night, then I'll go up there and take a look. If nothing looks out of the ordinary, we can introduce ourselves in the morning." Lou could see that Clara didn't like the plan, but she nodded her head anyway. Katie and Mort were with him. "Let's move back a little bit, eat some food, and get some rest. We'll take turns sleeping, two at a time. I want us rested for tonight. If things go bad, we may be doing a lot of running... maybe even some killing."

They crouch-walked to a clearing and began eating their meager supplies. Lou took the first watch, his mind filled with worst-case scenarios. It was definitely going to be a long night.

Chapter 9: A Bowling Ball

They moved swiftly down the street, the ever-pressing threat of the dead trailing them. They were on a four-lane road that threaded through the suburb of Beaverton. Functional, if unimpressive, houses lined the sides of the road, and it seemed as if everyone was home.

They had tried for the highway, but hundreds, if not thousands, of the dead lined the westbound Highway 26, shambling amid hundreds of stalled cars. It was a meat grinder if ever Tejada had seen one, and he had seen plenty in his day. This trip was going to take longer than expected.

Tejada and his men headed south on Cedar Hills Boulevard. The road would connect them with a street called Walker Road, which, according to his map, seemed to parallel the highway for some ways. They would follow that and then after a couple of miles, they would cut over and see what they could see of the highway. There were only a couple of ways from Portland to the coast due to the fact that the city sat in a valley surrounded by rugged terrain on all sides.

Cedar Hills Boulevard was passable and wide enough that they could bolt in any direction if they needed to. The side streets, while infinitely less populated, offered less routes of escape. The last thing they wanted was to be trapped on a street with houses and fences blocking off any chance of escape. If the dead filled the streets, they would have to break sideways, and that was much easier to do on a larger street.

Other than the steadily following trail of the dead, it was a pretty nice day. The weather was cool, and they had made good progress. The men, still haunted by the loss of Ramirez and Kazinsky seemed to be in good spirits, or as good as could be expected. Being on the move allowed them to forget the sorrow of their lost squadmates for the time being. For Tejada, the only thing that allowed him to forget about their deaths were the men he still had to keep alive.

His mind wandered to the pot of gold at the end of the rainbow, and he wondered how these men would manage if they ever found someplace safe. Would they be able to return to normal, or would they constantly be haunted by nightmares of the dead and those they'd lost? *First thing's first, get 'em to that pot of gold.*

In no time at all, they made it to the intersection of Walker Road and Cedar Hills Boulevard. Tejada spared a glance behind him, and his stomach dropped a little bit. It's like they were leading a damn parade.

Shopping centers stretched out before them, and Gregg said, "You think that Five Guys is open? I could go for a burger right about now."

"Shut up, dumbass," Brown shot back.

They turned west on Walker Road, and Tejada saw something that interested him. It was a bowling alley. Large, defensible, and relatively free of windows. If they didn't have a thousand dead people following them, they could have holed up there and bowled a few rounds if the electricity hadn't disappeared forever ago.

"Let's head through there," Tejada said. "I wanna shake this tail."

He jogged forward, and everyone followed suit. Based upon the ragged gasps coming from behind him, he assumed even Rudy was quickening his pace. That was good. It was the only way he was going to survive in this world.

"Break it open," he commanded. "Flashlights on. Looks pretty dark in there."

Epps and Day rushed up to a small glass door, and they took turns bashing at it with the butt of their rifles. The glass shattered, and then they were through.

****

They stepped into the cool darkness of a small bar. Andy eyed the bottles behind the gleaming counter with a wary eye. A drink would be good right about now. He followed the soldiers closely, hoping to be of use. They looked at him askance, as if he didn't belong there, but they didn't tell him to back off. That was good. That was a sign of respect. They were starting to realize he wasn't like Rudy and Amanda. He was actually worth something.

Light filtered in from the broken door, but it didn't go very far. They pushed their way through the bowling alley bar and into the main floor of the building. Flashlights reflected off shining lanes that still shone, though they hadn't been waxed in months. Their beams illuminated bowling balls and puddles of blood. This place hadn't been immune from the end of the world either it seemed.

As they passed a rack of bowling balls, Andy grabbed an orange one off the shelf. It was an eight-pounder according to the number stamped on the side. It glittered in his flashlight, and he hefted it with ease.

"We ain't got time for bowling, kid," Beacham said.

Kid. Good one. He doubted Beacham was much older than he was. "I'm not going bowling. This thing is perfect for bashing in Annies."

"You're going to tire yourself out in two swings," Allen said.

The conversation would have continued, but they heard a low groan from somewhere in the darkness. Then they heard the squeak of shoes shuffling. Andy looked around frantically with his flashlight, trying to see the source of the noise, then he spotted them at the end of one of the lanes. They were crawling underneath the pin-setters.

"They're coming up behind us!" Rudy yelled from the back of the line. He was closest to the bar they had entered through.

"Let's push through, people!" Tejada yelled.

126

Andy followed after the others. Confusion reigned in the darkness with flashlight beams shining this way and that. *It's like an Abrams movie with all these lens flares,* he thought, just before a crawling Annie lurched forward and took his legs out from under him. He fell to the ground, his flashlight skittering to the side, its beam of light spinning in the darkness. Rather than call out for help, which might come too late, he did the only thing he could think to do, he swung the eight-pound bowling ball downward and smashed the head of the thing wrapped around his legs. He heard the crunch, and then Beacham shined his light at what he had done.

The Annie's head was caved in, and blood and brains slid from the fractured skull, staining Andy's pants.

"If that ain't a strike, I don't know what is," Beacham said. With his good arm, he pulled Andy to his knees, and they continued through the bowling alley to the far end. There were a couple of flashes of light, followed by deafening thunder, and then they reached a set of glass doors at the west end of the building.

Andy stood with his back to the glass as the dead honed in on them. Rudy and Amanda ran past him, glancing at the blood-covered bowling ball in his hands. He sneered at them and readied himself as Tejada fiddled with the door.

"You want me to break it?" he heard Allen ask.

"No, I want to be able to close the damned thing behind us," he said.

Andy couldn't see what they were doing, but with his flashlight, he could see the dead getting closer and closer. He licked sweat off of the thin mustache growing on his upper lip, and as a dead man in a bowling shirt approached him, he swung the ball as hard as he could. It cracked the man in the face, and the Annie tumbled backwards. Andy enjoyed hearing the satisfying crunch of bones.

"We got it!" Allen yelled, and they all filed out backwards of the bowling alley. The dead pressed against the glass door as they pulled it shut behind them. "Find something to hold this damn thing closed," Tejada commanded. Rudy and Amanda sprinted over to a dumpster and began pushing it towards the door. The soldiers stepped in to help them out.

With the dumpster in place, Tejada turned to Andy and said, "Who the hell do you think you are? Walter Ray Williams?"

"Who the fuck is Walter Ray Williams?" Brown asked.

"The greatest bowler of all-time?" Tejada looked around at his men, hoping for someone to back him up, but everyone just looked at him like he was crazy.

"Who knows that type of shit?" Brown asked

Tejada just waved them away and said, "Come on. Let's get out of here."

"Yeah, come on, Walt," Beacham said.

Andy just smiled. A nickname. It was a start. All the greatest people in the world had nicknames. It just sucked a little bit that his was going to be Walt.

"Hey, Walt! I like it," Quigs said, and the men all smiled and repeated his name. He even saw Amanda and Rudy smiling.

They walked away, hundreds of dead locked inside a bowling alley, trapped by a dumpster and a door that opened inwards.

****

Amanda was happy for Andy. He seemed to glow under the appreciation and praise of the other soldiers. That was good. He had spent far too much time brooding. Ever since Chloe had tried to kill Rudy, he had become a completely different person. When they had been stuck in the movie theater, he had seemed a fairly regular guy,

128

maybe a little awkward, but normal. After the incident with Chloe, he had become withdrawn. It was as if up until that moment, none of it had been real to him. Then, overnight, he had become an entirely different person, and not the type of person that anyone would actually want to know.

He talked to no one. When everyone else was sitting around talking, he would be off in the corner just watching, a dark look on his face. Over the last week or so, she had begun to wonder if he hadn't gone crazy at some point. But to see the smile on his face was to see the real Andy. She hoped he stuck around because this version of Andy didn't seem like such a bad guy... just a little lost. And this wasn't the world to try and find yourself in.

They had no time to celebrate. The dead were always present, and the dumpster wouldn't hold them for long. Without a word of warning, Tejada broke into a light jog, and everyone followed, even Rudy. His baggy trousers swished back and forth with each movement, but Rudy moved as quick as he could. The loose ends of his rope belt jiggled back and forth, as did his chin. Sweat poured down his face, but when she looked at him, he smiled back at her.

The sun shone on them, and there was a nice breeze. It carried on it the stench of rot, but it felt good on her skin. They moved west up Walker Road, leaving the bowling alley and the potential horde of the dead behind them and out of sight. Andy cradled his bowling ball in his arms for a block before he stuffed it into his backpack. *How long was he going to keep that thing?* It was dead weight, but she had a feeling it was more than a bowling ball to him.

When they were three blocks away, having jogged for a few minutes, they slowed to a walk, and Amanda could see that Rudy was grateful. She worried about him. He was pushing himself hard, much harder than she thought him capable of. There was a strength inside of him, and though she hadn't noticed it when he had first appeared at her apartment door, it became more and more obvious every day. This was why she was attracted to him. *My God, did I just think that?*

She stopped in the middle of the road, her thoughts running through her head at a million-miles-per-hour.

Rudy, out of breath and covered in sweat, asked her if she was ok. She smiled at him and nodded, and they moved forward. She couldn't look at him now, for fear that he would see her staring at him and somehow read her mind. Rudy, poor pathetic Rudy. That's how she had thought of him at first, but he was more than that now.

But how much more was he?

They swerved around an upended beer truck. It sat canted, its rear end in a ditch. Hundreds of bottles of beer, most of them broken, lay in the ditch as well. She had never quite gotten the taste for beer, but she was so thirsty that she could go for one now.

"Sergeant? Can we?" Beacham asked.

Tejada looked at the spilled bounty, pursed his lips as if fighting the word no, and then said, "We got time for one a piece, no more. Drink 'em as we walk. Whiteside, the skinniest of the soldiers, climbed down into the ditch, careful to avoid the broken shards of brown and green glass. He picked among the bottles, tossing unbroken ones up to the waiting survivors above.

"Anyone got a bottle opener?" Quigs asked, looking dubiously at a brown bottle with a smiling cavalier on the front of it.

"Just use your teeth," Gregg said before sinking his own teeth down on the bottle cap, popping it off with a quick twist. Amanda cringed at this display of machismo.

Tejada yelled, "Don't use your goddamned teeth, you idiot. You see a dentist out here? You break one of your choppers and you're in for a world of hurt. Whiteside, gimme one of those."

Whiteside tossed him a bottle, and Tejada caught it in mid-air. He looked at the label and shook his head. "Of course you'd give me a damned IPA. What's a guy gotta do for a can of Coors Light? Lookit here." Tejada pulled his sidearm and wedged the butt underneath the bottle cap. "A soldier's sidearm is a man's best friend for more reasons than one." He twisted the handle downward, and the bottle cap popped off with a hiss. "Just make sure you got the safety on." He upended the beer, and the other soldiers used their sidearms as Tejada had done.

Whiteside tossed Amanda a bottle, and she bobbled it a bit before clamping her hands around the glass.

"Nice catch," Rudy said. She looked at him like she did it every day, and then turned to the soldier next to her and held the bottle out. He popped the top off using the trick Tejada had shared, and Amanda took it back. She held it up and looked at the label. It was a brand she had never heard of. The red and gold label featured the word "bitter," which she didn't think boded well.

Epps handed Rudy an open beer before catching another from Whiteside.

"Everyone good?" Tejada asked, not intending to wait for an answer. "Great. Let's walk."

"Bottoms up," Amanda said, looking dubiously at her beer. She wished it was one of those sweet-flavored numbers that her friends used to bribe their older brothers into buying for them. Rudy and Amanda clinked bottles, and then Amanda held the beer up to her mouth.

She wanted to spit it out immediately. As she forced herself to swallow the beer, she was struck by the sensation of three things: bread, piss, and ear wax. The draught had an initial bready flavor, which struck her as odd, but not as odd as the warmth of the drink. This was where the piss sensation came in. As she swallowed, the bitter aftertaste of the beer reminded her of ear wax.

Rudy gasped and spit his beer out on the road, where it foamed on the dusty pavement. "Bah!" he grumbled. "Tastes like shit."

"Don't waste it, Rudy," Epps said next to him. "What do you got there?"

"Dusty Mummy Imperial Stout," Rudy said.

"Here, trade me. You'll like mine better."

Rudy and Epps traded. Amanda watched Rudy take another swig, laughing at his grimace.

"What are you laughing at?" he asked.

"Nothing."

"I don't see you drinking yours," he said.

Amanda, always up for a challenge, tilted the bottle back. The bitterness of the drink must have screwed her face up something awful because Rudy couldn't contain his laughter. They walked down Walker Road, sipping their beers and eyeing the shadowy, overgrown yards of the houses to their left and right.

Occasionally, an Annie would appear as if from out of thin air. The clothes of the dead were bleached and tattered now. They blended right in with the brown and green, knee-high stalks of grass that jutted up from lawns that hadn't been watered for the better part of the summer.

A slight breeze set the overgrown grass to rustling, and the noise covered the approach of the dead as they pressed through the stalks of grass and other weeds. In one yard, a patch of giant sunflowers grew. Amanda caught sight of movement in several yards, without being able to see exactly what was moving. It could have been a dog or a cat, or maybe just a common squirrel. Or maybe it was a legless Annie crawling towards the sounds it heard on the road. Either way, she didn't feel safe.

Whiteside, drained his beer, and chucked it at the head of a distant Annie working its way through a patch of ivy that had grown onto the road. The bottle smashed off the poor bastard's head, and Whiteside pumped his fist.

"Why don't you show some class?" Rudy said.

Whiteside looked at Rudy sideways, smirking,

"Big boy, the next time one of those things is coming to make a meal out of you, by all means, show it all the respect you got. Me? I'll be shooting the fuckers."

They lapsed into silence, but when the other soldiers were done with their beers, they tossed them into the overgrown grass, not at the Annies. Whiteside didn't seem to notice. They pressed forward, enjoying the day, until they crested a hill and saw a line of black-walled fortifications in the distance. Twelve-feet tall, the blockade started at the corner of Walker Road and shot off to the west and south. It was a good sturdy wall. They could all see that.

But they could also see the hundreds of Annies that crowded around the wall as well. With another growing comet tail behind them, they had a decision to make. They stood in the middle of the street, their tail getting closer and closer.

"What do you boys think?" Tejada asked.

"Nice big walls. I fucking love walls right about now," Epps said.

"Nah, it's a trap. Those walls come down, and those things will be all over us, hundreds all at once," Brown said.

"But, if it's a safe place, we have to try, right?" Rudy asked.

Tejada scrubbed a hand across his stubbly face. "Yeah, but we don't know what's on the other side of those walls. We might jump over one wall and find hundreds of Annies just dying to get out."

"I say we give it a try. It's... providence. That's the word, right?" Quigs asked.

Whiteside punched Quigs in the shoulder, "I wish you'd quit readin' that damn Bible, you sumbitch. It's sucking all the fun out of you."

133

"Providence is right," Brown said. "I'm still willing to believe in a little bit of that God luck, what about you, Izzy?"

Allen ran a hand through his curly brown hair. He looked down at the wall in the distance, "My name is Ozymandias, King of Kings; look on my works ye mighty, and despair."

"What the fuck does that mean?" Whiteside asked.

"I wouldn't expect you to know," Allen said.

Tejada, annoyed by the by-play and feeling a little pressed by the Annies approaching behind him, said, "Alright. This isn't the fucking View. Let's do this the old-fashioned way. Anyone that wants to get over that wall, raise your hand."

They looked around as six hands went up. Tejada nodded. "Those that want to go around, raise your hands." 5 hands went up. "And what about you two?"

Rudy and Amanda looked at each other. Amanda had so many thoughts running through her mind at that moment, but the biggest concern of hers was not the men with the guns and the hard faces. It was not her own safety either. Her biggest concern was Rudy. He looked at her expectantly, waiting for her to make the call. She knew he wouldn't survive. He was too big, too out of shape, and she couldn't stand the thought of losing him, or even worse, seeing him become one of those things.

"This could be a good thing," Amanda said. "I say we give it a shot."

Rudy nodded his head. "I'm with her."

Tejada nodded. He had expected as much, but then he regarded them both with an eye as hard as bronze. "You know that if this thing goes south, that could mean more running."

They nodded.

"Are you up for more running, Rudy?"

"I'll do what I have to do," he said.

134

Tejada nodded. It was as he expected.
****

They turned down one of the side streets and circled around, trying to shake their tail. The plan was to hide inside an old elementary school they had seen, and if they couldn't get inside the school, they could always find a way onto the roof. Tejada wanted the men to be rested when they approached the wall.

As they walked, Tejada fantasized about what was on the other side of the wall. He imagined that there were other soldiers. He imagined that there were civilian families sitting in a cafeteria eating food from cans. Maybe there was even a little garden that was growing food. There could be anything on the other side of that wall, anything at all. It was too good an opportunity to pass up, until he thought of the alternative scenario... of an army of the dead waiting on the other side. He put the thought out of his mind and focused on the task before him.

They pushed through the backyard of a couple of residential homes, whacking the few straggling Annies with their rifles and sending them to the ground. They moved as silently as they could, but even so, Tejada could hear Rudy's wheezing behind him. Rudy needed a rest as bad as anyone. The boy was pushing himself, and Tejada, despite the needs of his soldiers, couldn't let Rudy run himself into the ground. If they found a safe place on the other side of that wall, Tejada would put the boy through his routines. He had come this far; it wouldn't do to not train him to survive on his own. Tejada wouldn't always be around; he knew that was a possibility. He would impart his knowledge to as many people as he could, even to Amanda if she wanted it.

It was the only sort of legacy he would have now. The chance of him having children was all but over. He cursed himself for being so dead set against starting a family in his younger years. He had indulged in the company of many women of course, but he had always held them in check, refusing to allow them to come between his career and what he had seen as his real family, the fine men and women of the United States Army. If he could find a place for his soldiers to live, maybe he could have that legacy. Maybe, after he was long gone, he would be able to live on in the memories of those he had served, and maybe their children would remember him as well. Hell, if they were the only people left, he would be the only grandparent any of those kids would ever know. He kind of liked the thought of that.

The walled compound was a bit close to Portland, but it was far enough away that he didn't think the hordes of downtown Portland would ever find their way to this part of the suburbs, not for a long time at least. Would the beach be better? Maybe. But this place certainly had its attractions. Close to shopping centers and unlooted stores, they could survive for years, giving themselves a chance to get their feet under them and strike back against the undead menace that plagued their each and every day.

Ahead of them, the low, functional structure of a school appeared. The pavement looked dry; shoots of persistent weeds jutted up and out from jagged cracks in the pavement. Waist-high glass windows ran up to the ceiling, reflecting the sunshine above while hiding the contents inside. Without having to be told, Day sprinted up to a window and bashed it in with the butt of his rifle. In the old days, this would have set off a silent alarm, and within minutes, police cars would be on the scene, their lights flashing blue and red in the daylight. But there were no more policemen. There were no more alarms. Everything you wanted was right at your fingertips, just a broken window or busted lock away.

Day swept the frame of the window free of glass with his rifle. Whiteside threw a towel over the frame, and then Whiteside and Allen climbed inside. Once they had cleared the classroom, they helped pull the others inside. Epps and Quigs boosted Beacham through the window, with Whiteside and Allen helping him in. Despite their best efforts, Beacham's face still screwed up in pain, but he managed to keep quiet. Next, they boosted Rudy up, his upper body lacking the strength required to climb in himself. As soon as everyone else was inside, Tejada ran and jumped, hauling himself into the window not a moment too soon, as the first of the dead shuffled into view. Everyone laid low on the floor, resting.

The classroom was warm; its large windows trapped the heat inside. The soldiers and survivors lay on the floor looking all around them. Rows of abandoned desks sat in neat rows, as if the students were going to come back any day. The whiteboard was empty, the outbreak having started at the beginning of summer. Around the upper edge of the whiteboard, a cardboard border ran. The alphabet was printed on it in cursive letters, and more than one of the survivors were hit with a wave of nostalgia.

Day and Gregg crawled across the ancient, wooden boards of the classroom, towards the door. Day rose into a crouch and pushed the door open. He tested the outside doorknob and found that it didn't turn. Gregg grabbed a math textbook from a bookshelf and wedged it between the door and the jamb to keep the door from closing behind them. They stepped into the cool darkness of the interior hallway, their rifles at the ready. There was nothing to see, except for chairs stacked randomly in the middle of the hallway.

The hallway ran down the middle of the building where there were no windows, so there was no need for them to hide. It was stuffy like the air inside a sealed mausoleum. The only air coming into the hallway flowed through the window they had broken and then through the door they had propped open. The bulletin boards along the walls were blank and unused.

"Spread out. Take a look around. We don't want any Annies creepin' up on us," Tejada whispered.

Day and Gregg, covered in dust from their crawl, moved silently through the hallway, though the weight of their bodies caused the old wooden floors to groan. They turned the knob of a door, but it wouldn't budge. All up and down the hallways, they found the same. The school was locked up tight, with the exception of the bathrooms, which were empty.

Day elbowed Gregg as they stood in the men's bathroom. "Check it out," Day said, pointing, "toilet paper."

Gregg and Day looked at each other before sharing a muted high-five.

With the building pronounced clear, the group took the time to rest in the hallway, eating and regaining their strength.

****

Andy basked in his newfound fame. He was one of them. The other soldiers finally saw him for who he was. It was glorious. He was no longer a weak nothing whose sole existence seemed to be to give rich kids something to punch. He was somebody now.

He sat, playing a quiet game of poker with the others. They referred to him as Walt now, and Andy wondered if they had ever truly learned his name to begin with. Most of the soldiers had just called him "kid" up to that point.

"Here you go, Walt. Try one of these; you earned it," Whiteside said. Whiteside held out a somewhat crinkled cigarette, and Andy just looked at it.

"Go on. Take it, man," Epps said. "That right there is like the highest honor one can give in this world. You know how hard it is to find cigarettes these days?"

It was true. Even in the grocery store, Andy had watched as Whiteside and the others had combed the grocery store looking for cigarettes. While there was plenty of food around, it seemed that humans, in their infinite stupidity, had found cigarettes to be more important than food because there were only a few cartons left lying around. For Whiteside to offer him one of his few remaining cigarettes was a high honor indeed... but Andy didn't smoke. He reached for it anyway.

"I've never..." he began, but then Whiteside interrupted.

"Why? Cuz you thought you were gonna get cancer?" Whiteside laughed. "Hell, we should be so lucky to die of cancer."

"You have a point," Andy said.

"Of course he does," Allen said from the corner where he was tying bundles of rope into intricate knots. For what purpose, Andy didn't know.

Andy held the cigarette up to his lips, between his fingers the way he saw others do it. It felt awkward. Whiteside lifted a lighter to the tip of the cigarette. Andy breathed inward, and his mouth filled with the disgusting flavor of smoke.

He leaned back and blew the smoke into the air.

"You didn't do it right," Whiteside said. "Breathe it in, man."

Andy tried to breathe the smoke this time, but he breathed it in too deeply, and he began to cough. He put his arm over his face to muffle the noise, and through the tears in his eyes, he could see Whiteside and the others rolling on the wooden floor of the hallway, their hands over their face to keep their laughter from floating outside and alerting the Annies to their presence. From the end of the hall, Tejada tossed them an annoyed glare, but they could see the trembling at the corners of his mouth as he stifled a smile.

Eventually, the coughing passed, and tiny spots swam in Andy's vision as he tried to regain the oxygen he had been deprived of during his coughing fit. He held the cigarette up to his lips like a boy about to have his first kiss. He breathed inward, slower this time, and the smoke made its way into his lungs, with only a slight burn in his trachea. He exhaled the smoke, knowing that he had done it right that time.

His head began to swim in the most pleasant of sensations, and he understood now why people smoked. Whiteside gave him a wink, nodding his head up and down.

"You in?" Epps asked him as he took another drag off of the cigarette.

Andy nodded his head, as Epps' brown hands dealt the cards.

"You like it?" Whiteside asked.

Andy nodded his head, incapable of speech through the spinning euphoria of his head.

"Yeah, well, the next one's on you. So keep your eyes peeled out there," Whiteside said.

****

Izzy Allen flipped and knotted the ropes using the knowledge that he had learned as a Boy Scout. He had learned much as a young boy, stuck among other boys who had never quite seen the world the way he had. It was funny which of those lessons had stuck with him. Tying knots was one of those things.

He disliked the feel of the nylon rope, its garish patterns sliding in and out of his hands as he looped, circled, pushed, and pulled. He would take coarse rope any day. Coarse rope, that cheap hemp stuff with the fraying edges and the prickly feel, that was what he liked to use. When you knotted classic rope, you felt like a snake charmer, taming something that was never meant to be tamed. With the nylon stuff, there was no such sensation.

140

Still, he twisted and he knotted, listening to the conversations of the men around him. The memories of Ramirez and Kazinsky were drifting away like the smoke around Walt's head, lifting upwards, fading into nothingness. But just like smoke, they were still there, a faint smell on the fingers and clothes that would intrude at the most random of moments, but eventually this too would fade. When we die, we turn to smoke.

It was a depressing thought. He cinched the last knot and then stood up and swung his creation around, testing it. When he was done, he stepped past Quigs who was engrossed in reading a small, pocket Bible.

"Come here, Walt," he said, "and bring that bowling ball."

Walt did as he was told, and Allen felt slightly guilty at not actually remembering the kid's real name. As far as he knew, there were only thirteen people left in the world, and he hadn't bothered learning all of their names. He supposed he was just protecting himself, trying to keep the smell of smoke off his clothes and hands.

Walt finished whatever game he was playing with Epps and Whiteside, and he rummaged through his backpack, lifting the 8-pound bowling ball out with a grunt.

"It's pretty heavy, huh?" Allen asked.

"Yeah," Walt said.

Allen looked at the kid, measuring him, as if seeing him for the first time. He was gangly, but you could see potential in him. He was like a caterpillar now, but Allen could see the butterfly that might emerge. "You plan on keeping that thing? It looks pretty heavy."

"Yeah," Walt said, smiling. "I was thinking about it."

Allen nodded. He had expected as much. "Well, then here." He shoved his rope contraption into the middle of Walt's chest.

He grabbed it and looked at it, trying to look pleased, but his confusion was obvious. "What is it?" he asked.

Allen took the woven rope back from him and said, "Let me see that ball." Walt handed it to him, and he slipped the ball into the mass of ropes. He stood up and twisted the ropes a few times, and then realization dawned on Walt's face.

"No way."

Allen stood back as he lifted up the bowling ball. The cradle that Allen had woven for him was perfect. "Now you don't have to get so close to the Annies when you want to kill one of 'em. And with this rope, you can let the bowling ball do most of the work."

"This is awesome. Thanks... uhh... I don't know your first name."

Allen laughed at this. "It's Izzy, but you can call me Allen, my last name. Whichever one you feel like."

Allen left the kid then, and he sat back down watching him test out the bowling ball. It wasn't perfect, but it was a damn sight better than having to run into the middle of a group of Annies swinging the ball by hand. He could get more power in his swing by rocking the ball back and forth, and if he swung it over his head and got the arc just right, he could pretty much demolish any of the dead that they came across. It was a weird weapon, for sure, but these were weird times.

With that, Allen sat down and leaned against the wall. He pulled his camo hat low over his face and crossed his arms, tucking his chin down on his chest. Sleep came fast for him.

****

Rudy and Amanda found themselves alone at the end of the hallway. They were quiet, both seemingly lost in their own thoughts. They had eaten already and then fallen

142

into an awkward silence. Neither was tired, though the soldiers were bedding down for the evening. Time was moving slowly, but no one seemed to mind. It just meant they would be alive for one more day.

Rudy fidgeted with his fingers. He had one thing on his mind, the same thing that had run through his head all day... Amanda. He thought of how to tell her what he was feeling, but every time he did, blood would rush into his face, and he would turn away from Amanda so that she wouldn't turn to him and see.

The words were there on the tip of his tongue, but he had no way of making them real. He couldn't speak them. He tried to think back to movies he had seen to remember how guys told girls they liked them, but all of the movies he had watched were action movies or horror flicks. In those movies, people just sort of had sex. To them it was as easy as waking up in the morning. There was no awkwardness. There was no sitting on the floor, flooding your face with blood at the mere thought of speaking your heart to another.

He looked at Amanda. Her skin, which had been almost lily white when he had first encountered her, was now a red-brown. She chewed on her lip apprehensively, and he could feel the tension in her. Was she freaked out by him? Was he exuding some sort of "Uh-oh, this guy is going to hit on me" pheromone?

Finally, he could stand it no longer, and he fled to the only place that he could, the restroom. It was dim in the bathroom. A scant smattering of light found its way into the plain, tiled room through a frosted glass window set high in the wall. The urinals were low to the ground to make it easier for little kids to use them.

Rudy looked longingly at the sink, wishing he could just turn the tap and splash some cool water on his face. Out of desperation, he gingerly grasped the tap handle and twisted it. There was nothing... just a brief, dry, sucking sound, and then it was gone. He leaned on the sink and looked at himself in the mirror. He was nothing but freckles and fat. He was nothing. He shouldn't even be alive.

There's no way she could ever like you like that. No way. His heart ached so bad that he thought he was going to cry. The emotions were things that he had never felt before, equal parts pain and elation. He felt like he wanted to rip his skin off in the hopes that this would let the emotions escape his body. He gripped the cool porcelain of the sink and squeezed his eyes shut. *Stop being such a pussy.*

Rudy jumped at a touch on his arm. He spun sideways, away from the touch. His heart was in the back of this throat when he realized that it was just Amanda... in the bathroom.

"What are you doing here?"

"You were gone for a while," she said. Her lips were so shiny, just a faint hint of wetness. He didn't know why, but it did things to him. "I just wanted to make sure you were ok."

He felt as if his entire body was just a giant sack of meat meant to contain the fluttering of a million moths. "I'm... fine."

She stepped closer to him, and he could swear he could feel the warmth from her body. She reached out and touched his arm. "Are you sure? You don't seem fine."

Her hand was like fire, the pads of her fingers branding his arm. He could say nothing. Her approach and her touch had the same effect upon him that headlights had on a deer. He was frozen. They stood that way for what seemed like an eternity, and Rudy looked anywhere but at her. Then, he felt her other hand turning his head by his chin, and he found himself looking into her eyes. There was something there, shining in those pools. She got closer to him, standing on her tiptoes, and then they were kissing.

Rudy didn't know what he was doing, so he mimicked Amanda, their tongues touching. His mind raced, weighing, cataloguing, questioning, and he found himself frozen in time. Then she stepped away from him, and his world was changed entirely. On her lips, she took with her the old Rudy and left behind someone different, someone rawer, more real. He felt as if she had stripped him of his skin and laid him bare in that bathroom. He wrapped his arms around her, and she wrapped hers around him. They kissed some more. In a bathroom at the end of the world, he freed himself of his prolonged adolescence.

****

Andy practiced swinging his new weapon, an 8-pound, orange bowling ball cradled in a lattice of rope. He had no idea why he had been drawn to the bowling ball in the first place, but it had called out to him, like the ring to Bilbo in the blackness of the caves under the Misty Mountains. The bowling ball moved in an arc. Once it was going, it actually didn't take too much energy to maneuver the thing around.

He had to hand it to Allen. The rope cradle was an ingenious device. Truth be told, he had been thinking about getting rid of the bowling ball. It was too awkward and too heavy to be relied upon in a fight, which made the load not worth bearing. The only reason he had considered keeping it was because it had done something astounding. It had made him a man in the eyes of the soldiers.

They called him Walt. It was a somewhat silly name, but he planned on going with it. Maybe this was just another part of becoming who he was. Maybe he was meant to be someone completely different with a completely different name. He was meant to be a man named Walt, not a boy named Andy. Walt was a badass name, right? It sounded like the type of dude that drove one of those giant Dodge pick-up trucks through riverbeds in commercials for some ridiculous reason, the type of dude that had a Budweiser in one hand and a woman's ass in the

145

other while he steered with his crotch. Yeah, if they wanted him to be Walt, that's who he would be.

He twirled the bowling ball in the air, getting used to the ebbs and flows of its momentum. It was a pain in the ass to start the ball in motion once it got going, so he tried spinning to keep the ball moving. It was awkward, but he thought he was finding a rhythm with it. He had already discovered that an overhand attack with the bowling ball was pretty dangerous. He had almost brained himself and cracked the ancient wooden floors of the school pretty good, which drew another disapproving look from Tejada who sat up and glared at him, his sleep rudely awoken.

Andy, or Walt, had just smiled at him, and Tejada pulled his hat low over his face, folded his arms, and let him continue his practice. No, overhead wasn't the way to go at all. Side to side, spinning the bowling ball in an ellipse, twirling to keep the momentum going, that seemed to work the best. He was almost able to keep the bowling ball spinning forever, but there was one transition that he just couldn't quite get right. His feet felt clumsier than he wanted them to be. Sweat dripped off his body, and after a final collision between his shin and the bowling ball, he decided to call it quits. He would need his sleep, and he wasn't going to get any better if he was tired. Besides that, his arms and shoulders ached, and he was developing blisters on his hand. He would have to keep his eye open for some gloves. Gloves would be handy for more than just spinning the bowling ball. They could also mean the difference between life and death when an Annie's bite factored into the equation.

He lifted the bowling ball and placed it down next to his backpack. He realized he was breathing heavily, and his back knotted up with tension as he settled into his sleeping place. The others slept dutifully, their games over, their worries gone for the evening. He settled into place, feeling the sweat on his shirt cooling.

Then he saw them, Amanda and Rudy. They came out of the bathroom looking flushed and... no, it couldn't be. He watched them through half-lidded eyes, as they returned to their belongings at the end of the hall. They held hands, and Andy couldn't help but feel a slight bit of jealousy gnawing at him. What right did they have to find love? While the entire world collapsed and burned around them, why did they get to have each other?

It wasn't that he was attracted to Amanda. He wasn't. She was a bad person as far as he was concerned. He just didn't think it was fair. But, being a hero was never fair he supposed. Though they were completely ridiculous, and the thought of them having sex repulsed him, he decided he would let them be. After all, they were just survivors. They were like children, and Walt and the other soldiers were their protectors. He smiled at the fact that he had just thought of himself as Walt. He wondered what his mother would have thought at him having given up his given name, a name of tradition and family. He would love to see the look on her face when he told her he had changed his name to Walt. But that would never happen would it? He was sorry about that; not because he cared for his mother, but because he would never get to rub it in her face that he had become someone important.

He closed his eyes and dreamed about telling his mother off. They were good dreams.

Chapter 10: Popcorn Eyes

The sun had gone down hours ago, but the night had fallen over them before that, the canopy of the trees above them blocking out the sun as it angled down to meet the earth. Their clearing became blue, grey, and then black, and in the darkness, they sat still as statues, listening for the approach of the living and the dead.

They had lapsed into silence, each person stuck in their own mind on the odd chance that someone was out looking for them. Lou thought that highly unlikely, but you never knew. It didn't hurt to be cautious. Lou listened to his heartbeat pulsing in his earlobes. He was warm, flushed. He felt like he was on the verge of cracking, grabbing his weapon and just running straight into the compound firing. But that would just get them all dead.

He had never been that great at stealth. He had always lived his life as straightforward as possible. If he had a problem with you, he would tell you straight to your face. If someone had a problem with him, he would confront them on it. No, stealth was not how he liked to operate in the world, but it was a necessity now.

He needed to know how many people were in that compound. He needed to know what they were about, but most of all, he needed to know if Joan was alive. If she wasn't, they had no need to mess around with those people. If she was hurt, well, he didn't know what he would do. Most of all, he didn't know what Clara would do.

"It's time," he whispered, rising from his spot between the giant roots of a tree. It had been a comfortable spot, but his body had slowed. He stretched his legs and his arms, getting the blood going again. He could only see a vague outline of the others, but he knew they watched him.

"Maybe we should all go with you," Mort said.

"No. It's easy for one to sneak in, but not so much for four." He popped his neck, and then said, "If I'm not back by the time the sun comes up, you should leave."

"We won't leave you," Clara said.

"Well, you need to. If I'm not back by the time the sun comes up, it's because I've been caught. If they catch me, then they'll know that you guys are out here. We don't know what Joan has told them, but they know we're here somewhere. We don't know anything about these people, except that they have Joan and seem well-armed."

Lou couldn't see their faces, so he didn't know if they agreed or not. The wind rushed through the branches above, and a cold breeze made him shiver a bit. "I'm serious," Lou said. "If I don't come back, you have to leave."

"We won't," Clara said, "so you just need to get your ass back here safe and sound."

"Yeah, we're not leaving without you," Mort said.

Lou knew he wasn't going to win this one. He left his backpack on the ground and made sure his boots were tied good and tight. When he was ready to leave, Clara came to him and wrapped her arms around him. "Good luck," she whispered.

"Be safe," Mort said before pressing his hand into Lou's and throwing an arm over his shoulder.

"We'll see you soon," Katie said before giving him a kiss on the cheek, which was odd, but not unappreciated. It was nice to know that there was something of a human inside Katie. She could be so cold at times.

With their farewells said, Lou turned and oriented himself. He moved smoothly through the night, picking his footfalls carefully. As if the gods were on his side, the wind picked up, shaking the trees and the branches, hiding his clumsy steps as he pressed through the black forest. He tried to memorize his route, but he didn't know how well of a job he was doing. It was simply too dark. The sky was black above with only the occasional star for illumination.

The trees gave way to the clearing in front of the compound, and he was greeted with a vision of a starry, moonless sky. He stopped for a second, awed by the amount of stars. When he was a kid, hiding on the streets while his dad and his friends partied the night away, he could only ever see a couple of stars, but in this place, there were more than he could count.

He only hesitated a second, and then he was on his way again. He had a job to do, and he didn't want to get caught out in the open. That would be death for him and maybe the others. He jogged to the left of the compound, keeping low until he was out of sight of the watchtowers by the main gate. In the darkness, he could see shadows atop the walls, backlit by the starry sky. He didn't think they could see him, and as he circled clockwise around the compound, they didn't move or acknowledge his presence.

He moved closer to the trailers encircling the compound. Their windows were blacked out, but from inside the compound, he could see the orange glow of firelight dancing on the underside of two trees that shot up from the center of the encampment. He looked for an opening in the wall of trailers, but there were none as far as he could tell. This was going to be harder than he thought.

Instead, he bent down and inspected the fill dirt that had been placed underneath the trailers. It was loose, and it would take some time to loosen it, but he could get in that way without exposing himself to the guards in the watchtower. He began digging, using his hands to scoop the dirt behind him. Time seemed to freeze, and he had no idea how long he had been at it. Sweat ran down his face, and his hands were caked in dirt, the fingertips aching from his efforts.

Digging was a strange sensation. It was something he had never done before. Growing up in the city, he had been bound by concrete, brick, and pavement. There was dirt in the parks, but the parks in his neighborhood hadn't been the type of place where kids would go to dig and play. They were the types of places that you stayed far away from, unless you happened to be with your father. But even then, you probably weren't there to play. If his father was in the park, that meant business. That meant running sandwich bags full of weed and other things across to people waiting in cars. That meant keeping an eye out for the police.

He was deep in his thoughts when it happened. He heard a twig snap behind him. As the wind shifted directions, he caught a whiff of something rotten, and he knew that one of the dead had stumbled upon his position. He sprang to his feet just as the dead thing tried to wrap its hands around his throat. Lou was able to shove his forearm up underneath the creature's jaw. In the night, he could hear the thing's teeth clicking. It was a big one, strong.

Lou stumbled over the piles of dirt on the ground, and they both tumbled backwards, Lou on the bottom. His back struck the side of the trailer with a clang. Anyone inside would be alerted now. He had to finish this quick. He rolled to his side, hoping that no more of the dead were around. With the dead thing under him, its flesh hard and dry, Lou fumbled for the knife that hung on his belt with his free hand. He grasped the handle and pulled it free. He jammed the blade downward as hard as he could, but the tip skittered off the skull. Cold hands pawed at his face, forcing him to lean backwards.

He reared back for another attempt, and this one skittered off the cheekbone. The zombie shifted under him, and Lou rolled to his side, coming to his feet, kicking up a cloud of dust. He readied his knife, but it was hard to see in the gloom of the night.

Suddenly, that was no longer a problem. Light flooded the area. From atop the trailer he had tried to dig under, bright flashlights shone into his eyes, blinding him.

He put his arm up to shield his eyes, and that's when the dead thing lunged for him. He landed on his back, his hand smashing into a jagged rock. The knife flew from his hands, and all he had left were his hands as he fended off the attack of the dead.

He struggled, pushing and repositioning his hands to keep the monster's teeth off his skin, burning up all of the energy he had.

"Take the shot," he heard a voice say.

There was a pause, and then another voice asked, "Are you sure?"

"Yeah. Do it."

There was another pause, and then he heard the click of a bolt-action rifle chambering a round. This was followed by a crack of thunder, and then blood covered Lou's face. The dead man on top of him stopped moving. It's full weight, now limp, crushed him into the dirt. He tried to push it off of him, but he was too exhausted. All he could do was lay there. Maybe if he sat still, they would think him dead.

"Well, hello there," a voice said. It was the voice of the man from the gate, the one in charge. Lou didn't feel like answering, so he remained silent.

"I said, 'Hello.' The least you could do is answer me. We just saved your life."

That was true. It was the least he could do. "Hello."

"There. Now that's a start." The voice lapsed into silence as the wind rushed through the trees. "Now what business do you have trying to break into our home?"

"I was looking for my friend. I tracked her here."

"Oh, you must mean Joan. Well, why don't we get you cleaned up and you can come inside and we'll talk. I'm sure Joan would be pleased to see you. Keith, Stan, why don't you go around front and help our friend?"

Lou tried to push the body off of him, and this time he was more successful. He managed to free his upper half from the corpse, when two dirty men appeared from around the corner.

"Now don't go running, mister," said the man on top of the trailer, still shining light in Lou's eyes. "It's a shameful thing to shoot a man in the back, don't you think?"

Lou waited as the pair of men lifted the corpse of the dead man off of his legs. As they did, the man atop the trailer said, "Bring that one inside. It'll keep us warm. You there, why don't you lend a hand?"

Lou got to his feet, feeling as if he was about to keel over. He was exhausted, but he bent down and picked up the corpse by its legs. The man across from him carried the upper half by the hands, trying to avoid getting blood on his clothes. They duck-walked around the perimeter of the compound. The man atop the trailers followed them, jumping the gap between trailers when needed, but never failing to shine the light on them.

They reached the main gate, and as they stepped inside, it rattled shut behind them, the chain-links jingling as it closed.

"Over there," the man said, pointing to a brick-lined fire pit. They shuffled over to the pit, and unceremoniously dumped the corpse on top. It went up in flames immediately.

"If we didn't live in a damn forest, we could get rid of them all with a flamethrower or two," Keith said.

It was true. The corpse, when he had been wrestling with it, had felt abnormally dry, its skin more like flexible leather than human skin. Fire would do wonders against the dead, but then again, it did wonders against the living as well.

Lou watched as the man atop the trailers leapt nimbly to the ground, a heavy flashlight in his hands. He smiled at Lou, but Lou didn't trust that smile one bit. He had seen that smile before in the streets. It was the smile of

153

a wolf. Meant to be disarming, that smile would disappear from the man's face as soon as Lou turned his back.

His arms spread open in greeting, and he said, "Welcome to Clarksville."

Lou just nodded.

"Is that all you have to say for yourself?" The man looked around at the other people in the compound, as if he were surprised. "Listen. Don't give me all this thug-life bullshit, man. I'm trying to be cordial here. I really am."

Lou said nothing. He sensed the unhinged nature of this man, and the cowering nervousness of the other people in Clarksville told him that he wasn't wrong to react in such a way.

"Oh, I get it," the man said with a smile. "We haven't been properly introduced yet. So let's take care of that bullshit right now." The man came closer to him and held out his hand for a handshake. "The name's Chad."

Lou held out his hand and shook it. It was a firm handshake, a bone-grinder for sure. Chad leaned in close to his ear and whispered, "Otherwise known as the man with whom you don't want to fuck." This was followed up with a punch to the gut that dropped Lou to his knees as his breath exploded from him.

"I'm sorry about that, mister, but that's a small price to pay for your sneaky little escapade out there." He leaned over, inches from Lou's face, daring him to spit at him or defy him in some such way. It's what he wanted. Lou knew this man. He had known men like him all his life. He was a small man, held down by the world at every turn. The only real power he had came from his anger and his ability to hurt people. He would be an expert at hurting people too. Once a small man found out they had that kind of power, they honed it like the edge of a knife.

"My name's Lou," he grunted.

"Lou, Lou, Lou. I don't think I've ever known a Lou," Chad said amiably. "Hell, with the way the world is

154

right now, I don't know that I'll ever get the chance to know another Lou."

The men in the compound laughed at this, as if it were hilarious, but Lou didn't find it particularly funny. Chad was the type of man who demanded that other people laughed at his jokes, whether they were funny or not. "Well, Lou. You said you were looking for your friend, right?"

"Yes, sir."

"Oooh. You hear that everybody, I'm a sir. I like that. Well, Lou. As soon as you tell us where the rest of your friends are, we can take you to see your friend. How does that sound for a bargain?"

"I told you, I'm here by myself," Lou lied.

Chad just nodded his head, as if that was what he had expected to hear. Suddenly there was a pop from the fire. Chad laughed and said, "I love that sound. You know what that was?"

Lou said nothing.

"That was the sound of an eyeball popping. Yeah, boy, when you toss one of those dead things on a fire, those eyeballs, well they just keep getting hotter and hotter and hotter until they just up and explode like a popcorn kernel." Just as he finished talking, the other eyeball popped. "Hey Stan, which one went first, the left or the right?"

"Looks like the left one this time, Chad," Stan said. He was a wiry dude with a severe underbite. He looked to be missing a few bars in the grate. Lou could spot a methhead quicker than most people could tell he was black. Unless he was some sort of chemist, Stan was cured of his addiction whether he liked it or not. Lou guessed some good had come from the end of the world after all... you know, until that guy got his hands on some model glue or something.

"The left one? Dammit! I totally would have bet on the left one, but I was too busy with Mr. Lou here. You just

155

cost me some money, Lou," Chad said while wagging his finger at him. "Now, Mr. Lou, if you don't tell me where the rest of your friends are in the next thirty seconds, I think I'm going to throw you on the fire next, and we'll see which of your eyes pops first. I got right. Anyone want any of that action?"

"I'll take some of that, Chad," Stan said.

Chad smiled. "Well, it looks like we got ourselves a wager. How does a hundred sound to you, Stan?"

"A hundred would be just fine."

Lou knew they were bluffing. There was something about the new world that made bluffing almost an art form. He admired the way that Chad and Stan had played their game. It was almost as if they had done it before, but Lou knew Chad was full of bullshit. What he didn't know was whether or not Chad was a killer. He had that look, that madman look, but hell, everyone had that these days. The last time he had seen his own face, he had nearly jumped in fright.

"I'll take some of that action," Lou said.

Chad turned to him and smiled, unable to believe what he had just heard. He pointed at Lou uncertainly and said, "You sure that's what you want?"

"How does two hundred sound?"

Chad just shrugged his shoulders, and then he and Stan lifted Lou up and dragged him over to the fire. They held him over the coals like a priest holding a new convert over the baptismal pool.

"You got the money on you?" Chad asked him.

"What?" Lou said, before he felt Chad and Stan let him go. He fell backwards into the flames, his back cracked across the hot, brick lining the circumference of the fire pit, and he felt warm heat envelop his entire upper torso. He tried to scream, but there was no air to scream with. He rolled over and plunged his hands into the burning coals of the fire, pushing his way up and out of the fire. Lou thought

156

he could feel his skin dying as he rose into the cool night air. He thought he felt his cells scream out in unison then fall dead, leaving exposed and damaged nerve endings behind.

He landed on the ground, his skin smoking in the coolness of the night.

Chad leaned over him, looking down at his ruined brown flesh. "Hey, no fair. That's cheatin'. You just cost me some money again."

Lou could say nothing. He squeezed his eyes shut, unable to concentrate on anything but the searing pain that ran through his body. Then the world went black.

"Hey, check his wallet," Chad said. "Maybe he has the money on him."

****

The sky was slate blue through the canopy above. The survivors shivered in the cold morning of the forest. A small mist kicked along the ground, disturbed every now and then by the squirrels who bounded their way through the world, oblivious to the fact that the dead walked the earth.

Katie leaned against the cold, mossy trunk of a pine tree that must have been two-hundred years old. It was as thick and round as two portly men standing side by side. She sat in a cleft between two thick roots that veered off into the loamy turf. In her hand, she rolled a cigarette back and forth. She wanted it bad, but then she felt that kick inside of her. It was still there. A boy or a girl, she didn't know. She questioned if she ever wanted to know.

But it still clung to life, and so must she. She wanted nothing more than a drink, a quick nip of something that would burn as it went down. But it would go down too far. It would go down into the baby, and no matter how she felt about her own life, she knew that the life of the baby inside wasn't hers to own. It was Zeke's. And though he wasn't here, she had a good idea that he would have wanted the baby to live. So she was willing to press on and suffer next to the others.

They were dead already, but they didn't even know it. She rolled the cigarette back and forth, wondering just how bad one little cigarette might be for a baby. Hell, mothers throughout the '60s and '70s had doused their children with nicotine for decades, but now it was suddenly bad. But that wasn't her choice. It wasn't her baby. She was just carrying it. Somewhere along the way, she would be freed of it, and when she was, well, she would be free altogether.

She put the cigarette in the inner pocket of her jacket and pulled her revolver free. It was fully loaded, and she trusted it more than she trusted the others. She sensed their distance the way a fish might sense a human on the shore above them through muddy waters. There was something there, but it was unclear, disturbing, and yet there was absolutely nothing she could do about it.

Clara and Mort slept peacefully, their breathing deep and untroubled, though it shouldn't be. They had all heard the gunshot in the night, and now Lou wasn't back. She guessed they would be packing up and leaving now. If Clara and Mort didn't want to go, she would head out without them. There wasn't any sense in kicking this hornet's nest, and that's exactly what it was. They all knew it, though none of them had said it.

Who knew what the men in that compound were capable of? She suspected she would very soon be on her own. This would complicate things when she had her baby, but at least she would have a chance to give birth if she left. If they went poking around that compound, they were likely to die... or worse.

She popped the cylinder open on the handgun, checked all the rounds, and then closed it back up with a flick of her wrist. Something gnawed at the back of her mind, some memory of what it had been like to be loyal, to dedicate her life to something other than herself. It was guilt eating away at her. It was why she hadn't abandoned the others, she hesitated to call them friends, days ago. They were all good people, if a little misguided, but she had seen what happened to good people.

It was safer to be bad. It was safer to not rely on emotions and feelings. Those things just seemed to get people killed. She was pondering her newfound philosophy when she heard the snapping of a twig behind her. Immediately, she spun around, her handgun up and ready.

"Wake up!" she yelled as she fired a round into the trees around them. Clara and Mort were on their feet in an instant, their weapons in their hands, their wild-eyes searching the forest around them. They were surrounded.

"Hold your fire!" a man yelled. "There's no need for anyone to die!" A skinny man, all country and cool cars, stepped from behind a tree. He had his hands in the air to show he was no danger, but Katie knew that wasn't the case.

"What do you want?" Katie asked.

"We just came to let you know that your friend had an accident. He sent us here to find you."

"Bullshit," Clara said.

"No, it's true," replied the man. "We saved your friend from one of the dead last night. You probably heard the gunshot. The fight must have exhausted him because he passed out and fell into our campfire. He's badly burned. If you put your guns down, you can come with us and see for yourself."

"We're not giving up our guns," Katie said.

Clara without saying anything tossed her gun on the ground. She stepped forward, ignoring the others.

"What are you doing?" Mort asked.

Without looking back, Clara said, "We have to go. Our friends are hurt."

159

Mort thought about this and then tossed his own gun on the ground. He followed after Clara. Katie stood alone, the weight of the revolver in her hand seeming to grow exponentially with every moment that passed.

"And what about you, little lady?" the man asked.

"I'm not a lady," Katie said, "and I'm not going anywhere without my gun."

The man just smiled at her, as if she were a big joke, and she wanted to put a bullet right through his teeth. "Suit yourself. But if you want to change your mind, all you have to do is hand that gun over to the guards at the gate, and you can walk right in."

"I'll be fine on my own."

Clara turned to Katie imploringly. "Katie, don't."

"You're a fool, Clara. Your heart is too big."

Clara turned and walked away. Mort looked over his shoulder apologetically at Katie as if to say, "What are you going to do?" The men from the compound surrounded the two, and then everyone melted into the trees, leaving Katie in the woods, her gun in her hands and no one else around.

"They left me," she said. She sat on the ground, her knees buried in the mossy turf. It was the first time she had truly been alone in months. It was so silent, so empty. She felt the swelling warmth of her belly, and she knew that she wasn't completely alone. That made it better somehow. She dropped the gun to her side, as tears flowed from her eyes. She tried to tell herself that she was just emotional because she was pregnant, but in her heart, she knew that the tears were real and justified. She had turned her back on the others, though they had deserved no such thing. Shame flowed through her, and she patted her belly, "Boy, you're getting to experience all the emotions today, aren't you?" Katie smiled. All of the emotions indeed.

Chapter 11: A Safe Place

In the relative quiet of the morning, Beacham kicked down the door. The door to the janitor's closet flew open, and the able-bodied soldiers rushed in and grabbed a ten-foot, fiberglass ladder. Day and Gregg carried it as they rushed out of the school that had been their home for the previous evening. All of their bags were packed, and they were ready to go. One by one, they slipped out of the window in the dull gray light of the morning.

The sounds of Beacham breaking down the door had already drawn several Annies to investigate. The soldiers sent them to the ground with the butt of their rifles. And they pushed through, already feeling the pressure of the dead as they attempted to surround and constrict the survivors.

They rushed through the backstreets, walking quickly to outpace the dead. The dead appeared before them, and they pressed through them violently and quickly, leaving them in their wake. The entire group was focused and ready. There was no conversation, only the solemn sense that they were on a mission, and they would not let it end in death.

Allen felt their purpose as if it were a tangible thing. They wanted to be somewhere safe, somewhere where they could laugh as loud as they wanted and not worry about the dead coming after them. They wanted freedom from the dead and from the dread that infused their souls with every waking minute. Most of all, they wanted to be able to smile, sit in the sun, and angle their faces up at it with their eyes closed without having to worry about a dead thing coming to take a bite out of their ass.

They turned onto Murray Road, the ladder clanking with each step. Gregg and Day had transferred the ladder to Rudy and Beacham who balanced the ladder on their shoulders, leaving the other soldiers free to gun down anything that got in their way. Any concerns they had about making too much noise went out the window. This was an all or nothing affair, do or die. They either hit that wall running and gunning and popped over it like it was three-feet tall, or they were going to smash headlong into it, breaking like waves against a cliff face.

As they neared the mass of dead scratching at the wall, the soldiers opened fire. The smoke and thunder of their press cleared out an area roughly the shape of a pie wedge. They stepped over bodies, firing their weapons at as many of the dead as they could. They picked their targets according to proximity.

Once they were at the wall, Tejada and Walt lifted the ladder off of Rudy and Beacham's shoulders and planted it firmly on the ground after they had kicked a dead body out of the way. Brains ran down the wall as the ladder went up. They sent Quigs up first. He was the eager one of the bunch, always ready to move onto the next pitfall so that he could be the one that said he had jumped first. He was the type of guy who, if you took him sky-diving, would jump out of the airplane before the instructor even gave the order.

He stopped on top of the wall and turned around, balancing on the edge to help the others over. "It's clear over here," the blonde-haired man announced. The wall was thick, but not as thick as one of Quigs' size-10 shoes. His toes stuck out over the edge of the wall. As each survivor reached the top, he lent them a hand to help them over the two-foot difference in height between the wall and the ladder. Amanda went first, followed by Rudy, then Beacham, who managed to climb the ladder with his one good arm, the other hanging in a sling.

Allen fired into the crowds of the dead. He was responsible for all of the dead to the south of the ladder. It was almost unfair. With his rifle, he was able to line up shot after shot, but even after unloading two full clips there

162

were still more. The ground was littered with the dead, yet more still came, and they were getting closer and thicker every second.

The other soldiers, including Tejada, climbed up the ladder until it was just him and Epps at the bottom. "You go," Allen said. If Quigs was always the first man into a door, Allen was always the last man out of the room. Epps shouldered his rifle and then clambered up the ladder. Once he was up, Allen did the same. At the top, Quigs bent over to help him up, the soles of his feet still balanced on the edge of the wall. A small rectangular book edged out of the pocket on his chest, hanging precariously and then falling completely. Quigs moved to catch it, over-committed, and lost his balance in the process. He fell forward and Allen reached out for him with his hand.

He grasped onto the inside of Quigs' shirt, but the extra weight pulled the ladder off balance. It began to tilt to the left and was in jeopardy of falling completely over, which would mean death for them both with the dead closing in.

From the other side of the wall, the others yelled at them, asking if they were ok. "Don't let me go, man!" Quigs pleaded. Allen and Quigs locked eyes, and then Allen did the unthinkable. He let Quigs go.

He moved quickly after that, fear nipping at his heels along with the screams of Quigs below. When he was at the top, he stepped to the side, balancing on the edge of the wall and spinning around. He leaned over and pulled the ladder up and over the wall. The ladder gave a loud metallic rattle as it hit the ground, and then he scanned the outside of the wall to find Quigs buried underneath a crowd of Annies. He had no shot, but Quigs still screamed, so he pulled his pistol and tried to kill as many of them as he could. One round after another, he fired into the mob of Annies feeding on his friend. He must have killed a half-dozen of them by the time he could finally see Quigs' face.

163

There wasn't much left of it, and the man that he had known as Quigs was no longer there as the Annies feasted.

Allen took aim and squeezed the trigger. It was all he could do. Guilt washed over him like a tsunami, sweeping away everything that he was. He knelt on top of the wall, his mind lost to him. He was raw emotion oozing with rage. The dead looked up at him from below, aching to reach Allen's flesh. He screamed so hard, he thought he would turn himself inside out, and then he fired into those faces. Man, woman, and child fell under his onslaught. And when his handgun clicked empty, he let it fall to the side. There were more here than he had ammunition for.

"Get down here, son."

It was the voice of Tejada, calm, sympathetic. He had never heard the man's voice like that before. It calmed him immediately. He hung from the inside of the wall by his hands and then dropped to the ground with a thud. Epps was there, putting his hand on his shoulder. Allen's eyes had gone blurry with tears, and he wiped his arm across his face, keeping his eyes on the ground.

No one needed to say anything. They had seen Quigs fall. They had heard the screams and the gunfire. They stood that way for a few minutes, until Allen sucked in the snot, dried his eyes, and said, "I'm ready to go." But he wasn't. None of them were.

****

They were surrounded by overgrown nature. Flowers, grass, and bushes grew wild. In the distance, they could see buildings rising up above nature's bounty. The buildings were large and the architecture strange. The closest building was a pristine white. It was all angles and lines. In the center, a large glass atrium rose. Inside, they could see shadows moving about in the morning light.

Their hearts fell. The dead were here too.

"Bring that ladder," Tejada said.

164

Rudy and Beacham tossed the ladder over their shoulders again, and they walked with their heads poking up between the rungs. They pressed forward through the grass, the soldiers scanning left and right, all except for Allen. His rifle hung at his side, and he had a blank look on his face.

Walt felt sorry for him. But he would keep an eye on the man. It was the least he could do. As they pressed forward, they began to see evidence of a large battle. Bodies lay rotting in the tall grass, their corpses keeping the grass underneath from growing. The smell of the dead hung in the air, and there was evidence of gunfire. Many of the corpses, in addition to the mutilations that lead to their birthing as the living dead, had bullet holes in their foreheads.

Andy noticed the name of the building to their right. It was called the Tiger Woods Center. Then he noticed the signs on the buildings around them, each emblazoned with the name of a famous athlete. If you knew what to look for, you would see the tell-tale swoosh symbol everywhere, both on the buildings and on the clothing and badges of the dead.

"I always wanted to visit the Nike Campus," Beacham said.

It all made sense in a weird sort of way. Only a company flush with money could have managed to create their own little compound with the end of the world going on around them. As they pressed forward, Andy stopped. "What is that sound?" They all stopped and listened. A faint mechanical whine could be heard. Then they saw the source; a small golf cart trundled towards them. At one point it stopped, becoming stuck upon the body of a corpse. A large man, dressed in the all black uniform of a security guard, hopped out of the cart and pulled the body of the corpse out of the way. Then he hopped back in, and the cart headed towards them once more.

"Be ready," Tejada said.

The soldiers checked their weapons, and Walt let his bowling ball drop to the ground. He pulled his handgun free and held it at his side. He would be ready if anything went badly.

"Hello there!" a round-faced man with a white beard called as the golf cart pulled to a stop in front of them. Now that the man in black was closer, they could see that he had a submachine gun slung over his shoulder. It was currently aimed at them.

"Hello to you," Tejada said, his voice letting the man know that he didn't much care to have a weapon pointed in his direction.

"Don't mind Harper here. You can never be too careful these days." The man looked them over with a careful eye. "I see we have some soldiers here. Are you good soldiers or bad? We've seen both."

"We're good," Tejada said shortly.

"We'll just have to see about that. Bad soldiers wouldn't tell me they're bad, would they?"

"I suppose not," Tejada said.

"Well, either way, welcome to Nike World Headquarters, not that there's much of a world left. But hey, at least we won't have any competition for a while. Not many other companies still holding together I suppose. Why don't you come on in and take a rest?"

"That sounds just fine," Tejada replied.

The trollish-looking man in the golf cart, hearing that they were welcome, let his machine gun drop. The soldiers did the same.

"Follow us," the man in the golf cart said. He spun his golf cart around, jiggling as he rolled over the arm of a dead Annie in the process. "Oops," he giggled.

Walt bent down to pick up his bowling ball as the survivors moved to follow the odd old man.

166

"That building over there is the Tiger Woods Center," the old man began as if giving a tour. "You'll find that it is not a place that you want to go. The dead are in there. As a matter of fact, most of the buildings here are not places you want to go."

"What happened?" Andy asked.

"Oh, you know. The same thing that happened everywhere," the man said wistfully. "We thought we were safe. We weren't, and by the time we had the situation under control, we had to lock up most of the buildings. It's a sad thing really. There are some truly great people roaming the buildings of this campus. But come, we can speak more of these things once we get to safety. The buildings are all sealed up tight, but with the living around, the dead can get a little agitated. And when they get agitated enough, they can escape. We've seen it before."

They followed the man in quiet, admiring the unique buildings and the campus, which at one time must have been beautiful to behold. The buildings still were, but the grounds, which were once faithfully manicured, had fallen into a state of overgrowth. The cart motored along a covered walkway.

There was a large lake to their left. Instead of ducks floating along placidly, there were bodies, floating face down. Their corpses were swollen and pale like gooseflesh. The late summer wind rippled across the water, and Walt felt a chill on it. They entered a building named Ken Griffey Jr., another glass behemoth of modern architecture. At the entranceway, the old man climbed from the cart, leaning on the arm of the security guard, who had thus far remained quiet.

They followed the toddling man inside the building. There were other people about, soft people who looked upon them with fear in their eyes. Walt thought that they were lucky to still be alive. He wondered if he had once had that look. Is that what the other survivors had seen when he had allowed them into the movie theater? A soft-faced boy, barely capable of wiping his own ass?

They filed through an entranceway and up a flight of stairs. They found themselves on a second floor. Small couches and chairs filled the spaces. Haggard-looking men and women lounged on the chairs, doing nothing other than looking upon their new visitors.

Walt nodded at each of them in turn, hoping to exude the confidence that he felt. These people were no threat to them.

"You still have power," Tejada said.

"Yes, yes. Before this whole thing started, we had just turned this place into a 100% green paradise. Only on the most cloudy of days do we not have enough energy for our needs. Now that there's no TV, no internet, no wi-fi, well, we really only need enough power for lights, cooking, and the water heater."

"You have hot water?" Amanda asked.

The old man smiled at her. "Yep. Water stopped working a month ago, but we were able to rig something up. After we talk, I'm sure we can arrange a shower for you and your friends. That's the great thing about having all these engineers and scientists on hand... nothing is ever truly broken."

Everyone brightened up instantly.

"But before that, we need to have that talk. So come with me."

They walked down a corridor, the chairs and sofas disappearing from view. They passed a wall decorated with hundreds of baseball bats and several golden baseball gloves, and then they were in a meeting room. The old man stood to the side as they filed in, and then he closed the door behind them.

At the head of the table, a man sat with wild eyes. He had the look of a hippy about him. He had a red and grey beard that was unkempt. A strip of red cloth was tied around his forehead to keep his shoulder-length gray hair out of his eyes... to Walt, he looked like if a businessman had gone feral. To his left and his right sat several pinched-face people, suspicious, their eyes darting from one survivor to the next, weighing and judging.

"Please, have a seat," the man said. "My name is Nike, and these are my trusted advisors."

The survivors sat in the chairs. They were soft and luxurious, and Walt could feel the tension release from his back.

"You said your name was Nike?" Tejada said.

The bearded man smiled. "It was not my birth name, but that name belonged to a different world, a different place. That name belonged to a person that died. We have all been reborn in this place, as many of you have probably been reborn as well, out there... among the dead. It's a different world out there than the one we were born into. A different name seemed fitting."

"Well, my name is Tejada, and these are my soldiers and a couple of people we picked up along the way. We lost a man getting into this place, and we don't have much time for bullshit, and that's what this place smells like... bullshit. Now what do you want from us?"

Nike laughed, his mouth opening wide as he threw his head back and bellowed like no man had ever bellowed before. The fucker was crazy. Walt could see that.

When he was done, Nike regarded Tejada with a good-natured smile. "Your directness is apropos. You know, in the time before all this, I would have been put off by such adroitness. I would have counted you a feeb and a simpleton. But I suspect that directness has probably kept you and your men alive thus far."

Tejada and the other survivors waited patiently.

"I won't waste any more of your time, Mr..."

"Tejada."

"Mr. Tejada. We have many problems here. You've seen the dead in the other buildings I suspect. We have everything here we need to survive. Walls, land for food, people, water... but what we don't have is people like you and your friends. People that can get things done. We were all pencil-pushers, people who worked with our minds, not our hands. When our friends turned, there was nothing we could do but lock them inside these buildings. But they are a danger to our way of life. We cannot live if they still live in death. Does that make sense?"

Tejada nodded as the other soldiers looked at each other, unsure of what was happening here.

"In short, Mr. Tejada, I want you and your men to kill the dead on these premises. I want you to be a part of our community, to train us, and help us survive."

Nike fell into silence, his underlings eyeing the soldiers expectantly as Nike's request sank in.

"What say you to our little deal?" Nike asked.

Tejada pulled his backpack off of the floor and unzipped it. He reached inside and pulled out a bottle of water. He twisted the top, the flimsy, ridged plastic crinkling in his hands as he tipped it back. He let out a great "ah" of satisfaction and then set the bottle on the table. Nike showed signs of impatience at Tejada's display. He was not a man used to waiting for a response.

Tejada wiped the back of his mouth with his hand, slapped the arms of the chair he was sitting in and said, "We'll sleep on it." With that he stood up and waved to the others. Walt was laughing on the inside, struggling to keep a straight face. *Absolutely badass,* he thought. Tejada had just emasculated this hippy turned leader without even trying.

Nike, for his part, showed no ill will other than the crinkling of the skin around his eyes as he attempted to hold back his displeasure. "By all means," the man said, "take the evening to dwell on my proposal. We have plenty

170

of food, and if you need to freshen up, we have plenty of water, which should make you feel more at home. We'll talk again in the morning. Zimmer, would you show these men around?"

The toddling old man nodded at Nike and then gestured at the survivors to follow him. They filed out of the meeting room. When Andy looked over his shoulder, Nike was still sitting there. The smile glued to his face was like a picture of Bigfoot, fake as hell.

****

Rudy had to hand it to the people at the Nike campus. They knew how to make some pretty good food with stuff from cans. He was famished, and for the first time in who knew how long, he could finally get down to the business of eating without worrying about tomorrow. Rationing your own supplies of food in the hopes that you would have something to eat the next day was practical, but certainly not the way that he wanted to live.

Speakers played some soothing music. It wasn't the type of music that he would have ever listened to, but he didn't mind it one bit. The song was simple, soft jazz. He normally hated jazz, finding its rhythms and instruments jarring and annoying. But he hadn't heard music in so long that he thought he could listen to this particular song for hours.

The soldiers sat around them, slurping up food that had been prepared by some of the denizens of the Nike campus. They were good, normal people, the likes of which he hadn't seen in forever, since everything had gone to shit at the Memorial Coliseum. They were the type of people that you would see walking down the streets, shopping in the grocery stores, and basically living a "normal" life.

He had never imagined such an existence for himself, but here, after having gone through everything he had gone through, he thought that maybe there was a chance that he could have a nice normal life. Maybe he and

171

Amanda could have that together. He scooped another mouthful of the ramen-chili concoction into his mouth. He had to hand it to the end of the world, food had never tasted so damned good... even if it was just chili plopped over a plate full of unseasoned ramen.

Amanda stuck a forkful of peas in front of his face, and he opened his mouth and made them disappear within. *Oh, so good!* He turned to her and smiled, and she bumped shoulders with him. They were both ecstatic.

The soldiers however were not in the same mood. They had lost a friend outside, and they spoke in hushed tones at the other end of the long cafeteria table they sat at. Andy, or Walt as everyone seemed to call him now, was down there with them. Whatever the soldiers decided, Rudy knew in his heart that he was going to stay. He hoped they would take Walt with them. He had changed subtly since they had left the movie theater. It had only been a few weeks since then, but there was something about him that just didn't seem right. The bowling ball incident had been dangerous, not awesome like the soldiers thought, and he had seen some of the disdainful looks that Andy had cast his way. Rudy knew those looks. He had experienced those for the better part of his life whenever he walked down the street.

It wasn't the sort of look where people just stared at you. It was the type of look where they couldn't even stand looking at you. Andy's eyes seemed to just slide off of him as if he didn't exist. *Well fuck him. If he wants to be an asshole, he can do it somewhere else.*

But then there were the others to think about. Mort, Lou, Blake, Clara and Joan. They were out there somewhere, and while the people here were nice and all, they seemed almost helpless, as if they lived in a fantasy land comprised of fairy tales. And there it was again, that nagging feeling like he was about to make a very terrible decision. It was the same type of feeling he had felt when

172

he had escaped from his apartment using the rusting fire escape... which had of course collapsed behind him as soon as he had gotten off of it. But he didn't have a choice then. He had a choice now. He didn't have to risk his life if he didn't want to.

"What do you think?" he asked, his meal suddenly losing its appeal.

"About what?" Amanda said around a mouthful of canned peas.

"Should we stay here?"

Amanda looked at him, and the smile left her face. He felt like a bastard for bringing up something that would make her unhappy, but he wanted to have this conversation before Tejada and the others asked what they were planning to do. He didn't want to have to figure it out on the spot. They needed a plan.

"Do you want to stay here?" she asked.

"It seems... normal here. Or as normal as any place can be," he said.

"As normal as any place can be where all the buildings are filled with the dead."

Rudy shrugged. "Everywhere we go is going to be filled with the dead. But at least here, no more are getting in."

"That's true," Amanda said. She looked around, trying to get used to the modern building. Its heartless architecture was fine for looking at, or even working in, but she couldn't imagine herself living there. "It's so weird here."

"How is it weird?" Rudy asked.

"It's just so lifeless. Everyone here seems afraid."

"That'll change," Rudy said.

"So you want to stay?"

"I think I do."

"What about the others?" she asked.

"You mean the soldiers or Lou and the others?"

173

"Both I suppose."

"Tejada and the others will be fine without us. It's not like we've been fitting in or anything. We're basically baggage to them. And Lou and the others... we don't even know where they are, or if they are even still alive?"

Amanda nodded and looked at the soldiers at the other end of the table. "Then maybe we should stay. Maybe this place will grow on me."

"It'll be nice to not have to worry."

"Yeah, I suppose so," she said. Rudy didn't think she sounded sold on the prospect, but it was a start. Things would get better.

****

Tejada had been chewing on the issue more than he had been chewing his food. He didn't like this place. He didn't like all the glass, all the buildings, the poor sight lines, the people who seemed about as capable of defending themselves as he was of shitting gold.

But his men were sad... beaten. They had seen three of their number die in the course of three days. How many more days was it to the coast? Who could say? A week? A month? How many of them would be left by the end of a journey like that? Quigs, Kazinsky, Ramirez... all dead. But they had been put down at least, not left to wander the world as rotting corpses. Allen had assured him that he had put Quigs to rest. That was something.

Now, here he was at a crossroads. Stay here with these soft people who looked on him and his men as nothing more than hired help, or make his way out in the real world, always looking over his shoulder to see if death was on his heels.

They could use him here, him and his men. There were women here, the promise of a future if the hordes of Portland never found their way over the hills. Maybe if they cleared this place... but no. The decision wasn't his.

He pushed his plate to the side and decided now was as good a time as any to clear the air. When he looked up, he found the soldiers waiting for him to speak. Tejada wondered how long they had been staring at him and waiting. He looked each of them in the eye before he began. "I want you to remember this. I am not in charge of you. You are all men. You are all capable of making your own decisions. There is no such thing as going AWOL anymore. The entire world is AWOL. There is no such thing as duty and honor, there is only living."

"Is there such a thing as loyalty?" Epps asked. He was a bright one. Perhaps the smartest of the bunch, and Tejada knew that Epps would know exactly where his speech was headed.

"Loyalty is for dogs. You are not dogs. You are men, and I want you to understand something else before we go any further. Learn this, and learn it well. There are no heroes in this world, only the living. I'll let you chew on that for a second."

He could see them thinking, digesting the words that he had said. They were hard words, but he felt they were true, and that's what they needed here, the truth. Though he had said loyalty was for dogs, he knew, other than the gear on his body and in his bag, it was all he really had. The only thing that kept him going was his loyalty to his men. "Do you understand what I'm saying?" he asked.

"I understand you, sir." It was Allen. The soldier hadn't said more than a few words since they had lost Quigs getting over the wall. "When Quigs fell off the wall, I had it in my head that I could save him, that I could jump off the ladder and somehow keep him alive. But that was a hero talking, and I'm no hero. But I'm alive. I have to carry the guilt of that for the rest of my days, but I'm alive. So, yes, sir, I understand you one-hundred percent."

"Then hopefully, you'll understand this as well. Tomorrow, you are each going to have to make your own decision about what you want to do. Do you want to stay here, or do you want to go back over the wall? It's not my decision to make, and I don't want you following me because you think you owe me something or because I saved your life once. That's a foolish way to operate in this world; it's a heroic way to operate, and goddammit, this world doesn't need heroes. It needs the living. So you decide what's going to be the best way for you to live, because I sure as hell am not going to make that decision for you."

The table lapsed into silence, each man lost in his thoughts.

"Have you made up your mind, sir?"

It was Walt. All the men turned to look at him, for he was one of them now. Tejada nodded his head at the young man. "Yes, I have."

"Well?" Walt prodded.

"Tomorrow, I'm going back over that wall." The soldiers nodded, and he knew several of them would come along with him, but he also knew that some of them would stay, and maybe they would be able to salvage this place before the lights went dark for good.

Several of the men just nodded, and he knew that they were now deep in thought. That was good. That's exactly what he wanted. "We'll meet in the morning, say our goodbyes." He looked every man in the eye, one by one. "And I'm dead serious about this. I don't want you following me out of some misguided sense of duty. If this looks like the type of place you want to be, then be here. Life's too short now to be playing by some playbook that didn't save our ass in the first place."

Tejada turned his back on his men and headed toward the area of the building where he had seen all of those couches and comfy chairs. He was looking forward to sleeping in something that was actually soft for once.

****

176

Never known for being the brightest star in the sky, Beacham sat on the table bench stunned. He couldn't understand what Tejada was saying about heroes and loyalty and all those other words he had never quite grasped. He kind of knew what those things were. They were good things, or at least they used to be. Now, Tejada made them sound like bad things.

All Beacham knew was that in the morning, he was going to have to make a choice, and for him it wasn't much of a choice at all. His arm was busted. He would die on the road. He had never broken his arm before, and he didn't know how long it was going to take to heal, but he was pretty sure that if he followed along with the others, he would die and become one of those things.

The idea of the others leaving him behind scared him. He hadn't been alone in a very long time, and the people on the Nike campus seemed smart, like the type of people that might look down on him or treat him badly.

He imagined that without his army friends, he would be stuck in a situation not unlike when he was younger, when everyone seemed to want to make fun of him for being slow. Somehow, he had managed to fumble his way through school, whether it was because the teachers felt sorry for him or not, he didn't know. But then, when the world had opened up before him, offering up all the opportunity he could ask for, he had found that he had no clue what to do. He had no direction, no desire. He just wanted to eat and be alive.

So his mom, unable to keep feeding him and taking care of him with the money she made working at McDonald's, had talked him into joining the army. That was probably the best decision of his life. He didn't have to think so much. There were other people for that. He was what they called a grunt, just a body capable of doing certain things that needed to be done. Best of all, no one gave him a hard time because he always did his job.

When the President had said he didn't have a job anymore, Beacham didn't know what to do. He watched the other soldiers bustling about, talking about going north or south or east, and he had no idea where he was. He didn't know which direction his mom was or how far he would have to go to get back home. So he had just sat, waiting for orders. If it wasn't for Tejada, he would still be sitting on that box, waiting for someone to tell him what to do.

But Tejada had asked him to come along, not as a soldier, but as a man. Tejada respected him for some reason, when no one ever had. Even the other soldiers never actually treated him like an equal. They all knew they were smarter than him, but he tried to be nice. That was the key. If you were dumb and mean, like his daddy had been, then no one would like you. But if you were dumb and smart, then some people would stand up for you when you needed it. His Mom had told him that, and he had generally found it to be true.

He listened as the others spoke, weighing the pros and cons of going or staying. All Beacham knew was that he liked it here with the walls around the place. He liked knowing that his arm would have the time to mend. He liked that there were more people here.

Arnold Beacham had always liked people watching. In his free time, he would often go to a park, sit on a bench, and watch the people go by. He would sit there listening to the wind as it rushed through the trees, as people went about their daily lives. He would create stories about where they were going and what they were doing.

Maybe staying here wouldn't be so bad. He could watch the people some more. With that, he made up his mind and rose up from the table.

"Hey, where you going, Beacham?" Epps asked.

"I'm gonna go get some sleep."

"Are you going with us tomorrow?" Epps asked.

Beacham shrugged uncomfortably. He didn't want to make Epps not like him. "I think I'm going to stay." He gestured to his good arm. "At least until this is better."

Epps just nodded, knowing that it was probably the right decision. Still, Beacham saw the disappointment on his face. He turned away from it and went to find a place to sleep. On the lower floor of the building, he found a couch that was long enough to accommodate his giant body. He lay down, resting his head on his good arm, ignoring the scratchy feel of his beard on his forearm.

It was a long time until he finally managed to fall asleep. In his mind, he kept seeing Epps' face, and he imagined them sitting around the cafeteria table making fun of him and calling him dumb. He knew they wouldn't do that, but he was still suspicious.

When he first heard the screams, he couldn't tell if he was dreaming or awake. The building's lights had been dimmed at some point. As he sat up, he had trouble trying to figure out what he was looking at. All around him, there was action. People were running and screaming. He saw a slow-moving Annie tear into one of the Nike people. When the smell of blood hit him, he knew he wasn't dreaming.

"Help me!" a woman yelled, locking eyes with Beacham. Her hand shot out to him, though he was a good ten feet away, and an Annie's gray hands pulled the woman in for a bite. She screamed in pain as it took a chunk of her shoulder meat. When the blood began to run down her dingy pink shirt, turning it a dark red, he finally understood what was happening.

He popped to his feet, gasping in pain as his nervous system reminded him that his arm was broken. He drew his pistol with his good hand and thumbed the safety off. There were screams coming from all parts of the building, but he could only focus on the middle-aged lady in front of him, with her pleading eyes. He held the pistol up and squeezed the trigger. Her brains covered the glass window behind her. Then Beacham leveled his pistol at the Annie that had killed the woman. As he was about to squeeze the trigger, he felt something pulling him backwards by his shoulders. His shot went wide, and he screamed as he attempted to regain his balance by windmilling his arms.

His broken arm fell from his sling, and Beacham grit his teeth against the pain which was so intense that it made his head swim. He felt more hands on his body, trying to pull him down, and then he began to panic. He held his pistol up, firing at anything that moved, alive or dead. Round after round he fired, missing more often than not, and still the arms gripped him, their weight bearing him down.

When his gun clicked empty, he spun around, waving it at his attackers' heads. He tried to push them off, but with only one good arm it was impossible. They were rotting things, smaller than him, but still strong. He counted four or five. It was hard to see between the cold hands that were pawing at his face. He cracked the largest one in the temple with the butt of his gun, but it didn't do enough damage to even stagger it. Before he could take another swing, he screamed in pain. He looked down as his broken arm was bent backwards. The corpse of an old man held onto it as it backed away gnawing at his arm.

The pain was too much, and he screamed even louder as he watched the old man try to walk away with his broken arm, the weight of the other Annies holding Beacham in place. The skin of his arm stretched, and just before one of the Annies dug a hand into his eyes, he saw the skin tear and snap apart like an overtaxed rubber band, and then it was off, the rotten old man falling away, holding his arm like a trophy.

He finally fell to the ground, his screams just one among many that echoed throughout the building.

****

180

Amanda awoke with wild eyes, panic fluttering in her chest. She immediately reached over to Rudy, shaking him by his large shoulder. He sat up, gasping for air as if he had been drowning.

"What is going..." he began, the words dying on his lips as more screams began. He scrambled to his feet, and Amanda followed.

They were in a dark office in the large building. The thick office door was closed, but they could see a sliver of light underneath it.

"Shhh," Amanda said not wanting to draw the attention of any of the dead, for that was the only thing that it could be.

"I'm going to take a look," Rudy said. He stepped gingerly across the carpeted floor, avoiding the shadowy shapes of office furniture. When he reached the door, he paused with his hand on the door handle. The screaming in the building intensified, and it seemed closer now. From other parts of the building, they heard the sound of gunfire.

Amanda felt like her heart was going to burst out of her chest like one of those aliens in that old science fiction movie. She couldn't quite remember the name of it. She placed her hands on her chest in the hopes that she could keep her heart where it belonged.

Rudy pressed the door handle downward and opened it just a crack. Blue-white light flooded inward, and Rudy, ever so carefully, opened the door wide enough so that he could poke his head out and see what was happening.

Immediately, he withdrew, slowly closing the door behind him.

In the darkness, Amanda could see him shaking his head. "What is it?" she hissed.

"They're out there."

"Should we bar the door?"

"I think so."

181

Quietly, they moved across the room, grabbing the edge of the only substantial furniture in the room, a giant desk that seemed much too large for the size of the office they were in. They half slid, half carried the thing across the room, and then they pressed it against the door. Amanda stood quaking, her arms pressed against the desk and her head hanging. She felt Rudy's soft hand on her arm, and she clung to him.

The screams reverberated off the walls, and she was glad he was here with her, safe in this space, just the two of them. They whispered about random things from the world they had left behind. They talked in hushed whispers, sharing secrets like children trapped in a closet while playing hide and seek, blocking out the horrors on the other side of the door. But the horrors were still there, and they would have to face them sooner or later.

****

Walt, formerly Andy, ran with Day and Gregg. To Walt, they seemed to be the two most normal people of all the soldiers, which was probably why he liked them the best. They didn't think about him. He never caught them analyzing his existence, trying to categorize who or what he was. The others did, but never Gregg or Day. They accepted him as just another person.

They rounded a corner, and suddenly, a wall of the dead rose up before them. Walt reached for his pistol, but Gregg put his hand out and yelled, "Don't! There's people on the other side." Walt could see people rushing about in a hallway on the other side of the dead that might as well be the other side of the moon. In the tight confines of the hallway, their guns were now a last resort. Walt told them to step back, and he set his bowling ball into motion, spinning and sliding as he built the momentum of the eight-pound ball. He was thankful the building had tall ceilings; it gave him more room to maneuver. When he felt the

182

moment arise, when the ball's force was ready to be unleashed, he swung it at the first of the dead. The poor thing's head caved in like a watermelon dropped from a three-story building, its left eye springing outward on its optic nerve as the pressure of the blow forced it outwards.

Without stopping, Walt spun, wrapping the rope around himself, keeping it tight and in motion. He spun away, his back to the dead momentarily before he faced them again and brought the ball crashing down in an overhead arc. The ball crushed the top of an Annie's head, collapsing the skull so that brains flew out its ears. It too fell to the ground, but Andy had lost the momentum on his weapon.

"Hold them back," Walt yelled. Day and Gregg stepped forward, swinging at the dead with the butts of their rifles and pushing them backwards. The Annies had bunched up now; they were a solid mass, a slow-moving wall of death. When they were packed in tight, they were unstoppable.

"We got no choice," Day said. "We have to open fire."

And they did. Walt dropped his bowling ball to the side and pulled his handgun free. Their fire lit up the gloomy hallway, and the dead fell to the ground. The ones behind them trod over them as if they were nothing. Their uncoordinated movements made it difficult for them to traverse the corpses, and the rotting beings toppled to the ground.

Through the ringing in his ears, he heard Gregg yell, "Get the ones on the ground, Walt!"

Walt concentrated on the Annies that stumbled and fell, tripping over the bodies in the hallway. He watched them as they crawled forward, too hungry and uncoordinated to rise from their prone position. He aimed his pistol at their heads, squeezed the trigger, and flinched as he popped their skulls. Blood sprayed, but still they were

183

forced to move backwards. Walt kicked his bowling ball backwards. He was going to need it soon, and just as this thought occurred to him, his handgun clicked empty.

He shoved the gun into the waistband of his pants, where the hot barrel singed the flesh above his crotch. He bent over and picked up the bowling ball. He hefted it in his hands until he got a good bead on one of the crawlers. Then he lifted it over his head and brought it crashing down upon the dead thing's skull. Using the rope, he pulled the blood-soaked bowling ball to himself, lifted it again, and brought it crashing down upon the next unfortunate soul.

Time slowed to a crawl, and they fought back the tide. Sweat dripped from their brows. Walt's hands were sticky with blood. Then suddenly, they were standing in the hallway alone. The only noise was gunfire and screaming from other parts of the building. Walt blinked sweat out of his eyes as he looked at the hallway full of carnage. Blood had splattered every inch of the hallway, and gun smoke hung in the air.

"Holy shit," Gregg managed to say, and all Walt could do was nod his head.

****

Tejada nodded in and out of sleep on a soft loveseat that someone had graciously left open for him to sleep in. Though he had dreamed of sleeping on something soft, the reality was that his body, which had become hardened with sleeping on floors and in the back of vehicles, disliked the soft loveseat.

So when Tejada heard banging, he didn't have far to go to drag himself to consciousness. He sat up immediately. His first instinct was to grab his rifle. He checked the magazine and then stood to see just what the hell was going on.

He stood, his back popping like fireworks as he rose. He walked to the top of the stairs where he saw

184

people looking downward. They looked at him, like they expected him to do something, and Tejada knew it was an Annie situation. "What's going on?" he asked.

The civilian shrugged at him, and Tejada resisted his urge to punch the useless fucker in the face. He hightailed it down the steps, his boots clomping on the marble staircase. As he reached the bottom, he saw a crowd of people huddled around the front entrance. The banging was coming from the other side of the crowd.

"What the fuck are you people doing?" he asked as he pushed his way through the crowd.

"It's Manny Gibson?" a young, bookish man said.

"What?"

"You know, the basketball player."

The crowd parted, and Tejada saw what the man was talking about. On the other side of the front door stood a giant beast of a man. He must have been seven-and-a-half feet tall if he was an inch. He had a body that was twice as wide as the bookish young man that had informed him who the man was. Even dead, Tejada recognized the man from the myriad Gatorade commercials and Nike ads that he had been featured in. He didn't remember the name of the team that the man had played for, but that didn't matter now because he was dead as fuck, and the last he had checked, the NBA had played its last season.

The dead basketball star pounded on the glass door in front of him, and Tejada could see that there were quite a few other Annies around him, their faces pressed to the glass, their features flattened by the translucent material. A crowd had gathered in front of the doors, standing there like dumbasses.

"Back away from those fucking doors!" Tejada began. But he was too late. With a massive fist, the reanimated Manny Gibson punched a hole in the glass, and with that, the entire structural integrity of the front door was compromised. It wasn't long before the rest of the

185

shattered glass gave way. Tejada managed to put a bullet through the massive dead man's forehead, but then there was a scramble as the Nike workers pushed backwards, knocking Tejada to the ground as he swore heavily and creatively. Someone helped him to his feet, and then he was stuck in a headlong rush away from the front of the building. If he stopped to go against the flow, he would be trampled.

He chanced a look over his shoulder and saw the dead streaming in through the broken door, jostling each other to be the first to eat human flesh.

"Wake up!" Tejada yelled. "Wake up! We got Annies in the building!" As the crowd fled in different directions, Tejada bounded up the stairs, knowing that he wanted to reach the high ground. He spun and pushed a gawking man out of the way. "If you're not going to kill 'em, get in a goddamn office and barricade yourself in. We'll let you know when it's safe." If the man had had a tail, it would have been tucked between his legs as he scurried off.

Tejada took aim at the dead, mowing down any that he could get a bead on. From his angle on the staircase, he couldn't get a bead on many, but none of them were getting up the stairs. He made damn sure of that. However, the bulk of the Annies, sensing less resistance in other parts of the building, broke off and headed in directions that Tejada couldn't cover from the stairs. It was a giant mess, and still the dead were streaming through the front door.

****

Epps hopped to his feet at the first gunshot. He shook the boot of the man sleeping next to him. It was Max Masterson. Max rubbed his eyes sleepily, and then sat up, his rifle magically appearing in his hands. Together they rose and scurried into the hallway as Whiteside, Allen, and Brown stepped out of the room across the way.

186

They had slept on the first floor, their bellies full of food and drink from the night before. Epps felt as if he hadn't been asleep for more than ten minutes. He looked at the hands of his watch and saw that it was four in the morning.

Outside it was still dark. Epps jumped as he saw a set of hands press against a window, then another, then another. Soon there were dozens of hands pressing against the ground-floor windows.

"We're in for a world of hurt boys," he said, clutching his rifle and waiting for the inevitable sound of cracking glass.

"Load 'em up," Allen yelled.

Epps was glad to hear Allen say something. Izzy had been quiet all evening, kicking himself for being unable to save Quigs. He couldn't blame the man; he just hoped it didn't turn into anything worse than a little guilt. Allen was a good man. If he had to choose one soldier to have at his back, it would be Allen.

The glass broke and the dead tumbled inwards, flopping onto the marble floors. Civilians scattered every which way, screaming and generally causing nothing but confusion. "Let's put 'em down!" Epps yelled just before he fired his first shot. It went wide, and he swore under his breath. "Remember to take your time," he warned the others.

The dead erupted into blooms of red. Flesh and blood decorated the walls as their rounds ripped through dead bodies. Still they tumbled inward.

"We got more coming down the hallway!" Whiteside yelled over the sound of their exploding rifles.

"I'm empty!" Masterson yelled.

"You ever seen that movie Signs?" Epps shouted to him.

"Yeah, you want me to dump water on them?"

"Swing away!" Epps shouted. Masterson flipped his rifle around, ready to bash in the skull of any Annie that got too close. From his left, Epps could hear Brown praying. Epps, never really a religious man, joined him. If anything, the act of prayer settled his nerves a bit as he took aim again and again, pulling the trigger.

"Me and Whiteside will take the hallway," Allen yelled, and then they were gone.

They heard screams from the other parts of the building, and Epps couldn't help but think, *This is bad. This is seriously bad.* His rifle clicked empty, and he found that his spare magazines were all gone. He looked down at his feet in the hopes that he had dropped one, but no... they were all out of bullets. *This is seriously fucking bad.* As a big-nosed man in a cardigan sweater lunged at him, Epps swung his rifle, breaking the man's jaw and knocking him to the side. He stomped on the man's face three times until the man's arms stopped clawing at him. He hoped the others were doing better than he and Brown were.

****

Tejada and the others stood over the corpse of Beacham. Tejada had put a bullet in the gentle man's skull himself. He wasn't the only person that had died that night, but he was the only one they had known. Tejada could see the dejection on the men's faces. Brown knelt over Beacham's corpse, muttering some words of prayer.

A fat lot of good that'll do him, Tejada thought, but he let Brown finish anyway. Suddenly, Tejada felt tired, more tired than he had felt since this whole thing had begun. He stood with his hands on his knees, and for the first time in a long time, he felt tears brimming in the corner of his eyes. He didn't have the words to say what he was feeling. He was incapable of comforting his men, and he saw it on all their faces. Kazinsky, Beacham, Quigs, Ramirez... there were a hundred other names to add to the

188

list, but those four had meant as much to him as any of them. Less than a handful of days, and he had lost a third of the men he had dragged from the brink of self-destruction.

The look on his men's faces said it all. They were done. They were past the point of wanting to be out in the real world, past the point of dreaming and hoping for a better future.

"Sergeant, I have to thank you for your help. Without you, we would all be dead by now." It was Nike, that smug bastard looking just as prideful as he had the day before when he had begged them to stay. He wasn't thankful for Tejada and his men. He wasn't thankful for Beacham's sacrifice. Nike was just glad he was alive. On any other day, Tejada wouldn't begrudge the man his joy, but today was not that day.

"Save your thanks. We just lost a man, and you and yours didn't do shit to help."

Nike's mouth opened and closed as he attempted to say something clever. But there was nothing clever that he could say that wouldn't get him knocked the fuck out. He knew this, and Tejada knew then that Nike wasn't as dumb as he thought. Nike turned on his heel and walked out, a big, mean-looking bodyguard following behind him.

"These fucking people," Epps said.

"We ought to just leave 'em to die," Allen added. "We lost two people just fucking around with this place, and there ain't a damn one of them worth one of the ones we lost."

Much to his surprise, Tejada could feel the tide turning. He knew that all of his men were ready to hop over those walls and hightail it to the coast. But that wasn't what Tejada wanted. He wanted his men to be safe. He wanted them to be happy. He didn't like hearing his men become bitter and angry. That was no way to live a life. He should know. He had lived that way for the past twenty years. "I

189

don't want to hear any more of that shit." The men looked at him, confusion on their faces.

"I thought you wanted to leave, sir," Whiteside said.

"Yeah, well. Look around. Ain't many of us left, and this trip ain't even halfway over. That's got me thinking, maybe we shouldn't be so quick to leave this place."

Masterson and Gregg bent down and lifted Beacham's body. Without speaking, everyone knew where they were going. The soldiers followed, stomping through the broken glass on the front of the Ken Griffey Jr. building. Outside, the sun rose, turning the slate-gray sky a brilliant orange and pink above them. *It's a damn sight more beautiful today than it ought to be.*

The men carried Beacham's giant body towards the edge of the lake. Bodies floated there, swollen and pale in the middle of the water. If they were going to stay, they were going to have to do something about that. When they found a suitable spot, the soldiers began to dig.

They used their hands, digging into the soft dirt of the campus common. Tejada got down on his knees, the morning dew seeping through his pants as he pushed his hands into the dirt. He couldn't tell if tears or sweat rolled from his eyes, and he didn't care.

Behind them Tejada sensed a crowd swelling. He turned and glared at the corporate fucks who stood outside their building. He wasn't in the mood for any of their shit. They stood watching, their faces drawn and sad, about fifty of them, a damn sight less than there had been the night before. From out of the pack, two men broke, shovels in their hands.

They approached Tejada and handed the shovels to him. He accepted them gratefully, and then they went about finishing Beacham's grave, each of them taking turns at widening and deepening the hole. When they were done, Whiteside and Gregg hopped into the grave. Epps and

Brown lowered the man down, and they set him upon the damp earth below.

They stood that way for a while, not saying anything, just looking into Beacham's grave, each man lost in their own thoughts. There were no jokes, no remembrances, just silence. Tejada picked a shovel up from the ground and threw the first shovelful of dirt on his body. He passed the shovel to Allen, and one by one, they filled in his grave.

By the time they were done, the sun was overhead, and the crowd had gone inside. In the distance, Tejada eyed the building that the dead had escaped from. He knew it had to be one of the campus' stupid buildings that had failed and not the wall. If it had been the wall, they would all be dead by now.

"Come on," he said. The men followed him without asking as he set out across the unnaturally green lawn, tall grass swishing at his legs. They reached the building, a flat squat structure. It looked like one of the older buildings. The inside smelled like rot, but it's what was on the floor of the foyer that really caught his eye. The floor was covered in glass. "Son of a bitch."

"What is it, sir?" Epps asked.

Tejada pointed at the glass on the ground. The front door had been busted from the outside.

"What the fuck?" Epps said.

"Sabotage?" Allen asked.

"Who the fuck would do something like that?" Epps asked.

"Who the fuck indeed?" Tejada said, thoughts running through his head at light speed.

Chapter 12: The Compound

Clara and Mort looked down at Joan and Lou. Joan was awake and conscious, her leg severely broken. Mort couldn't look at Lou for long. His skin was blistered and peeling. He had been burned severely.

"What happened to him?" Mort asked.

"He passed out. Fell in the fire," Reed said.

"He didn't just pass out," Clara spat.

"Believe what you want to believe," Reed said, "but that man right there passed out and fell in the fire."

"Why are you keeping us here?" Clara asked.

Reed laughed behind Chad, a squawking, weird sound that sounded frightfully unstable. "We're not keeping you here," Chad said. To Clara, it actually sounded like he meant it. "As a matter of fact, this guy is going to have to stay outside the gates."

Chad was pointing at Mort. "Why?" he asked.

Chad just smirked at Mort. "I'll tell you why. Come with me. Outside." Chad turned and left the trailer that Lou and Joan shared. He stepped outside and Clara and Mort followed, stepping into the clearing in the middle of the camp. The trailers were dust-covered, and the windows were ringed with mildew. Chad spread his arms wide and said, "This is why."

Women moved through the compound, hauling water from a spring while armed men walked alongside them. Some tended a garden that was growing off to the left of the massive fire pit.

"Notice anything?" Chad said. Reed smirked behind him. To Clara, he seemed like a giggling monkey or that weird creature that always sat jabbering by Jabba the Hutt in that Star Wars movie.

"It's nice here," Mort said.

"You're goddamn right it's nice here. And we aim to keep it that way. You see, you people are running around like you're living a nightmare. Us? We're living a dream."

Mort's confusion showed on his face. Clara started to feel uneasy in the pit of her stomach.

"Only problem is there ain't no dark people in my dream, you get my drift?"

Clara's stomach dropped. She couldn't believe it. The end of the world, nothing but a few hundred people alive as far as she knew, and one of them was a racist.

Chad continued, saying, "Now, don't get me wrong. You got every right to live and try and make your way in this world. I ain't gonna stop you. Neither is my brother Reed." Chad looked at his brother, but he was silent. "But you got to do your living outside the walls. If you want to stick around until your friends are alright, then that's fine. During the day, you can come in and visit and trade, but as soon as it starts getting dark, I want you out of here."

"Why?" Mort asked, genuinely confused.

Chad just shrugged his shoulders. "That's the way it has to be. You see, I think the whole reason the world is in the shape it's in is because no one knew their place. Everyone's looking over into other people's yards and saying, 'Ooooo-weeeeee! I wish I had that man's barbecue.' When what they really should have been saying is, 'I'm gonna build myself the best damn barbecue that anyone has ever seen.' And if my neighbor gets jealous, I'm going to shoot him in the face."

Mort was still confused.

"Mort's not going to take your barbecue," Clara said. "He's just worried about his friends. He's one of the most trustworthy people I know."

Reed giggled at this, saying, "There aren't enough people left in the world to make that a significant statement."

193

Clara could have stabbed him in the face. She was about to explode when Mort put a reassuring hand on her arm. She turned to him, and he said, "It's alright, Clara."

"No, it's not alright."

Chad raised his eyebrow at this. His smugness and confidence were repulsive, and Clara could tell that he got off on the power of running the place.

Mort continued. "Yes, it is. We're gonna be fine. Besides, Katie's still out there, and I think it's a bad idea to leave her alone."

Clara nodded. Then she wrapped her arms around Mort, realizing just how much she had come to care for the big man. She buried her head in his chest, and his scratchy beard brushed the top of her forehead.

"It's gonna be alright," Mort said. "I gotta go now, see if I can find Katie and find some place to hole up tonight. I'm not a big fan of sitting in the woods in the dark." How he was able to smile, Clara didn't know, but he did. She smiled right back. Then he left. She stood in the courtyard of the compound feeling more alone than she had ever felt in her life.

"I like that guy," Chad said, oddly cheerful.

"Just not enough to let him stay here, right?"

"My backyard, my rules," he said, as if that ended all possible conversation.

Clara turned and headed back inside the trailer. Chad and Reed followed along. They made her nervous. Reed was obviously unstable, but Chad seemed to be the true danger. Something was off, and she knew that she would find out what it was soon enough.

Inside, she smiled at Joan. It was so good to see her. She walked around the edge of the tiny bed she and Lou lay on, and she took up Joan's hand and squeezed it with her own.

"Where's Mort?" she asked.

"We'll talk about it later."

Chad stood outside the door, leaning a shoulder on the door frame. Clara could tell he had more to say.

"What now?" she asked.

For the first time, Chad hesitated, trying to find the right words.

"Spit it out," Clara said.

Chad did not take kindly to Clara's demand. "You're a mouthy one, aren't you?"

"I like 'em mouthy," Reed said from an unseen part of the trailer. It was too small for them all to be in the trailer's tiny bedroom.

"Shut up, dipshit," Chad spat over his shoulder in a weary voice. Then he turned back to Clara and said, in warning, "Now don't go getting the idea that you can treat my brother like shit just because I do. I love the little guy."

Clara stared Chad in the eye. His eyes were blue, but not a cold blue. There was life in those eyes, a twinkle. He might be crazier than his obviously crazy brother she finally decided. "Why don't you go ahead and lay it on us?"

"Lay what on you?"

"The big secret that you've been trying to tell us but which you can't seem to actually say."

Chad leaned his head against the wall, the tension sucked out of his body. "Am I that obvious?"

"More so," Clara said. Joan squeezed her hand tightly, warning her not to push the man too far.

Lou grumbled, but his eyes stayed closed. Chad looked at him and then wiped a hand across his brow. He took a deep breath and let it out slowly. Then he locked eyes with Clara. "Alright, here it is."

"Oh, boy!" Reed said from the other room, earning himself another admonishing glare from Chad.

"Look, we've got ourselves a philosophy here, and this may sound crazy to you guys, but I don't know, to me, it just makes perfect sense. I mean here we are, just a bunch of people trying to get along while the world is dying around us..."

"Get to the goddamn point," Clara said.

Chad stopped talking and nodded. His next words were spit out at a million-miles-an-hour, so fast that Clara wasn't sure she had heard him right. "If you're going to stay here, you're going to have to breed."

"What?" Clara asked.

"I said, 'If you're going to stay here, you're going to have to breed.'"

"Whoa, whoa, whoa," Clara said, rising from the bed, her hands put out against any sort of advance Chad might make.

"What the hell is wrong with you?" Joan asked.

At their protestations, Chad suddenly became a different man. "Listen. Shut up. Just shut the fuck up. Who do you think you are?" He pointed at them, spittle gathering at the corner of his mouth as he continued. "We saved her! We kept your friend alive. She would be in the stomach of one of those things if we hadn't come along and saved her. And here you are getting all high and mighty."

Chad's voice was a roar. Clara imagined that she could feel the windows of the trailer shake as he his voice rose. Reed giggled like a madman in the other room. "Oh, you're in for it now!" Reed called, his voice fading as he rushed from the trailer.

"This is the way it is. We are here to repopulate the world and make it the way we want it. No more freeloaders. No more letting the rich take advantage of us. It is our duty. I don't know if you noticed this, but there aren't a lot of women running around these days. If you stay here, it's under our rules. So what's it going to be?"

That had come to a head quickly. Clara looked at Joan and the unconscious Lou. "Look at them; that's no choice at all," she said.

"Well, it's the only one you got."

196

"We'll go," Joan said, attempting to rise from the bed and grunting in pain.

"No," Clara said. "That's ridiculous. You wouldn't last two minutes out there with a broken leg." She turned to Chad. All pretense at being a regular guy had left him, and Clara saw him for what he was, a petty, wannabe despot standing at the end of the world. "You say we have a choice, but if we go out there, we're dead." Chad said nothing, so she continued. "How about a little compromise?"

"What did you have in mind?" Chad asked.

"You let us stay here, get better, and then, when we're healthy. We'll decide."

Chad shook his head. "Uh-uh. It's not a fair deal."

"Why?" Joan asked.

"Just look at yourselves. Two of you are damn near useless. You're going to be eating our food, drinking our water. What do we get? The pleasure of your company? That's not fair at all."

"I can work," Clara said.

"You do the work of three people? I'd like to see that," Chad said, still unconvinced.

"I'm a doctor," Joan said. "You've got pregnant women around here. I can help."

Chad nodded. "Now that is worth something. "And what about this guy here? Assuming he recovers."

"He's tough. He's a leader. You need someone out there guarding you, he's your man."

"And what about those others, the black fella and the woman? They gonna be any trouble?"

Clara shook her head, knowing full well that Katie was nothing but trouble. "Mort wouldn't hurt a fly. And Katie, well, Katie's pregnant. I don't think she'll be causing you much trouble."

Chad looked thoughtful for a moment, weighing his options. "Alright. You can stay here for as long you need to heal up. But when the time comes, if you decide to stay, it's under my rules, and I don't want to hear any pissing or moaning if you stay. How's that sound?"

They nodded their agreement.

Chad stuck his hand out. "Shake on it."

They each shook his hand, and then he stepped over to Lou. "I assume this guy will abide by our agreement as well." He leaned forward and shook the unconscious man's hand. With that done, he turned and smiled. "I'll leave you two to catch up. When you're done," he said, talking to Clara, "I want you to come outside. I got some work for you to do. You can find me in the big house."

Clara nodded, and Chad turned to leave, the screen door of their trailer slamming shut behind him. They waited until he had been gone for a few moments, and then Clara sank to the ground, exhausted. This was not good, in any way. She knew that. Chad's agreement had the ring of truth to it, but she didn't trust him one bit.

"How are you doing?" Clara asked Joan.

"I need you to take a look at my leg for me."

"Why?"

"I don't know that any of these people know what they're doing."

"Ok, what do I do?"

Joan threw back the covers, and Katie gasped looking at her leg. It was bruised, battered, and swollen. It hurt just to look at it.

"What am I looking for?"

"I need you to run your hands along my leg, see if anything feels out of place. Don't be gentle, or you might miss something."

Clara did as she was told. Joan's leg was hot, like fire. She slid her hands upward, cringing at the thought of causing Joan pain.

"You're going to have to do it firmer than that," Joan said.

Clara nodded and then she wrapped her hands around Joan's leg, sliding them up towards the knee. When her hands hit a rough protuberance, Joan screamed in pain.

"What? What is it?" Clara asked.

It took a moment for Joan to stop thrashing in her bed, and when her grip finally relaxed on the sheets, she finally spoke. "Did you feel anything?" she asked.

"There's something sticking up," Clara said. "I don't know that your leg is straight."

"Fuck," Joan said, her head falling back on her pillow.

"What? Talk to me, Joan."

"It's not set properly. Dammit." Joan looked off to the side, wishing that there was another option, but there wasn't it.

Clara had some inkling of what she was going to have to do, but she dreaded the prospect. "You need me to set it."

"Yeah," Joan sighed. "If you don't, I may never walk again, or I'll have one real mean limp."

"What should I do?" she asked, perspiration gathering on her upper lip.

"You're going to need to pull my leg, and then press down where you felt the break."

It sounded simple enough, but Clara was feeling lightheaded at the mere idea of pulling on Joan's broken leg, but it had to be done. She figured there was no time like the present. "Ok. Here goes nothing." Clara grabbed Joan's foot and immediately Joan's hands grasped the sheets of the bed, every muscle in her body straining to stifle the scream that she wanted to unleash. Clara pulled on Joan's foot with her right hand and pressed down on the broken section of her leg with the palm of her left. The pain was too much. Joan screamed, her voice echoing off the cheap walls of the trailer. The broken part wouldn't slide into place, so Clara pressed harder. There was a small pop, and then Joan's leg was smooth again.

"I think I got it," Clara said. But Joan didn't hear her. She was unconscious, sweat dripping down her forehead. Clara rose up and pulled the blankets over her. She checked on Lou, but she had no idea of how to help him. His skin was shiny where he had been burned, which, as far as she could tell, seemed to be everywhere. The area around his eyes was swollen and blistered. She gave up, and then left to find Chad and see what he had in store for her.

****

She shielded her eyes as she stepped out of the cheap trailer. The courtyard was packed dirt, walked over many times. Only a few sparse tufts of grass grew in the place. On the watchtowers, men with red, sunburned faces stood guarding the gate. A couple of big-bellied women tended the garden, and Clara knew that Chad wasn't lying about his desire to repopulate the world. *What a fucking nightmare that would be if the whole world was populated by Chads.*

They didn't look particularly miserable, but they didn't look like the type of women who would be able to survive on their own. They were probably just happy to be alive. Clara walked across the dusty courtyard, enjoying the sunshine. It was a cool day. It must have been the middle of September. She could smell fall in the air. She jumped as one of the men on the watchtower hooted, and then yelled, "I got one!" He hauled a bloody spear upward as his partner congratulated him. The rifles on their backs would only draw more of the dead, but they would be good to have if the dead or the living ever showed up in overwhelming numbers.

In front of her was an old dilapidated house. Its windows were covered in boards, and through the cracks in

200

the boards, she could see that the glass was gone. Plastic sheeting snapped in the steady breeze, and the trees around the compound rustled in their indifference to Clara's plight.

She climbed a rotting wooden porch and knocked on the door. She heard boots stalking across creaky, wooden boards. There was no better security system than a house with creaky floorboards. The door was pulled open with a horror movie creak, and Reed stood there, looking at her like a goon. Behind thick glasses, his eyes wandered all over her body. He had a sick, sour smell to him, like he was constantly sweating.

"Entrez-vous," he said, and he stepped aside to let her in.

The inside of the "big house," as Chad had called it, was less impressive than the outside. The wooden floorboards looked rotted, and many of them seemed like they had recently been the object of a termite feast. The walls of the cabin were splattered with graffiti. She imagined that at one point, this had been the place where people had come to smoke dope, drink, or fuck when they were in high school. It had been cleaned up a bit, but it was obvious that the place had long been abandoned.

"Chad's in back," Reed said, that goofy smile on his face. She walked down a hallway, peering in doors until she found Chad in one of the back rooms. Chad sat in a rickety chair. On the floor was a sleeping bag. A gas lantern sat on a table with uneven legs.

"Ah, hello again," he said, as if they were friendly acquaintances.

"What did you want to see me for?" she asked, ready for this whole charade to be over.

Chad sighed. He looked weary. "Why do you have to be like that?"

"Like what?"

"Like you want to kill me."

Clara shrugged, not saying anything.

"Can't we just pretend to be civil. Maybe you don't want to be here, but here you are. If we just pretend, maybe we'll actually come to appreciate each other."

"You want me to pretend? I can do that." Clara cleared her throat and plastered her fakest smile on her face. "Hi, Chad! Did you need me to do something?"

Chad stood up and clapped her on the shoulder. "See? That wasn't so difficult was it?" Whether he was just fucking with her or not, Clara didn't know. "Follow me," he said.

Clara followed him to another room in the back of the house. "What was this place?" she asked.

"Oh, this? This used to be a ranger station. I don't know why they stopped using it, but they did. Since then, it's kind of become me and my brother's own special hangout, along with every other kid in the county. But they're probably all dead now, so I figured we'd just move in. This place is special to me."

"Why is that?"

Chad moved to a locked door. The brackets were new, the screws shiny. A padlock secured the door. Chad reached into his pocket and produced a small key. "Oh, this is where me and Dez first kissed. You never forget a thing like that."

"Dez?"

Chad turned the key in the padlock. It clicked open, and he undid the latch that held the door closed. "Dez. My wife." He pushed the door open. "Come on. I'll introduce you."

Chad stepped inside, and Clara followed. From another part of the house, she heard Reed laughing at something. He was mad as a hatter she decided. The first thing that hit her when she stepped inside was the smell. The small room reeked of body odor and shit. Immediately, her hand came up to her face.

202

"You don't like the smell, then get out, bitch." These words came from a woman who was covered in grit and grime. Her hands were bound to a headboard. Her feet were similarly bound so that she lay on her back spread-eagled under a blanket. On her face was a look of pure hatred.

"Is this your new sow?" the woman spat. "How long until she starts poppin' 'em out?"

"Don't mind her," Chad whispered conspiratorially. "Dez. This is Clara. She's going to take care of you."

Dez snarled as she said, "I don't give a fuck who she is. If you were a man, you would take care of me yourself with a bullet, just like you did my parents."

As she looked at the hateful woman, she noticed that she was pregnant. Telltale bandages were wrapped around her wrists, and Clara knew why she was tied up.

Chad nodded at Clara to exit the room, and he closed the door as she exited. She stood in the hallway, wondering just what sort of nightmare she had gotten herself into.

"You meet Dez?" a voice asked. She turned to see Reed hanging in a doorway, a suspicious wet stain on the front of his trousers.

"Yeah, I met her."

Reed whispered the next words in a conspiratorial tone. "She's a real bitch, ain't she?"

Clara said nothing.

"She didn't used to be like that, until she got pregnant. I think she's got temporary crazy up in her from that baby. You gonna take care of her?" he asked, a hint of hope in his voice.

"I guess so, if that's what I've gotta do to stick around here."

"Cool. Cool." He stopped talking to her and cocked his head as if he were listening to some unheard voice. "I gotta go, but I guess I'll be seeing you around." His let his arms fall from where they were gripping the doorjamb above, and he disappeared into a side room.

From inside Dez's room, she heard the muffled shouting of Chad. She tried not to listen, but the walls in the abandoned ranger station were so thin that she couldn't help it.

"Just shut up! Shut up! I did what I had to do! You know that!"

"Why won't you just kill me?" Dez moaned, begging, pleading.

"You know why. You've got my child in there, and I will see it born."

"It'll be a monster."

"It'll be my monster," Chad said.

"Fuck you! Fuck you! Fuck you!" Dez shouted. She too appeared to be insane. Clara stepped further from the door as she heard the sound of approaching footsteps. Chad threw the door open and stepped into the hallway as if everything were fine.

"Sorry about that. She's been a little crazy recently."

"I guess so," Clara said.

"I guess you saw the marks on her arms." Clara nodded. "I don't want to keep her tied up. I love the woman, despite all appearances, but right now, we just need to get her through this pregnancy. Your job, since you're doing us the favor of sticking around, is to take care of her. Whatever she needs. But do not, under any condition, untie her. Last lady that did that got her jaw broken. We clear?"

"I got it."

He pulled his shirt down, attempting to straighten it, even though no iron in the world could have gotten all the wrinkles out of his frayed khaki shirt. "Good. For today, you can hang out with your friends. Tonight, come back here, bathe her down, feed her, keep her company."

"Keep her company?"

"I don't know, all that girl shit you guys do. Talk about boys, first kisses, whatever the hell you guys are into." With that Chad brushed past her, and she was left on her own.

She walked back to the trailer feeling as if she had just given up her freedom. She felt the weight of her captivity between her shoulder blades, and she was beginning to get a headache.

****

Mort heard the chain-link fence slide closed behind him. The guards on the towers didn't offer anything in the way of goodbyes. He was on his own now, and it scared him. The forest ahead of him seemed dark and ominous. He checked his rifle. At least they had given that back, though he didn't have much in the way of ammunition. He still had his hammer as a last line of defense.

It was still early yet, the sun not having yet reached its peak. Mort wanted to be out of the way and safe by the time it began to go down. He put one foot in front of the other and stepped into the woods. The hair on the back of his neck stood up, and he suddenly felt like he was being watched. He couldn't tell if it was all in his head or if there was someone actually watching him.

He took heavy steps, making sure to leave footprints and disturbances in the mud and foliage, so he could find his way back if he needed to. He pulled his hammer from his belt loop, leaving his rifle slung over his shoulder, and he began to pound markings in the bark of the trees. He thought about making a map; he still had Blake's notebook in his pocket. Sometimes, when it got dark, he would pull it out and hold it, but he couldn't bring himself to actually flip it open and look at the messages he had shared with Blake when he lost his hearing.

He wished Blake were there now. Those good ol' boys in that compound would have loved him. With Blake at his side, they would have had to let him in. Those bastards. Racism had ceased to be a problem for Mort when he had become homeless. When you were homeless, you were the lowest of the low, and nothing anyone said or did could make you feel any less like shit. Therefore, when someone was racist to you, all you could do as a homeless person was laugh, and thank the gods that people could still see you, because any other time the regular people of the world would just ignore your existence. Being homeless was like being a ghost cursed to walk the world.

But now he was bothered. Because of the color of his skin, he had been cast out into the world on his own. He had to find his own way now, at least until Joan and Mort got better. And he did want that. He wanted to be with his friends. He wanted to see them all again. He wanted to make it to the beach and see them all smiling in the sunshine with no worries about the dead or the living, just a chance to rest and walk on the sand.

He bashed another divot in a tree with his hammer, using more power than he probably needed.

"You're going to break your hammer," a voice said.

He spun around to find Katie behind him, staring at him with her cold, dead eyes. She held her pistol in her hand, and for a moment, he thought she was going to shoot him.

"Katie," he said, but he didn't have the words he needed to let her know how happy he was to see her. Truth be told, he didn't know if he was happy to see her or just relieved that he wasn't alone.

"Good to see you too," she said.

They talked underneath the swaying trees, and Katie listened as he told her everything he knew about the compound. When he was done telling his tale, she stood up and stretched her back, and Mort noticed the taught swelling of her belly.

"Should you be out here like that?" he asked.

"Like what?" she asked.

"You know... pregnant."

She laughed and slapped her belly with the barrel of her revolver, harder than Mort thought was good for her, and then she said, "This old thing. This is nothing. Gimme a couple of months, and then we'll start worrying. It'll look like I'm smuggling a basketball, but even then I wouldn't go in there... even if they had all the macaroni and cheese in the world. You know why?"

Mort shook his head.

"Because the place you described to me... that's a prison. That's a place where a woman is treated like a subhuman, and I won't live like that again. I got this," she said, referring to her handgun, "and that's all I need."

She took off into the forest, walking deliberately through the underbrush.

"Where are you going?" Mort asked.

"Come on," Katie said. "I found us a place."

Mort looked all around him, as if he could spot a better option, but all he saw were trees. He put his hammer in his belt loop, the end still sticky with sap, and he followed Katie into the forest.

****

They walked for a while. Mort didn't know how to tell the time underneath the canopy of trees, but he felt as if they had walked for an hour. Halfway through, they emerged onto an old gravel road.

"How did you know this was here?" Mort asked.

"I used to come camping up here."

"You don't seem like the type," Mort said.

"I wasn't." Katie turned away from him then, to hide the panic that showed on her face as memories of her past life came back to her. They were painful, and her first instinct was to run away. "I recognized that building in their compound. It's an old ranger station. It became unnecessary once people started building in the hills here. We're not too far from where my..." The memories came back then.

"Where what?"

"Oh, nothing," she said.

They walked down the gravel road a bit, until they came to a point where the road was washed out. It was quite a tumble to the bottom of the washout. Mort crept to the edge, ready to jump backwards at a moment's notice if the ground beneath him felt like it was going to give way. He peered over the edge, and twenty feet below him, a dented and battered pickup truck was wrapped around a tree. Two dead things peered up at him their bodies buried up to their waist in the mud and rock from the washout.

Before he could tell her not to, Katie had turned to face the wall of rock that rose above them. She stepped out onto what little bit remained of the road and began to skirt sideways.

"Where are you going?" he asked.

"You'll see," she said, smiling at him. It was a weird smile.

Mort turned and did the same, though his fear of falling into the washout was damn near debilitating. In his mind, he saw himself broken and twisted but still alive, while the dead feasted on him. He pressed his face against the cool rocks, sliding his feet along the ledge of the road. The back half of his feet hung in the air, only his toes keeping him from tumbling to his death. Though the skin of his cheeks, the only part of his lower face not covered by graying beard, scraped against the rough rocks, he dared not lean backwards even an inch. He searched for handholds with sweaty palms as perspiration dripped from his forehead and into his eyes. Then he was across. He looked back at the washed-out road and dreaded going back that way again. On the bright side of things, it was a handy way to keep the dead from following them. He turned and found Katie waiting for him, her face grim. Her skin was paler than usual, which was saying something, and she looked like she was lost in her own mind.

"You ok?" he asked.

Katie jerked into consciousness as if she hadn't even seen Mort there. "Yeah, I'm fine. Come on." Katie set a quick pace, and Mort could barely keep up with her, which left him feeling a little ashamed. Soon they were walking up an overgrown gravel road. It hadn't been used in some time as weeds were poking up between the gravel. It rose for fifty yards and then doubled back upon itself. Up and up they went, hugged by trees and greeted by the hoots of songbirds in the afternoon.

Then the forest gave way, and Mort's mouth dropped open. He stood in front of a beautiful old house. It was a large, three-story affair. One couldn't help but be stricken by the feeling of home when looking at it. The bottom floor was nothing spectacular. Cords of wood sat neatly stacked underneath the wraparound porch of the second floor, which seemed to serve as the main floor of the house. The third floor was all peaks and gables, and sneaky windows looking out onto the forest.

"How did you know this was here?" Mort asked.

"I stayed here once." More memories flooded Katie's mind, and she squeezed her eyes shut and blinked her eyes rapidly, hoping that no more would follow.

"You stayed here? Was you rich or something?"

"Hardly," she laughed. "It was with a large group of teachers and their families. We all sort of pitched in to give the kids..." Katie trailed off.

Mort was worried about her. As they neared the house, she had seemed to become gradually more fractured, confused. Now she was leaving off her sentences right in the middle. He didn't know how to comfort her. He didn't know if she wanted to be comforted, so he did the only thing he could do. "Let's see if anybody's home."

Mort took the lead, climbing the wooden steps that led up to the wraparound balcony. The steps were firm and solid. He didn't hear Katie climbing up behind him until he was near the top. He pulled his hammer from his belt loop and reached for the doorknob, only to find that it was locked.

"What do you think? Should we bust in?" he asked. There was no answer from Katie. When he turned around, there were tears in her eyes, and the sight of them brought him to an awkward standstill. She put her hands up to her face and began to cry quietly, her shoulders shrugging with her muffled sobs. Mort edged closer to her and placed a comforting hand on her shoulder. She didn't shrink from him the way he imagined she would, so he wrapped his arms around her. She buried her face in his chest and began to cry uncontrollably.

Behind them, he heard a banging on the glass door, and he knew that someone was indeed home in the house hidden in the woods, but they could wait. Katie needed him. Still, he rocked her around so that he could keep an eye on the front door. The top half was paneled glass, the inside hidden by a lacy, white curtain. Behind that curtain he stared into the eyes of one of the dead.

They stayed that way until the glass broke. Mort let Katie go, and when she raised her pistol to fire at the dead thing slashing itself upon the broken glass of the window, he gently put his hand out and pushed the barrel of the gun down. He pulled his hammer from his belt loop and approached the door. He swung five times, bashing out the framing of the window, then it took two more swings to get the thing to stop moving. He waited patiently to see if any more were inside, but he heard nothing.

Mort reached inside the door and unlocked it, ignoring the stench of the rotting woman. The dead woman at his feet was an older lady. The skin on her face was sunken, but there appeared to be no bite marks on her. Her arms and body were emaciated, and as he dragged the body out to the porch, her shirt came up and her hip bones jutted out like the breastbone of a picked clean turkey. He had seen bodies like hers before on the streets. She had died of starvation. How long had she huddled in her house hoping for someone to come and save her? At what point did she realize she needed to go out and find food, only to find that she was too weak to do so? This world was no place for the elderly. If he could find a shovel, he would bury her. He seemed to have nothing but time on his hands. He didn't know how long they would have to wait until Joan and Lou were able to leave that place.

They stepped inside the house. The first thing that Katie checked was the kitchen. The cupboards were bare. On the counter, there were empty spice bottles, the old lady's last meal Mort guessed.

"I knew her, you know?" Katie talked as if she were somewhere else, reliving memories that made her squint as if she were in pain. She rubbed her belly unconsciously, and Mort waited for her to speak more.

"She was the caretaker here. She kept the yard tamed. It must have been a full-time job. Come on, I'll show you."

They walked through the living room, past comfy-looking furniture that had an old country feel to it. A colorful red Afghan rested on the back of a rocker that sat next to a bookshelf with aged, leather-bound books. The room was devoid of the knickknacks that one would find in a regular home. There were no pictures on the walls, nothing that spoke of personality, and there was no TV. The only decorations were a few paintings on the walls, some flowers, a mountain painting, the type of stuff you'd see in a hotel room.

They walked across the polished wooden floors and reached the backdoor. Katie pushed it open, and they stepped out onto the back deck. Mort's breath was taken away. The porch jutted out into a backyard that was unlike anything that Mort had ever seen before. A gentle field of grass sloped down and away to a river bank, still looking inviting despite its overgrown state. Decorative trees and shrubs of all sorts of colors framed the edge of the grass, and cleverly manicured trees rose to the sky, their bases covered in circles of bark dust. A small stream ran down the north side of the house, creating a border to keep the encroaching forest back.

"It's beautiful," he said.

Katie just nodded, her memories rushing through her so fast that she had to grip the wooden railing of the deck. She looked out onto the field of grass and she saw them, her husband and her son playing Frisbee with another family. She saw their faces as plain as if they were actually in front of her. She squeezed her eyes shut, no longer wishing to relive the memories, but her mind replayed the scenes anyway. She became dizzy and lightheaded, and she fell to her backside, her teeth clacking together painfully.

Mort rushed to her side. "Are you alright?" Katie could say nothing. Mort picked her up and guided her upstairs to one of the bedrooms. They were small, but there were many of them. He lay Katie down on a bed, and then went to find a blanket. He found one in a hall closet, and then he rushed back to Katie and spread it over top of her. She curled into a fetal position and brought the blanket tight around her. Mort could see tears rolling from her closed eyes and down the bridge of her nose. A teardrop hung there for a second and then fell onto the magenta comforter, turning it a dark red color.

He backed away and left her to her sadness, knowing that there was nothing he could do for the pain that she felt. It was inside her. He couldn't reach in there and fix it. All he could do was wait around for her, to be there when she needed him. He closed the door behind him and, after another quick check of the house, went downstairs and closed the front and back doors.

He found a door that led downstairs. It was dark, even though there were windows. He found some spare wood and then set about searching for some nails. In a corner, among a bevy of yard maintenance equipment, he found what he was looking for and returned to the second floor. He dropped the plywood on the floor and proceeded to cut it to shape using a hand saw he had also taken from downstairs.

Mort worried about Katie as he worked. She had proven to be volatile emotionally, and he was worried about her. He hadn't known many women like Katie on the streets, but the ones he had known were dangerous; they could explode at any point, harming themselves or others.

He finished boarding up the broken glass of the front door and then went and sat in the rocking chair. He pulled the Afghan from the back of the rocker and spread it over himself. It was warm, and after a night spent in the woods, he fell asleep.

****

Reed was pleasuring himself to thoughts of the new lady when his brother entered his room. He quickly threw a blanket over his disrobed lower half and looked at Chad angrily. He pushed his glasses up on his nose with his jacking hand, smelling the funky odor of his penis as he did so.

"Put away your pecker, Reed. We've got some things to talk about." His brother sat down on the edge of his bed.

Reed sat up, his erection fading. "What do you want?" he spat.

"We've got some work to do."

Reed knew what was coming next. Over the last month, after they had managed to bring all the trailers up,

213

he had had talks like this with Chad before. Chad needed something dirty done. This was fine with Reed, as he had long ago gotten rid of whatever conscience he might have had, and Chad always rewarded him well. Perhaps Chad would let him take another spin with Dez. He never knew being with a pregnant woman could be so erotic, but there was something about her that made him hard every time he looked at her.

"What kind of work?"

"The kind you're good at," Chad said. Chad made a show of looking towards a corner of the room as Reed pulled his pants up under the blanket. He enjoyed the feel of the zipper on his balls, and he regretfully stuffed his gear into his pants before he zipped up. Everything he did lately felt sexual, everything.

Reed was only good at a few things, getting loaded, fucking, and hurting people. He had always known about the first two, but the last one had been something of a fortunate discovery.

Chad continued speaking. "We've got a problem."

"When do we not have a problem?"

"We have to kill the black guy," he said. Reed just listened. "Those girls are good stock. The one is a little mouthy, but that's a good thing in a child, I suppose. Don't want our offspring to be docile and stupid. But, if that black man wakes up and tells what I did to him, we're going to lose a couple chickies."

Reed smirked. "We can just take them. What does it matter if they want to stay or not?"

Chad looked at Reed with that big bro look on his face. Reed had seen that look three or four times a day since they were teenagers. That look served two functions. On one hand, it told Reed to pay attention to something important. On the other hand, it let Reed know that his brother loved him, despite all of his quirks.

214

"We have to get them to want to be here because we need them to breed, and a woman that is forced to do things against her will doesn't make a very good mother. In fact, they might actually hurt themselves to hurt the baby."

"Is that what happened with you and Dez?"

Chad cuffed him on the back of the head, as he had done off and on since they were knee-high, and Reed knew he had opened his big mouth just a little too wide.

"Never you mind about me and Dez," Chad said.

"So what do you want me to do?" Reed asked.

"The way I figure it, we got two days, maybe less to get that burned up bastard. After that, there's a chance he wakes up and sings."

"You want me to just go in there and kill him?"

"No, that would just piss 'em off."

"What then?" Reed asked, his mind trying to conjure ways to get into the trailer unseen to kill the man.

"I'm going to have to figure out a way to get the one with the broken leg out of there. The other one, she's easy. I've got her taking care of Dez, so once they're both out, we can take care of him."

"How are you going to get her out of there? She's got a broken leg."

"Let me think about that," Chad said. "In the meantime, I want you to go looking for the other black guy and the pregnant lady."

"You want me to do 'em both?"

"Definitely the guy, but the girl, if there's a way to manage it, see if you can bring her here. She is pregnant after all. We need as many humans as we can get. Besides, we don't want to get all inbred in here. You know what happens when brothers and sisters start fucking."

Reed nodded his head. Living in a trailer park, you tend to learn about the drawbacks of genetic homogeneity. "You get webbed feet and chinless weirdoes with two dicks."

Chad just looked at Reed and shook his head. "What goes on in that head of yours?"

"Speaking of which, what's my reward for this little caper of yours?"

"What do you want?"

"I want the one with the broken leg."

Chad just laughed. "What makes you think she's going to want you?"

"You let me worry about that," Reed said. "I just don't want you or any of the others muscling in on my action."

Chad patted him on the knee and then stood. "You won't have any competition from me, not that it would be much of a competition if I threw my hat into the ring. I'll pass the word along to the others to keep their hands off for now."

"For now?"

"Yeah, if you can't seal the deal, we can't very well let her field go unplanted."

"Fair enough."

Reed waited until Chad left, and then he went back to work. He thought of Dez's big belly, and her full breasts with the dark nipples. He bit his lower lip, and thought about killing and making love.

Chapter 13: It Was Nice While It Lasted

Tejada and the boys finally finished fishing all the corpses out of the lake. Their departure had been delayed indefinitely it seemed. Most of his men were without ammunition now, and besides that, he had some unfinished business on the Nike campus. In Tejada's mind, his men had been set up, and there was only one person on the campus who could have pulled it off... Nike.

Nike had been overjoyed to hear that they were going to stay. That was fine. Let him think that they had been won over. In reality, Tejada was just biding his time. He had a dead soldier to avenge. He looked over at the plot where they had buried Beacham and made a promise. He wondered if Beacham could hear it, or if he were just wasting his thoughts.

The bodies in the lake did not receive the honor of burial. There were too many of them. There had been quite a firefight here, and Tejada was confused as to where all that firepower had gone. The only guard he had seen was the one they had first encountered when they hopped over the wall. Wearing batting gloves they had found in the Ken Griffey Jr. building, they stacked the corpses into a pile as high as Tejada's head. When he gave the order, Masterson flicked a lit cigarette onto the gasoline-soaked pile.

He surveyed the field as black, noxious smoke drifted over the campus. He saw much. He saw Rudy and Amanda sticking with the soldiers. He saw Walt busting his ass, his face harder and more severe than when they had first met. His body was changing too. He was becoming hard, chiseled, in his heart and his body. He saw the residents of the Nike campus taking care of their own, digging with some shovels they had liberated from an unoccupied maintenance building. He saw that most of the other buildings were occupied. But most of all, he saw the cameras situated around the campus.

If all these buildings were running on solar power, there was a good chance that one of those cameras had captured video of whoever had broken the front door of that building. That meant there was proof somewhere, and now he just needed to find it.

"You need anything, sir?" Epps asked.

"Not right now, Epps. But why don't you see if you can buddy up to these people. find out who they are. I have a shitload of questions, and I need to have answers fast."

"What kind of questions, sir?"

"Oh, you know, do those cameras work? Where do they feed to? How can we see what's on them? Who wanted to set us up? You know, the usual." Epps just nodded and pulled his gloves from his hands. Tejada watched as he tapped Allen on the shoulder and whispered in his ear. Allen nodded his head, popped a peek at Tejada, and then stripped his own gloves off.

"Rudy! Come here. I want to talk to you for a second."

Rudy bumbled his way over, hiking up his pants as he came. "Yes, uh, sir?"

"You don't have to call me that. You're not a soldier. Just call me Tejada, everyone else does."

Rudy nodded, his awkwardness still present despite all that they had all gone through together. "What do you think of this place, Rudy?"

Rudy gave the question some consideration before he answered. "I think that it's a good set-up. But I also think that there's something not quite right about it."

"How so?"

"I mean, how the hell did they get all these people locked up in those buildings? Where are all the people that killed all of the corpses we found, and why are the people here so damn secretive?"

It was a good analysis, as good as any that had been kicking around in Tejada's head anyway. Tejada put a hand on the man's shoulder and brought him in close. "Those are good questions, Rudy. If we're going to stay here, we need answers to those questions, and we needed them yesterday." From the corner of his eye, he saw Nike's head of security step outside. "I want you to find those answers for us. As far as these people can tell, you're not one of us. They don't trust us; they don't even seem to want us here."

"They were glad you were here last night."

Tejada nodded. "Yeah, I noticed. A little convenient if you ask me. Anyway, I want you to pal around with these people, ask the questions that need to be asked, but quietly. We don't want anyone to get suspicious, you know what I mean?" Rudy nodded. "Good. Now, as much as I appreciate your help, why don't you make yourself scarce until you've found some stuff out. And, if you need to badmouth me or the other men to give yourself a little more credibility, it ain't gonna hurt my feelings none."

Rudy nodded and then walked away from Tejada. He whispered into Amanda's ear, and then they peeled away from the soldiers. Nike's head of security watched them go, and Tejada watched him without looking like he was. The smoke blotted out the sun, the smell clinging to everything in sight. You never got used to the smell of burning human flesh, but once you smelled it, you'd recognize it wherever you went. He stared at the Nike people. They looked like mice, cowed and scared. They were going to have to get over that shit, and fast, if they ever wanted to stop inhaling that stench.

****

In a back room, where blood still dried on the walls, Rudy told Amanda what Tejada wanted from them. He told her how they had to befriend the Nike people and figure out

219

what was going on. He told her how they were to distance themselves from the soldiers.

"It's like we're spies," Amanda said.

"I think it's exactly like that," Rudy said. "Who knows? Maybe there isn't even anything to find. Maybe it was all just one big accident."

Amanda laughed. "I don't believe that any more than you do." They lapsed into silence. "Do you think we're putting ourselves in danger?"

"I think that no matter what we do, we're in danger. At least this way, we're doing something about it."

Amanda nodded again, then took him by the hand. With a smile that made his heart feel like it was going to erupt, she dragged him from the small side room and said, "Come on. Let's go make some friends."

****

As they stepped outside, Amanda marveled at what the world had become. The feeling of having been magically transported to a completely different world didn't come to her often, but when it did, it hit her like a hammer to the sternum. Here they were, standing on the campus of one of the most powerful companies in the world, and on its lawn, piles of bodies were burning in great, big, smoky heaps. The employees of that company were now either dead and trapped inside buildings or on the lawn digging graves for those that had died in last night's attack.

She walked with Rudy across the lawn. "Just do what I do," she said. She knew that Rudy wasn't the right choice to infiltrate a group of people. He had all the social grace of a hobo covered in horse shit, but she could make up for his deficiencies, and if he just followed her lead, perhaps they could figure out what was going on.

Amanda walked up to a man who was covered in sweat and dirt. His shirt was soaked with perspiration, and she could tell that he was exhausted. "Can we help?"

220

Amanda asked. The man looked at Amanda, and though he seemed dubious as to Amanda's ability to actually help, he willingly parted with his shovel. His hands were red and blistered from his work. Amanda grabbed the shovel, and Rudy walked off to find someone else's burden to relieve.

She jammed the blade of the shovel into the hole that the man had been digging. He sat down roughly on the grass, too exhausted to keep himself standing. There had been a lot of graves to dig that day. On the grass, to her left, there was a body. A bullet hole had punctured the forehead of a middle-aged woman. The dead had fed upon her left arm until it was nothing more than bone highlighted by a few stubborn tendons and blobs of flesh. Her skin was gray. Her dead eyes stared up at the smoky sky.

"Did you know her?" Amanda asked as she tossed a shovelful of dirt off to the side. The man nodded, still too tired to even speak.

"I knew most of them," he said. Tears came to his eyes, and he pulled his glasses off to wipe them away. Amanda dug in silence from then on out. It was hard work, and after ten shovelfuls, she could feel her hands revolting at their ill use. The webbing between her thumb and forefinger was red and already protesting.

She looked up to see Rudy taking the shovel from a sobbing woman. He patted her on the shoulder, and the woman collapsed in his arms, tears streaming down her face. He gently lowered her to the ground and began digging. *Boy, we're going to be one hell of a pair tonight.*

"You came here with the soldiers, right?" the man asked.

Amanda nodded.

"I haven't had a chance to thank them, but then again, how do you thank someone for being in the right place at the right time? It just seems ill-conceived."

"Oh, I don't know about that," Amanda said. "There's always room to show your appreciation, especially if you get to breathe another day."

"That's the thing," the man said. "I don't even know if I want to be alive... I don't know if I should be thanking those men or cursing them."

Amanda hopped into the hole she had created. It came up to her shin now. "Hey, you might feel that way now, but think about the future... what did you say your name was?"

The man pulled his glasses off and wiped his eyes with the back of his hand again. The soot smeared away along with the tears, and he looked like a man who had gone sunbathing and forgotten to take his sunglasses off. "They call me Ceres, but my real name is Nathan. Stupid Nike had us all choose new names when this all went down."

"Yeah, what's with all the names?" Amanda asked.

"He says that the old world is dead, and that we are the new world. Nike says that the people we were are gone, and that we're all new people with new names, but I don't know, I just liked being called Nathan." He wiped a drip of snot from his hawkish beak and said, "Hell, I've been called Nathan all my life. It seems stupid to go changing it now."

"Well, Nathan, on the issue of thank-yous, you might not feel it now, but sooner or later, there's going to come a time when something comes along that makes you happy." She looked at Rudy sweating in the murky light of the smoke-filled afternoon. "And when that happens, you're going to feel like saying thank you, but by then, if you haven't said it already, it's going to sound fake as shit, and you're going to feel like an asshole. But if you do it now, and you get it out, maybe even if you don't mean it, then everything is going to be alright."

The man nodded, his eyes crawling over the corpse on the ground. "I knew her, you know? She was a real sweet lady. She worked in the payroll department. She always smiled and said hello. I saw her here every day for the last ten years, and every day she had that damn smile on, even if I didn't. It didn't matter to her, you know?"

Amanda just let the man talk. She chopped through an ancient tree root with her shovel, slicing it in half and digging around it.

"Funny thing though. Until this all happened, I never even asked her name. I didn't know who she was until the entire world had died. She didn't smile so much then. She had a family and all. Here she was kind of lost."

Amanda felt like the man himself was getting lost, talking about nonsense that didn't matter anymore. But maybe that's exactly what he needed to do. Maybe he needed to unburden himself of these thoughts, these memories. Maybe he needed a clean slate, even if it was just for a few minutes. She hacked some more at a stubborn root, stomping on the shovel with her heel until the blade sliced through it completely.

"Hell, I think we're all kind of lost. Did you know this is the first time that the majority of us have been outside this building in weeks?"

Sweat dripped down Amanda's back, taking a ride all the way down the crack of her ass. "Yeah, why is that?"

"Oh, that's how Nike wants it." Nathan plucked at a handful of grass, ripped it free from the soil and then tossed it on the ground, something Amanda bet would have never happened before the dead had started living.

"I thought it was because of all the dead in the buildings."

"No, no. They can't get out. That's bulletproof, shatterproof glass. Do you know the amount of security we had around here before this whole thing happened? Hell, you couldn't jog the track around the perimeter without a badge for more than two minutes before security guards showed up. We had a lot of movers and shakers in here. It wouldn't do for one of them to take a bullet. That's not good P.R."

Nathan said this last as if it were a well-worn company mantra, the type of thing that would be appended to every memo ever sent. "So then why was everyone staying inside?"

Nathan just shrugged, his eyes wandering over to the dead woman's body again. His eyes clouded over, and Amanda continued to dig. He lapsed into silence, his eyes tracking the smoke of the burn pile. Amanda jammed the shovel deep into the dirt, cranking the blade back and forth, lifting it up over her shoulder, and depositing the soil on the grass. This was going to take a while.

****

Rudy had never been one for physical labor, not because he hated it or anything, but because he had never needed to. Foster parents occasionally asked him to take out the trash or clean his room, but they seldom asked him to do more than that. They had never loved him enough to want him to do those things. He was at fault for that; he knew that now. He had been thinking a lot about the person that he used to be before all this.

The end conclusion? He had been an asshole. Somehow, it had taken Amanda's unconditional acceptance of him to realize this. He had been offered olive branch after olive branch by one person or another during the entirety of his childhood, and he had spit in the face of every single one of them. Why? Because he was afraid he would be left again. But Amanda hadn't left. Even when he was lying unconscious on the Burnside Bridge, she had fought for them to take him along.

He doubted she would ever leave. He looked over at her, lost in conversation with a sad-eyed man who had the face of an accountant. No, maybe his face was more lawyer-ish. Not the type of lawyer that would stand in the middle of the courtroom and piss fire in the judge's face, but the type of lawyer who would know what to do with a stack of unfiled folders. Hopefully, she was getting some good information. The woman he had relieved just sat on the ground, lost in her own sorrow. He might as well be invisible.

The prospective tenant of the grave he dug reclined on the grass. Flies crawled over the flesh caught in the man's teeth. One flew to the bullet hole in the man's temple, crawled in for a peek, and then crawled back out. The whole scene gave him the chills.

He rested the handle of the shovel against his shoulder and wiped his brow for the hundredth time. He looked at his dirty hands, trying to find what was making them hurt so bad, but all he saw was red skin. He went back to work, lost in his own thoughts and regrets, wondering just who he would have been if he had let people into his heart when he was younger.

"Want some water?" a man asked. It was Nike. Immediately he blushed, as if he had been caught masturbating in his bedroom.

"Uh, sure. Thanks," he said, reaching out for the proffered glass of water.

"Don't worry," Nike said. "It's purified."

"From the lake?" Rudy asked doubtfully.

Nike laughed like a good-natured grandfather. "Of course not. It'll be a long time before that water is ever potable again. It's from some rain barrels we keep on the roof. Once fall hits, we should never have to worry about water again. Which is good, because once the sodas and the energy drinks and the Gatorade run out, we're all going to be mighty thirsty."

"Cheers," Rudy said as he upended the water into his mouth. Water had never tasted so good. It was cool, fresh.

Nike squatted at the edge of the grave Rudy was digging. "I want to thank you for all that you've done."

At this Rudy had to laugh. "I haven't done anything."

"You're doing something now."

"Yeah, well, a lot of good it's going to do."

Nike blinked at Rudy, as if he wasn't used to anyone voicing a real thought in his presence. "What do you mean? We're safe. The threat is taken care of. We have water. We can plant crops in the spring. We have a wall that keeps us safe."

"You think that guy feels safe?" Rudy pointed at the corpse on the lawn.

Nike looked at the corpse, as if seeing it for the first time. "I knew that man. He used to be a software engineer. He would make all sorts of wonderful, Nike-themed apps for us. He invented a pair of shoes that would keep track of how far and how fast you ran. You ask me if he feels safe? I tell you he did. That's why all these people are here... because we promised to keep them safe. Many of these people could have gone anywhere else, but they chose to come here. When things got bad, we sent out the word that we were building a wall, that we had security, and that we would weather this storm together, the Nike family."

Nike blinked once, the memory of those days fading away. "He felt safe, but we let him down. I don't foresee that happening again. I think with the help of your friends, and the help of people like yourself, we can make this place great again."

It was then that Rudy realized just how out of touch and insane Nike was. Here he was surrounded by the dead, and he believed that everything was going to be ok. Somewhere in that soft brain of his he probably believed this place would probably start making shoes again. "You actually believe what you're saying, don't you?"

Nike just laughed. He reached down and patted Rudy on his shoulder. "I like you. You have no filter. I'm going to call you Perry. Do you like that name?"

"No..."

"Do you want to know why I'm going to call you Perry?" Rudy didn't even have a chance to answer before Nike began again. "Your lack of filter puts me in mind of a delicious unfiltered pear cider I had in Corvallis some years back. At first look it was ugly, unattractive, but when I spent some time with it, I found it refreshing and unlike anything I had ever drank before. It also gave me quite a buzz." Nike laughed as he walked away from Rudy. "See you around, Perry."

Rudy shook his head and gripped the shovel with his aching hands. The hole wasn't going to dig itself.

****

Allen and Epps helped digging graves as well. Of the soldiers, they were easily the most personable. When Whiteside came over to help out, Allen waved him away. Whiteside was a good guy and all, but he had a way of putting his foot in his mouth. He never shut up, and he always seemed obsessed with pushing people's buttons. Whiteside just shook his head and turned the other way.

The soil at his feet was dark and thick. It was hard clay, harder than a dream unrealized. Allen smiled in the hole, though his hands and back were straining.

"You think that's deep enough?" Epps asked.

"You bring a measuring tape?" Allen asked.

"No."

"Then it's deep enough."

They hoisted themselves out of the hole and stood on the edge of it, flexing their backs and dropping the shovels like they were live snakes. The smoke from the fire had died down some, and the sun was finally able to make it through. To Allen, the hole looked like a mouth sprung from the earth. "Feed me," he imagined it saying.

They lifted the grave's unfortunate occupant, Allen standing by the man's legs and Epps at his feet. They swung the body from side to side, ready to deposit the body in the earth's maw, where it would be digested and transformed into nutrients.

"You're not just going to toss him in their like that? Like a sack of garbage?"

Allen looked at the woman who had spoken. She was attractive, like a sparkling crystal bowl filled with peanut M&Ms. She had personality; he could sense it... that or he just really needed to eat something.

"No ma'am," he said. "Wouldn't think of it."

Allen nodded at Epps, and they set the body on the ground. He hopped into the hole, his earlier metaphor making the earthen walls around him feel somewhat dangerous. Epps lowered the body down to him, and he fumbled with the heavy corpse until he was able to lay it down gently on the bottom of the grave. Then he pushed himself out of the grave, wishing he could just lie down on the grass and soak up the sun. But a soldier's work was never done. You learned that early once you enlisted. You thought you were going to be able to take a nap and then bam, there was someone ordering you to do some mundane task. Being a soldier wasn't difficult because you had to kill people and maybe be killed; it was difficult because you never had enough damn sleep.

He stood upright, and he looked down at the shovel on the ground. He imagined that when he went to pick it up, it would be like Thor's hammer, immovable, no matter how hard he strained. No such luck though. He picked the blasted shovel right up as if it were comprised of air.

"Thank you," the woman said.

He wiped some sweat off his brow and then set about filling in the hole. This was the easy part. "Not a problem," Allen said.

"You know, the first thing we lost was civility."

Allen cocked an eyebrow at the woman. Epps just kept his head down and filled in the hole. "Civility?"

"Civility is humanity. Without it, we're just animals that can manipulate objects, nothing more than chimps in a forest of our own making."

Allen liked this chick. "There are some that would say civility is a luxury, and that it was just a game we played to fool ourselves into thinking that we are somehow nobler and more important than apes."

The lady smiled at him. "Do you believe that?"

Allen stopped and leaned on his shovel. "Beliefs are straightjackets for the mind. They keep you safe, and make you feel comfortable, but in reality, you're imprisoned for the sake of safety and reason."

The lady nodded and approached. She stuck out a dirty hand to him. She had clearly been helping out with burying the dead. "My name is Diana." Allen shook her hand.

"This is my man Epps." Epps waved at her. "My name is Allen. Well that's my last name actually. My real name is Izzy."

"Pleased to meet you. Perhaps, after you're done here, we could grab a bite to eat."

"I think I'd like that," Allen said.

"How very civil of you," she said with a smile. Then she turned and walked away inside the Ken Griffey Jr. building. Allen watched her the whole way. The sway of those hips did things to him that even his poet's mind couldn't put to words.

"You want to come eat with us?" he said over his shoulder to Epps.

"Nah, man. That weirdo is yours, man. All yours."

"You think she's weird?"

"I think you two will get along just fine. Now stop watching that ass, and help me fill in this hole."

Allen did so, but in his mind, he replayed Diana's walk over and over again. The work wasn't all that bad.

****

Tejada had never been one to be bullied. It wasn't in his nature. As the bodies turned to ash and the smoke cleared the sky, he caught Nike's head of security, a force that seemed to consist of one lone security guard with a face like a troll, looking at him with that look in his eye. It was the look that said, "Listen, asshole. I'm the big kid on the block, and sooner or later I'm going to pound that reality into you."

Tejada had always been short, but he had always carried himself like he was the largest man in the world. It wasn't pride or cockiness. It was just that he didn't have the patience or the time to waste on something as worthless as fear. Life was too short for that bullshit. And as he stalked across the trampled grass of the Nike campus, headed right for the security guard, he could see the man tense up.

Tejada barely came up to the man's flabby chest, but he came as close to the man as he could without touching him. "I see you looking at me."

"Yeah. So?" the man said.

"The only real question is are you looking at me because you want to or because someone else wants you to?" Tejada looked at the man's face. He had a bulbous nose, and his lower teeth looked like the underbitten maw of a bulldog. His balding head was covered in black hair swept over the top of a shiny pate.

"What's it matter?"

Tejada got so close to the man that he could smell the fabric of his shirt. "It matters because once I'm done pounding the shit out of you, I need to know if I have to pound the shit out of someone else as well."

The security guard tried to push Tejada away and get out of the situation, but Tejada kept his proximity, daring the man to take a swing at him. "Get the fuck off of me," the man said.

Tejada didn't back up. "Answer the question."

The security guard cocked his arm back, and then Tejada sprung into action, jumping upwards and bashing the top of his head into the man's bulldog jaw. As the man fell backwards, Tejada grabbed his arm, swung his legs up around the man's chest and took him to the ground. With his legs wrapped around the man's torso, he yanked his arm backwards. The security guard was going to tell him what he wanted or he was going to break the man's arm.

"Tell me what I want to know." The man strained against Tejada's hold, and Tejada sensed the other people around him. The entire campus had stopped working. They watched the confrontation between the two of them, but no one came to the man's aid. The man had no friends; men like him never did. He pulled tighter on the arm, holding it at the point where it hurt real bad but wouldn't break.

The security guard strained. His pale face had turned red, and the top of his head looked like the bulbous end of a thermometer.

"Gentlemen," a voice said, "this is unnecessary. Stop this."

Tejada turned and looked at the placid face of Nike. He was like a father chiding two unruly children. In his face, Tejada saw pity. If Nike hadn't held a low opinion of Tejada before, he did now. Tejada gave one quick jerk to the security guard's arm, and he screamed in pain. Then Tejada untangled his legs and popped to his feet as if nothing had happened.

"Are you ok, Harper?" Nike asked. The security guard, Harper, rose to his feet, flexing his arm. It would be sore for a week or two. Tejada had made sure that the security guard would remember this little lesson. "Sergeant, what is this all about?"

A crowd had gathered around them. "I think you know."

Nike laughed at this. "I haven't the slightest idea what could have caused you to resort to such barbarism. Is this how the army trains its soldiers?"

The slight was a weak one, and it had no effect on Tejada, but he could see the other residents of the campus tense up at this. Nike was a man that was used to getting his way, used to being able to say whatever he wanted to say. Even though Tejada had showed the man how piss-poor his security was, he was still the same man. Cockiness or stupidity? Tejada didn't know, and he didn't particularly care either. "The army trains us to do a lot of things. Listen to mouthy old men with a superiority complex isn't one of them. If you'll excuse me."

Tejada turned his back on the man, knowing that this was the ultimate knife in the ribs for Nike. A man like that was used to having his questions answered. No one ever turned their back on Nike, but Tejada had, and he smiled as he stepped into the Ken Griffey Jr. building.

"Back to work people!" Nike yelled. Tejada could hear the anger in the man's voice. He wished he could turn around and see that smug look gone from his face, but that would ruin everything.

Inside, he headed to the cafeteria. He wanted a cup of coffee, so he ordered one. One by one, his soldiers returned. They sat at a table all their own as the people of the Nike campus came and went, grabbing food and drink and staying far away. That was good. He had set himself up as the heavy now. Fear was good. It kept people from doing stupid shit, up to a point. Sooner or later, he was going to have to show these people that he and his men were the good guys, but for right now, that fear suited him just fine.

Epps and Allen strolled in grabbed some food and then sat down at the table. "You guys hear anything?" Tejada asked.

"No," Epps said. "But Allen here got himself a date."

Allen blushed, and Tejada's eyes wrinkled at the edges as he smiled. "It's a start, I guess. Anyone see which way Nike and his pet gorilla went?"

Brown said, "I saw Nike heading up to the offices upstairs. Harper went with him. He looked like a whipped dog."

Tejada nodded. "Brown, Masterson, I want one of you two on those people at all times. They want to watch us, then we're damn sure going to watch them. Don't turn your back on them for even a second. If, what's his name?"

"Harper," Brown supplied.

Tejada snapped his fingers in recognition. "If Harper walks off and leaves Nike alone, stick with Harper. He's Nike's hands. If Nike's up to something, it's Harper that's going to be carrying it out. That's how these rich fucks work."

Tejada watched as Amanda and Rudy walked in. They followed a wormy looking fellow in spectacles across the cafeteria, got some food, and then sat down at the same table. "Everybody, Rudy and Amanda are officially off limits. They're still with us, but I don't want it to look that way. Walt, you look the least like one of us, so I want you to talk to them when they're alone sometime and see if they've learned anything."

"You got it, sir."

"Alright, let's eat up and get some rest here. I'm sure we've got a long day tomorrow of dealing with some more bullshit. Each of you give Masterson and Brown some of your food; they've already had a long day, and it's about to be longer."

233

Tejada spooned his food into his mouth. It was flavorless. His mind was on other things.

****

The tiled floor of the locker room was cold. Diana said that the locker room used to be used by athletes who came to visit the Nike campus. The lockers themselves were tall, metallic, and a bright green. Diana stirred, her head resting in the crook of his arm. They had rutted passionately. There was very little foreplay before they had gotten down to business. She was older than him by some ten years, but in bed they were perfectly matched.

When they were done, they had fallen into a quiet rest, and Allen had basked in post-coital clarity for the first time in months. He was no fool; there was no relationship here, just two ships looking for a night's portage during a storm.

"So are you guys good guys or bad guys?" Diana asked.

"Good guys, obviously. Why?"

"It's just that, the people we had here earlier, we thought they were good, but it turns out they were bad. Even Nike's weirdness was more preferable than their... brutality."

Allen could feel Diana's words as they fell from her lips, like syrup dripping slowly from a tapped maple tree. She had the words, but it was hard for her to let them leave.

"What happened?"

Diana sat up then, placing her arms on her knees. Her breasts hung down, and Allen resisted the urge to grab them. That wasn't what he was here for, though their coupling had been a pleasant interlude from all the death and dying.

"At first, the people here were overjoyed at having found a place to be safe. When things went bad, and they went bad fast out here, the company sent out a mass email

234

saying that they had some sort of contingency plan. Our families were invited. The campus was going to be safe."

She looked off into the distance, seeing the past in her mind. "It was for a while. The company hired a security firm to protect everyone and to man the wall. Of course, while they were looking outside the wall, someone neglected to keep an eye inside the wall. One of our older employees passed away in their sleep, and this led to a chain reaction of death. Before we knew it, the security team was running the show. They were brutal."

Diana swallowed hard. There was a sorrow there. He imagined it like a knot in a piece of wood, an imperfection that grew from some wound, some irritant, and created something beautiful, even though it was a scar. He could see that the events of the campus' early days had left these knots in her, both beautiful and sad at once.

"They executed many of the older people. If someone became sick, they would kill them too. We became like prisoners. But Nike knew what to do. He recruited his caveman, Harper, to do his dirty work for him. At night, Harper killed them while they slept, but he didn't "kill them" kill them. He left them to rise. Nike had Harper lock the doors to the security building, and in one night, all the security team was gone, except for Harper and a handful of others who were on duty. But they're gone now too."

"What happened to the others?" Allen asked.

"Harper killed them too. There's no proof of it. Nike keeps the door to the security room locked, but we all know he ordered it. Now Harper is the biggest goon on the block, and people are too afraid to do anything."

"Why?"

"Because Nike knows all. He sees everything. The locker rooms and the bathrooms are the only places on the campus where Nike can't watch what we do and what we say."

She lapsed into silence then, and Allen sat up as well. He placed a naked arm over her bare shoulders, and then pressed his lips to hers. They were cold and dry. He thought they were going to go for round two, but she pushed him away, not roughly, but enough to let him know his cock wasn't needed at the moment. "That's not why I brought you here," she said.

"Well, it was nice the first time."

She bit her lower lip before saying, "Nike will kill you all."

This sent Allen's disappointed libido into hibernation. "What are you talking about?"

"He's all smiles now, but he doesn't want what happened before to happen again."

"How do you know this?"

She smiled at him, an ironic sort of thing with a hint of sadness. "Because I'm his daughter."

Allen's head hit the wall behind him, and he began to wonder just what he had gotten himself into.

"He won't allow you to take over, but he needs you. Without you, we're not safe. But he also knows that with you and your friends here, we're not totally safe either."

"So how is he going to do it?" Allen asked.

"He's going to use you until he gets what he needs, and then he'll throw you away."

"And the people? They'll go for this?"

"They're afraid. They lost family members, co-workers, children to the last men with guns. That memory doesn't go away. Sometimes, even I wonder if my father might be right."

"But you know he's not."

Diana shook her head. "I'm just guessing here. If I'm wrong, then it's my ass."

Allen closed his eyes, his head still leaning against the cool locker room wall.

"Are you going to sleep?"

He shook his head.

"Then what are you doing?"

"I'm thinking about a time when people didn't fear each other, a time when you could trust that the person across from you wasn't out to screw you over. I'm thinking about a time when a woman didn't fuck you because she wanted you to kill for her."

"I never said anything about killing," she said defensively.

"Didn't you?" He opened his eyes then, ignoring Diana's beauty. "You know, your name is appropriate. Diana, goddess of the hunt. You've been hunting me since we got here haven't you? You've been hunting down the perfect weapon to take out your father."

She turned and faced him, shaking her head. She was flustered and sputtering denials, but Izzy pressed onward. "You say you don't want us to kill your father, but that's exactly the situation you're setting up here. What did you think? That you would hand over all this information, and we wouldn't do something about it? That we'd keep playing this game your father is playing? Just how stupid do you want me to think you are?"

She stood then, her fists on her hips, her breasts jiggling invitingly. She glowered down at him imperiously and said, "I was trying to help you."

"By helping yourself."

"Yeah, so what? My father... my father is going to get more of us killed, just as he's gotten the majority of us killed already. He needs to be stopped."

"Have you no love for your father?"

"He lives in a fantasy world. He is stuck in a reality where he was in control, he was in charge, and everything worked according to his plan, but the world doesn't work like that. He doesn't need to die. He just needs to know he's not in charge."

"I guess the apple doesn't fall far from the tree." He hated to use the cliché, but when the shoe fit... something something.

Then Diana did the oddest of things. She sat upon him and wrapped her arms around him. She smiled. "Listen, all I'm trying to do is keep more people from dying. My father, he's one man. He's a dinosaur, large, cumbersome and completely unsuited for this world." She grabbed him down there, one arm still wrapped behind his neck, and slipped him inside her.

"Do you always talk about your dad when you fuck?"

She slapped him then, and then she was gone. He caught one final glimpse of her backside as she bent over and grabbed her clothes, and then he was left alone, on the cold tile floor. He leaned his head back against the wall and dozed for a bit. Oh, well. It had been nice while it lasted.

Chapter 14: Last Breaths

The black man's trail was easy to find. He took big steps, and he was heavy. Reed followed the trail for a while, and then it became even easier. He spotted the wounds on the tree bark quickly. They were fresh, the wood underneath a bright yellow. He followed these signs for a while, and then they just disappeared.

He scanned the ground, noting the disturbances in the undergrowth. Someone else had joined up with the black man. There were a lot of signs to track, so it was fairly easy to see which direction they had gone. He noted that once his two targets had met up their path was less meandering than it had been before, almost like they knew where they were going.

When he stepped out onto the gravel road, he spotted two distinct sets of footprints, confirming that the black man and the pregnant lady were both together. He also knew where they were going. They were going to the old lady's house.

He smiled to himself as he walked casually down the lane. He remembered her. He remembered her pleading, her nasty wrinkled face begging him to leave her some food. In the end, he hadn't. He had taken everything she had, even sitting on the kitchen counter to eat a good majority of the food in front of her. He had laughed with a full mouth as the old lady had cursed him. Such a vile string of swears from such a fragile old lady. He had thought about hitting her, maybe strangling her for her impertinence, but in the end, leaving her without any food had been an even better punishment.

For days after that, he would visit her house, watching from the woods with his hand down his pants, doing the dance that he loved so much. He watched her waste away, and when three days had passed, he crept closer and watched her as she lay on the couch in her living room, too tired to get up and try and find food. He had tapped on the window, his pants around his ankles, and all she had been able to do was wave a weak arm at him, middle finger extended. What great fun it had all been.

He wondered what type of fun he would have with the couple that lived in his house now. He thought of it as his now. He had earned it with his cleverness and cruelty. That he was clever was never in any doubt. He knew he existed on a plane far above most people, and that was before everyone had started dying.

At first, Reed had been scared. In his mind, he saw this new plague as something biblical, but when they had killed Dez's parents and nothing but good things seemed to happen, he understood then that there was no God. This was no plague sent upon man to punish him for his wicked misdeeds. This was just nature gone wrong. He was thankful for that. The only thing that had ever kept him from being an even more wicked person, and he knew he was wicked, was the fear that there might be something after life, some place where he might be judged for all the things that he had done.

Reed didn't want to be judged. He had already experienced enough of that in his life. Going to prison, going to the mental hospital up at Ridgewood, those hadn't been terrible experiences. It was the judging that he had found so painful. He still remembered the faces of everyone in that court room as he had been sentenced for his crimes. Fat faces, pale faces, disapproving faces. If he could have found every one of them, he would have shown them what he thought of their judgment. How dare they judge him? Who were they? They were nothing, just as everyone in this world was nothing, just sacks of meat for his own entertainment.

He knew he was wicked, but he loved the way the word sounded, and whenever he found himself in the middle of one of his experiments, he would say to himself, "This is wicked," over and over again.

The thought of his wickedness made him hard, and as he inched across the washed-out road, hugging the side of the mountain, his erection scraped uncomfortably against the rocks. Somehow, this only made him harder. He stepped across the gap and then went to find who was living in his home. He wondered if this was how the bears in Goldilocks felt as they approached their house only to find that little tart sleeping in their bed. Oh, what wicked things he would have done to Goldilocks.

He hit the road that led up to the front of the house. He smiled as the footprints continued up the driveway. He disappeared into the fringe of trees and underbrush that encircled the home. He knew his way around there well. He had watched the old lady for some time before making his presence known.

On the backside of the house, he spotted the black man digging a grave. He frowned a little bit. That means they had found his surprise and killed it. He didn't like the thought of someone undoing his work. He had toiled a long time to make that lady what she was. Who were they to come along and undo all of his hard work?

He pulled his rifle free and suppressed a giggle. He held the gun up and took aim. His sight danced in front of the back of the man's head. "Boom," he whispered, smiling from his vantage point in the woods. It was that simple. All he had to do was pull the trigger, and job #1 would be done.

But he didn't pull the trigger because that wouldn't be any fun. It would be downright boring. Sure, there would be a splash of blood, and his rifle would crack like thunder sent down by the gods themselves, but then it would be over.

He let his rifle fall, suspended on his shoulders by its strap. He pulled a buck knife from a sheathe tied to his leg. The knife was shiny. It had been a gift from his brother. He had used it for all sorts of things, but he had never killed a black man with it. He departed from the trees, his stomach filling up with that good feeling, the feeling of doing something wicked. This was a wicked thing he was about to do, and he would gladly add it to the list.

He thought briefly, in a moment of clarity about the time before he had discovered his wickedness. Reed hadn't always been bad. It was the drugs that had done it to him. Never in his life had anything come close to the euphoria he felt with every new drug he discovered. When he was wasted out of his mind, it was like disappearing from reality altogether and existing in a completely different dimension. The memory of the joy and exhilaration he felt when he was on meth was something that would never leave him, but he had overcome that addiction, not through any means or willpower, but through the lack of product. He had never been much of a chemist, and with the way the world was now, he doubted he would ever get another taste of that wonder drug.

That was ok though. He had found something else, something that gave him the high that he so desperately needed. He had found his wickedness, and as he approached the black man from behind, he smiled a wicked grin, his knife glinting in the sunlight.

He was two feet away when he heard a voice say, "Uh-uh."

He froze, his knife hanging uselessly in the air.

"Drop the knife," the voice said. Reed turned to see the woman standing there, her hands gripped around a silver handgun. The darkness at the end of that barrel seemed huge, like a cave that he could get lost in, and for a brief moment, he wanted it. He wanted that cave to burp fire at him and burn him to a crisp. He just smiled at the lady, taking note of her stomach and the bump of pregnancy that was so obvious there.

Then he saw the woman's eyes, and he thought, *Here too is a wicked person.* And he fell in love instantly, the way mad men do.

He dropped to his knees and held his precious buck knife out to the wicked woman the way a peasant might offer a king the last of their food because they knew the only other option was death.

"I said drop it." Her voice was like chewed gravel. Her eyes were smoldering pits, but her hands were steady, unflinching. She had no fear of her gun. She had become friends with it a long time ago. He could see that as plain as he saw her pregnant belly. He let the knife slip from his hands, and then he was tackled to the ground by the black man.

He let all of this happen. He was having such a good time. When the black man was done, they had him dressed like a turkey and left him lying on the cool grass of the once manicured lawn.

His prey stepped off to the side, out of earshot, and they had a quick discussion, about what to do with him. They finished their conversation and returned to him, ready to carry out whatever little plan they had come up with.

"Why shouldn't we kill you now?" the pregnant woman asked.

"Ask him. He knows the answer."

"That's the main guy's brother," the black man said.

"So?" the woman asked.

"So if you kill me, you can be assured of two things. My brother is going to come looking for me, and he's going to kill anyone that doesn't give him the answers he wants. And your friends back at the compound? They're going to die too, but not before we have a little fun with them."

"Why are you out here?" the woman asked.

"I was just doing a little reconnaissance, checking out some of these houses. Then I saw that guy there, and I thought I better see who our new neighbor was."

"You saw me back at the compound," Mort said.

"Yeah, but you had your back to me. It doesn't pay to make assumptions these days." The pair looked unconvinced, so he said, "Look. I had a rifle. If I wanted you dead, I could have just shot you."

"You're so full of shit, I'm surprised your teeth aren't brown," the woman said.

Reed laughed. That was a good one. He would file it away for a later day. God he loved that woman.

"So what do you suggest we do?" the woman asked.

"First, tell me your name." It was a simple demand, but he had to know the name of the angel he had the pleasure of addressing.

"My name is none of your business."

"My name is Mort," the black man said.

"I don't care about your name," Reed replied. "You're nothing to me, but you," he said addressing the lady, "you're something else entirely. I must know your name... or you can just kill me now and see what happens."

The woman glared at him with those eyes, those wild, soulless eyes of fire. "My name is Katie."

Reed nodded. It was a good a name. "And the child, have you picked a name out for the child?"

The woman's arm fell to her side, and the rage and fire was gone from her eyes instantly. It was as if one person had been replaced by another. Reed didn't love this new woman. There was nothing there to love. Oooh, she was as damaged as damaged could be, but every bit as wicked as the woman she had been before.

"Why would I name something that isn't even alive yet?"

"Are any of us truly alive anymore?"

The woman kicked him then, hard in his ribs. The pain was intense, and it shot through him. He felt something he hadn't felt since the day this had all began, and Old Lady Bronson had come to feed on his brains. He felt fear. He felt powerless, and he hated this new woman, wishing that the other would come back.

"We're not here for your philosophy, you little freak." The cold woman, the woman of ice, cocked the hammer of her gun, and she squatted down beside him. Mort looked on with concern, and Reed could see the fear in his eyes. Through that fear, Reed knew that Katie was fully capable of killing him right now. She was a wicked lady indeed.

"Please, make her stop," he pleaded.

Mort stepped forward and placed a hand on Katie's shoulder. She shrugged him off violently, pushing Mort away. Then she squatted down and poked the barrel of the gun painfully into Reed's eye. He screamed in pain and she pressed it slowly and forcefully into his eye. "If you have any suggestions, I'd love to hear them," Katie said. "Or else, I'd just as soon take my chances with your brother."

"You'd lose," he said.

"I don't give a fuck," she said back, cold and quick, so that Reed knew that she meant it.

Reed screamed in pain as the barrel pressed deeper into his eye until he thought it was going to burst. "Stop! Stop!" he screamed in panic. "We can make a deal! I'll make you a deal!"

And just like that the pain was gone. A dull ache shot through his eye, and when he opened it, a black shape floated in his vision, but he could still see.

"This isn't a fucking game show," Katie said. "So you show me the door that the good prize is behind, because if you show me a deal that sucks, we're going to go right back to making your life unbearable."

Reed could see how uncomfortable Mort was with this all, but he knew that Katie was the real power here. She was the one that was calling the shots, but he hated Mort more because he just stood there, watching Reed's abuse. Tears fell from Reed's eyes, and he hated himself and the others for it. *No more crying,* he thought, but he couldn't stop.

"I was sent to kill you," he said referring to Mort, "and I was supposed to bring you back with me because you're pregnant."

"Kill me? But why?" Mort asked.

"I don't know," Reed said, and in truth, he had never really questioned the order. He had just seen another opportunity for his wickedness. "They don't need you. Maybe they think you'll talk the others out of staying. I really don't know."

"I'm not going back with you," Katie said.

Reed nodded through his tears, snot dripping from his nose and onto the emerald green blades of grass in front of him. "You don't have to. If you let me go, I'll go back and say that I did the job. But you have to stay hidden. When your friends are healthy, I'll come find you, and you can all leave together. I promise!"

"What's to stop you from going back there and telling your brother that he should come out here and kill us?" Katie asked, waving her gun in Reed's face.

"Look at me," he pleaded. "I'm a total fuck up. I can't go back and let my brother know I failed. I just can't."

Katie nodded, and Reed felt hope for a second, and then he felt nothing as she blew his brains out.

"Jesus," Mort said.

"Grab his rifle," Katie commanded, and Mort did as he was told. "Finish burying the woman, but leave this one alone. I have an idea."

Mort didn't argue with Katie. Something about the man had made her snap, and he knew better than to argue with her while she was like this. She left and went inside the house. Mort left Reed's corpse lying in the overgrown grass and walked over to the grave that he had already dug for the woman. He continually looked over his shoulder as he finished the grave. That gunshot could have been heard for miles. If there were any dead out there, they could arrive at any moment.

Katie appeared with a gardening tool in her hand. It looked like a small, handheld version of a rake.

"What are you doing?" he asked.

"Don't worry about it," she said. He turned his back as she squatted over Reed's body and began mutilating his face with the metal rake.

With no ceremony, he shoved the woman's body into the grave and then worked as fast as he could to fill it. When he was done, they rushed inside as the first of the dead appeared at the edge of the forest. The monster was broken and twisted, its fingers and arms sticking out at jaunty angles as if it had experienced some sort of fall, and he knew that he was seeing one of the dead from the highway. He wondered how many more of the dead had survived the tumble down the side of the ravine.

It was going to be a long night.

****

Chad heard the gunshot. It sounded like it was a mile or two in the distance. He couldn't quite place it. The canyons and trees made it hard to pinpoint the source. He waited a few minutes, sitting in the inner courtyard of the compound and listening for another shot. His mind spun with possibilities. Reed had been successful. Reed had died. Someone else was out in the woods. All of these possibilities had him on edge.

When he couldn't stand sitting there any longer, he stalked up to the watchtowers and relieved Dale. Dale, thankful for the break from staring into the forest for hours on end, headed into the compound, and Chad took up his watch. The trees swayed gently, and he kept waiting for Reed to appear. As the sun began to go behind the trees, someone brought him some stew. It was made from things they had grown themselves, along with the last of the venison from their last kill a few days earlier.

It was good and filling, and as he licked the last bit of stew off of his spoon, the sun disappeared behind the trees. The dead were here now, and rather than kill them, Chad was forced to disappear behind the barricade. They pounded on the chain-link gate. They pounded on the trailers. The people in the compound had a harried look about them because death itself knocked at the door. Chad poked his head up over the wooden railing of the watchtower and scanned the faces of the dead, looking for his brother. But he wasn't there. He was missing.

The gunshot had drawn unwanted attention all throughout the forest. Maybe he was holed up out there; maybe he was trapped, waiting for his brother to come and save him one more time. He leaned his head against the wooden watchtower and closed his eyes. If something had happened, he would have felt it. Isn't that the way it worked in the movies? One brother dies, the other feels it? They were that close. They knew each other's secrets. Sure, Reed had more of these, but Chad felt as if they were pretty much even-steven on that one. Chad's secrets... were troublesome, more extreme compared to Reed's standard-issue fuck ups.

As the dead continued beating upon the walls, he stood in awe of how one gunshot could bring the dead tumbling out of hiding. Perhaps they hibernated when no one was around, just shut down like a laptop not in use for fifteen minutes, only to spring back to life once you pressed the spacebar.

He popped his head over the railing and scanned the faces of the dead again, hoping not to mark the face of his brother in the crowd. His brother was nowhere to be seen, and for the tenth time, he hoped his brother had found some place to hunker down. Then he went through the cycle again. *I'd know if he was dead. He must be caught up somewhere. We'll see him tomorrow.*

The people in the compound were looking to him now. There were too many of the dead at the walls. They would have to be dealt with. If his brother was ever going to get back into the compound, they had to do it soon. He had a vision of Reed trapped in the bough of a tree, the dead waving ineffectually at his dangling feet as he straddled a branch above them.

It was darker now. The glow of twilight had disappeared in the blink of an eye. The groans of the dead sounded even worse when there wasn't a face you could put to the sound. They sounded like wounded animals stuck in a trap. Chad had experience with that; for a time, that's all he and his brother did, sit and watch the animals they trapped as they tried to free themselves. He shook his head. No, they didn't sound like trapped animals at all. They sounded like the dead. Trapped animals had more urgency in their squeals, the type of urgency that could get your blood going, the way hearing a blood-curdling scream in real life could make the flesh on your arms do weird things. The dead had no such urgency, but the effect of their groans had the same effect. He rubbed the gooseflesh on his arms as the men lit the bonfire.

Shadows danced off the dusty trailers, and his people were there, looking up at him like a god. He knew he wasn't a god. Hell, he had been told he wasn't shit his whole damn life. But for one moment, he almost felt like he really mattered, like he was more than just a farmhand on some bastard farmer's parcel of land. He felt like someone with power, someone that people looked up to. It was intoxicating, but he didn't let it get to his head. That was Reed's forte. *Damn, where the fuck is he?*

He stood and placed his hands on the railing as he overlooked his people. "Alright, we got ourselves a problem. We got a lot of dead over here, and they're gettin' to be more than is safe for us to let alone. With all that ruckus they're puttin' up, I figure it's probably a good idea to put some of 'em out of their misery. Let's grab the spears and see if we can't make it a little quieter around here for the womenfolk."

Dale and Steve carried a bundle of spears out to the area around the campfire. Each man grabbed a spear while the women tended to the fire, their bellies big and round in the growing firelight. It was good that they were there. The men ought to be able to see what they were fighting for whenever they looked over their shoulders.

Chad hopped down from the watchtower and headed to the pile of spears. "Alright now," he yelled as the men geared up, "I only want one man per trailer. Can't have these roofs caving in, especially seein' as how we're only a few months away from winter. Hey, hey, hey, what do you think you're doin'?" The dark girl, Clara, had reached down to grab a spear before he even realized what was happening. Chad wrapped his rough and callused hand around her wrist and held her in place.

Clara glared at him and said, "I'm going to help."

Chad gripped her wrist and squeezed. He knew he was hurting her, but she didn't drop the spear. She was a tough one. That was for sure. "Drop it."

"I can kill them just as good as any of you."

Her words made him smile; he couldn't help it, and to be honest, it never even crossed his mind that he would piss her off with his attitude. "I doubt it," he said.

She shook free of him then, and he sniffed inward and looked away from her, thumbing his nose as he did. "But I guess if you want to earn your keep around here, we'll let you. You can be in the watchtower with me, so I can keep my eye on you."

She followed him with the spear in her hands, and, whether it was his own hubris or some defect in his brain that made him think he was God's gift to women, he imagined her checking out his backside as he strutted up to the walkway. Clara, of course, did no such thing. She concentrated on not ramming the wooden spear through Chad's back.

When they were on top of the walkway, Chad set the spear against the railing. He reached into his back pocket and pulled out a set of leather work gloves. Those gloves had served him well for the last couple of years. They had mended fences, driven tractors, tossed hay bales, felt up Old Man Bronson's daughter and been covered in so much blood that they were a permanent rusty brown color. He pulled them on and wiggled his fingers until they became like a second skin.

"Usually, I got my brother up here with me."

"Yeah, where is your brother?" Clara asked as she hefted the spear in her hands.

Shit. Me and my stupid mouth. "Oh, he's around. Probably just waiting until we clear out this mess before he comes back in. He likes to wander."

If Clara thought anything untoward about his comments, she kept it to herself. Chad turned back towards the campfire and called over his shoulder, "Hey, Belle, you wanna get that doctor out here? It might help to have her around if anyone gets hurt." A large woman with thighs that reminded him of an elephant rose from around the campfire. She called to another woman, and they set off to roust Joan from her trailer. With those wheels set in motion, he turned around to Clara and said, "Now don't go just stabbin' around. You do that and you're liable to get that spear ripped right out of your hands. You gotta tease 'em a little bit, make 'em want ya some."

He leaned over the railing and looked into the eyes of a dead woman. She looked up at him, her arms raised as if she would catch Chad if he leaped down from the watchtower. "When you get 'em like that, that's what you want. Then you take your spear, and aim for the eye, ya see?" He held his spear up in front of him, both hands wrapped around the shaft. He took aim, and then drove the spear downward. The point entered the dead thing's eye socket, and it crumpled to the ground, sliding off the end of the spear.

"Now you try," he said.

Clara raised her own spear above her head and waited for an opportunity to present itself, but the dead creature below her kept clawing at the wall. "You gotta get its attention. Wave an arm at it. Make it think it's gonna get some dinner."

Clara looked doubtfully at Chad, but then she let her spear drop to the side. She leaned over the railing and dangled her hand just out of reach of the dead thing. It looked up at her, and it had all the hunger in the world on its face.

"There you go," he said. "It's ready." Clara stepped back and raised her spear. She drove it downwards, and it glanced off the creature's cheekbone.

"Nope, not good enough. You gotta be quicker than that."

She brought the spear back again, raised it up high, and then plunged it downward again.

"Yeah! There you go, girl! Just like that!" Clara's spear had punctured the orbital bone of a raggedy woman. The corpse slumped to the ground, sliding easily off the spear. "Now when you do that, make sure you hold on good to that spear. Sometimes, they don't just go limp like that. Sometimes they buck and spasm, and they can rip that damn spear right out of your hands. We run out of spears and we're up shit creek without a paddle."

Clara looked at him. He could see the determination on her face. It reminded him of Dez... at least, how Dez

252

used to be. He liked that look. He liked it a lot. Reed could have Joan, but this one was his. After that, they worked in silence. There must have been thirty or forty shamblers out there. It was the most they had ever seen, but their defenses had held up.

"Where the hell are they all coming from?" he wondered aloud to himself. If Clara knew, she didn't answer.

With each of Clara's kills, he congratulated her and encouraged her, secretly hoping that he was winning her over the way one might tame a wild dog. When the last thing was dead, he stood back and let his spear rest on the wooden boards of the watchtower. He pulled his gloves from his hands and reached into his shirt pocket. He pulled a pack of cigarettes free. He had pulled them from the shirt pocket of one of the dead after he had put a bullet through its head, so there was some dried gore on the package, but beggars couldn't be choosers, and he had no issue sucking down the smokes of a dead man.

"You want one?" he asked.

She wiped sweat from her brow, and in the quiet of the compound, he could see a fire in her eyes. She had the fever, the fever of killing. He had seen that look in his brother. He doubted he had the same look in his eye. He derived no pleasure from killing the dead. "Yeah, I'll take one," she said.

He lit the cigarette and put it to his lips. He took a long drag, and then passed it to Clara. "Ain't enough for me to just be giving these away, but I'll share it with ya." He marked the disappointment on her face, but she took it anyway. They stood that way in silence, passing the cigarette back and forth. When it was done, they jumped down from the watchtower. A chill had fallen upon the compound, the type of cold that made you want to crawl under your blankets all the way, head and all.

He noticed Clara's hands. The skin was shredded from the rough wood of the spear. "You ought to have your friend look at your hands. You don't want to get an infection. Not a lot of antibiotics goin' around, ya know?" Clara nodded, and he watched as she headed on over to Joan and sat next to her.

They looked glorious there by the firelight, two angels sitting in the orange glow. He stood and walked away from the light, a plan burning in his heart.

****

The interior of the camper was cold, but he heard the raspy breathing of the man he had thrown into the campfire just two days before. He walked through the gloom of the camper, resisting the urge to turn the light on.

"I'm sorry about this pal, I really am." Chad put his hand to the man's head. He was burning up. Chances were that the man would die from his wounds, but chances were things that he didn't take anymore. It was too dangerous.

He stood there in the dark, wondering what he should do. He didn't want to do it; he had never liked to kill anything. See 'em hurt, oh yeah, that's just good fun. But to actually kill something that was still alive, let alone a man... he had no stomach for it. Now if Reed were here, that would be a different story. But Reed wasn't here. He was holed up in a rundown house somewhere, probably doing things to the pregnant woman that he didn't really want to know about. He knew about Dez and Reed. Hell, he had put him up to it basically, in the hopes that maybe Dez would move on from him and find some spark of who she used to be, but she was even worse after Reed fucked her.

He knew he and Dez were done, or else he wouldn't even be in here. He wouldn't be standing over this poor bastard wondering if he should kill the man first and then stab him in the brain, or just stab him in the brain right off

254

and get the whole thing over with. Decisions, decisions. In the end, he decided to smother the man.

He pulled the pillow from behind his head, and he placed it over the man's face, pressing down firmly, but not firm enough to crush anything. The man's arms shot out, clawing at him, and Chad suppressed a giggle. Had the man merely been sleeping? *Well, how about that for a stroke of luck?* The bastard could have awoken at any moment and ruined all of his scheming.

Chad stood that way for several moments, and then he slowly backed away from the dead man on the bed. He would let them find him; it was their right.

****

Joan tended to the wounds on Clara's hands, but her mind was elsewhere. Her mind was on Lou. Just before the large lady and her friend had come to carry her out, he had stirred. His eyes were damaged beyond all repair. He would be blind for the rest of his life. This was a certainty.

When Lou had groaned in pain, she had said, "I'm here."

"Who is it?" Lou had moaned.

"It's Joan."

He smiled then. It had broken her heart, to see this man, this great man knocked so low. He was suffering, but still he was able to smile. His hand pawed the air, and she grabbed it, squeezing his hand.

"Did you kill them?"

"Kill who?"

"The man that did this to me?"

Joan shook her head, tears forming in her eyes. But Lou couldn't see it. "No, we're still in the compound."

His face became grave. He squeezed her hand. "You have to get out of here. This place is no good."

Lou had fallen asleep then. As she digested his words, a large pregnant woman and her friend barged into the trailer. They had that look on their faces that women immediately recognized, that of the tortured and spiteful. They didn't like Joan because she wasn't like them. She didn't have the face of a pig and the limbs of an elephant. Despite the fact that Joan had no intention of staying here now, she knew that these women saw her as a threat. She could see it in the gruff manner in which they spoke to her. She could see it in the looks on their faces. They were threatened by her, and they would do anything they could to take her down a peg. That she was on the lowest rung on the ladder didn't matter to them; they would want her off the damn thing completely. They had lived their whole lives as balls of insecurity, and now, with the world the way it was, they had become important... simply because of what was between their legs. Now with Joan and Clara in the picture, they felt their importance diminishing, and for this, Joan would have to pay.

"Come on, princess. It's time to do some work," the larger one said. She had a face like a trailer park queen, fashioned through years of eating McDonald's and drinking Coors Light. She was beautiful in her own way, Joan decided, like one of those velvet Elvis paintings or the unnatural sheen of melted Velveeta.

"What do you mean?" she asked.

"Chad wants you out there in case anyone gets hurt." With that, the large lady and her friend came and lifted her out of bed. She thought about protesting, but these women could manhandle her in the condition that she was in, and there was nothing she could do about it.

They carried her from the trailer, Joan's arms looped over their shoulders while the larger lady supported her broken leg. It still hurt like a motherfucker, and Joan thought then and there that she could easily kill the two of them if it meant getting the materials to make a proper cast for her broken leg.

They carried her down the stairs and out to the campfire. They placed her in an ancient Adirondack chair. It creaked under her weight, and the larger woman, Belle they called her, brought her a stool to keep her leg in an elevated position.

"Comfortable, princess?" Belle asked this with no warmth, no derision, no judgment. She was just doing her job. Joan nodded her head. All around her, men were moving, climbing ladders that led to the tops of the trailers. They had spears in their hands, and battery-operated lamps glowed a brilliant white as they set them upon poles on top of the trailers, freeing their hands up for killing.

It seemed all Joan could do was wait. In the meantime, Belle and her friend tended to the campfire, dropping logs in occasionally, and it suddenly struck Joan... this is as close to camping as I'll ever be. She had never been a particularly outdoorsy person. Most of her outdoor activity had consisted of a jog here and there through local parks, and while these jaunts could technically count as being immersed in nature, she had never been more than a mile from buildings and civilization. The illuminated undersides of trees disappeared into an impenetrable darkness, and she suddenly felt small.

"So you're a doctor, eh?" the other woman asked her. Belle shot her a look that said, "Don't talk to the prisoners," but if the other woman saw it, she didn't react.

"I was a doctor," she said conversationally, seeing no advantage in giving the two ladies even more of a reason to hate her. "What about you?"

"I was a waitress. Nowhere fancy. Applebee's."

Joan just shook her head. What else could she do? Applebee's? Not much to talk about there. "What was your name again?"

"Theresa," the woman replied.

"I'm Belle," the large woman said begrudgingly.

"I'm Joan," she said with a smile that only an idiot couldn't see was fake. Neither Theresa nor Belle seemed to notice. "So how did you guys wind up here?"

"See that guy up there?" Theresa asked. Joan turned and looked at the top of one of the trailers. A man in a plaid shirt plunged a spear downward. When it came back, it shone wet in the lamplight.

"Yeah," Joan said.

"That's my brother, Keith. He lived in the trailer park where Chad and Reed lived. When things started going down, the people in the trailer park didn't know what to do. But Chad knew. He got the bright idea of getting all the trailers mobile and dragging them out here."

"The roads weren't all clogged up?"

"Plenty of road around here, Joan. You just gotta know the right ones. The highways are fucked, but there are more than enough logging roads to get from here all the way to the coast. You just gotta know the right way," Belle said, as if she had just imparted a trade secret.

Theresa added, "My brother was a logger. He knows the way, but it was still slow going. Trailers aren't so easy to move, especially not up logging roads, but we did it."

Theresa was proud of this fact. It was plain to hear in her voice. Joan was unimpressed. They had simply relocated a trailer park to the middle of nowhere. "Did you ever think about going to the coast?"

"What for?" Belle guffawed. "You in the mood for some clam chowder?"

The two cackled like witches, loud and obnoxious. Joan envied them this freedom. She couldn't remember the last time she had laughed as hard as the two ladies had, over a poor joke even. She also envied their relaxed nature in general. She had seen too many horrors in the last couple of months. Even now, she felt like she should be on top of the trailers with Clara making sure that none of the dead breached the walls.

These two had seen none of that. They had stayed with these men and played house. That's why they could laugh like that. She sat there through the night, listening to them go on and on like a couple of madwomen, talking about things that didn't matter anymore. They were content. They were happy, but Joan was none of these things. Lou's words ran through her mind, and she worried for him. Even if he survived his burns, he would be a blind man in a world where the dead could appear as if by magic.

She watched as Clara and Chad jumped down from the barricade. She followed him from the corner of her eye. The man disappeared into the shadows that surrounded the trailer she had been living in for the last day. She wanted to scream at Clara to stop him, but she knew that would just get them both in hot water.

Instead, she had to do the harder thing. She had to sit there and pretend like that man wasn't going to go in there and kill Lou. But she knew that was what he was doing. She knew that she was sacrificing Lou for herself and Clara, and she hated herself for it. She despised this place. She wanted to see it burn to the ground, with these cackling heifers sizzling in the middle.

As she cleaned and bandaged Clara's hands, tears sprang to her eyes, but she willed them away. When she was done, she stared into the fire, and when the men atop the trailers called a halt to the work, she sat there meekly as they told their stories. They made themselves sound like conquering heroes; Achilles and Hercules had nothing on these men. They did not fear the dead. They made the dead their "bitches," as they were so fond of saying.

As Chad reappeared, Joan swallowed the words she had in the back of her throat. She swallowed the hate that flowed in her gut and threatened to suffocate her. She smiled at Clara as if everything were ok, though it wasn't.

Later, as the men smoked dope and most of the women went to bed, Belle and Theresa carried Joan back to her trailer. Clara followed along, her spear long since put away. There was no need of it, after all.

Belle and Theresa continued their inane chatter. "Dale's going to want a piece of me tonight, I bet," Belle said. Joan wondered which one was Dale. Was he Theresa's brother too? Who else would want a piece of these ogres?

"Oh, you wish," Theresa said.

"You're just jealous because no one wants a piece of you," Belle shot back.

As Theresa yanked open the door to the trailer, someone did take a piece of Belle. It was Lou, on his feet, groping with his hands. He found Belle's long greasy hair, and Joan was dropped unceremoniously to the ground. Belle's screams were not unlike the cackles she and Theresa had shared earlier, loud and insane. But this time, the pain came through. This time, Belle saw the horror that she had been missing out on within the cozy confines of the compound.

Then Joan screamed in pain as she was yanked backwards by her hair. Her hands shot up to grab the fists knotted in her hair, and this lessened the pain somewhat. She looked up to see Clara pulling her backwards, and she knew she was going to be alright.

The men came rushing, coughing up marijuana smoke, their faces red, their eyes uncomprehending, all except for Chad. He knew what was waiting in that trailer. He knew Lou was dead because he had killed their friend himself. He rushed past Clara and Joan, spear in his hand. Men raised burning sticks high, as Chad rushed in, a dashing hero to them, an evil villain to Joan.

By firelight, Chad jammed the spear through Lou's skull. He fell to the ground, his face covered in blood. Belle got up screaming. Her large, floral print muumuu was covered in her own blood, and she screamed and screamed.

And for the first time in a long time, Joan laughed a laugh that could not be contained, a big throaty chuckle that contained within it all the irony the world could muster.

Later, the men, disturbed by her callousness, would explain it away as a sort of delirium, a woman's weakness at seeing violence. But in their hearts, they knew the truth. Their new doctor had no love for them and would be happy to see them all die.

As Belle was led away, Chad ordered two men to bring the doctor. Joan laughed as she was picked up and carried into the big house. She laughed as the men set her down. Chad slapped her hard across the face, and Joan tried to kill him with her eyes.

"Save the baby," Chad said.

"It's already dead," Joan replied.

"Save it, or your friend is next."

Joan looked to Clara who had followed her into the house. "I'm going to need some things."

"You name it," Chad said.

She listed off the things she would need, and then the men went to work sterilizing her tools. Belle screamed the whole time, and from another room, Joan could hear another woman cussing up a storm.

"Shut that fucking hog up!" the voice screamed.

When she had everything she needed, she went to work.

****

Clara crawled into bed after Joan. It had been a long procedure, bloody, brutal, and one-hundred percent futile. The tools that the men presented her with were nothing like the sort Joan had needed to try and successfully do what needed to be done. They were sterile though, not that it mattered. Halfway through the procedure, Belle had passed away. They tied her arms and legs as her body cooled, so that her corpse, when it reanimated, wouldn't attack them.

261

The baby had been born stillborn. It was a boy. It did not come back to life. Joan was thankful for that. Whatever this disease was, it was not present in the newborns. Whether they would carry it once they were born into the world was another mystery that would have to wait. Clara guessed that it would. The disease was in all of them. Each of them, when they died in their turn, would reanimate again... but at least a fetus was still protected from this hell by the barriers between mother and child.

"They killed Lou," Joan said.

The words didn't surprise Clara. She had noticed Chad's absence, and she had known it was no good.

"They were the ones that threw him into the fire," Joan said.

Clara squeezed her eyes shut. A cocktail of emotions flooded her system. She wanted to scream. She wanted to cry. But most of all, she just wanted this nightmare to be over with. They were dropping like flies here, and now there were only four of them left, if Katie and Mort were still out there somewhere. Who knew? By now they could be dead as well. They might be the only ones left.

One thing she knew was that they couldn't stay here. "We have to get out of this place."

Joan sniffled in the dark, and then she spoke. She sounded tired, beat down. "We can't leave. I can't survive out there with my leg like this. Even if the roads were clear, I wouldn't be able to go more than a mile a day, and the roads aren't clear. They're clogged with cars and the dead."

"I know." She had known all the reasons why they couldn't escape before Joan had even said them.

"What are we gonna do?" Joan asked.

"We're going to do the only thing we can do." She placed her hand on Joan's shoulder. "We're going to survive." In silence, they shed their tears for Lou.

262

Chapter 15: The Journal

Tejada sat on the lawn of the Nike campus. In his head, thoughts rolled around like thunderheads. There was definitely a storm coming. The only question was, could he ride the lightning and bring his men out unharmed on the other side?

The biggest problem so far had been his loyalty. His men came first; there was no question about that. But after that, how important was anyone else? He had meant it when he had said there were no heroes anymore... but did that mean that he shouldn't try? Were the people of the Nike campus expendable? Could he do what thousands of generals over the history of humanity had done to survive and just take what he wanted and not give a fuck about who he was taking it from?

He shook his head. First thing was first. Time to clear out the armory. His sources had collected enough information that Tejada had been able to fill in the blanks. Soon after the shit had hit the fan, the security had turned on the regular civilians of the Nike campus. Nike had set it up so that they all died, chewed to death by their own men in their sleep. How he had accomplished the particulars of that feat was still a mystery, but the word was that Nike's goon Harper had a hand in it. He suspected some sort of drugging. There was no way that a security force, no matter how shitty would just keep sleeping while their fellow guards were killed. The dead did not maintain operational silence... they caused fear and screams wherever they went. Even if they had been that shitty, there wasn't a single person left in this world who wasn't a light sleeper. It just didn't add up.

That meant that Nike had his supporters, his conspirators. The only question was, what would happen to these people once they left? Tejada and his soldiers would leave; that was a certainty. This place was a dead zone.

263

Those walls wouldn't last forever, not if the dead from Portland made it this way. They would eventually, he was sure of that. It might not be today. It might not be tomorrow, but someday, the million dead bodies that were in and around Portland would show up on the doorstep, and then those walls weren't going to be worth a piss in a hurricane.

"We're ready, sir."

Tejada pushed himself up off the ground. His bones were sore. It wasn't just fatigue; it was a result of getting old. He had aches now, constant aches in his shoulders and hips. Some mornings were better than others, and today wasn't one of the good ones. *Christ, will I even live long enough to get old?*

"Let's move 'em out."

The men walked across the courtyard, heading to the former security building. In their hands, they held baseball bats, liberated from the Ken Griffey Jr. tribute wall. They weren't doing anyone any good stuck to the wall, and half his men had no ammunition, and the other half were nearly out. Tejada hoped that they would be able to restock in the armory of the security building, but first they would have to clear the damned thing out.

From the corner of his eye, he saw a man rushing up to him. It was Nike. He was trying to make it look like he wasn't in a panic, but Tejada suspected the last time that man had moved that fast was some time ago.

"Sergeant? Sergeant, I need to talk to you!"

"So talk," Tejada said.

"Just what do you think you're doing?" Nike asked indignantly. Tejada had heard that type of voice many times over the years. It was a politician's voice, a voice used to thinking they were the brightest, smartest, and best person in the room. Tejada knew that Nike was none of these things. He knew that Nike was a piece of shit.

He stopped his walk across the campus. His men kept going, but Tejada wanted Nike to see his face when he talked. "We're going to clear out that security building. You said you wanted our help here, well, we can't do that without weapons. So there it is."

"You can't do that," Nike said.

"And why the hell not?"

Nike was flustered. He fumbled for an answer, and the one that he came up with was about as useful as a dick on a toadstool. "Because you're putting us all at risk."

Tejada nodded as Rudy and Amanda walked past, baseball bats twirling in their hands. "At risk?" Tejada could hardly believe the temerity of the man. "At risk? Motherfucker, you're at risk here every second of every day. Did you not learn anything from what happened the other night? Each one of these buildings is an abscess, an infection, and if we don't fix it up now, sooner or later this whole place is going to die, including your pampered, spoiled rotten ass." Tejada said this last part so loud that the civilians that watched couldn't help but overhear it. Some of their hands went to their mouths, but most of them seemed satisfied with it. They didn't want Nike here anymore than Tejada did, not all of them. Tejada suspected that wouldn't be a problem for very long.

"You're making a mistake," Nike said with finality.

"Sometimes you have to." With that, Tejada turned his back on the man and caught up with his soldiers.

"You going in with that bowling ball, Walt?" Tejada asked.

The young man smiled at him, hefted his bowling ball and said, "Bowling balls don't break. Baseball bats do."

It was good logic. Tejada had Masterson go and pull a dozen more bats off the wall, just in case. He came back carrying them like an armload of firewood.

"Anyone breaks a bat, don't be a hero. Hightail it back here, grab another and get back in line. You got that?"

"Yes, sir," came the chorus.

"Would you do the honors, Nike?"

Nike stepped forward, the keycard around his neck held in his hands. "You're making a big mistake."

"He heard you the first time, asshole," Whiteside said.

Nike bent down and placed the keycard over a nondescript square reader, then he backed up. As he passed Tejada, the sergeant snaked a hand under the lanyard around Nike's neck. "I'll take that," Tejada said. Nike didn't argue. The dead were already at the doors.

"Alright, open it up!" Tejada yelled as Nike turned and ran.

Rudy, their heaviest man let the door open a crack, and one of the dead stumbled out. Rudy and Masterson pushed the door closed, and it locked with a click. The dead man had that military look about him. Large chunks of flesh were missing from his neck and arms, but he was mobile enough.

"Come and get it, motherfucker," said Gregg as he moved backwards, drawing the dead man's attention away from Rudy. The zombie stumbled after him as Gregg danced backwards, watching each step as he backpedaled down the small flight of steps that led up to the building.

"Batter up!" Tejada yelled.

Whiteside ran forward, baseball bat at the ready as the dead man hit the last step. He took a swing and the dead man rocked sideways, somehow still standing on its feet. Whiteside danced away.

"Next batter!" Tejada shouted.

This time Brown ran up. He clocked the damn thing so hard one of the dead thing's eyeballs popped out of socket. It crumpled to the ground, and a cheer went up from the onlookers behind them. Tejada smiled and waved at them.

"Get him out of there!" Tejada yelled.

266

Amanda and Allen, wearing yellow rubber gloves that went up to their elbows, pulled the man off to the side.

"Check its pockets, then douse the motherfucker," Tejada snapped at them.

The two rifled through the man's pockets, producing a lighter, some loose rounds of ammunition, a pocket knife, and a pack of smokes.

"We got smokes!" Whiteside yelled.

"Don't get too excited. No one touches anything until that building is cleared," Tejada said. Whiteside's head dropped, but he was raring to go in the blink of an eye.

Amanda and Allen had finished going through the man's pockets. They doused his body with gasoline and then lit him up. Inky black smoke spread into the air. Allen looked at it going into the sky. Tejada wondered what he saw with that poet's brain of his.

Tejada shouted, "Send out the next one, Rudy!" He tossed the key card to Rudy, and he looped it over his neck. He bent down and touched the card to the reader, there was a small click, the door opened, and another Annie came shooting out the gates.

"You want some of this? Come on, ugly!" Epps yelled at it, leading it down the steps.

"This one's yours, Walt!" Tejada yelled.

Walt, his skin brown from the sun, stepped up, twirling the bowling ball as if it were nothing more than an orange on a string. He changed the direction of his twirling and then suddenly, the eight-pound ball was crushing the side of the dead man's head. It dropped to the ground, and Amanda and Allen dragged it out of the way.

"Home run! Nice one, Walt!" Day yelled, and he held out his hand for a high five, which Walt gleefully returned.

Brown chided Whiteside. "See that, hillbilly? One swing. You think you can do that?"

"Oh, bring it on! Most homers gets them smokes," Whiteside said.

Things continued that way for some time. A pile of possessions accumulated on the ground, and more smoke filled the sky. His men were having a good time, perhaps too good. Tejada turned around for a second to keep an eye on what was going on behind him. He saw the Nike residents standing there, their hands shading their eyes in the midday sun. The look on their faces did not match the looks on his men's faces. They were not celebrating; they were not having a good time. They were revolted.

Tejada sucked on his teeth, and he wondered if he should give a fuck. There was going to be a lot more revolting business before this was all over and done. There were at least 15 buildings to clear out before Tejada would call this place safe, well, fifteen buildings and a couple of rats.

He supposed it was his training that made him reign the men in, that and a little embarrassment. These people had been human after all, and they had made a game of killing them. "Alright, let's tone it down a bit! We got an audience."

His soldiers looked over their shoulders at him, but they nodded. The hooting and hollering stopped, and they were serious once again.

Another hulking man stumbled out the door as Masterson pushed it shut behind him. Whiteside stepped up and swung his bat. It broke across the man's giant skull, but the man kept coming. "Aw, hell no," Whiteside said.

Tejada could see what he was going to do next, and he yelled at his man. "Leave it, Whiteside!"

Whiteside took the broken handle of his bat and ran at the dead man. He jammed the sharp end of the bat into the creature's face, but he missed anything brain related. The Annie wrapped two gray hands around Whiteside's throat and squeezed, despite the baseball bat sticking out of its mouth. Whiteside's eyes bulged out of his head, and Tejada pulled his pistol from its holster. He took the shot, and the big man fell backwards, his hands locked tight around Whiteside's neck. Whiteside fell on top of him, pummeling the man with his fists. His face was turning blue.

Epps was the first one there. He yanked on the Annie's fingers, but Whiteside was in a true death grip. Epps gave up and said, "This is going to hurt."

He kicked at the Annie's hands, connecting with Whiteside's face in the process. By the second kick, Whiteside was unconscious, but Epps had managed to break the dead Annie's grip around his throat.

"Check his pulse," Tejada yelled.

Brown and Epps squatted next to Whiteside as they rolled him onto his back. "He's still breathing," Epps said.

"Thank god for that," Tejada said. "Alright, Epps, Brown, take Whiteside inside. Everyone else take a breather."

Walt walked over to the pile of possessions they had found on the dead. He plucked the pack of cigarettes from the pile, and Amanda said, "What are you doing?"

"It's for Whiteside, when he wakes up. I owe him some anyway." Amanda nodded.

They waited in silence, the reality of their situation suddenly striking home. When Brown and Epps returned, Tejada gathered everyone around him and made sure they drank some water and rested their bodies.

"I just want to remind you guys that we're not playin' around out here. One stumble, one trip, and it could be over for you. Whiteside almost found that out. Don't ever get comfortable with these things. When you think you know it all, when you think you got it all figured out, that's when you die. You understand?"

"Yes, sir," came the chorus.

"Now, we've got a couple more on the ground floor to take care of, and then it's time to sweep and clear. We find any keys on the one's we killed?" Tejada asked.

"Plenty of keys, but I'm not sure which ones will open the armory," Allen said.

"Well, we'll worry about that when the time comes. Let's divide up our ammo, we're going to do this place one floor at a time. I don't even want a closet left unturned. You see a toilet bowl with the lid down, you flip that fucker up. I don't want someone going to take a shit and getting their ass bit."

They laughed at this, and Tejada took the opportunity to drive his point home. "You think I'm joking. I am not fucking joking. Take this seriously people."

They nodded and then took their positions again. Rudy pulled the door open, and an Annie came stumbling out. As Gregg lured it down the steps, Walt bashed its brains in with his bowling ball. Amanda and Allen dragged it out of the way, and Rudy let the last visible Annie out. The process continued, without incident, and then, when the last two Annies were smoldering on the pile, the soldiers checked and rechecked that their rifles and sidearms were locked and loaded.

"Let's go see what Santa brought us," Tejada said. The soldiers entered the security building. Rudy and Amanda stood outside waiting apprehensively, trying to not make eye contact with the Nike people who stood on the campus lawn, watching all of the proceedings.

****

Epps stepped into the foyer of the building. The floor was cold concrete, rough so that you could see individual stones. He broke to his left, heading for the west wing of the building. Masterson and Gregg clung tight to him, covering his back and sides. He pushed open a door handle, and the door swung inward. Nothing pushed back,

270

which was a good sign. He stepped into a room full of cubicles. Computers sat dark and unused. He spotted a monitor with a bullet hole in it. Blood smeared the floors and the walls.

"This place must have been a slaughterhouse," he whispered. He stepped inside, and they cleared each cubicle, popping into each opening set in the five-foot high walls. The paneled ceiling above was splattered with dried gore. The smell of death hung in the office, and they knew something dead was there. Whether it was mobile or not was the real question.

He found nothing in the first cubicle, but in the second, he found a man dressed in a black security uniform. His legs had been separated from the upper half of his body. The upper half was still functional, and Epps put a round in his skull without thinking twice. The gunshot brought movement from other cubicles, and Epps watched as heads popped up over the cubicle walls. They took their time lining up shots, and when they were done, there were four more bodies to add to the pile. Their gun smoke clung to the air, and they pushed through the office making sure no more crawlers were left. That was what Masterson had called the half-man; it was as good a name as any.

They looked under desks and behind chairs. They pulled weapons free from bodies and slung them over their shoulders, thankful for the additional rounds. Epps preferred to use his own weapon, but if he ran out of ammo, which he would with two pulls of the trigger, he wanted something to fall back on besides his dick.

When they were sure that the office was clear, they moved back to the first-floor foyer, being just as careful as when they had come into the place. In the foyer, Masterson stood guard at the staircase. If anything came down those steps, Masterson would vent their heads. Gregg watched the office doors, and Epps waited until the other groups returned from sweeping the other part of the ground floor.

It took a while, but after a few gunshots, they came back grim-faced and holding more weapons. Tejada gestured to Epps, and they knew that the rest of the floor was clear. With Masterson in the lead, they pushed up to the second of three floors.

The second floor was where the important people worked. Here there were nameplates bolted to the walls. Each office had its own door. This would make things both safer and more difficult. While the odds that the dead would come swarming out of the offices were low, each office offered its own surprise, especially since the lights were off in most of them.

Epps switched on the flashlight attached to the end of his rifle as they approached the first such door. He gave Gregg the signal, and he threw the door open. Epps shined his flashlight into the murk, but there was nothing there as far as he could tell. The spring-loaded door began to shut on its own.

"Get the lights," Epps said.

Gregg reached in and flipped on the lights. They saw a regular office, untouched, normal, no signs of violence.

"Let's get the next one," Epps said. This time they rotated positions. It was Epps' turn to throw open the door while Masterson and Gregg waited with their flashlights. Just as he reached for the door handle, he heard a gunshot. It caused him to flinch. Masterson leaned back into the hallway and looked to see if there was any trouble. He gave Epps the thumbs up, and he turned his attention back to the door just in time to see an Annie's face pressed up against the rectangular glass window. Gregg fired off a shot immediately, and Epps felt it whistle by his head.

The glass shattered, and the face of the Annie disappeared. "You fucking, halfwit. You could have killed me," Epps hissed.

Gregg said nothing. He knew he was in the wrong.

272

"Is it dead?" Masterson asked.

"I don't know. I was too busy having my life flash in front of my eyes." Epps depressed the door handle and tried to push inward, but a rotten arm burst through the shattered glass of the door's window and grabbed Epps' arm. It squeezed with great pressure, and Epps lowered his shoulder into the door, slamming it backwards as hard as he could. He felt some resistance, and then whatever was on the other side bashed into the wall. Epps and the door rebounded off the creature, and it finally released its grip on his arm. Epps fell to the ground and scrambled backwards. The door slowly closed on its own.

"Fuck," he muttered, his heart fluttering in his chest. "Shine those lights on there."

Masterson and Gregg painted the black rectangular square with their lights as Epps edged closer to the door. His forearm throbbed from the Annie's attack, but the skin wasn't broken. Something fiddled with the door handle. "Here, Annie, Annie." He continued calling the dead thing until an arm shot out of the window. He grabbed the arm and sunk to the ground with it until the Annie's face was framed against the window. "Get it," he said as he struggled to hold onto the dead arm. Its flesh was cold and clammy and covered in a slick layer of something that could only be described as rot.

Masterson lined up the shot, and the round punched through the Annie's head. The creature's arm spasmed in Epps' hands, and then the Annie fell away, thumping to the ground on the other side of the door. Epps got to his feet, wiping his hands on his fatigues. He pushed open the door, still being careful, still following protocol, Sergeant Tejada's warnings about being careful ringing in his ears. He flipped the light switch, and the florescent lights came on.

In the corner, another body sat slumped on the ground, a handgun in its hands. Its face was unrecognizable, and Epps couldn't tell if the body belonged to a man or a woman. Flies buzzed in the room and maggots crawled across the corpse. The smell was awful. They could come back and check the bodies later. This room was clear.

They continued clearing out the offices, finding only two more bodies, and no more Annies. They rendezvoused with the other soldiers, and then it was time to tackle the third floor. Epps would be glad when this was all over. His nerves were getting to the point of being shot. This was the time when mistakes were made. He shook his head and told Masterson and Gregg to take a breather, while he guarded the staircase. He didn't want their fatigue leading to their demise or his for that matter.

When everyone had caught their breath, they climbed the stairs to the third floor, hoping that this was where the armory was. As they reached the landing, Epps could barely hide his disgust. Bodies lay in beds, chewed to nothing. The entire third floor had been converted to a bunkhouse with about as much privacy as you'd see in an old prison movie.

Twenty double-decker bunks lined the walls. The smell was dreadful, and Epps reached into his pocket to grab a bandana to tie over his face. Once it was in place, it barely helped. The smell was still so strong that it penetrated his makeshift mask. They pushed forward, but Epps could make neither heads nor tails of the carnage he saw. Body parts lay strewn about like a child's play things left out at the end of the day. He couldn't tell what piece went with what body. The soldiers stepped through the mess, none of them making a single noise. They trampled through dried blood puddles because there was no other way to move through the makeshift dormitory. The carnage was so brutal that many of the security guards hadn't even come back to life. He didn't know if they were lucky on that account or not.

274

Across the way, he saw Tejada stop at a door set into a back wall. Tejada waved at Epps, and he approached the door yet again, hating that he had been nominated for this duty once more. It was much better to be the person taking aim with a gun than to be the door-opener he had decided. He grasped a silver doorknob and made eye contact with Tejada. Tejada nodded, and Epps threw the door open. The lights were still on in this room.

At first, Epps thought the room was clear. As he stepped into the room, he realized they were in an armory. Beautiful guns of all sizes and shapes sat like shadows on racks, their black stocks and barrels pristine and new. Then Epps noticed the blood on the floor as Gregg and Masterson followed him into the room.

From behind a counter in the center of the room, a shape rose up. It was fresher than the other dead, its body not nearly as gone to rot. It showed little damage, but for a small wound on its hand. It stumbled towards Epps, and Epps raised his rifle to his eye, aimed, fired, and watched as the man fell to the ground, his jaw crashing into the counter on its way to the ground.

"Clear!" Epps yelled, hoping that today's nightmare was almost at an end. He thought perhaps he would need something extra to sleep tonight. It was becoming tougher and tougher for Epps to try and catch some good shut eye. He was reminded of when he used to go rock climbing with his friends. On one particular day, he had been halfway up a cliff face, when he had stopped on a ledge to plan his next move. His leg, so filled with tension for the last half-hour had started bouncing back and forth uncontrollably. Climbers called it sewing machine leg. His whole body felt like that these days. He had been tense for so long, seen so many terrors, that he didn't know how much more his body could physically take. He jumped as Tejada slapped him on the shoulder.

"Looks like we found the armory," Tejada said smiling. "Maybe we can get the fuck out of this place after all."

"Sir?" Epps asked.

Tejada looked at him, one eyebrow cocked.

"You're not planning on abandoning these people, are you, sir?"

"It's not abandoning if you never joined them in the first place," Tejada said in reply.

Epps just kept quiet. It was not the way that Epps thought about the situation, but he owed the Sergeant that one. Who could ever question the guy? Certainly no one in this building.

"Get a load of this," Gregg said.

They moved to the other side of the counter. On the ground, there were empty food wrappers and water bottles scattered about. Old bandages lay crumpled on the floor along with an empty bottle of antiseptic. A gray Moleskin journal lay on the floor, a couple of bloody fingerprints marring its cover. Tejada bent down to pick it up. He flipped the cover open and read the first page, his lips moving as he read.

Tejada closed the cover and then said, "Burn the bodies, keep two guards on the front door. You see that Harper fucker coming your way, put a bullet in his head. That asshole's not getting shit from here, and neither is anyone else."

"Yes, sir," Epps said. He picked out Allen and volunteered himself for guard duty. He wanted to be out of the building anyway.

Tejada removed himself to another room to read the journal. The first words sent a chill up his spine.

****

I left them there sitting at home, my family... the money was too good. I thought by leaving Sue and the kids

276

with my brother Bobby, they would be safe, and once this whole thing blew over, we'd be rich. But this thing isn't blowing over.

We finished getting the wall up today, and just in time. Martial law has been declared, but we haven't seen anyone from the army for a couple of days now. The skies are clear, no more airplanes, no more helicopters. In the first week, we saw several small prop planes fleeing from the city, now there are only birds in the sky. They don't sing like they used to. They sit silently in the trees, watching and waiting. Gives me the fucking creeps.

****

June 16th

The dead are at the walls right now. They press themselves against it as if they know there is food on the other side. I don't know how they know. Everyone is silent. When people talk, they do it in whispers.

There are too many people here, and my men are nervous. Maybe Sue and the kids are better off with Bobby out there. This place is like a powder keg. You can feel the tension. The employees here look at me with fear in their eyes. They are afraid of my gun, all of our guns. I bet before this, the closest any of these college-educated liberals had been to a gun was on the TV.

The CEO is assuring me that they'll get used to us, but what the fuck does he know? What the fuck do any of us know?

The men want to clear the walls, but I think it's better to save our ammo for when we need it. We're safe in here. Based upon what's happening on the news, that's a rare thing.

****

June 17th

We had to shoot some people today. A couple people tried to climb the walls. Nike said they had to die. I would have been happy to let them in, but he made a good point. We didn't know if they were infected or not. The men that killed them are shaken.

Most of these guys are tough, experienced, but they've never been in a position to kill Americans, especially not Americans just looking for a safe place to survive. I have to admit I'm not looking forward to sleep tonight. I expect nightmares. The guilt I carry is twofold. For the deaths of that family and for the fact that I left my own family out there. I can't get a hold of Bobby.

Maybe I should take my toys and leave.

****

June 20th

There's a lot of smoke coming from the west. Portland must be on fire. There's more smoke around us, but so far, we haven't had to deal with any fires. Still, I got the men rigging hoses around the campus just in case. We'll drain the lake to put out a fire if we need to.

The CEO is calling himself Nike now. He's insisting that everyone takes new names. My men laughed at the idea. I had two guys arguing over who gets to be Wolverine. I'm beginning to hate that CEO.

I tried to think of a mythical figure that abandoned their children. The idea seemed fitting, but I couldn't come up with one. So I just kept my regular name. Nike argued with me about it. Thought about killing him, but I don't know what that would do to the people here. They look to him for leadership. I'm just a pawn in their eyes, a foreigner, a stranger. They might stick with me if I killed him, or they might turn on us. I just don't know.

We killed ten more people trying to get over the wall today. They had kids with them. Fuck, what are we doing here?

278

****

June 23rd
Haven't been good about writing in this thing. My thoughts are almost constantly with my wife and kids these days. I can still see their faces. I got a picture of them on my phone. When I look at it, their eyes seem accusing, harsh. I can't look at it for long without my eyes tearing up. Still nothing from Bobby, phones aren't working, but I've got a radio here. I put Tate in charge of it.

I may have to rotate that position. All the man hears is distress calls and horror stories. There's some guy out there broadcasting a radio station, lots of oldies. I'm pretty sure he's trapped somewhere and just trying to keep from going insane. I get it.

The days are blending together now. There's no more Mondays or Tuesdays. There's just Hellday, and we get seven of them in a row before we get another seven.

We only killed five people today for trying to climb our walls. I guess it was a good day.
****

June 24th
The power is out. The lights flickered on the campus, and everything went dark. The solar power collectors kicked in, and we at least have lights and enough juice to prepare food. At night it's dark, so dark that you can't see anything outside the wall. All you can hear are their groans and their constant scratching at the walls.

Had a couple of men kill themselves today. They were smart about it though. They put the bullets right through their brains so that they wouldn't come back. We buried them behind the security building. I talked to the men, tried to let them know that suicide wasn't the way out... but hell, it's not like I haven't thought of it from time to time.

279

The only thing that keeps me from doing it is the hope of an afterlife. I don't know much about religion, but I know that you don't get to heaven by killing yourself. If there's any truth to religion, I hope to see my kids there... of course, I'll probably go the other direction for leaving them, but if there's a chance, I'll take it. Maybe I should start doing some good things.

****

June 25th

Nike found out about the suicides. He blames me. He says that the news spread to his employees. He still calls them employees. What an asshole. Now he's worried that they're going to start offing themselves. He's probably right. But what can I do? Dammit, Jim! I'm a soldier, not a counselor.

Even if they did start killing themselves, it might be a good thing. I had one of the men go poking around to take stock of our supplies. There's not enough food here to feed all of us for however long we're going to be here. At this point, this might be my new home. Hell, the way things are going, I'm probably going to die here. I'd rather do that with a head of gray hair, but it is what it is. Anyway, there's not enough food here to feed us all, and last I checked, it's a long way to spring if we're planning on growing things.

I'll have to start thinking about putting together teams to do supply runs... but that could mean more men dying, which I'm not keen on. But people have to eat. All I can do is shrug my shoulders and wait.

****

June 27th

It happened. One of those damn employees offed herself. Nike says she took an overdose of pills and went to sleep... the selfish bitch. Wasn't long before she was awake again. Now we got a whole building locked down full of the

*dead. We're lucky they didn't spread across the campus.
Nike assures us that the building is secure.*

*Fuck, my heart never pumped so hard as when we
were running across to secure the building. If it wasn't for
Nike and his damn cameras, we never would have known.
I'm going to start putting guards on patrol on the
perimeter. If this happens again, it could easily overrun
this whole campus. There are just too many people here.
On the bright side, that's a hundred less mouths to feed. I
feel like an asshole saying it, but things are different now.*

*I had my men tear down all the cameras in our
building. We're keeping this place safe. I don't need that
asshole spying on us. He's got Harper for that. Pretty sure
Harper is relaying everything we do and say to Nike. I
should probably just get rid of him, but that's a precedent I
don't want to set.*

****

June 30th
*It happened again. Only this time, way worse. Nike
says this time some old person just up and died in their
sleep. We fought like hell to get this place under control.
The dead were thick. I lost a lot of men, and still the dead
are all over. The lake is filled with them. A group of Nike
employees tried to survive by sailing out to the middle of
the lake. Damn thing is no more than six-feet at its deepest
point. Probably due to some sort of liability issue.*

*I'm glad they went out there though. The water
slowed the dead down. It was, for a lack of a better phrase,
like shooting fish in a barrel. We couldn't save the poor
bastards on the lake, but they saved us. I'll have the men
fish them out tomorrow, give them a proper burial. If it
wasn't for them, we'd all be dead.*

*Still, I lost a lot of damned good men yesterday,
more than I should have. I think we've got a traitor. Several
of the men I had placed on guard had their throats slashed.*

I suspect Harper. He's the only one that could have gotten close enough to kill those men. I should shoot him in the head now, but I've been too busy making sure these buildings are locked down tight.

The people are scared out of their minds, and I have to admit I am as well. This is a shit show, plain and simple. Things are about to get pretty hectic, but first we have to get all the buildings locked down.

****

July 2nd

Things have calmed down now. Harper works for Nike. It's official. Nike says that Harper is under his protection. When I asked to see the security footage, Nike just laughed at me, said this was a corporate matter and that the footage was off limits for someone of my pay grade. I almost shot him right there.

Things are coming to a head here. It's us or them. The poor employees here are going to be caught in the middle. They're not bad people. They're just fucking useless. I feel like I'm guarding a bunch of cattle... maybe sheep is more accurate.

****

July 3rd

Nike ordered it. My men carried it out. We rounded up the old and the infirm. Executed them on the lawn. It was Nike's order, but I'm hearing from the men now that Nike's telling everyone we did it on our own.

That's the last straw. Tomorrow we take this place from Nike. I'm gonna send his privileged ass outside the wall, see how long he lasts. The men are done here. Most of them want to leave. But where the fuck would we go? We haven't heard anything on the radio for days. Hell, even that old-timer's radio station went dead. It's just a bunch of static on the frequency. We haven't even had to shoot anyone trying to get over the wall in a while.

Maybe we should just leave. We could do it tonight. Take the food and the supplies that we need, blast our way out of here. I want to, but I can't just leave Nike in charge of these people. Who knows what will happen with Nike and that monkey Harper in charge? We'll figure this shit out in the morning. The men are too amped up, too raw to make good decisions. I don't want them killing any employees if we don't have to. They're suffering right along with us after all.

****

July 4th

Happy Independence Day. That's a laugh. I woke up to the sound of yelling and screaming in the night. They must have drugged our food. I can see no other way that they would have been able to kill this many of us. I don't even hear any gunshots.

When I went to investigate, I found myself surrounded. Damn bastards bit me, so I know I'm writing on borrowed time here. I never should have come here. I want to put a bullet through my brain to keep myself from turning into one of them, but then there's that whole heaven and hell thing.

The infection is moving fast. I can feel it inside, burning. It's only a bite on my hand, but I know what's going to happen. No one who has been bit has ever not turned, so it's curtains for me. Haha! Curtains for me! Apparently, this disease turns you into some sort of '50s gangster.

I hope that when I turn, I'm completely dead. It worries me that I'll be stuck in my skull, conscious but unable to do anything about it. Sue, Jeff, Natalie... I'm coming for you. Any second now.

****

Tejada closed the journal and set it on his desk. He had everything he needed. Conscience was no issue now. He would finish what this man had started.

****

Allen watched as Harper strode across the Nike campus.

"Shit," he heard Epps say next to him.

"Tejada said to shoot this bastard," Allen replied.

They looked at each other. "You want the shot?" Epps asked.

"Not especially," Allen said.

"Then we'll both do it. On three." They aimed their rifles at Harper who kept coming right along, as if nothing were out of the ordinary. "One." Harper raised his hand in greeting, and Allen felt sick to his stomach. "Two." When they didn't wave back, a strange look flitted across Harper's face. It was almost as if he knew. "Three." They fired in unison. Both shots took the man in the chest, and he fell backwards onto the green grass.

"I'll make sure he doesn't come back," Allen said. Epps stood guard while Allen ran across the short distance to where Harper lay. He was on his back, his legs flailing weakly in an attempt to get himself upright.

Underneath the smoke of the burning body pile, everything had a sepia feel to it, everything except for blood. Harper's life squirted onto the green and brown grass, vivid and otherworldly compared to the drab feel of everything else. Allen stood over the dying man, offering no words, no comfort. When the man finally stopped struggling, his head fell to the side and Allen knew he was gone. He pulled his sidearm free, aimed it at Harper's skull, and pulled the trigger.

He dragged the dead man to the burn pile, and after going through his pockets, Allen tossed him on the smoldering mess. He didn't think anyone would mind.

284

It took a while for his body to catch fire, but it went up eventually. He watched as the fire caught his clothes first. Next would come the flesh itself. It would sizzle and pop before it turned black. The lips would peel back from the man's teeth, shriveling up like the feet of that witch that Dorothy had crushed with her house. He began to see shapes in the flames, and he didn't notice when Nike approached him.

"What the hell did you just do?" Nike demanded.

Allen blinked, looked at the old man and then went back to looking at the flames. He watched as the skin split on Harper's skull and steam rose from his eyeballs. It was really a beautiful process.

Nike grabbed Allen by the front of his uniform and began to shake him. Allen looked down at the foolish man, grabbed him by the wrist and forced him to release his grip on his uniform. He shoved him backwards gently, and when Nike was out of range, he went back to staring at the fire.

At this point, Nike turned to head to the security office, presumably to find Tejada. He needn't have bothered. The door to the security building banged open and Tejada came striding out with Masterson and Gregg behind him. His face was devoid of any sort of emotion, and he strode forward purposefully, his hand on his sidearm.

"You!" Nike said pointing an accusatory finger at Tejada. "What is the meaning of this? Your man killed Harper. What are you going to do about it?"

Tejada didn't smile. He didn't lord it over the pathetic figure of Nike. He was matter of fact as he said, "Nothing. As far as I'm concerned. He got what he deserved."

"What are you talking about?" Nike sputtered.

"And you're going to get what you deserve as well. Nike, you're under arrest." Masterson and Gregg moved to

285

take hold of Nike. When their hands touched him, he sank to his knees, unable to keep his mind and his body working at the same time.

"No! You're making a mistake!" Nike screeched, as he attempted to shake off the hands of Gregg and Masterson.

Tejada bent down to look into Nike's face. "The only mistake I made was not killing you when I first saw you." He hauled the man to his feet.

Allen watched as a crowd started to gather on the lawn. They had worried, confused looks on their faces, and Allen could sense that they didn't like what was happening to one of their own. The Nike employees' faces were easily readable. The confusion and worry faded to outrage. They were angry at how Nike was being treated. Diana was there. He tried to make eye contact with her, but she wouldn't look at him.

The crowd pressed forward at some silent, unknowable signal. Allen held his rifle at the ready, covering the crowd should they do anything violent.

"Everyone take it easy now!" Tejada yelled to the soldiers and the crowd. But the crowd didn't want to hear any of it. Tejada, sensing that a massacre was inevitable if they stayed outside, gave up trying to reason with the mob. "Everybody fall back to the security building."

The crowd, emboldened by the fact that they hadn't been shot yet, pressed forward. Allen could feel that things were about to get ugly. Masterson and Gregg took control of Nike from Tejada, and they basically carried the man up the steps to the security building. They opened the doors and carried the man inside, as the other soldiers followed suit.

Allen and Epps were the last ones inside. They stood at the door, watching the angry mob outside.

"You think we're going to have to shoot these people?" Epps asked.

"God, I hope not," Allen said.

The mob spit at the door and threw objects at it, but they didn't dare come close enough to place their hand on it. They hurled vile words at Epps and Allen. Allen hoped that this would all be over soon.

Chapter 16: Death in the Compound

Clara tried to get through the next day like nothing awful had happened the night before. The men all gave her a little more respect than they had the day before, so that was something. They still undressed her with their eyes every chance they got, but at least she wasn't being eyed like a piece of meat anymore... it was actually more like a piece of meat that could also kill things.

She stepped into the big house to check on Dez and see if she needed anything. According to Dez, she needed a big bottle of pills and a bottle of wine to wash them down, but Clara didn't think that would be such a good idea for the baby or for Clara's own personal safety.

"Fuck the baby," Dez said.

"Now why do you want to go and say a thing like that?" Clara asked.

"Because it's half son of a bitch, and I don't want that bastard's spawn inside me," Dez spat.

Clara set about cleaning up Dez. With a moist sponge, she wiped down her skin. She held the bedpan for her while she went to the bathroom, and the whole time, they argued about whether or not she should live.

"You know, even though it's half his kid, there's half of it that's yours. Who's to say it won't be more like you than him?"

"Why would I want it to be more like me? So it could wind up falling for some psychopath? So it could wind up knocked up and tied to a bed?"

Clara removed the bedpan from under Dez, placed it on the floor, and she cleaned her up with a rag. "Listen. I don't have the answers. I'm just here until my friend heals, and then I'm out of here."

This set Dez to laughing. "You think you can leave here? You think Chad is going to let you leave? You're madder than he is."

Clara had nothing to say to this. So she continued cleaning up Dez. She knew what would happen if she stayed here. She would wind up like Dez sooner or later, only there was no one here that she would willingly let impregnate her. No, when the time came, they were getting out of here one way or another, even if that meant leaving bodies in their wake.

She sensed a presence in the doorway, and she turned to find Chad standing there. His face was grim. His eyes were two chunks of coal. "My brother never came back," he said.

Clara felt no sympathy for this man. He was a piece of shit as far as she could tell. "What do you want me to do about it?"

Chad's face became even more grim, even though Clara didn't know how that was possible. "Those people, the black man and the pregnant lady, what can you tell me about them?"

Clara just shrugged her shoulders. "There's not much to tell. Mort was a homeless man before this all began. Katie, she doesn't talk about her past, but she has housewife written all over her, right down to the mom jeans." There was much more to tell. She could have told him that Mort was a warrior, capable of killing the dead with a single hammer blow. She could have told them that Katie was a coldhearted killer when she needed to be... and sometimes when she didn't need to be. She could have told him that Mort was the most gentle soul in the world, and Katie, quite possibly, was the most damaged. She could have told him that if Reed had crossed paths with those two and tried to do them wrong, that he would most likely be dead by now. But she didn't tell him any of this because there wasn't time enough in the day, and she didn't want to help him in any way. Let Chad think they were just a pregnant lady and a black man.

"Do you think they would have killed my brother?"

Clara laughed at this. "Listen, I barely know the two. What I do know is that they're probably long gone by now. Besides, what would your brother be doing looking for those two anyway?"

Chad didn't answer. He just turned and left, purpose in his stride.

Dez, speaking calmly for the first time ever said, "I don't know who your friends are, but I know what's going to happen to them." There was a slight pause, and then she said, "He's going to kill them."

Clara threw back the curtains to let some sunlight into the room. Dust motes danced in the air as weak shafts of light found their way through the boards on the windows and flooded the dim chamber, splashing across the yellowed, sickly skin of Dez. "He can try, I suppose."

When she was done, Clara went to find some food for herself and Dez. As she exited the big house, she saw Chad and some of his men throwing their rifles over their shoulders. She crossed her fingers and hoped that Mort and Katie would be alright.

****

Chad was furious. He knew that those two had killed his brother. He put his money on the black man. Maybe he should have been nicer to the man, but no, fuck that. He didn't know this guy from a fucking hole in the wall. But maybe... no, he wasn't to blame for this.

He shook his head and then signaled for the others to spread out. They circled around the compound, one person dragging a body while another covered them with their rifle. In no time at all, they had the bodies stacked up and ready to be burned. But it was too soon for that. The smoke inevitably drew the dead, and before they lit those

290

bodies on fire, he wanted to do a little scouting and see if he could find his brother anywhere.

He looked off into the woods. "Reed... where are you, buddy?" They fanned out in the forest, walking in pairs, just in case anything happened. The rules were simple, don't use your gun unless you have to. They carried short spears with them. They were a good five feet long, but slimmer, more maneuverable than the ones they used to clear the compound. One gun shot in these woods could have dire consequences with the growing number of the dead in the area.

Chad felt jumpy and pissed off at the same time. Each shift in the wind, each rustle of the branches around him, made him more tense. He scanned the underbrush, pushing aside bushes with the butt end of his spear. Reed had to be out here. He should have been home by now.

They headed west, pushing towards the old road. When they stepped onto the road, he sent men to the north and the south after a quick radio check. He took Dale along with him as his backup. He liked Dale. He didn't talk, never argued with his orders, and he could kill them dead things like nobody's business.

They would check the campsite first. Perhaps the black man and the pregnant lady had holed up there. It did have its own bathroom. Women loved that sort of thing.

The campsite was really nothing more than a bunch of cleared spaces marked off for out-of-towners to park their RVs and pretend they were camping. It wasn't real camping as far as he was concerned. It was just some bullshit designed to help city folk feel like they were communing with nature. They might as well sit in a parking lot outside of Wal-Mart. But the joke was on them in the end he guessed. All those city folk were gone by now. He was thankful that he had grown up a country boy, freed from the things that city folk craved.

He didn't need a mansion. He didn't need wi-fi or electricity. All he really needed was good people, some guns, and his brother. But now his brother was missing.

There were a few vehicles parked in the area. Chad saw the tell-tale signs of carnage. They were easy to spot now. A camper with its door wide open. Supplies scattered and left in the open. A bloody handprint on the side of a camper's tan siding.

A few of the dead had gathered here. They stood still, just waiting for something to draw their attention. Chad, with Dale guarding his back, snuck up on one and jammed his spear through its neck, severing the spinal cord. It was still alive, but its arms and legs no longer worked.

The noise of the body slumping to the ground was enough to draw the attention of the other corpses in the area. "Let's rock and roll," he said. Dale grunted his agreement. He liked that about the man. He didn't flap his gums too often. A man who knew the value of silence was a good man to have around in Chad's opinion.

The dead honed in on them. There were only four of them. None of them were his brother. He didn't know whether to be thankful or annoyed that his hunt still had to continue. Reed was the hunter. He knew how to track things down, find things that other people would have missed. Chad was more of a fisherman; he liked to bait the hook, catch the fish, reel it in, and watch as it flopped around on the shore gasping for breath. That intensity, that struggle for life always fascinated him.

He remembered the lake where they used to fish when they were younger, when their parents still gave a rat's ass about them. They would make a day of it. Chad would sit on a bucket with his old man, just casting and reeling while the sun worked its way across the sky. He always caught something. As the sun would go down, Reed would appear, some sort of dead animal in his hands, a beaver, squirrels, sometimes something larger. He didn't know how he did it, but he envied his brother that skill.

The first of the dead approached, and Chad sidestepped its clumsy attempt to grab him. He stuck the spear between the creature's legs as he circled, yanking it sideways so that it fell to the ground. He raised his arms in the air and drove downward with the spear. It punctured the creature's skull at the temple, and then it was dead for good.

Another came, perhaps the wife of the bearded man he just killed. She waved her arms wildly at Dale. Dale flipped the spear in his hands and swung it like a baseball bat. It crashed into the dead woman's head, and she fell sideways to the ground. Dale jumped on her, stepping on her neck with his boot. Its arms grabbed at Dale's jeans, and he drove his spear home. She stopped moving.

From there, the rest of the dead were easy pickings. Just children, they were a lot easier to knock down and dispatch. He felt sorry for them, in a distant part of his mind. He never felt good about killing the young ones, but they were just as dangerous as the older. He had seen that shit first hand at the trailer park when a couple of kids fell sick, only to attack their parents in the middle of the night. He and Reed had been the only ones capable of killing them, but after that, everyone sort of got the picture. He was sure that it was his ability to do what needed to be done that had allowed him to become the leader of his motley crew of trailer park residents. Without those kids, they all would have been dead long ago; he was sure of it.

It's funny how things work out. There I was, just a nothing slaving away on some asshole's farm, and now I'm the king of it all. He smiled at the thought.

"You want I should take a look at the bathroom?" Dale asked.

Chad nodded, and Dale took off, a handheld flashlight in one hand, his spear in the other. Chad watched the trees sway in the breeze for a second, and then he approached the camper. There was still a bunch of good shit in there. He found a can of Pringles that was still unopened. He reached down and grabbed them from the bloodstained floor of the camper.

"Pizza flavor?" He shook his head, pulled the plastic lid off, and then ripped open the foil seal. He reached inside and pulled out a stack of Pringles. He popped them in his mouth and shrugged his shoulders as he chewed. "Not bad."

He put the lid back on the Pringles and then began rummaging through the rest of the crap that was left. He had an eye on the cooler in the corner. Who knew what good shit would be hiding in there?

He was bent over reaching for it, when he felt something touch his elbow. Immediately he spun, his fist cocked back to deliver a blow, but it was just Dale.

"Jesus, Dale. Use your words man. You scared the fuck out of me." Then Chad noticed Dale's face. It was white, the color drained out of it. "What is it?"

"You should look," Dale said.

Chad's heart sank in his chest. He knew without having to be told what he would find in the bathroom. Shit. He walked over to the entrance to the bathrooms. It was dark inside, and he paused. "Are you sure I need to go in there?"

Dale just nodded.

Chad fumbled in his pack for his flashlight. Finding it, he took a deep breath to steady himself. He didn't want to go in there, not one bit. He clicked the flashlight on and a brilliant beam of light shot off into the gloom. "Ain't nothing moving in there, is it?" he asked, delaying the inevitable.

Dale shook his head.

Chad wiped a cold sweat off his brow and then pushed forward into the darkness. The beam only managed to light up a small portion of the bathroom. The first thing he spotted was the blood. Then he saw a boot, Reed's boot. As he panned the light up his brother's body, the light began to shake. Then the beam touched his brother's face.

He dropped the flashlight altogether and then backed out of the bathroom. It was too horrible. Even though he couldn't visually see Reed's body anymore, the image was still in his mind. It was a mess, a smashed and devoured mess. Something had been feeding on him, but he couldn't tell what. He didn't want to know. Animal or dead thing, it didn't matter. He dropped to his knees and retched, spitting bile into the dirt in front of the bathroom.

"Holy God," he moaned. Trying to look anywhere but the bathroom. "Oh, Jesus." He looked up at the trees, but even there, he could still see his brother's mutilated face. He closed his eyes, but the face was there as well.

"Yeah, we found him. We're down the road a bit... at the campground." It was Dale, speaking into the walkie. He might as well be in another galaxy as far as Chad was concerned. He squatted in the dirt, trying to make sense of the world he was in.

He didn't know how long he sat like that, but when he came to, the others were around him. They had grim looks upon their faces, and they were obviously concerned about him. He was ashamed at showing this weakness to them, and anger unfurled in his chest where the pain had been before.

"Gimme some light," he said as he walked into the bathroom. They followed him, lighting the way. He squatted down to take a good look at the mess that used to be his brother.

"You think one of the dead got him?" a man asked him.

The face was definitely shredded, but the lines were too straight, too perfect to be from the teeth of the dead. Chad reached out and turned his brother's head from side to side. The back of his skull was gone. Animals didn't do that. Bullets did.

"Someone killed him. Look at that," he pointed to the back of the skull.

"You think it was those people?" Dale asked.

"You seen anyone else out here?"

Dale didn't need to say anything to that. *Why would they cover it up?* It made no sense. They must have known that Chad had sent Reed to find them, so why go through all of this trouble? They must be afraid of him, and well they should be.

He suspected they were staying somewhere close. Most likely, they didn't want him to know that they were out here. Fear was the only logical explanation he could come up with to explain their clumsy attempt to make him think his brother had been killed by the dead. Their stupid attempt at covering their tracks was pathetic, and he would make them pay for it. He would do to them what they had done to his brother, only they would be alive while it happened.

"Come on. Let's get you home, little brother." Chad leaned down and hefted his brother's body off the floor. Even though Reed wasn't a big man, he still weighed what seemed like a ton. He threw the body over his shoulder, and they began the long walk home.

****

For a while, Dez slept. After she had eaten, she had fallen into a silent, brooding mood. Clara wondered what would happen if she let Dez go. She cared nothing for the drama of this compound. If Dez wanted to kill herself, she had every right. It wasn't something that Clara would ever consider, but who was she to rob someone of what they truly wanted? If Dez wanted to die, let her.

That she was pregnant didn't even enter the equation. The way Clara saw it, it was criminal to even bring a baby into this world. It was a selfish and misguided act, but then it always had been in her mind, even before the world had died. But society had to start up again sooner or later, or else they were all just part of a species slowly going extinct.

Looking back on everything that she had seen, maybe that was a good thing. She shivered at her own morbid thoughts.

"You look like I feel," Dez said sleepily.

"Yeah, well, we all got our problems, don't we?"

"You know what I miss the most?" Dez asked. Clara said nothing. She didn't want to have this conversation. She had heard it enough to be sick of it. "I miss the smells of the morning. My parents would always get up before me. I was supposed to go to college, so they didn't bother trying to teach me the farm life. But those smells, they would always wake me up, even though I could have slept in. I can still see them there, my father sitting at the table reading his newspaper, drinking a black cup of coffee. That coffee smell would just crawl right up my nose while I was sleeping, and it would always wake me up, didn't matter how late I had gone to sleep. I miss the clink of glasses and forks and knives as they ate. I miss the smell of sizzling bacon and toast warming in the toaster."

"Stop it," Clara said. "You're depressing me."

"You weren't depressed before?" Dez asked. "That's a miracle."

They lapsed into silence, Clara looking through the cracks between the boards that covered the window. She could see the womenfolk out there. That's what they called them, right? Womenfolk? They went about their duties, gardening, hauling water, preparing the evening meal. The sun had moved over the big house so that it was dark in the room.

"Grab that bedpan. I have to shit," Dez asked.

Clara turned and grabbed the bedpan from the floor. Dez was in the act of squirting out a runny shit when the door burst open. A demon stood in the doorway, covered in blood. For a moment, Clara thought it was one of the dead, but then the demon pointed at her and yelled, "You!"

That's all there was. No other words accompanied the demon's declaration, and then it flew across the room, knocking her to the ground. She slapped at the demon as it advanced upon her again. It picked her up and threw her into the wall. She fell to the side, knocking over an end table. An ancient lamp fell to the ground, breaking into a dozen pieces and cutting Clara's legs.

The demon picked her up again and punched her in the ribs. Then it dragged her through the big house, out the front door, and down the rickety, wooden porch. She tried to fight, tried to stop what was happening to her, but she couldn't. Her heels hammered on wooden floor boards and then dirt, but he was too strong, too violent.

He threw her down in the courtyard, and Clara resisted the urge to fight back. Everyone watched, the pregnant women, the slack-jawed men. She was powerless. Everything in the compound stopped, and it was quiet, but for the buzzing of insects and the songs of birds in the trees.

Chad bent over and looked her in the face. "You said they weren't killers!" he yelled.

"They aren't," she spit back, not sure what had changed since Chad and the others had left. He grabbed her by the hair and dragged her to her feet, hauling her across the courtyard of the compound and through the open gate. She stumbled, falling, gashing her knee on a rock, but Chad didn't stop. She would be following him one way or another, on her feet or on her knees, so she pushed herself up and stumbled after.

"Then why is my brother fucking dead?" he said as he dumped her on the ground next to a corpse.

It was Reed. She recognized him by his clothes and what was left of his hair. His face was damaged beyond recognition. "It looks like one of those things got him."

Chad stalked over to his brother's corpse and lifted it up, turning its head, so she could clearly see the exit wound. "How do you explain that?"

She couldn't explain it. It was obvious. Chad kicked her hard in the ribs. He balled his hands into fists tightly, and she wondered just how far this would go. He punched her, the sound echoing across the silent courtyard. The impact struck her across the jaw, and she tasted blood in her mouth.

He picked her up again, shaking her. "Tell me why I should let you live."

She had no answer, and now wasn't the time to lie to Chad. He was on the verge of murder. She could see it in his eyes. "You shouldn't," she said.

Chad stared at her, trying to figure out what game she was playing, and then he saw that she wasn't playing a game. She was simply being honest. He let her drop to the compacted dust of the courtyard. There were too many people here for her to do anything to try and escape. All she could do was wait out the storm and hope that she made it through to the other side.

"Put her in the trailer," Chad said, though it seemed to take all of his strength to utter the words instead of beating her some more.

A couple of men rushed to pick her up off the ground. They dragged her to the trailer and threw her inside. She heard the sound of a padlock clicking as they locked the door behind her. She dragged her battered and bruised body to the bed in the back of the trailer.

Joan was awake and concerned. She got one look at Clara and said, "My God. What's happened?"

Clara was too tired to say anything. She lay on the bed, nursing her ribs. They burned with fire as she lay

299

down on the mattress. Joan reached over to her to see if she was alright, but Clara just batted her hand away. Then she drifted off to sleep, letting the pain turn into blackness.

****

Chad stalked across the compound, unleashing a cavalcade of swear words. His rage was consuming; his anger sought to overwhelm him.

"You oughta just kill them," Dale said.

Chad pulled up from his pacing and looked Dale in the eye. "Don't tell me what I ought to do."

Dale took a step backwards, and Chad ran his hands through his hair as if trying to physically pull the anger out of his skull. He threw his hands at the ground and looked up at the sky. A couple of men grabbed some shovels and began digging a grave.

He sat then, his mind churning up horrors and revenge fantasies. Sick thoughts flooded his brain. He ought to cut Clara's hand off. Reed was like his own right hand, and now he was dead. Shouldn't she lose her hand? Wasn't that fair? Shouldn't she have to pay for what her friends did?

The doctor was off limits. They needed her. She had skills that none of them had. Sure, people had been having babies without doctors for the better part of humanity, but just in case something happened during delivery, she was still needed. The last thing they needed was someone dying in child labor with people all around them when they turned into one of those things. Maybe they would have to tie down the pregnant women when they gave birth, but that was a problem for another time.

Right now, his problem was revenge. He could go in there and make them a part of this whole thing, but that would defeat the purpose of this whole compound. It's not that he was against rape as a means of punishment, but he needed them functional. He needed them to be good mothers. Children needed mothers. They needed people that would care about them and feed them. Rape children would not be cared for. They would grow up crooked and twisted, despised by their own mothers.

The raspy sound of the shovels hit his ears, and another thought crossed his mind, a dark twisted thought that finally brought a smile to his face. The plan came to him, unfurling in his mind like a time-lapse video of a flower blossoming. Tomorrow... tomorrow would be a good day to execute his plan.

****

Katie heard them moving through the woods. They were searching for her and Mort. They were riled up, agitated. She regretted that her plan to mutilate Reed's body hadn't worked. It would have made things so much easier if Chad had believed his brother had been mauled by the dead. She had heard Clara's cries of pain as Chad had beaten her. She felt guilty for that, and while it wasn't a welcome sensation, it was at least a different emotion than she had felt for the last few months.

She knew why she was up in the tree with her handgun clutched in her hands. She knew why she was spending valuable effort trying to free these two women who had shown nothing but tacit acceptance of her existence. They had finally made her feel something other than depression. Katie knew she was a drowning woman, and the only thing that had kept her afloat these last few months had been the presence of others. She wasn't best friends with Clara and Joan, but she didn't like the thought of them being stuck in the compound either. They couldn't stay in there, and Mort and Katie couldn't stay outside. Something was going to have to give... and it certainly wasn't going to be Katie.

From her vantage point, she could see them moving through the forest. Mort had boosted her up into the tree as

301

the branches were too far off the ground for her to reach. It was an old tree. The stumps of branches, shed long ago, stuck out of its sides, and once she had made it into the tree proper, it had been easy enough to make her way up higher into the tree.

She had smiled at the look on the man's face as he had come out of the bathroom. She knew that pain; she had felt it herself, but damn was it good to see that pain on someone else's face. From their vantage point in the woods, she had been forced to put her hand to her mouth to suppress a little giggle. Maybe that made her evil, but then again, maybe evil wasn't even real.

From their vantage point, they had watched as Chad picked up his brother's body and carried it home. They had heard the cries from inside the compound and seen the rage on Chad's face.

Then everything had quieted down, but Katie knew that the fight wasn't over yet. They had taken one of his; now he was going to try and take one of theirs. Mort and Katie had gone home to plan that night. The only problem was that they didn't know if Chad would come after them or do something to one of their friends in the compound.

They had planned for both. As it turned out, Chad was coming for them.

The men from the compound entered a clearing, and they found what Katie and Mort had left for them. She couldn't see their faces, but she knew that the little surprise they had left would make them pause for a second.

She watched as Chad stood up from the corpse they had left in the middle of the clearing. He cupped his hands to his mouth and shouted, "We know you're out there!"

And so they were.

"We've got your friends! Did you forget that?"

Mort and Katie maintained their silence. She couldn't see Mort across the way, holding onto the rifle of the man they killed, but she knew he was hearing

302

everything that was being said. It had taken a lot of work on her part to even talk Mort into this plan.

He had moped and seemed out of sorts when she had killed the boy. But he would have done the same to them. He wasn't sent to spy on them. He was sent to kill them, and eventually she convinced Mort of this. It was still difficult getting him to go along with her plan, but eventually he relented. He was too gentle, too nice. If he could harness that great strong body of his, he would be a force to reckon with.

The voice in the clearing continued, "I got a little game for you to play. Tomorrow morning we're having a feast. There's gonna be music, beer, maybe even a little hanky panky. You're both invited."

The voice lapsed into silence, and Katie took aim at the man's head with her revolver. She had never shot anyone from that distance before, but she thought the gun was strong enough.

"But let me tell you now, if you refuse our invitation, your friends are going to die!" He let the words hang there as Katie lined up her shot. "Party starts at noon! Don't be late!"

Katie squeezed the trigger. Smoke and fire erupted from the barrel of her gun. She missed. The clearing erupted into a flurry of activity as another shot came from the other side of the clearing, Mort's shot. There was a scream of pain, and then the men from the compound were scrambling away.

"Don't be late!" they heard a voice yell as they disappeared into the forest, dragging their injured man.

They sat in the trees for a long time. They had agreed to this for safety, just in case the men from the compound left anyone behind in an effort to be sneaky. Katie doubted they would stick around. The confusion caused by the multiple shots would put the fear into them.

Fear. Her shoulders shook as she laughed silently to herself. She hadn't felt fear for some time.

She knew why. In order to feel fear, you had to have one thing, a reason to live. She didn't care if she died or lived, but she knew her friends did. She needed them on some primordial level that she couldn't explain. *Did I actually use the word 'friends?'*

When the sun turned orange and started to disappear behind the trees, and she heard the shuffling of the dead below, she lowered herself from her perch. She rushed to the clearing, looking at the mutilated corpse they had left tied to an ancient tree stump with no legs and no arms.

It had been a dangerous game, knocking the dead thing to the ground and cutting its arms and legs off with a machete they had scavenged from the vacation house. She looked at the poor creature's face, its lips shriveled back from its jagged and broken teeth. On its forehead, she had carved the words, "You're next." She raised the machete above her head and brought it down as hard as she could on the creature's skull. Its eyes finally stopped following her.

At the crack of a branch, she spun with her revolver in her hand. It was just Mort, lumbering through the trees, his eyes big and round. "We gotta go. There's dead out here."

She nodded, and they headed back to the house, dodging the dead that had been drawn to the gunshots from the road above. They didn't appear immediately, but once they showed up, they were constant. If a person fired a gun and stood in one spot, they would find you. They had learned that the other night after they had killed the boy behind the house.

A dozen of the dead, not too many to handle, but enough to make things difficult had made their way to the house. They had huddled in the dark, the windows blacked out as they heard the dead bumping into the house, trying doorknobs. In the morning, most of them had moved on.

Katie wasn't afraid then, and she wasn't afraid now as they moved through the gloom, silent as death. When they reached the house, they pushed the door open and checked everywhere for the dead. One good thing about setting up the trap in the clearing, they had drawn all of the dead away from the house.

In the dark they sat, eating the food they had taken from the RV down by the campsite where they had left the big man's body. They were silent for a long time. The two, despite being on their own, hadn't quite managed to hit it off.

"You hit anyone?" Mort asked.

"Nope. Missed."

"I hit someone," Mort said. He didn't sound proud of the fact. "Got him in the shoulder I think."

They lapsed into silence again. Katie ate another stack of Pringles. They were good. They weren't the type of thing she would have eaten in the before world, but she was eating for two now. She thought she felt the baby move, but it was too soon for that. The feeling made her nervous.

"What are we gonna do about tomorrow?" Mort asked.

"I guess we're going to go to a party," Katie said.

"You think it's a trap?"

"I know it's a trap."

They sat in silence, and then Katie reached over to Mort and pulled him close to her.

"What are you doing?" he whispered nervously.

"Don't worry. I won't hurt you."

Mort let himself relax, and Katie did all the work. They slept through the night on the floor of the living room. Katie had dreams of a past life, one that made her brow wrinkle in her sleep. When the sun came up, she was back to being herself and ready to party.

****

That evening was a nightmare. Clara hardly slept a wink as Joan busied herself with fixing up an injured man, and since she couldn't get around on her own, Clara had served as her helper. They could hear Chad ranting and raving in the courtyard, his rage echoing off the trailer walls. She could hear voices trying to calm him, but he wouldn't be calmed.

The man who had been shot, Keith, grimaced in pain as Joan tested out his arm. Blood dripped onto the blankets that covered the bed she shared with Clara. The man's teeth glowed yellow in the lantern light as he grimaced. Joan tested the mobility of his arm, but it was no good. The shoulder was shattered, broken by a bullet.

The best she could do was immobilize the arm. Luckily for Keith, the bullet had gone clean through. She recommended drinking some alcohol and sleeping sitting up... painkillers seemed to be scarce in the compound. She packed the wound with some rags that they had sterilized in boiling water, but Joan told the man that the chance of infection was pretty damn good without some antibiotics.

When the injured man left, aided to his own trailer by a couple of other men, she and Clara lay on the bed, wondering what sort of nightmare they had gotten themselves into. Still, they heard Chad swearing up a storm in the courtyard.

"I think we're in danger," Clara said.

"I know we are."

They had spoken little of Lou's passing, but they both felt it. Clara tried to catch a few hours of sleep. She was awoken periodically by swearing and cursing in the courtyard. Even after the voices in the courtyard had faded and the night went calm, her dark dreams caused her to jerk away several more times.

When she awoke, she readied herself for another day of wiping Dez's ass. As she exited the trailer, she felt a strange energy about the camp. Some of the women smiled at her, which was a rare thing. Ever since she had jumped on board the watchtower and speared the dead, they had avoided her like the plague, as if she had broken some sort of taboo commandment. Thou shalt not be a woman and kill the dead. Today, the women looked positively pleasant as they said hello or waved at her.

She walked over to the campfire and prepared some instant oatmeal for Dez. She didn't speak to the other women, but she noticed them glancing at her from the corner of her eye. Something was up. She grabbed a small, dull knife from the pile of silverware and slipped the blade into the oatmeal, concealing it so that only the plain handle was visible.

Then she noticed something else peculiar. The men of the camp avoided eye contact with her completely. Usually, whenever she turned her head, she could spot one or another of the men eyeing her with that look that men had. Today, it was as if she didn't even exist in their eyes. She might as well be a ghost walking around the courtyard as far as the men were concerned.

Something was definitely up.

She walked inside the big house, and Chad was there. He was gearing up. On a table in the main room, he had placed all of his weapons. There were a lot of them. He had rifles. He had knives in sheaths, and he had hundreds of rounds of ammunition set out before him.

"Going hunting?" she asked, trying to hide her concern for the others.

He just smiled at her as he fed rounds into the magazines on the table. She walked past him, the steam from the oatmeal billowing in the chill morning air of the big house.

She pushed open the door of Dez's room, panic building in her chest. She wanted to run to Joan and drag her out of this place, but she knew that was a stupid plan.

Joan couldn't go anywhere. She felt trapped. She felt dread, and there was nothing she could do about it.

"What's wrong with you?" Dez asked.

"Nothing," she said.

"You're a terrible liar," Dez said.

"I didn't have much practice before all of this."

Dez nodded as she swallowed a mouthful of oatmeal. "Oh yeah, I can see it now. I bet you were a real firecracker before all this, never had to watch your mouth, always able to speak your mind. You know, it's funny how things like gender equality and feminism get tossed out the window once the only thing that matters in this world is your ability to survive."

"Fuck that."

Dez laughed again. "What? You think if our roles were reversed, you wouldn't be in the same position that I am? Think again, girlie. I ain't no Barbie Doll. I'm every bit as tough as you are. If it wasn't for Chad's goon squad out there, he would have been dead some time ago."

"Yeah, well, that would be nice."

Dez smiled at her, oatmeal stuck between her teeth. "What's up your ass?"

"I think something is going to happen to me today."

The smile fell from Dez's face. "Well, you know what to do about that."

Clara looked Dez in the face, and she saw a killer there, a madwoman who had been treated like an animal. Her eyes were ferocious, and her jaw was set like the side of a mountain. "What do I do?" Clara asked.

"You kill as many of those bastards as you can when the time comes. They try to put it in you, you cut the fucker off and stomp on it."

Clara fell silent and spooned more oatmeal into Dez's mouth. She could hear Chad's boots clomping around in another part of the big house. Clara held a knife up in front of her face, showing it to Dez. "I'm going to put this here," she said as she slid it under Dez's pillow. "If I don't come back, I want you to fight your way out of here. I don't know what your plans are for the future, but no one should have to live like this." Clara loosened the knot on Dez's wrist, enough that she could free her hand if she needed to. "For when the time comes."

Dez smiled at her, her brown eyes gleaming in the dingy room. "For when the time comes."

Suddenly, the door to the bedroom was kicked open and Chad stood there, geared up like a one-man army. There was a knife in a sheath on every part of his body. The barrels of two rifles crisscrossed as they rose above his back. Belts of ammunition crossed his chest. He smiled at her, and for a moment, she thought he had heard everything that they had been saying.

"Come with me," Chad said, and he held his hand out to her invitingly. "The men have been working on something just for you."

She walked around Dez's bed and took Chad's hand. Together they left the room. Clara tossed a look over her shoulder at Dez. The woman's eyes locked with her own until she was out of sight of the door.

As she stepped out into the sunlight, she knew that something major was happening. All of the men were decked out just as Chad was, their arms legs and shoulders bristling with weapons. Joan was there too. She sat in the middle of the courtyard, her meager medical supplies sitting on the ground next to her, concern evident on her face.

Chad led her past them and out the front gate. A hole had been dug in the ground. She turned to Chad, not comprehending what was happening. The hole wasn't a grave, but it was big enough for someone to stand in. He smiled at her again, a crooked thing that spoke of a capacity for cruelty that she had never encountered before.

"Get in."

Clara wanted to scream, but she had done plenty of that already. She wished she hadn't. Behind her, she heard the clomp of boots on the watchtowers that overlooked the front gate. She wanted to turn around and look at Chad, but she couldn't.

From somewhere, she heard a generator start, its dull thrum reverberating through the ground. She squeezed her eyes shut, fear threading its way through her body.

The sun wasn't yet high enough to cut through the canopy, but it cast enough diffused light to allow her to see into the trees. A song began to play, something twangy... something country... something loud.

She was going to die out here.

To be honest, Mort was glad for the music. It covered his clumsy footsteps as he moved up the tree. Katie was out there somewhere. They had taken in the scene in front of the compound for only a few moments before Katie had grasped what they were going to do. Like it was nothing, she had come up with a plan. It was a dangerous plan, but it just might work. As the hole was halfway filled in, they had crept to the other side of the compound.

He was now perched in a tree, overlooking the stronghold. He tried to remain as still as he could. He had chosen a nice leafy tree with plenty of large branches to help conceal him. The rifle he held in his hand was dull, its barrel covered in a layer of mud to prevent it from glinting in the sunshine that filtered through the branches overhead.

He wasn't comfortable with the gun yet. It felt like a live snake in his hand, and he was nervous around it. *They're burying Clara, man. These people are fucked up.* He wished it could be any other way. There was no reason for any of this. There was no reason for the men in that compound to want any of them dead. He didn't understand any of it. If they had been a threat, if they had been dangerous or mean, then maybe he could understand it.

Katie had told him that this would be the end. Either they won, or they died. Mort didn't know if he was ready for that. The old Mort would have left. He would have climbed out of that tree and gone home... home being whatever quiet, out of the way place he could find. But he couldn't do that now. He had become a part of something for the first time in his life. And being with Katie had taught him one thing... he never wanted to be alone again. So if this was what he had to do to make that happen, then this is what he had to do.

He shook the thoughts out of his head, and squinted down the sights of his gun. He only hoped that Katie found what she was looking for.

****

Katie ran through the forest, machete in her hand. She ran as fast as she could up the old country road that ran past the vacation house and the campground. The dead were moving now. They honed in on the sounds coming from the compound. Even this far from it, she could hear the faint sounds of music. The dead turned to follow when they saw her, but she moved past them.

She had to get to the highway. She was sure she would find what she was looking for there. The old country road led to the main drag, but it would also lead to the deadly traffic snarl that they had escaped from.

Her back was killing her as she ran, and she hoped that the baby inside her would be alright. She wasn't so far along that a little jogging would hurt the baby, but exhaustion could. She swerved through a group of dead, ducking out of the range of their hands when she spotted something moving in the woods to her right.

She smiled as she advanced upon the dead thing. She hefted the machete in her hands and stepped forward.

The dead creature across from her was clad in a leather outfit. On its head, it wore what she was looking for. She knew what Chad was planning, she didn't know how, she just did. Maybe she was as twisted as he was. She stepped up to the creature, and its arms reached out for her.

She brought the machete down on the creature's left forearm, and it didn't exactly cut through the thick leather biker jacket, but it did break the creature's arm. She spared a look over her shoulder to make sure the group of dead that she had recently passed wasn't breathing down her neck. They were closer, but she still had some time if she was quick. The second slice of her machete managed to completely slice off the right arm of the dead thing, just below the elbow. Black blood, dead blood, dripped from the wound, and then she shoved the creature on its back.

She stood perpendicular to the prone corpse and brought the blade of the machete down on the creature's white neck. Its head slumped sideways, black blood running down its torso. The arms and legs stopped moving, and it fell to the ground, but she knew the thing inside the helmet was still alive. The head was still attached, and it took her three more blows with the machete to sever it completely.

With the dead advancing upon her, she didn't have time to pull the head out of the black motorcycle helmet, so she tucked it up under her arm like a football and ran back to where she had left Mort.

****

Clara heard them first. They crunched through the dry, dead leaves of the forest, kicking piles of dead pine needles out before them with each of their shambling steps. As the first one appeared, she squeezed her eyes shut and

312

remained stock still, hoping that they wouldn't notice her head sticking up out of the ground.

How the fuck did I end up here? How did this happen? Death was coming her way at a slow walk, but she couldn't open her eyes and look.

****

Chad wasn't sure that they were going to show up at this point. If they were going to show, they would have shown up before the dead did. The forest was crawling with the dead now. It sounded as if the forest had come alive. For a moment, he considered killing the music, but hey, he had promised a party and he was going to deliver.

He turned around and looked inside the compound. His men were ready, stationed on top of all the trailers. There wasn't an approach from the forest that wasn't covered. Joan glared up at him from the courtyard. If it wasn't for the fact that she could deliver babies and fix up the injured, he would have put a bullet through her forehead right then and there... just because of that glare. *Where did she get off glaring at him like that? He was the one that had lost a brother. What did she lose, a black man and her lesbian friend? Shit, she should be thanking him.*

There was no doubt in his mind that Joan and Clara were lesbians. Never in his life had he experienced such a negative sexual energy from a woman before, let alone two of them. Oh, well. He turned back to Clara, her brown hair shining in the sunlight. He wished he could see her face as the dead approached, but the tactic would prove more effective this way. They would take one look at the fear on her pretty face, and they wouldn't be able to resist.

He smiled at his own ingenuity. She looked like a mole poking its head up out of the ground.

Where are you, you bastards? Show yourselves. He wanted to see them try and save her. What a delightful TV show that would be.

313

He saw it playing out in his mind. They would burst from the forest, panicked looks on their faces, digging at the ground while fighting off the hordes of the dead. *Oh, this was gonna be awesome.*

Just then, a gunshot rang out, and there was a scream.

****

Mort looked down, expecting to see one of the dead. Instead, he saw Katie, struggling to pull something from inside of a motorcycle helmet.

"I got it," she hissed up at him, holding the helmet up like a trophy.

Mort watched as she reached her hand into the helmet, jamming and pulling at the head stuck inside. Her hand came out bloody, and he could see her biting her lower lip as she strained. He was about to climb down to help her when the head came out with a sickening sucking sound, skinny strings of liquid rot trailing after it. She threw the head on the ground, its jaw opening and closing.

"Ok, we're ready," she announced.

Mort nodded. Now came the part that he dreaded. He took aim with the rifle at the nearest man. His target stood in the open, walking along the top of a trailer, and Mort thought the man was a fool. He was perfectly visible, his body outlined against the whiteness of the trailer and the brown dirt of the compound, and Mort felt sorry for the man. But his friends were in need, and if this is what had to be done so that he would never be alone again, then so be it.

"I'm sorry." He pulled the trigger, and there was a microscopic delay between the sound of the gunshot and the crimson cloud that erupted from the man on top of the trailer. The man stood for a second, his eyes locked on the cloud around him, and then the red stuff started to flow down his chest. He fell to the ground, screaming. Mort

314

wondered how long it would be until he stood up again. He had just killed a man... he had just killed a man.

He didn't have time to think about it. He quickly scampered down the tree as gunshots peppered the spot that he had fired from. Katie was already gone, running through the woods. He hung from the last branch, but it broke under his weight, and he fell backwards to the ground. Mort landed inches from the severed head that Katie had pulled from the motorcycle helmet. His eyes went wide as it opened and closed its jaws, still trying to feed, and then he was up. He scrambled through the forest to the next position, scanning the trees for the dead as he went. They were out there; they were coming.

****

Chad heard the gunshot, but it took him a moment to put together what had happened. He turned to see Larry standing stock-still on top of a trailer on the other side of the compound, then the man slumped to his knees. Chad saw blood pouring out of his back and down his shirt, and without thinking, he aimed his rifle into the woods and began shooting. The others followed suit, their panicked yells disappearing under the booms of their gunfire.

It had begun. His enemies had drawn first blood. He would be damned sure to draw the last.

He emptied his rifle into the trees, into where he thought the shooter might have come from.

"Dale! Check him out!" he yelled while he fed shells into his rifle. His ears rang painfully from all of the gunfire, but he didn't care. He scanned the forest around him. There was movement all over, but he couldn't figure out what was from the living and what was from the dead.

"Take 'em out!" he yelled. "Take 'em all out!" As he turned, he saw Dale put a bullet in Larry's head. He was dead for good now. He turned around to keep his eye on his section of the compound, the section where Clara was buried. The dead were closer now. He held off on shooting them. Let them eat her first, then he would take them out. He watched the show play out before him, fighting the urge to turn around and take in everything that was going on.

****

Katie ran through the woods, dodging the dead and kicking them out of the way when she had to. There were more of them now. The music was drawing them, and time was now a factor. She carried the putrid motorcycle helmet with her, its insides slathered in the rot of the dead. A large woman, who seemed to be mostly composed of large saggy breasts stepped in front of her, and she bashed her across the face with the motorcycle helmet, swinging it like a kid who had just picked up his first Wiffle ball bat. Kevin had a bat like that.

The corpse fell over on its chest, its feet going up comically in the air as it high-centered on its breast meat. Kevin... she knew that name.

She approached the front of the compound, but stopped in her tracks as she saw the man atop the watchtower scanning the forest. It was the main man, the bad man. She pulled her handgun free, but knew that would be a death sentence right now. It would draw the dead to her like ants to the rotting core of an apple. Her only option then would be to run into the open area of the courtyard, where the men atop the trailers would mow her down.

She heard another gunshot from outside the compound, and immediately the men began firing into the woods from whence the gunshot had come. All except for the bad man. He kept watch over Clara, his eyes scanning the woods.

"Shit," she muttered. She only had one real option now... and it was basically suicide. She smiled. It was what it was. She pulled her handgun from her side and dashed into the clearing.

316

Chad saw the pregnant woman coming from a mile away. He smiled at the object she had in her hand. It was a dark black motorcycle helmet. *Clever, but not clever enough..* Too bad she wasn't going to make it.

He looked down his rifle, tracking the woman as she ran. He would try for the shoulder of the hand holding the gun. Maybe then she would live. After all, there was still a child inside her. She fired her gun as she sprinted at him, a look of desperation on her face that almost made him feel something inside. He tensed his finger on the trigger, and then something strange happened.

Blood flowed down his chest. He tried to take a deep breath but ended up choking on something salty and metallic.

He tried to look down to see where the blood was coming from, but he couldn't find the source. He turned around and saw someone standing there. It was Dez, a small knife in her hand. There was blood on the blade, and as he reached out to her, he stumbled. Blood jetted from somewhere in his body, covering Dez, and she looked him in the eye. There was nothing there for him. Just hate. He fell to his knees, and she remained dialed in on him.

"Fuck you," were the last words he heard before he fell on his face, and he realized she had slit his throat. He put his hands up to stop the flow of blood, but it was too late.

****

Katie didn't know who the woman was, but she had her thanks. She smiled at the sight of the big man's blood squirting into the air. Then she ran forward and slid to a stop where Clara's head poked up out of the ground. She didn't have the time to say more than a few words to her, but she managed to say, "Don't move, it's the only chance you have," before she slipped the putrid helmet over Clara's head.

Then she ran and began to climb the watchtower. The wooden structure offered plenty of handholds. It was designed to keep the dead out, not the living.

****

Clara had no time to respond to Katie as she slipped the helmet over her head. Hazy darkness enveloped her. The inside of the helmet smelled like death, and she could feel the coldness of rotting ick in her hair and on her skin. The visor of the helmet was down, and she could see shapes moving towards her. She remained still as the dead filed past her, kicking her in the head with their clumsy footsteps.

She fought the urge to vomit and tried to will herself to go somewhere else, to disappear into her mind. It was the only place she had left to go. She thought of the world before, of a man who had loved her more than anything else. She thought of hours sitting at a computer screen writing up case briefs and analyzing previously tried cases. She thought of family members she hadn't thought of in years.

She cried silently, as the dead absentmindedly kicked the helmet sticking up out of the ground, never stopping to wonder why it didn't move when they kicked it.

****

Joan saw the woman walk across the courtyard, limping as if she hadn't walked in a long time. She saw the knife in the woman's hand, but she didn't say anything. The pregnant women were huddled inside the trailers, and she was the only person to see the woman, who looked like one of the dead herself, bury the knife in Chad's throat.

She sat there, not calling attention to the ordeal as the men had their backs to the inside of the compound. The

318

threat wasn't supposed to come from the inside. It was outside, and Joan didn't want them to think any differently. There were six men left now. Firing indiscriminately into the woods, bringing the dead down upon them.

She watched as the woman calmly turned around and walked back into the house, shutting the door behind her. She watched as Katie's head appeared over the watchtower wall, and then tears of hope came to her eyes. Katie picked up Chad's rifle, hopped to the ground, and crept over to Joan.

Katie put a hand to the side of Joan's face and looked her in the eyes. When she placed the rifle in her hands, Joan knew what she had to do. She nodded at Katie, and then Katie went to stand behind her back, so that they could cover the whole compound.

"Now," Katie said, and they began to fire.

Her first shot went wide, but her second shot didn't. It struck a man in the chest and he fell on top of the trailer. The man on the next trailer over, sensing that something was wrong spun around with his rifle in his hand. But in the time it took for him to figure out that the two women in the courtyard were not on his side, a bullet ripped into his skull. He fell backwards and tumbled off the trailer completely. They fired until there was only one man left. As Joan was racking home another round, in the bolt-action rifle, he turned around and without hesitating threw the rifle down and put his hands into the air.

Joan took aim at him, and then she hesitated. He was unarmed. He was a human being. She had sworn to never willingly harm a human being. But that oath was a relic from a different time. When his face turned from fear to supplication, she shredded that oath in her mind and pulled the trigger.

He fell down to the ground, and then suddenly, it was quiet. She looked over her shoulder, and Katie stood there panting, her gun hanging at her side, her free hand pressed to her back. She sat on the ground, and they listened to the sounds of the dead. They had won. They had fucking won.

****

The women came out of the trailers then, tears in their eyes, hands on their pregnant bellies protectively.

"Why?" Theresa cried. "Why did you do it?"

There was no answer they could give, and it wouldn't have been heard over the noise of the dead anyway. They pounded on the trailers, creating a thunderous sound that was sure to draw more flesh-eaters their way.

"Spears!" Joan yelled, for she knew that they had them stored in the big house.

The women stood there, mute and shocked.

"Get the spears, or we're all going to be overrun!"

One of the pregnant women, with a face like a Disney witch pointed as a corpse began to rise. It was Chad, his eyes cold and dead. He pushed himself up on the watchtower, and then stood, looking left and right. His eyes locked onto the pregnant women, and he tumbled from the watchtower wall. When he rose, his left arm was broken, but that didn't stop him from advancing. He came at them, gnashing his teeth.

Katie lifted her handgun, but it clicked empty, the hammer hitting the brass casing of a spent shell. She frantically tried to reload, when a shot boomed out next to her. She jumped, fumbling her shells, and the dead men on top of the trailers began to rise as well. She saw Chad's corpse slump to the ground, a sizable portion of his skull missing. Smoke wafted up from the barrel of Joan's rifle.

Theresa waddled out of the big house with the bundle of spears. She dropped them next to the women, and they each grabbed one. They stood in the middle of the compound, fear lighting up their eyes. The dead came at

320

them slowly, and by the time they had entered the circle, Katie was slamming the cylinder of her handgun closed.

She began to take aim and fire, killing two of the things with the six shots she fired. Still more came. Joan, who couldn't move from her spot, had the worst angle. She couldn't see around the pregnant women huddled around them, and for this reason her rifle was useless. The women grabbed spears, but they seemed not to know what to do. They poked and prodded the dead. One woman jammed a spear into the gut of one of the creatures, and it pressed forward, the spear sliding through its guts as if it were made of Jell-o. It sunk its fingers into the flesh of her shoulders, squeezing so hard her skin popped and they could hear bones break, and she screamed a blood-curdling scream.

Katie saw all this as she tried to reload. There were still five of them, soon to be six if the pregnant lady turned. Katie didn't want to think about what would happen to the fetus inside the woman, but she did. She slammed the cylinder shut again and shot the pregnant woman in the head. Her life was over anyway. She took better aim this time and was able to put three more down.

The remaining pregnant women batted at the dead with the spears, pushing them back and holding them off. Joan waited patiently for a shooting lane to open up for her. When one of the pregnant women fell to the ground, she was finally able to get a shot off. She squeezed the trigger, and there was only one remaining.

"Dale!" one of the women cried as a dead man advanced upon her. She was unable to carry out the execution of the dead man, and she sank to the ground with her hands over her head as he fell upon her.

Katie was out of ammunition, so she snatched a spear from one of the ladies who stood there dumbfounded and in awe as Dale ripped the woman apart. Katie stepped up and drove the spear through the man's eye socket, pressing him back until he was lying on his back. She pulled the spear out to get a better angle at the writhing dead man, and then she plunged the tip of the spear all the way through his skull.

The mauled pregnant woman lay on the ground, blood wetting the compacted dirt below her. No one seemed to want to do anything about the fact that the woman was going to be dead soon. Katie stood there with the bloodied spear in her hand.

Loose flesh hung from the woman's face as she looked up at Katie. "No," she pleaded. "I want to live."

The pleas fell upon deaf ears, and Katie advanced upon the woman. She put up mangled hands in defense, the left one missing fingers, but Katie wouldn't stop. The cries of the woman cut her, but she had to make sure everyone was safe. She stabbed the woman through the throat, and she fell onto the ground gurgling, still trying to plead for her life. When the light faded from her eyes, she plunged the spear into the woman once more, ending her life for good.

Katie turned to find the women staring at her in disbelief. She hated them, those soft, doughy faces looking at her. They hadn't earned the right to look at her like that. They had spent their time hiding from the dead, playing house with a bunch of losers, and now they wanted to judge her. She had survived worse than dirty looks.

"Grab a spear. Get on top of those trailers. This isn't over yet." As if to punctuate her words, a trickle of dirt tumbled to the ground from underneath one of the trailers as it shifted. They left the dead in the courtyard, and they climbed the ladders that led to the rooftops.

"No guns!" Joan yelled as one of the women went to take one from a dead man's corpse. "That'll just bring more of them. And will someone please cut that fucking country music?"

As Katie climbed to the top of the watchtower, she began to think about Mort. The dead were too thick around the compound for him to safely make it inside. She hoped he was somewhere safe. Maybe he was hiding in a tree. Maybe he was back at the house. She supposed it didn't matter. They wouldn't find out his fate until they managed to clear the dead from around the trailers. As she stepped onto the wooden planks of the watchtower, she was greeted by a hundred dead faces. Through them, she caught a glimpse of the motorcycle helmet she had placed over Clara's head. It was still in the same place... all the more reason to dispatch the dead as quickly as possible.

She picked out the strongest and heaviest zombies first, plunging the spear into their upturned faces. They wanted her. They wanted everyone inside the compound. She heard the strained grunts from the other women. Dust kicked up and hung over the compound along with the smell of blood and decomposing flesh. The country music came to a stop as the generator lapsed into silence. All Katie heard were the groans of the dead, the grunts of the other women, and the crunch of wooden spears as they penetrated the skulls of the dead.

Every ten dead or so, she had to climb off the watchtower and trade her spear in for a new one as the point became blunted. Her hands were worn ragged, and blisters and bleeding cuts crisscrossed her palms. Sweat covered her entire body, and her clothes were turned a muddy brown as the dust mixed with the sweat.

The sun traced a slow arc over the sky, and more and more dead came to join the fray. After a while, she stopped seeing faces. She stopped seeing them as people and only as something that needed to be put down. The bodies piled up outside the walls, stacking up quickly. The dead stepped over their fallen brethren, gaining height with each body that Katie speared. The rotten corpses underneath squelched under the weight of the dead; the liquids pressed out of them until a river of red blood ran from underneath.

The smell was nauseating. The dead had made it through a summer of heat, rotting in the sunshine. Katie found herself retching as she continued spearing the dead. The whole time, she kept her eyes on the motorcycle helmet, hoping that the person they found in there would still be alive. She had no love for Clara, but she respected her. She had always been the most honest about their relationship, and she appreciated that... even if they did hate each other.

While the others had given her crooked looks and pretended as if everything was alright with her, Clara had always called her out for her perceived madness. As she wiped the sweat from her brow, she wondered at the change that had come over her. Was this survival? Or was this something more? Was she simply insane? Was that what had driven her to make an all-out assault on the compound, or was there something more there?

Was the old Katie peeking through? She jammed the spear into the face of a housewife with tiny bites on her arms. She knew what had made those bites, someone small, someone fragile, someone the woman had probably sacrificed her life for over and over again. The woman fell dead, and Katie wondered if there was something after death. Would that mother find her children again on the other side? Would she be able to face the end with a clear conscience?

As the sun turned yellow, she continued slaying the dead. She called out to Clara, "Just hold on. We just have to clear out the dead, and then we'll dig you out." She didn't know if Clara heard her; the helmet didn't move.

****

Mort spent a harrowing night in the trees. It was pitch-black out, the clouds obscuring the small sliver of moon enough to make the forest floor murky and dark. He could see the glow of the compound's campfire in the distance, and he longed to be near it. He longed to be there and discover if their plan had been successful or not.

The wind rushed through the trees, but the sound of branches brushing against each other couldn't hide the sound of once-human hands pawing at tree bark. He was very thankful that the damned couldn't climb. He was in for a long night.

Mort tried not to think about the exploits of the day. He tried not to replay the scenes of carnage that he had seen, but they wouldn't stop coming. He huddled against the trunk of the spruce tree, trying to keep from freezing to death as the scene played out before his eyes once again.

After they had fired off their first shots, Mort had climbed down from his perch. ducking his head as shot after shot was fired into the woods, as if ducking would protect him if any of the bullets actually struck him. Once he hit the ground, he had run through the forest, dodging in and out of the dead, the underbrush clinging to him as he ran.

He had almost screamed out loud as he lurched directly into the path of a stringy old lady who shambled around a tree just as he was passing. He pushed at her and struggled to free his hammer as two more of the dead approached through the trees. He knew he was wasting precious time, but his hands didn't seem to want to work correctly. His movements felt awkward and clumsy.

He felt the hands of another dead thing on his back as he finally pulled his hammer free. He clonked the old lady on the head and shoved her away. She fell into a tangle of blackberries, and he only barely had time to spin around and hit his second attacker under the chin with the head of his hammer. Its teeth shattered, and Mort pushed this one away as well. Time was running short. He should be in the second tree already, but the dead were out in full force.

He dodged the remaining dead man, and he ran to the next tree, the one he had marked earlier as being the easiest to climb with the strongest branches. Up he went, fear chasing him quicker than any of the dead could. As he pulled himself up on the first branch, he felt hands grasp his ankles. He kicked his legs, struggling to pull himself higher.

For a second, he thought he was going to be pulled down, but then he landed a lucky kick on his attacker's face, and it stumbled away, giving him the freedom he needed to climb higher. He sat on the lowest branch of the tree, sweating and looking down at the crowd of the dead that had gathered around him. Despite the fact that the compound was still blasting country music and firing off the occasional shot into the forest, these dead didn't care. They saw him. They probably smelled him at this point, and they were going to wait for him.

Once his arms recovered enough strength to carry him upwards, he began his ascent, careful to test each branch as he went. The last thing he wanted was to fall from the tree into the clutches of the dead below. He pushed upward, fear still bouncing around in his body. He didn't stop until he came to a spot that allowed him a view of the compound while still providing plenty of cover. He looked down at the unruly mob below him, and they looked up at him. They were partially obscured from his line of sight, as he was to them, but they knew he was there, and they showed no sign of giving up, even though he was out of their reach by a good forty feet.

He took a deep breath and forced the sounds of the dead out of his mind, and then he fired his shot. One shot, one blessed shot. It tore through the man's chest and he toppled to the ground. He said a little prayer, thankful that he was able to do his part.

Mort scrambled then, moving around to the backside of the tree as more shots came his way. He hoped he had caused a good enough distraction for Katie to do what she needed to do, but right then, with bullets whizzing past his head, all he could think about was escaping.

He used the trees to escape, creeping along the thickest branches he could find to move from one tree to the next. The dead still followed him, but with each tree he reached, there were less. They had difficulty tracking him through the trees, which worked to his advantage. He came to a spot in the forest where it became dangerous to move on. The only option he had was to jump. A few feet away, there was a branch that looked like it was thick enough to take his weight. He inched out across the branch, holding onto some weaker branches above him to steady himself. He was almost there when a bullet hit the branch that he was on. The bullet didn't break the branch in half, but it did enough damage to weaken it. He felt himself slowly sagging, and, having no other option, he made a leap for it. The branch came at him quickly, and he wrapped his arms around it. For a second, he thought he was safe, but then there was a great snap, and he was plummeting downwards, his back to the ground, his arms flailing for anything to break his fall.

Mort's back slapped off another branch, and his world was sent tumbling. The ground was coming up fast, and he had no chance to brace himself. With a great thump, he impacted the ground. Panic rushed through him, and he had no time to think. He rose up on his feet, shaky and unsteady as the dead that had been trailing him closed in. The rifle on his back was useless. The barrel was clogged with dirt from the fall, so he pulled it over his head and left it on the ground as he fumbled for his hammer. He knew the hammer was still there because he had a fiery pain in his hip where he had landed upon it.

He pulled it free and took a clumsy swing at the nearest dead thing, his hip cramping in pain at even that weak attempt. He ended up smacking the creature in the side of the head with his forearm instead of the hammer, but it was enough to knock the creature off-balance. He turned to run, but all he could manage was a brisk, stumbling walk. Stars still danced in his eyes, and his breath came in great ragged gasps.

Mort had no thoughts left. He moved like a cornered animal, dodging the dead and lashing out at them as they pawed at him. For all he knew, he ran in a great circle, and then a single thought crossed his mind. *Get off the ground, Mort.* He cast his eyes upwards, examining the trunks of the trees around him, but none of them were suitable. He had lost all sense of direction during his fall, and for all he knew he was running right into the hundred or so dead that were surrounding the compound.

He made his hammer sing as it rang off the side of a dead man's skull, and then he was clambering up the side of a young, healthy tree, his hip screaming at him. His head spun as he climbed. He felt as if the entire world were rocking side to side, as if someone had picked up the earth and set it afloat in gently rolling water. With his hammer tucked into his belt, he pushed upward, groaning in pain as he flexed his bruised hip. The dead pawed at his boots and calves, squeezing and trying to bring him to the ground, but with the great strength and desperation of one who knows they are about to die, he was able to pull himself out of their reach.

Now he sat in the dark, listening to the dead below trample on dried leaves and shuffle through mounds of old pine needles. He could hear their bony digits scrabbling at the tree bark, and all he wanted to do was see another living face. It didn't matter who it was, Katie, Clara, Joan, anyone would do.

He leaned back against the tree, trying not to breathe deep as his aching ribs burned with each deep breath. His hip felt like it was locking up, and he knew that if no one ever found him in this tree, he might well die there. His body was too wrecked to be any good for the next day and perhaps even the day after that. By the time his body would be healed enough to move, he would be dehydrated and starving... not the best way to try and survive. But he still had hope. Somehow, Mort, the man who had lived his life as a homeless runaway scared of others, had found an unending source of hope in this world. He still had friends, and they still cared for him. They would find him. They had to. He shut out the sounds of the dead and tried to keep his eyes from closing, for if they did, it might be for the very last time.

Chapter 17: The Trial

Epps felt nervous, as if things were coming to a head. The soldiers had holed up in the security building with Nike in their possession. All night long, the other residents of the campus had pelted the building with rocks. Fires burned in the night, and the shadows of the dead in the other buildings were restless.

He was afraid, not for his own life, but for the fact that he was going to have to kill people, actual living people who had, so far, done nothing wrong. While he had formed no friendships with the people of the campus, he recognized their normality. It felt like something that should be protected. But it wasn't his place to make decisions. It was Tejada's burden, and he was thankful that he wouldn't have to make such a choice.

"You ok?" Day asked him.

He and Day had never known each other before this all began. Even on the bridge, he had stuck mostly with Brown, Beacham, and Allen. "Yeah, I'm alright," he said. But he wasn't. He was tired, as tired as tired could be. He wanted to turn to Day and tell him all the things he was feeling, but Day wasn't like that. Day was a normal man, about as average a man as you could find. Without even having to ask, he knew the man liked football, barbecuing, and drinking beer. He liked his women plastic and fake. He liked his food plain and unseasoned. He was a cardboard cutout of a human.

No, he couldn't discuss his misgivings with a man like that. A man like that would hear his complaints and think him weak. It was a man's lot to look on a situation with grim impassivity and emotionless fatalism. He shook his head. *Allen and his stupid vocabulary must be rubbing off on me.*

As he thought this, a woman parted from the mob. It was the one that Allen had been banging. He corrected himself in his own mind. It was the woman he had been sleeping with. That seemed more... proper. Never one for political correctness, Epps had grown to miss the trappings of civilization. While before, it might have been fine for him to say that Allen and this woman were banging, now he found it base. He found it to be yet another of those things that men had devised to hide the fact that there were these things called emotions and feelings, and that they all had them. That his friend Allen had emotions and feelings did not bother him anymore. In fact, he was pleased to partake of them and be witness to them. For there were precious few men among them that could show these things now. The world, the way it was now, had all but killed these things in the other soldiers, but in Allen, the death of the world had refined them and brought them to the forefront. He wasn't afraid to show emotion anymore. For that reason, Epps vowed not be afraid to show his own emotions, but on a man like Day, they would be wasted.

The woman calmly walked up the stairs, and for an instant, Epps had a vision of a queen climbing the steps to her throne. She had the look on her face of one who was not used to being trifled with, and he didn't relish answering the door. But she knocked, and it was such a civil gesture during a time of rampant uncivility that he pulled the door open for her.

Day stood ready with his rifle, his sights dancing over the skull of the woman.

"What is it?" Epps asked.

"I want to see my father," Diana said.

"No one sees the prisoner," Day spat at her.

She looked at him the way a teacher might look at an unruly pupil. Day shrank a little bit. "This is our place. We decide who is a prisoner and who isn't," she said.

"That may be so, but right now, this is our place, our building," Epps said. "Sergeant Tejada is talking with him right now. If you have a message, we'll pass it along, but other than that, no one is getting in here."

Diana looked at him and smiled. It was a plastic smile, and he knew she was furious at being rebuked. "Tell my father that I came to talk to him, and that you wouldn't let me see him. Tell him that's the best I could do."

With her message given, she turned and left the way she came. The people outside seemed impatient for her return. Epps wondered how many of them thought that they were going to kill her. He saw Diana shake her head once, and the faces of many in the crowd changed, morphing from obvious outrage to one of grim determination. It was not the change he wanted to see, and Epps knew that things were about to go from bad to worse.

"Stay here. I have to talk to Tejada," Epps said to Day. "Brown!" he shouted. "Get down here and watch the door."

Brown rushed down the stairs, sensing the urgency in his friend's voice.

Epps patted Brown on the shoulder as he passed him on the stairs. "Make sure no one gets in."

****

Tejada sat across from Nike, their eyes boring into each other's souls. Tejada wondered if Nike saw something as empty as what he was seeing in the man sitting across from him. "What do you want, Nike?"

Nike tented his hands in front of him, looking as smug as the day they had been introduced in the meeting room. "I don't want anything."

"Oh, come on. Cut the shit. You must want something." Tejada slid the journal across the table. "A man who wants nothing doesn't spend his time making sure that every guard in his employ is murdered in the dead of night."

332

"You call it murder. I call it compartmentalizing. I saved this place," Nike said, leaning forward, ignoring the journal in front of him.

"Saved it? By killing everyone inside except for a hundred or so individuals? You murdered those people."

Nike nodded, hearing what Tejada said as if for the first time. "It wasn't murder." There was a silence, and then Nike began again. "What would you have me do? There wasn't enough food. The trucks we had ordered, the refrigeration units we had ordered, never showed. There were too many mouths and not enough food. I could have told everyone. I could have done that, but in the end, the result would have been the same. We would have lost people. They would have turned on each other, started fighting over resources. I could have sent people out to find food, but some of those people would have come back infected, and people still would have died. Nothing would be different."

"And that makes it ok?"

Nike leaned back in his chair, turning his head away from Tejada's steely gaze. "Oh, fuck you."

They sat in silence for some time until there was a knock on the door. Tejada got up and opened it. Epps stood at the door, and right away Tejada could tell that something was wrong.

"What is it?" he asked.

"I think we have a problem, sir."

"Go on."

"Nike's daughter came to the door, and she said some real cryptic shit. I told her that she couldn't come in to see her father, and when she left..."

"Spit it out, son."

"Sir, I think the people out there are planning something."

Nike just laughed in the corner. Tejada ignored his bullshit for the moment. "I'll put a stop to this right now."

He turned and grabbed the journal from the table, and Nike stopped laughing.

"What are you doing?" he asked, suddenly worried.

"If this turns to shit, it'll be because they know the truth," he said back. "Epps, stand here and guard this bastard. If he tries to escape, give him a beating."

Epps smiled at the older gentleman. Tejada had told them what had become of the security force that had risked their lives to secure the Nike campus, and he relished the thought of putting his knuckles through that smug mouth.

Tejada grabbed the book and rushed down the stairs. There was a lot of noise outside. As he approached the glass doors, he saw what he had feared, an angry mob stealing themselves to make an assault on the soldiers inside. They had torches and wielded baseball bats liberated from the Ken Griffey Jr. tribute wall.

"What do we do, sir?" Day asked, but Tejada didn't even stop to give him an answer. He thundered through the front doors of the security building into the black of the night.

As soon as the doors opened, he was greeted by outraged shouts. They called him murderer and tyrant, all the things people called someone who had the ability to shape their own lives without their say-so. He understood that. They felt put upon, left out of the loop. They felt taken advantage of. He and his men had been guests here, and now it would seem that they were calling the shots. But they weren't, and they had no intentions of doing so.

Still, he would like to know who had whipped up this mob because the people he had seen throughout his short stay on the campus had shown themselves to be a weak lot, even if they did have a certain hardiness about them. This was not a natural outpouring of rage. Someone had wound them up, and he had an inkling of who that someone might be.

334

He held the journal up in his hand as the first rocks came flying his way. "I understand you're angry," he began, dodging the thrown stones.

"You don't understand shit!" a woman yelled from the back of the mob.

"No, I do. You think we come here to rule you, to put you to death when we think you've done something wrong, but that's not true."

"Then why do you have Nike locked up?" a different woman yelled.

Tejada nodded. "I have him locked up because we have more information than you. It has come to our attention that Nike has been doing more than just looking out for you good people. He has been doing much more than that."

He held the journal up so that the mob could see it. "When we cleared this place, we found this journal. There's some interesting stuff about Nike in here that you all ought to know. I'll leave this out here for you." Tejada set the journal upon the ground. "Tomorrow, there will be a trial, so read it, study it. Because we won't be deciding the fate of Nike. You will."

With his message sent, he turned his back, hoping that no one out there had a gun stashed away. He heard murmuring among the crowd. They were unsure what to make of what he had just said, but he knew that eventually curiosity would win out in the end. He pulled the doors open and stepped inside.

To Day he said, "When they come up to grab the book, don't shoot them, unless they come up to touch the door."

Day nodded, and Tejada began his climb up the stairs. He was tired. Every bit of him ached, but it was his mind that was the most exhausted. He didn't know how much of this he could stand, but he knew that just over the horizon, he and his men had another slog through the countryside ahead of them. He wondered if it would finally do him in. He hoped not.

Inside the room, he relieved Epps of his duty and sent him off to grab some sleep. He sat down across from Nike. Nike looked at him like a dog that had just been kicked.

"What did you do?" he asked.

"I haven't done shit. It's you that has things to answer for. My conscience is clear."

Nike looked like he was going to bolt for the door. But then he thought better of it and remained in his seat. "I do have things to answer for. Yes, yes I do. I have to answer for bringing all these people here in the first place. I have to answer for saving their lives when everyone else around them died. And how do you think they'll punish me for this?"

"I don't know. I don't care," Tejada said.

"Oh, life must be so simple for you. Wake up. Follow orders. Decide who to kill." Nike sneered at him, as if he were but a piece of shit on the sole of one of his one-hundred-and-fifty-dollar pairs of running shoes. "I was responsible for all of this. I was responsible for bringing people here. I was responsible for keeping them safe. That meant tough decisions had to be made."

"You're preaching to the choir."

"Then why are you doing this?" Nike asked, exasperated.

"I'm not doing this for you. I'm not doing this for them. I'm not doing this for myself. I'm doing this for all the people that came before, all the ones that didn't have a chance to live. I'm doing this because this is the way things were done before the world went to hell. Just because we're living in hell doesn't mean we act like demons. You should have thought of that before you cost hundreds of people their lives because you were afraid."

"This world needs people like me."

"We'll find out tomorrow, won't we?" Tejada rose then, he was through listening to this man. He was a nothing, a petty, self-involved nothing.

As Tejada closed the door, Nike wept softly.

****

Masterson and Whiteside reported that the mob had departed peacefully last night, taking the journal with them. There had been no sign of them since.

Amanda clung to Rudy's arm as the morning broke gray and cold over the Nike campus. They watched as the broken and somber Nike was led down the stairs.

"I'd hate to be in his position," Rudy said.

"You never would be. That's the difference," Amanda said.

Allen and Epps led Nike onto the green grass of the campus. The smoke from the previous day's burnings had all but gone, though the smell still remained. For his part, Nike didn't struggle. He was led to the grass as meekly as a lamb on a leash. Tejada came next. He sent Whiteside and Masterson to get some sleep before ordering Gregg and Day to find their way to the roof to provide covering fire should things go wrong. Everyone else followed Tejada out to the campus green.

They only had to wait but a moment before the people of Nike began to file out of the Ken Griffey Jr. building, which sat directly across from the security building. Amanda watched them coming. Their faces were grim, and they shuffled forward as meekly as Nike had. Tejada stopped Nike in the middle of the field and sat drinking instant coffee from a tin cup as the crowd gathered around.

Amanda wondered how Tejada could smile the way he did, nodding reassuringly at the people as they began to congregate in a semi-circle around the accused Nike. This all felt familiar to Amanda, and she couldn't help but think

337

of Chloe. Sometimes she felt guilt for what she did, but at other times... she looked over at Rudy, the most unlikely of loves, and she felt absolutely justified for the actions she had taken.

The people finished filing out of the building. Tejada dumped the dregs of his coffee cup on the grass, drawing a disdainful look from Nike. Then the soldier began to speak.

****

Walt stood next to Brown, his finger getting itchy. He didn't like being out in the open, but Tejada seemed calm, so he tried to keep calm too. He looked around the field, marking the shadows in the glass windows around them. There was still a lot of work to be done, and he felt like they shouldn't be wasting their time playing games with Nike. He was a murderer. He should be dealt with accordingly. A bullet was all he deserved.

Brown, who he had been talking to more and more, didn't feel the same way. Walt had never been a religious person, but he had found Brown to be so. He kept saying "God was the only real judge," or some such bullshit. To be honest, he had tuned the man out as soon as he had offered up religious babble. How the man could still believe in a god after everything they had gone through was a mystery to him, but he supposed that some people would believe right up until the moment they died... simply because they hadn't yet died, as if that were indisputable proof of God's greatness. But Walt was willing to bet that on their deathbed, God offered little consolation even to the most pious of the believers.

Walt scanned the crowd, his eyes crawling across Amanda. She had been responsible for something like this at one time, and Walt had hated her for it. He understood now. He understood about justice, about caring for the others around you so much that you would do anything to

338

make someone pay for hurting the people you cared about. Truth was, before he had met Tejada and his men, he had never had anyone care about him. His time with the other soldiers had changed him, in a good way he hoped. It was such a short time, but so much had happened to open his eyes. His feeling of hatred for Amanda and Rudy was gone.

He spotted Rudy standing next to her, and though the pair still looked somewhat silly, they also looked right together. Rudy had proven himself capable and far more of a survivor than Walt had ever expected. When they had asked him to man the door to the security building, he hadn't even batted an eyelash.

"I'm not going to give you a speech. If you've read that journal, you know why we're here," Tejada began. The crowd remained silent, attentive. "This man, according to that journal, has been toying with your lives since the day you arrived here. Look around, and you can see the fruit of his actions." The crowd looked around at the shadows of the dead standing in the windows of the surrounding buildings.

"We are here, to determine guilt or innocence. If he is found guilty, you shall determine what we do with him." The crowd remained silent, and then Tejada stepped back and said, "But I'll not punish anyone without them getting the chance to speak their side. So Nike, the floor is yours."

Walt decided this was a wise move on Tejada's part. This way, people wouldn't have any misgivings about what happened. If he had demanded Nike to stand there silently and be judged, people would have had their doubts. Walt waited expectantly to hear what Nike would say.

The man stood still, forming his thoughts, the wind ruffling his curly brown and gray hair. His face looked tired underneath his overgrown beard, but there was still something of the worm about his face, something completely and totally untrustworthy. No, it was less worm and more reptilian, Walt decided.

Finally, he spoke. "You people know me. Where would you be without me? Without the walls I have provided?" He let the words hang there as the crowd filled in their own answers. He was a great speaker, his voice carrying a natural authority that was almost soothing, and Walt wondered if maybe Tejada hadn't made a mistake. "You'd be dead. Don't fool yourselves. Each and every one of you owe your lives to me, ten times over. I gave you safety. I gave you security. I gave you food and a roof over your heads. Did some people die in the process? Yes. And for that, I'm terribly sorry. I never wanted anyone to die, but this is what being a leader is about. Sometimes you have to make sacrifices for the greater good."

"Fuck you!" a woman shouted. She pushed her way forward. She was a stout woman, matronly in many ways. Her face was screwed up in anger and outrage. "My brother was one of those sacrifices thanks to you."

Nike listened, never breaking eye contact as the woman continued. "He died because you had to be in control. You had to make sure that you were always in charge, and so now my brother is dead. What do you say to that, bossman?" The crowd cheered her on, nodding and supporting the woman's outrage.

"I say this. If your brother were here now, and he had a choice to save your life by giving up his own, what would he do?" The woman said nothing. The crowd looked to her to see what she would say, but she clenched her jaw and stared straight at Nike. "You see? It's like I said. Most of the people in those buildings, if they knew they were going to be saving the rest of you, they would gladly give up their lives."

"What about the security guards?" a man asked, adjusting his glasses on the bridge of his nose.

"What about them? They were dangerous. They were too powerful. Sooner or later they would have been running the show. And then where would we be? Men with

340

guns, they might be necessary at times, but sooner or later, a man with a gun gets it in his head that he wants things, that he needs things. We saw it before they died. They ate more than the rest of us. They demanded more than the rest of us. And it was only a matter of time before they wanted more than just our food and support. Sooner or later they would have wanted us, our bodies, our freedom, they would have taken it all."

He lapsed into silence as his words echoed through the crowd's mind. "If you want to know if I killed the guards, then yes, I did. But understand this. When a master craftsman is done with his tools, he doesn't leave them sitting out to gather rust so that his child can come along and hurt himself with them. He puts them away. And that's what I did. When we didn't need them anymore, when our home was carved from the city, I put them away so that the children wouldn't hurt themselves. I put them away so that they wouldn't rust and become dangerous. I did what had to be done... for you." He looked into their faces, his own face suddenly humble.

Walt smirked at the man, at his saccharine words, so sweet, so misleading. But he saw that there were those in the crowd who were swayed by his words. There were those in the crowd that were still loyal to Nike, still appreciated that he had saved their lives because, in the end, they were only alive because he had brought them to the campus and put up the walls in the first place.

"That's all I have to say." Nike took a step backwards and clasped his hands in front. He seemed completely calm and in control, as if he already knew the outcome of his little speech.

Tejada stepped forward. "You've heard the charges; you've seen the proof. He has admitted his part in the deaths of the security guards and the people of the campus. At this time, does anyone else wish to say anything?"

341

Diana stepped forward, and Walt was once again jealous of Allen. He couldn't believe he had slept with that woman, that lucky bastard. Walt had put out some feelers to some of the women on campus, but none of them had reciprocated his clumsy attempts at romance.

She walked to her father and then turned and faced the crowd. "My father has done things for the good of all of us. While we may not agree with those things, he has never done so out of spite or for a reason that did not include our safety. Is he guilty? I think so, but guilty of what? Trying to protect us? Well, then we ought to put these soldiers on trial as well. They killed Harper in cold blood. Where was his trial? Or were they simply trying to protect us from him as well? It's just something to think about."

A man pushed forward, glasses on his face. He was small, unassuming, and had a face like a buzzard. "Nike claims he did this all to protect us. I accept that, but let's not overlook the fact that every act he took to protect us led to the deaths of others, people he had also claimed he was going to protect. If we don't find him guilty, who's to say that the next time we need 'protection' that I won't be the one to go, or you or you?" he asked pointing to people in the crowd. "We're all adults here. I am not a child. I do not need my actions or safety lorded over by some relic of a world that's dead. If I need to be protected, then teach me how to protect myself. If I need to make a sacrifice for the good of the others, then I damn well want to make that sacrifice with a good idea of what it is I'm sacrificing for. This man, though he claims to be protecting us, when it comes down to it, he's killed more of us than any of those things have. He's guilty as fuck, and if you can't see that, or you want to pussyfoot around the issue, then maybe you're just as guilty." He said this last to Diana, and she glared at him as if he had struck her.

"Anyone else?" Tejada asked. The crowd lapsed into silence. "Alright. It's time to vote. Raise your hand if you think Nike is guilty. Walt watched as some people debated internally about whether to raise their hands or not. Most hands went up immediately, but a few took their time about it. In the end, there wasn't a single hand that wasn't raised in the air, including Diana's.

Nike stood on the campus grass looking bewildered. His words couldn't change the facts, and everyone knew he was guilty, whether they owed him their lives or not. He seemed to realize that now. It was as if all the life had left him, and he stood on the grass looking like a lost old man who had been betrayed by his children. Walt felt a small sense of sympathy for the man, but not enough to care what happened to him. He had made his bed; now he would have to lie in it. That's what his mother had always told him after he had taken a beating from the boys in town, as if he could have avoided it in some way.

"The verdict is guilty," Tejada proclaimed. "Now it's time to determine the punishment. So let's hear it. This is your man, not ours, so it's your punishment to dish out."

Walt felt this was another good move on Tejada's part. His manipulation of the people was inspiring.

"Kill him!" a voice from the crowd yelled. A few other voices shouted their agreement.

Diana stepped forward and announced, "We ought to strip him of his power, but let him stay here. We owe him that much." No voices shouted support for Diana.

The man in the glasses stepped forward again. He waited until he had the crowd's complete attention, and then he spoke again, squinting in the gray morning light. "There's been enough killing here. We've lost too many people to keep killing. While this man has saved our lives, he has also cost us the lives of many of our loved ones. Let him see what life is like without us, the people he sought to use. Let him see what life is like out there, where he has no power, where no one cares who he was before the world died. Let him be exiled from here."

Many in the crowd nodded at the man's wisdom. He stepped back into the crowd, and people clapped him on the shoulders for a speech well spoken. Tejada, sensing that no one else would come forward and speak after the man in the glasses, held a vote. In the end, it was decided that they would send Nike over the wall. The soldiers would clear enough space for him to get away, and maybe he would have a chance at survival.

The old man sank to the grass then, his lower lip quivering with either fear, sadness, or rage. Walt couldn't tell which. Maybe it was a combination of all three.

Many in the crowd turned their backs on Nike, content with letting the soldiers carry out the punishment. Diana and a few other campus people brought Nike some supplies. He changed out of his comfortable business shoes and slipped into a pair of running shoes that Diana set before him. They filled a backpack with canned food and bottled water. Tejada himself handed Nike a baseball bat. Through it all, Nike remained silent, pensive, as if he were already dead.

They marched him to the edge of the wall; only the most vengeful of Nike employees followed along to see that the job was done well. Using ladders, the soldiers situated themselves at the top of the wall. They opened fire at the dead milling about outside, obliterating them with the new weapons they had taken from the security building. When a space was cleared, large enough for Nike to reach the ground and get a good head start, they sent him up the wall with his backpack and his baseball bat in his hand. He went meekly, like an animal being led to slaughter.

At the top he turned around and locked eyes with Diana. "I did it all for you," he said.

"I know," she replied.

"Will you come with me?" he asked.

"No." Tears came to her eyes.

344

Nike nodded, and then he went over the wall, dropping to the ground easily. Then he was off. They watched him jog toward the cookie-cutter townhomes across the way, which were separated from the road by a tall wall that acted as a sound barrier from the once-busy road. He disappeared through an opening in the wall, and then he was gone. Just like that, Nike was no more.

Walt and the others left their positions on the wall, and they headed back to the security building. Tomorrow would be a full day. They would be clearing the dead out of the other buildings. Tejada had already stated that he intended to have this place Annie-free by the end of the week. They needed to be well-rested so that they didn't make any mistakes.

They passed by Diana who sat on her knees in the tall grass close to the wall, tears in her eyes.

Chapter 18: The Rescue

It was night by the time they managed to clear out the dead. But there were more out there in the forest. The women, emotionally and physically spent, had called it a night. There would be more killing in the morning. Katie still had one more thing to do before she could rest. She crept down off the wall, landing on the bodies of the dead. She moved carefully to avoid twisting an ankle on the squishy mass below her. She made it to the blood-soaked ground, moving slowly and quietly.

It was dark out, too dark to see much, and Katie expected one of the dead to come shambling out of the forest at any moment. She should have stayed inside. She should have waited for daylight, but she had to know. She had to know if Clara was still alive. She crawled across the dirt, moving to the spot where Clara had been buried. She felt for her in the gloom of the night, and her hand fell on the black, plastic helmet.

The head inside the helmet jerked and moved, but that didn't mean anything. If she were dead, it would do the same. She lifted the helmet off of Clara's head and then waited a second before asking, "You still alive?"

In a voice as quiet as the rustle of fabric, Clara said, "Yes."

Katie was overjoyed to hear her response.

"Get me out of here," Clara said, her voice trembling.

"We can't."

"What do you mean you can't?"

"It's too dangerous. Too dark. All that noise pulled a lot more of the dead from the highway than we counted on. We don't know how many are out there, and it's too dark to work out here without lights. We could be surrounded in a heartbeat, and then we'd both be dead."

Clara hissed then, "Get me the hell out of here."

Katie wanted to, she really did, but she already heard rustling from the forest. "Tough break, kiddo. But don't worry. I'll be keeping watch all night. Nothing will get close to you. But, just in case, I'm going to put this helmet back on."

Clara's muffled "no" disappeared abruptly as Katie pushed the helmet down onto her head. She felt awful about it, but it was too dangerous to work out here. She heard a groan from her right and sprinted back to the wooden watchtower. She climbed as if the dead thing were right on her heels, and then she was up and over, disappearing around the waist-high wooden railing of the watchtower. She lay sweating on the wooden planks, feeling cold in the middle of the cool night.

She sat up and looked into the middle of the compound. The fire pit was dark. The women of the compound, overcome with sadness, fear, and their own cocktail of conflicting hormones had taken themselves off to bed after a tense moment when they had all stared at each other, weapons in their hands, waiting for the other side to make a move. But neither did, and now all was quiet.

Joan still sat in the middle of the compound, a rifle in her hands and a blanket over her lap. Katie climbed down from the watchtower and walked over to her. It was hard to tell if she were still awake or not in the shadows of the night.

Katie jumped when Joan asked her, "Is she still alive?" It sounded to Katie as if she had been crying.

"Yes."

"Thank God."

She could have said something about God and the dubiousness of his existence, but she kept her lip zipped. "We'll get her in the morning. It's too dangerous out here now."

"You can't just leave her out there." Joan sounded shocked at the idea.

"It's ok. I'm going to keep an eye on her from the watchtower all night and make sure that nothing happens to her."

"I'll stay with you."

"As awesome as that would be, I don't see any way to get you on top of that watchtower, unless you learned to climb steps with a broken leg." Joan was silent, and Katie wished there were enough light so that she could see her face. "Come on. I'll help you to bed, then I have to get back up on that wall in case Mort shows up or Clara needs help."

She bent down and picked up Joan, wincing at the oniony smell that emanated from her. Together, they walked/hopped to Joan's trailer. They bumped through the trailer in the dark, Joan cursing in pain as they hit the edge of the counter. Katie set her down as gently as she could, and Joan laid back with a sigh.

"What happened to Lou?" Katie asked.

"They killed him." Joan seemed to want to say more, but she didn't.

Katie wanted to feel something. She wanted to feel anything at that moment, but they had already killed Chad and his brother. If she had known what they had done to Lou, she would have stopped and enjoyed it more.

"What do you know about these women? Are we safe here?" Katie asked.

"I don't know. They're not killers if that's what you're asking. They sat around while the men did all the killing, so I don't know if they'll come after us or not."

"I guess we'll see in the morning."

Katie left then, but she returned quickly with the rifle that Joan had used earlier. She placed it in bed with Joan and said, "If anyone but me comes in that door, you shoot 'em. Ok?

Joan didn't say anything, but Katie trusted that she would make the right decision when the opportunity presented itself. She went back outside, cursing the inky black sky. She climbed back up on the watchtower and stared into the darkness of the area around the compound. It was quiet enough that she could hear every footstep out in the woods. They would have more work to do in the morning, and she was glad that she hadn't tried to rescue Clara in the middle of the night.

In the solitude of the night, she replayed the events of the day. Did she have a death wish? Was she just sane enough to make the insane happen? By all means, they should all be dead. Somehow, she had won out; somehow, she had saved the friends that she could.

She was sorry about Lou. He had been a good person. He, out of all of them, had accepted her for who she was... and exactly who was she? The question seemed to come out of nowhere, and, as questions frequently do to those sitting in the dark with nothing else to focus on, it seemed to take on an importance of its own. It was as if the question itself were life or death, something that could destroy her if she didn't manage to answer it correctly right then and there.

She knew who she used to be, a doddering old housewife, a plain Jane running through her life never thinking about anything. But who was this new Katie? Feelings of guilt began to creep and crawl through her soul as she thought about all of the things that she had done since this had all began. Killing people... that was easier than killing the dead. The living knew what they were doing, and they deserved the punishments that she had dealt out to them. But the dead, they were artless, just stumbling blocks of meat. She killed them out of necessity. But the people.

You're full of shit, girl. She looked down at the ground willing her mind to not disappear into the realm of justifications for the things she had done since the end of the world. She thought about the people she had killed and realized very few of the killings had been justified. They had been the actions of someone who truly was insane.

Katie imagined her heart as a pulsing organ floating in the stars above. On its surface, she could see the scars that were left from not so long ago. A dark light pulsed along those scars, and she knew that she would have to face them or they would eat her up as sure as one of the dead would.

For the first time since it had all begun, she thought of her child, her glorious son. He had been everything to her, her world, her reason for being. She hadn't been forced into being a housewife. She had wanted to be. She had wanted to give up everything of who she was so that her son might have the best life possible. She recalled her husband, a hardworking man who had only shown herself and her son love. Her life had been perfect.

That's why her scars ran so deep. She allowed herself to cry in the darkness for what she had lost. For the first time, she allowed herself to relive the memories of everything that she had lost. She allowed herself to feel the guilt of everything she had done since she had killed them. Katie began to heal.

****

Clara's night was pure hell. She longed to move with every inch of her body, but the only part she could move was the one part of her body that she didn't dare to. There was an ache in every muscle of her body from sitting still for almost a whole day. Though the earth supported her, she felt as if it were crushing her to death with its cold embrace.

She could see nothing through the death-filmed visor of the motorcycle helmet on her head. But she could hear the dead milling about in the forest, crushing branches and dry leaves. Katie had said she would be close, and a couple of times in the night, she thought she heard sobs. Though they filled her heart with sorrow to hear, she was grateful to know someone was out there watching over her.

Clara too cried as the dread of not being able to escape began to crawl through every inch of her body. She tried to stifle it, to shove it down, but doing so only seemed to make it worse. First, the tears came to her eyes, and she felt as if her entire body were going to explode if she didn't move soon. Then the thoughts began to creep in at the edge of her consciousness... thoughts of the dead finding her underneath that motorcycle helmet and eating her face, their grubby hands groping to gouge her eyeballs from her skull.

She began to hyperventilate, until she was sure that the only way to stop her erratic breathing was to scream. Tears fell from her eyes, snot ran from her nose, and she had no means to wipe either away. The feeling of being trapped intensified steadily, until she thought that it would be better to scream and get it all over with than to spend another second in her tomb.

Just when she was about to throw it all away, she saw a glint of orange light rising over the trees in front of her. She locked onto that glowing light with a single-mindedness that helped her keep from screaming. Clara soaked up the glow of the sun, locking onto it with her eyes as her tears dried up and her breathing began to slow. It rose higher in the sky, giving her hope.

They would be coming for her soon. They would get her out.

When she heard the shuffling footsteps behind her, Clara thought, *Thank God,* and she tried to turn around to see Katie. She realized her mistake almost immediately, as the dead thing behind her moaned and fell to its knees, pawing at the helmet on Clara's head.

Clara screamed.

****

Katie woke with a start. Immediately, she knew she had fucked up. She stood on the watchtower and saw a beefy man pounding on the motorcycle helmet on the ground. The creature looked like a gorilla having a temper tantrum.

"No, no, no," she repeated over and over. She grabbed a spear just as women began pouring out of the trailers to see what the noise was. Without thinking, she hopped over the railing of the watchtower. What she really wanted in her hands was one of those guns, but she knew that she couldn't draw any more attention to the compound and still have a chance of rescuing Clara.

She was three feet away when the bulky dead man ripped the helmet from the ground. For a second, Katie thought that the monster had ripped Clara's head clean off, but then she saw cascading brown hair glowing orange in the morning sunshine.

With no time to think, she jammed the spear at the back of the large man's skull. It did nothing but shred a roll of fat on the back of the man's head. He went to his knees, his hands pulling at Clara's hair, oblivious to Katie's efforts to kill him for good.

Katie circled to the front of the dead man as he yanked the hair out of Katie's scalp, along with a sizeable piece of flesh. Panic welled up within her as Clara's blood began to flow from the wound. As the dead man shoved the chunk of flesh into his mouth with one hand, he reached for another handful of hair. Katie gave it everything she had, thrusting the spear through his eye which regarded her as nothing more than an inconvenience, the way families used to look at the telephone when it would ring during dinner. The spear entered his eye, broke through the orbital bone and then sent a shockwave up her arms as it drove through brain and impacted the back of the man's skull. He fell over sideways, one hand still locked in Clara's hair.

Her head was yanked to the side, and she was crying. "Don't worry, I'm going to get you out of here," Katie said, digging at the ground with her bare hands. Blood ran from Clara's scalp wound, it was the size of a fist, and Katie had no idea how they were going to deal with a wound like that.

"Get me outta here!" Clara commander, her eyes wide like a spooked horse.

"Help!" Katie yelled, knowing that any hope she had of extricating Clara quietly was now blown. She drove her hands into the dirt, hoping that the women inside the compound would come to her aid. She dug deep, thankful that the earth had already been dug up once. It was loose enough for her to make some progress with her bare hands.

"There's another one!" Clara sobbed, panic in her voice.

Katie got to her knees and pulled the spear from the dead man's skull. She spun around to see a one-legged child crawling upon the ground. Bits of dirt-covered flesh from its missing limb trailed after the monstrosity, and she drove the spear into its skull. Morbidly, she noted how much easier it was to drive a spear through a child's skull.

With that done, she took a good look around her, spotting a handful of the dead moving towards her through the trees. She returned to digging, but kept the spear close to her.

Clara was in tears. Katie tried not to look at her face. She focused on the task at hand. "You're going to be alright," she said trying to comfort her, though she had so far only managed to uncover the top of Clara's shoulders.

"There's too many of them!" Clara wailed.

Katie looked up from where she was digging to find the pregnant women of the compound standing on the watchtower, looking out at them.

"Are you going to help us or just stare at us like a bunch of fucking cows?" Katie yelled at them. The women on the wall did nothing. They were cows.

Then the dead were upon her. She rose from the ground with the spear in her hands, knocking the dead backwards and clubbing them on the side of the skull with the heavy length of wood. There were too many of them for her to risk stabbing them in the head and losing the spear. But she knew she couldn't hold them off for long. Her arms would be exhausted before she ever managed to kill them all.

If this is how I go, then fuck it. She swung the spear again, knocking the nearest of the dead to the ground, but it got right back up again. She fought tooth and nail, striking and pushing the dead back, until her arms were rubber, but still no one from the compound came to help her. She fought like a wild animal, hitting them when she could. The entire time, she kept her own body straddling Clara's exposed head. They would have to get through her to get to Clara.

Those cowardly bitches will pay when I'm done. But she knew she was already done. She knew she was losing this fight. She could barely lift the spear in her hands, and she wished she had brought the gun with her anyway. She imagined how easy it would be to take a step backwards and shoot them all in the head, and then, as if her thought had made it happened, she watched as the head of the ghoul to her right exploded in a shower of crimson gore. She stood there, shocked and uncomprehending.

"Get her out of there!" a voice yelled.

Katie cast her eye at the watchtower for just a second to see a sweat-soaked Joan leaning against the railing, a rifle in her hands.

Immediately, she fell to her knees, and though she was dead tired already, she managed to find some reserves to try and dig Clara out of what could very well be her grave. "You gotta start wiggling," she told the woman as another gunshot rang out.

"I'm trying," she said, her shoulders bunching.

Katie's fingernails chipped and broke as she plunged her hands into the dirt, clawing it upwards and out of the hole. More gunshots rang out, and Katie knew that she was fighting a losing battle. The gun wouldn't hold them off forever. Sooner or later there would be too many of the dead upon them, and then it wouldn't matter; they would both be dead.

She dug and she clawed, and then a miracle happened; Clara was able to free one of her arms.

"Keep wiggling," Katie said. "Keep trying to get yourself out of there."

Together they worked, Katie digging and Clara trying to break herself free. Groans echoed through the forest all about them, and the wide, panicked eyes on Clara's face told her that the dead were getting closer. When they finally had Clara's torso free, Katie said, "Hold on. I'm going to try and pull you out." She hopped to her feet and circled behind Clara. "Give me your hands."

Clara raised her hands above her, and Katie grasped them. She pulled and pulled, yelling through the exertion she was putting on her already broken body. "Come on!" she yelled through gritted teeth as another clap of thunder split the morning air.

"Look out!" a voice yelled. She didn't know if it was Joan or one of the others, and she didn't have the time to figure it out. From behind, cold hands grabbed her around the torso. There was another thunder crack, and then she felt fire in her shoulder. She screamed in pain, falling to the ground. *At least that thing isn't touching me anymore.*

"Get her! Help her!" a voice yelled as Katie's blood spilled down the front of her shirt. Her world tilted and then she was on the ground, fire erupting in her shoulder. She looked at the world sideways, an army of the dead flooding from the trees as Clara used her hands to push against the ground to try and lift herself out of the hole those bastards had buried her in.

She blinked a couple of times, and then she felt a couple of strong hands lift her up off the ground. Katie, now on her feet, tried to go back for Clara, but the hands propelled her backwards, towards the compound away from the woman buried in the ground. She saw more women rush past her, and she caught a glimpse of Joan standing above her on the watchtower, lit by the morning sun, the rifle in her hands and a grave look on her face. Her hair blew in the morning wind, and she looked like one of those action heroes in the movies her husband and son used to love watching.

Then she was through the gate, and they dumped her on the ground. She watched as the red stain on her shirt grew bigger and bigger. The pain wasn't there yet. She didn't know if that was a good thing or not.

"Did they get Clara?" she managed to ask before everything went dark.

****

Joan had her work cut out for her. Katie had a gunshot wound and Clara was dehydrated and bleeding profusely from her scalp. She could see her skull where the dead man had ripped off a chunk of skin. It sent chills up her spine every time she saw it.

The first order of business was to stop the bleeding of Katie. She lay on a blanket they had spread on the ground, blood jetting from the wound. The gunshot wound was the only way Joan could have saved her. When she saw the dead woman clamp her hands around Katie, she had been left with two options, shoot or let her get bitten. She had taken the shot. Had she saved her life or killed her? She didn't know yet.

356

There was something else on her mind as Katie drifted in and out of consciousness. The bullet. It had gone through a dead woman's head and then into Katie's shoulder. Was there enough infectious material on the bullet to turn Katie? She could worry about that later though. If she didn't manage to stop the bleeding, it was a moot point.

With help from Theresa and the other women of the compound, she was able to staunch the flow of blood through both the exit wound and the entrance wound. It would need packing, and she had no idea about the state of the bones underneath.

She turned to Clara. The wound was large, and it was going to be impossible to close. It had to be cleaned, but first they need to clean all the crap out of Clara's hair. The amount of screaming she was about to create was sure to bring more of the dead their way.

"I need some people on the walls," she said. "This is about to get loud." The women brought Joan a bucket, and she slowly and carefully washed what was left of Clara's soiled hair, hoping that whatever sort of slime had been in the helmet was not still infectious. She was working with a lot of "ifs" here, and she hoped that she wasn't just prolonging the inevitable.

Clara screamed as they washed her hair, the soap making its way to the ragged edge of her wound. Clara gripped Joan's wrist, squeezing impossibly hard. Once it was clean, it was time for the hard part.

"This is going to hurt," she said to her friend. Clara looked her in the eye and nodded. She was tough as nails, but Joan knew this would be more than most people could handle. She hooked her suture needles through the ends of the wound and then she pulled making the stitches as tight as she could.

Clara kicked and screamed. Joan called Theresa over to hold her still, but it was like fighting a bucking bronco. She was only able to get two stitches in before Clara passed out. She wondered how it hadn't happened before. Her friend was dehydrated, had lost a lot of blood, and experienced more fear and terror in the last day than many of them had experienced in their entire life.

Clara's unconsciousness was a blessing. She was able to pull and kneed the scalp wound securing the raw edges of flesh in place. She could still see a large portion of skull, but it was the best she could do, and all that was left was to wrap it in a clean bandage.

With that done, she turned to Katie. Her skin was pale, and she lay unconscious on the blanket. She double-checked the wound and packed it with more gauze. She couldn't close it up yet. It needed time to heal. Her wound would heal though. She just had to make it through the day.

When she was done, she looked like one of the dead herself. Her clothes were covered in their blood. Her leg hurt, and she realized just how much pain she was in. She had hopped her way to the watchtower, cursing at the passive women who were standing there and watching. Climbing one-legged up the steps had also ruined her back and her shoulders. She felt like she could pass right out herself.

She looked around her and saw the women on top of the trailers, stabbing downward with spears. She wiped an arm across her brow, trying not to get blood on her face. She looked at her two patients, one was a friend and one was not, but she valued them both equally. She hoped she had done enough, but most of all she hoped that neither were infected. They would know in the next day.

Joan reclined in the dirt, too tired and too hurt to make her way back to her trailer. She noticed gray clouds in the sky, and then a drop of rain hit her face.

"Where's Mort?" a voice asked. It was Katie, stirring from her unconsciousness. Her voice was weaker than a wind produced by the buffeting of bee's wings.

"I don't know," she replied, pained that none of them were well enough to go looking for him.

****

He was cold and shaky. He didn't think he could stay in the tree anymore. His energy was low, and he had strained all night to stay in the tree, getting next to no sleep. He heard the gunshots, and he hoped that this would draw away the crowd of dead that huddled underneath the tree. It worked for a couple of them, but there were two that stayed there, looking up at him with their dead eyes.

He tried to stand. His muscles were stiff, but he flexed them as well as he could. Despite his battered ribs and the knotted bruise of his hip, this was the best chance he was going to have. When he had gotten his blood going, he began his descent, which was tough, as he refused to let go of his hammer. He held it in his right hand as he searched out branches that would hold his weight.

As he reached the lowest branch, out of range of the dead, he paused to regain the strength in his arms. He took a couple of deep breaths, and then the rains came.

"I don't know who you guys are, and I'm sorry for what I'm about to do to you, but I can't stay here no more." He spoke to the dead, but they didn't speak back. When he was ready, he jumped from the tree and rolled to his feet. He grunted in pain, but forced himself to get to his feet to meet the first of the dead. He was too tired and too hurt to run. Running would be a last resort, but he knew he could still swing his hammer. The first approached him with its arms out in the classic monster movie pose. He swiped its hands to the side with his free hand and then stepped into hammering range. He swung the hammer hard, popping the creature on the side of the skull. The creature tumbled to the ground.

Then the next was upon him, pawing at his face with clawed hands. He backed up, trying to keep his balance, his hip flaring in pain. The dead man was shorter than him, and he swung overhand, the head of the hammer pounding the top of the skull. It made a pop sound that echoed through the dead man's mouth, but it kept coming. It ripped at his jacket, his trusty military surplus jacket that had been with him since the beginning.

He brought the hammer up under its chin, knocking it backwards. Its jaw slammed shut and two of the teeth shattered, but the dead man didn't notice. Mort cocked his arm back for another swing, and then he let loose. It hit the side of his head with a dull ping, and it fell over on its side. It did not get up again.

Mort's breathing was heavy, and he looked around frantically, ready to fight the next wave of the dead. But there were none. He was free, for now. He moved in the direction of the compound, limping and clutching his ribs with his free hand. At least, he thought it was the direction of the compound. In his flight through the trees, he had become turned around, which was why he hadn't tried to escape earlier when the sun had come up. But then he heard the gunshots through the rain, and he strained his ears to hear where they were coming from.

Mort readied himself for the possibility that what he would find would be a slaughterhouse. He readied himself for the fact that his friends might already be dead. But if that were the case, he would try to make them pay for it. He would die in the process most likely, but he would rather do that than be alone.

For the thousandth time, he wished that his buddy Blake was still alive. He could have killed all those people from the trees. *I shouldn't want to kill people.* But he felt that it was the only way to bring peace to the situation. People had to die so that others might live.

The rain covered the approach of the dead, thousands of raindrops bouncing off of leaves, turning the forest into a symphony of dripping and splatting. He remained relatively dry underneath the forest's canopy, but it seemed that for every twenty feet he went, another of the dead appeared out of nowhere.

He was able to sneak up on them most of the time. They couldn't hear him coming with all of the noise from the rain, and he scored several single-shot kills with his hammer, driving the dead home the way a carpenter would drive home a nail.

Suddenly, the forest opened up, and he found himself looking at a sight that would burn in his memory forevermore. Women wet and dripping, their shirts clinging to their swollen bellies, drove spears downward into the dead. No men were in sight. The bodies lay ten-deep around the trailer compound. Wet rivers of blood trailed their way across the muddy ground outside the circle of trailers. He had come out to the backside of the compound, and his heart lifted for a second upon seeing the women.

It fell as he got closer and realized he didn't recognize any of the women atop the trailers. He ran forward, not caring about himself any longer. He pushed forward until the woman atop the nearest trailer saw him.

"Stay back!" she shouted as he skidded to a stop in the mud around the compound. She brandished her spear at him, and he stood there, out of her range and clueless as to what do next. The dead spotted him and marked him as easier prey than the women atop the trailers. They turned towards Mort.

"Just tell me! Are my friends ok?" he shouted. The woman looked at him. She had a big brown mole on her cheek. It looked like a glob of shit.

She had no sympathy for his situation, and she said, "We're all dead. One way or another." Mort didn't know what to make of that, so he backed up as the dead came closer. He knew that if he stayed, he would die. So he turned around and headed into the woods, alone and frightened. He didn't know where he would go now or what he would do. He thought of the house in the woods, and it seemed like the best option. He circled the compound until he came to the front, then he began looking for his markings.

More than once, as he dodged the dead, he thought of just giving himself up, but he knew that he couldn't. Blake wouldn't want him to. Clara, Katie, Lou, Joan, none of them would want him to give up. Besides, if he died, then the memory of Blake died, and he would cease to exist altogether. He owed the man his life, and he wouldn't throw Blake's gift away.

He carried his old friend in his heart, and it wasn't just himself he was living for anymore. He pushed through the woods, the dead groaning as they pursued him.

Chapter 19: The Deal

Izzy Allen watched them come and go from the roof. The Ken Griffey Jr. building had turned into his own personal ant farm. The Nike campus residents were in a busy state. The lines had hardened once Nike was gone. The soldiers weren't as welcome as they had once been, and everyone knew they were sitting in an untenable situation. He had tried to talk to Diana and see what was going on, but so far, she had rebuffed him at every opportunity.

But now there was this flurry of activity in the Ken Griffey Jr. building. The people moved quickly through the building in pairs or threes, talking furtively with each other.

Eventually, it got to the point where Allen figured he ought to tell Tejada. He stepped back into the security building, pounding down some metal stairs until he was on the top floor. Brown and Gregg looked up at him as he entered the barracks. They had drawn the dubious honor of scrubbing away the carnage that still marred the floor and the bunk beds.

They could clean it all they wanted; Izzy would never sleep there. That was too much bad energy. He had found a nice clean office in which to set up his bedroll.

"Is he in there?" he asked the men.

They nodded at him, and he stepped inside the armory. Tejada stood at a table breaking down and cleaning the supply of weapons that had gone without maintenance for a couple of months. They would still fire as there was nothing wrong with them, but Tejada was having them all stripped down anyway. Allen bet that Tejada had just gotten bored watching his men sit around doing nothing.

Tejada looked up from his work and asked, "Aren't you supposed to be on the roof?"

"Yes, sir, but I thought you might want to know that something is going on in the Griffey building."

"Something like what?" he asked.

"I don't know. The people seem real animated. It just seems like they're up to something.

"Oh, I wouldn't worry about them. It's just a bunch of bees buzzing around cuz their queen left. They'll find a new queen, and then they'll settle down."

"Respectfully, sir, I disagree."

Tejada finished reassembling an assault rifle, and then he set it upon the counter the way a father might set their baby down when they needed a changing. "Alright. I've never had reason not to trust your judgment. Why don't we go and check out what's going on? Grab Brown and Gregg. I'll be there in a second."

Allen stepped into the hallway and told Brown and Gregg the great news. They rose to their feet and tossed their towels and spray bottles on the ground, glad to be freed from the drudgery of cleaning. It was something that every soldier got used to, but no one ever learned to like the mundane responsibilities of being a soldier.

Tejada came out of the armory holding a locked and loaded M4 assault rifle. Allen and the others checked their own weapons, and then without a word or a signal, they followed Tejada out of the barracks. They went down the stairs and out onto the campus.

The people had gathered, and Allen felt his shoulders tense. He hoped this whole situation didn't go sideways. The people looked at them the way one might look at someone who had kidnapped their dog. They weren't happy, and it was obvious on their faces. At the front of the group was Diana. Off to the side, standing like a whipped dog was a bruised and battered man. It was the man with the glasses that had spoken out against Nike.

"Who are you here to kick out now?" Diana asked.

"No one," Tejada said through a tight smile. He held out the rifle as they approached, but he presented it as if it were a gift. "I brought you something."

Diana stepped forward to accept the weapon. "What's this for?" she asked. Her fire all but gone, doused by Tejada's actions. As she reached out for it, Tejada pulled it away.

"I thought you ought to have the means to defend yourselves. Are you the leader now?" Tejada asked.

"I'm the leader for now," Diana said. "What good is one gun going to do when there are hundreds of those things in the buildings and outside the wall?"

"Well, we have plenty of guns to give you, but I'll be damned if I'm going to hand them over to a bunch of untrained, ignorant civilians and get my ass shot off the next time someone sneezes."

"So you're going to keep all the guns?" Diana said sounding unsurprised.

"Now I didn't say that. You ought to be careful about assuming things. You know what they say." Tejada looked at the group of people around Diana and said, "Are you sure this is who you want leading you? She doesn't seem like a very good leader."

Some people murmured, but no one stood up to defend Diana. She looked over her shoulder, suddenly self-conscious about the lack of support. "The guns?" she prompted.

"Oh, yes. The guns. The guns are all yours, but you have to prove you can use them. So I'm proposing a deal." Tejada stopped talking to Diana and spoke to the assembled people. They listened to him like they never would Diana. "The way I see it, you guys have a problem, and we have a problem. For us, we don't want to be here any more than you want us here. But we're low on ammunition, and to survive out there, we're going to need a shitload of it."

Allen winced at the swear words, but if the people of the Nike campus got their panties in a wad over such things, then they had bigger things to worry about.

Tejada continued, "Your problem is that you're all fucking useless, and you got a thousand zombies around you right now at this very moment."

"And your proposal?" Diana prompted, not willing to cede any authority to Tejada.

"My proposal is that we stay here, train you until we feel like you can handle yourselves, and then we'll leave when you're good and ready, taking with us enough ammunition and rifles to get us to our destination. We'll leave the rest for you."

Diana nodded. She turned to the people of the Nike campus and asked, "Does anyone object to this proposal?" No one spoke. "Then it's done." Diana held out her hand to shake Tejada's, but he simply placed the rifle in her hands.

"This is the safety," he said, pointing to the latch on the side of the rifle.

Some people crowded in closer as Tejada went through the functions and different features of the rifle.

In the end, the deal was struck, and the people and the soldiers drifted away. Allen stood on the field, trying to catch Diana's eye, but she still refused to look at him.

The man in the glasses eventually walked up to him, his eyes black and bruised, but he seemed un-cowed. "She's a snake. You guys must know that. She's not any better than her father was," the man said.

"Everyone I trust is in that building behind me," Allen said.

"That's smart. My name is Nathan, by the way."

"I'm Izzy," Allen said holding out his hand.

"Well, nice to meet you," Nathan said, turning to head back inside the building.

"What happened to your face?" Allen asked.

"Oh, this is what happens when you do something that Queen Diana doesn't approve of." Nathan walked off, his head held high.

366

Allen liked the guy. What he didn't like was the thought that Diana would throw a beating a man's way simply because he had spoken up. He shrugged his shoulders, wondering what would happen on the morrow when those people turned out to train under the watchful eye of Tejada and his soldiers?

He smiled as he thought about it. Those people were in for one hell of a surprise. Army training doesn't start out as guns and fistfights. It's a slow build. In all likelihood, Tejada would have them running the perimeter of the campus for hours on end. It would be weeks before they learned anything useful or even touched a weapon.

That was by design though. A good soldier had to be indoctrinated. They didn't need to be broken the way they did it in the old days, but they needed to suffer with their fellow man. They needed to get used to following orders so they could function as a machine rather than as a group of individuals.

One thing was for sure. It was going to be a long time until they were free of this place. He looked westward. Hills and mountains rose up in the distance, and he wanted to be walking there. He wanted out of this death trap where the dead roamed in numbers that they could never hope to defeat. He wanted to make it to the beach, find a woman that looked like Diana, but who wasn't totally fucked up. He wanted to have a life, but first they were going to have to train these people to survive on their own. It was the right thing to do.

They could have left in the middle of the night, taking all the weapons they wanted, but Tejada was too honorable for that. He wasn't going to allow the people of Nike to die, and without someone to teach them how to survive in this world, that's exactly what would happen. Diana might know how to scheme and bully people, but if she ever wanted this place to truly be safe, she was going to have to learn. He just hoped she would learn to be a good

367

leader as well. There was no better example for that than Tejada.

The sky began to turn gray above. He felt a drop of rain on his face, and then he turned to walk inside. They wouldn't be getting out of here until the spring by his estimation. He didn't look forward to a winter fighting off the dead, but it was better than fighting them from behind a wall than in the mountains and the snow. The door clicked shut behind him.

Chapter 20: Interrupted Sleep

Joan sat with Theresa in the trailer that she had shared with first Lou and then Clara. Katie and Clara slept fitfully, but Joan felt that something was wrong. Joan herself was exhausted, her hands cracked and dry from washing them over and over with soap after putting the two survivors back together.

She had shared her fears of infection with Theresa, who despite their rocky beginnings, had shown herself as one of the only women in the compound with any common sense. She wasn't just a breeder. She was smart in the way that a particularly tough street cat might be smart. She would survive no matter what.

Now Joan was exhausted. Her head drooped on her chest. She wanted to keep watch over her two friends, but she was struggling. She had finally come to terms with the fact that Katie was indeed a friend. After all, she had saved them, saved Clara from a death that would have broken her heart. She drifted in and out of consciousness, the day's events catching up to her.

Her eyes closed, and Theresa took the rifle from her hands, letting her sleep.

****

Theresa watched the two forms on the bed. They had tied them down, making sure that they weren't able to get at one another should they awaken as the living dead. The women had lapsed into unconsciousness in the courtyard. They had not stirred even when they had carried them into the trailer. Theresa could see that neither woman was well. Their breathing was heavy and raspy.

Sweat poured from their brows, and they groaned fitfully in their sleep.

She had them all right where she wanted them. She could end this whole charade right now. Theresa turned and aimed the rifle at Joan, centering the barrel on her forehead. *Do it! Just do it!* Her finger tensed on the trigger. But she couldn't do it. She would be stupid if she did. She returned to her watch.

It was only a matter of time now. And as she thought this, one of the shapes on the bed began to stir. Theresa looked at Joan, wondering if she should wake her up. But she couldn't. It would be better for Joan if she didn't have to see this.

She felt a stirring in her belly. It was Chad's baby. None of the other men had wanted anything to do with her, but Chad had believed in his plan of repopulating the world. She didn't mind. She had only been with a couple of men, and most of them when they were drunk. The two weeks when Chad had dutifully attempted to impregnate her had been the best of her life.

Now, here she was without a father for her baby. Maybe she should just kill them all now. As the form on the bed groaned and struggled to release itself from its bonds, she turned the rifle on Joan. It was their fault that they were without men now. Now, they would have to learn to survive on their own, unless someone else showed up at their camp. But that was unlikely. The camp had been chosen for its remoteness. Unless you knew it was there, no one would likely stumble across it.

No, they were on their own, and her baby would need a doctor if it were to survive. It would also need killers. The other women in the compound were scared, meek things, with the exception of Dez, but Theresa didn't fully trust her. She didn't trust the woman that had killed her baby's daddy. These other women had survived among the dead. They had uses.

She came to a decision, and she aimed the rifle at the form on the bed. She pulled the trigger, and blood splattered the back of the trailer.

Joan jumped at the sound of the gunshot. By the weak lantern light, she saw what Theresa had done. Her hand came up to her mouth, and all she could think to say was, "Oh God," over and over as if the words could bring back the dead.

Theresa put a comforting hand on her shoulder. "It's ok," she said. "I'll help you bury her in the morning." She handed Joan the rifle and began untying the corpse on the bed. Theresa dragged the corpse through the trailer by its feet, kicking open the flimsy metal door to the trailer.

"What happened?" a woman asked from outside.

"One of 'em turned," she said sadly. "Help me with the body."

As they exited, the metal door slammed shut, and Joan shook with sadness.

In the night, the dead outside groaned, reinvigorated by the sound of the gunshot.

"Oh, God. Oh, God. Oh, God..."

A Word From Jacy

Thank you for reading This Rotten World: No More Heroes. If you've made it this far, I'm guessing you enjoyed the ride. Please leave an honest review for the book, as it's the best way to help indie authors like myself!

The next story, WINTER OF BLOOD, will be the fourth book in the series, and it will be followed by one more installment called CHOKING ON THE ASHES. In WINTER OF BLOOD, our survivors must contend with the living as well as the dead. In addition, as winter closes in, supplies begin to dwindle, and our survivors must battle mother nature herself. It is available now.

In addition, check out my other apocalyptic novel, THE DROP. It's about a boy band that kills the world with their music. Told through a combination of news articles, journal entries, and video transcripts, the apocalypse in The Drop is every bit as brutal and frightening as This Rotten World. Enjoy!

The Drop is available on Amazon!

Get Free Stuff from Jacy Morris

Building a relationship with my readers is super important to me. Please join my newsletter for information on new books and deals plus all this free content:

1. A free copy of This Rotten World: Part One.

2. A free copy of The Lady That Stayed, a horror novella inspired by real life.

3. A free copy of The Pied Piper of Hamelin, a twisted fairy tale like nothing you've ever seen before.

You can get your content for free, by signing up for my newsletter at jacymorris.com

Also By Jacy Morris

In the This Rotten World Series

This Rotten World

A sickness runs rampant through the world. In Portland, Oregon it is no different. As the night takes hold, eight men and women bear witness to the horror of a zombie outbreak. This Rotten World is the zombie novel that horror fans have been waiting for. Where other zombie works skip over the best part of a zombie outbreak, This Rotten World revels in it the downfall of humanity, dragging you through the beginnings of society's death, kicking and screaming.

Available on Amazon in ebook, paperback, and audiobook!

This Rotten World: Let It Burn

It didn't take long for Portland, Oregon to fall. Amid a decaying and crumbling city, a group of survivors hides amid the smoke and the fire. They need to get out of the city... which is easier said than done with thousands of zombies blocking the path. Witness the terrifying flight of these survivors as they leave the city behind and Let It Burn.

Available on Amazon in ebook, paperback, and audiobook!

This Rotten World: No More Heroes

With the smoking ruins of Portland behind them, our survivors find that they have a new enemy to contend with... other survivors. With the dead hounding them at every step and humanity struggling to hold onto its civility, the survivors face their greatest challenge yet. At the end of this battle, there will be No More Heroes.

Available on Amazon in ebook, paperback, and audiobook!

In the Enemies of Our Ancestors Series

The Enemies of Our Ancestors

In the mountains of the Southwest, in the time before the continents were known, the future of the entire world rested upon the shoulders of a boy prophet whose abduction would threaten to break the world. As a youth, Kochen witnessed the death of his father at the hands of a gruesome spirit that stalked his village's farmlands. From that moment forth, he became a ward of the priests of the village in the cliffs. As he grew, he would begin to experience horrific visions, gifts from the spirits, that all of the other priests dismissed. When the ancient enemies of the Cliff People raid the village and steal Kochen away, they set in motion world-changing events, which threaten to break the shackles that bind the spirits to the earth. A group of hunters are sent to bring Kochen back to his rightful place. As Kochen's power grows, so too does the power of the spirits, and with the help of an ancient seer and his hunter allies, he seeks to restore balance to the world as it falls into brutal madness.

Available on Amazon in ebook, paperback, and audiobook!

The Enemies of Our Ancestors: The Cult of the Skull

With the world balanced after the tragedies of the year before, two tribes attempt to come together and form a whole. But as an ancient foe from the past reappears and a new threat from the south snakes its way to them, the Stick People and the Cliff People must do more than put their differences aside... they must come together to survive. As fantastic as it is violent, The Cult of the Skull picks up right where The Enemies of Our Ancestors left off.

Available on Amazon in ebook and paperback!

Standalone Novels

The Drop

How many hearts can a song touch? How many ears can it reach? How many people can it kill? When popular boy band Whoa-Town releases their latest album, no one thinks anything of it. They certainly don't think that the world will be changed forever. After an apocalyptic disease sweeps the world, it becomes clear that the music of this seemingly innocuous boy band had something to do with it, but how? Katherine Maddox, her life irrevocably changed by a disease dubbed The Drop, sets out to find out how and why, to prevent something like The Drop from ever happening again.

Available on Amazon in ebook, paperback, and audiobook!

The Abbey

In the desolate mountains of Scotland, there is an abbey that time has forgotten. Its buildings have crumbled, and the monks that once lived there, guarding the abbey's secret, are long dead. When the journal of a crazed monk is discovered, so is the secret of Inchorgrath Abbey. There are tunnels underneath the abbey and in them resides a secret long forgotten. Together with a group of mercenaries, her would-be boyfriend, and her cutthroat professor, Lasha Arkeketa will travel across the world to uncover the secret of The Abbey.

Available on Amazon in ebook, paperback, and audiobook!

The Pied Piper of Hamelin

A sickness has come to the village of Hamelin. Born on the backs of rats, a plague begins to spread. As the town rips itself apart, a stranger appears to offer them salvation. But when the citizens of the town fail to hold up their end of the bargain, the stranger returns and exacts a toll that is still spoken of to this day. That toll? The town's entire population of children. This is the legend of the Pied Piper. It is no fairy tale. It is a nightmare. Are you prepared to hear his song?

Available on Amazon in ebook, paperback, and audiobook!

Killing the Cult

At any one time, there are 4,000 cults operating within the United States. In Logansport, Indiana, one cult is growing. When The Benevolent recruit Matt Rust's estranged daughter, he journeys to their compound to free her, one way or another. Unfortunately, for Matt Rust, his checkered past threatens to derail his rescue mission. When word gets out that Rust has reemerged after spending the last decade in the witness protection program, drug tzar Emilio Cartagena sends his best men after Rust. Will he be able to save his daughter before Cartagena's men arrive? Find out as Matt Rust tries Killing the Cult.

Available on Amazon in ebook and paperback!

The Lady That Stayed

Land has a price. It's always been that way. When J.S. Stensrud and his wife Dotty buy a piece of land on the Oregon coast known as the Spit, they come to know that price. As Stensrud tries to build a legacy on his island amid the background of the Great Depression, he is visited by a Native American woman who helps him learn the bloody price of land in the most painful way possible.

Available on Amazon in ebook, paperback, and audiobook!

An Unorthodox Cure

Cancer will touch all of our lives at one point or another. It may affect someone you know, someone you respect, or even someone you love. In the case of the Cutters, it has systematically invaded every cell of their daughter's body. When the doctors admit there is nothing they can do, the Cutters bring their daughter home and prepare to wait for the inevitable. Just as they accept defeat, a mysterious doctor appears at their door, offering a miraculous cure and kindling hope in their hearts. The only catch? The Cutters have to decide what is more important, their daughter's life or her soul.

Available on Amazon in ebook and paperback!

Be sure to check out

THE

ENEMIES OF

OUR

ANCESTORS

By

Jacy Morris

Here is a sneak preview:

THE ENEMIES OF OUR ANCESTORS

Prologue: The Night Whispers

Kochen walked through the night, his bare feet testing for sharp rocks before he put his full weight on the ground. In this way, he moved through the black-chilled air. Wind blew through his obsidian hair, and his dusky brown skin raised gooseflesh in response. Kochen looked up and saw the outline of the canyon's rim against the night sky, the faint hint of blackness against a dark blue. More stars than he could count looked down at him. It was the time of the Lynx moon, the time of the bobcat. Its full, round face rose into the sky, bringing with it the onset of spring. He could smell the change in the air. Though he was only six-winters-old, in a world where seasons meant everything, he had learned the signs of change at a young age.

He walked through the empty farmland, away from the mud and stone houses that his ancestors had carved and molded into the cliff, his toes sinking into the loose brown soil. Kochen lived on the lowest terrace of the village nestled among the cliffs, so he needed no torch to descend down the variety of stone ladders that led from the highest level to the rough stone ground. He had simply walked out of his family's small room where his mother and father slumbered, inched down a single, thirty-rung ladder, and he was on the ground.

The farm soil had already been broken up for the spring. The soil felt cool and soft against his toes as he plodded through the loose farmland, avoiding the budding shoots of corn. He stopped to relieve himself, pulling his

383

loincloth to the side. His urine steamed in the night as it pattered to the ground, impossibly loud.

Behind him, he heard someone doing the same. He turned to look and saw his father.

"What are you doing out here?"

"No, what are you doing out here?" his father shot back.

Kochen had been told over and over to not wander far from their house to relieve himself in the night. No one had ever explained why; they just said not to.

"I had to go. Besides, it's good for the crops." Kochen finished up his work and let his loincloth fall back into place. His father did the same. Kochen walked in his direction, and his father cuffed him on the back of the head.

"That is for thinking you know it all. Get your skinny rear-end back into the house."

Kochen ran in the night, lest his father's ire turn into more than just a simple cuff. He was usually slow to anger, but tonight he seemed different.

"Next time, you go from the ledge like everyone else."

Kochen heard the words, but dared not give a response on the odd chance that it would be seen as disrespectful. As Kochen put his first, rough hand on the ladder, he heard a noise, a low rumbling. It was not a noise he had ever heard before. It echoed through the canyon and across the farmland. A gust of wind blew the hair on his head backwards as he turned around to see what was making the noise.

In the faint light of the moon, he could see the blue shine of his father's skin running towards him. The tilled farmland was darker in the night than the untilled earth of the canyon floor, and when his father reached the edge of it, the earth opened up. A shape emerged, maggot-white, and twice as tall as his father. At first it seemed like a massive white worm, erupting from the ground, but then he noticed the arms Twisted and corded with segmented veins, the creature's arms were all twisted muscle and bone. In place of hands, the shape had sharp spikes, hooked like the backwards limbs of a praying mantis, and its eyes were black bulbs in a misshapen skull that was covered in skin the color of fresh-washed mushrooms.

Before he could even scream a warning to his father, the creature had shoved a claw through his father's middle, the other claw wrapping around his throat. Kochen's sob caught in his own throat, as his father descended into the ground in the embrace of the creature. The soil parted for him, and it was as if he had sunk into the river instead of the farmland of the village.

Kochen climbed the ladder, and reached the edge of the limestone landing. He sat on the edge, his feet safely on stone, watching and waiting for his father's hand to appear from the ground. It was a good harvest that year.

Be sure to check out

KILLING
THE
CULT

By Jacy Morris

Here is a sneak preview:

KILLING THE CULT

Chapter 1: A Letter in the Mail

It was the letter that started it all. It was the proverbial snowball that turned into an avalanche. Matt discovered the letter in his mailbox one sun-drenched afternoon after finishing his daily three-mile jog. At first, he had been ecstatic; the letter was from his daughter, Cleo, whom he hadn't heard from in ten years. He sat on the couch with a brass letter opener, his hand shaking with anticipation. The letter opener was his wife's. It was a gaudy piece, not the type of thing he would have bought himself. The handle was shaped like an eagle feather with the blade in the shape of a claw. She hadn't wanted it when they got the divorce, but not because it was ugly and stupid. She hadn't wanted anything. She could still hear her saying, "You can have it all, Matt. I don't want a single item that will remind me of you. I just want to pretend like we never even met." He thought it was a stupid sentiment. After all, she already had one thing that would always remind her of him... their daughter.

But that's the way things were. That part of his life had gone dark, the light snuffed out the moment they drove away with only their clothes and personal items in the car. So now, here Matt sat, a letter from his daughter in his hands... the first communication from his daughter in ten years. He had dreamed of this moment so often over the years that he couldn't believe it was finally here. He hesitated, the blade of the letter opener pressed against the plain white paper of the envelope. *Bad news or good news?* he wondered. Maybe his wife was dead. Maybe his daughter wanted him to be a part of her life again. Maybe he was forgiven for the past. The idea made him shake, and his ears and face flushed with warm blood simply from allowing himself to hope for such a possibility. He knew his fantasies were pathetic. Ten years was a long time, certainly long enough for a wife and a daughter to forget about a man like him. It was probably just a request for money.

He rose from his recliner, leaving the envelope and the letter opener on the coffee table. He didn't want to open the letter, and he couldn't, not yet. Matt walked to the kitchen to grab a beer instead. He tried not to look at the piles of dirty dishes and the empty Chinese takeout boxes on the counter, but the buzz of flies told him these things were there whether he looked at them or not.

He yanked the refrigerator door open and pulled out a bottle of Budweiser. He popped the bottle cap off and threw it into the open garbage can. It bounced off the pile of garbage and clanked onto the floor. Rejected, just as he had been once. Matt just left it there. That's all it really deserved.

Through the back window of his kitchen, he could see the backyard, a wild and unkempt place that had once been a beautiful playground where beautiful memories were created. He looked at the old rusted swing set and remembered when it had been brand new, right after the move. He saw his daughter, tiny, so fragile, flying into the air and then back down again, in a semi-circle of happiness as he put his hand in her back and pushed her forward for another ride to the moon. "To the moon, Daddy! To the moon!" That's what she always squealed whenever he had pushed her on the swing. Maybe that's what the letter was. Maybe Cleo had become an astronaut.

Matt took a sip of his beer, enjoying its bitterness. It paired well with the bitterness of his old memories. He stood in the kitchen, drinking and letting his regrets wash over him. He killed the beer in fifteen minutes and then set the empty bottle down on the counter next to the others. It was only right. Empty bottles belonged together.

He walked back into the living room filled with purpose. Without giving himself time to second guess, he grabbed the letter opener, jammed it under the flap, and ripped open the envelope. He pulled the letter free and unfolded a single yellow page. The handwriting was small, neat, just as her mother's had been.

He read through the letter once, and then he read it again, looking at every word as if some sort of code were hidden among the words. But there was no code. It was what it was. He sat down in his recliner and leaned his head back, a thousand thoughts running through his head. *What the hell had happened? How could this be?*

Matt picked the letter up again, hoping that he had experienced some sort of temporary brain embolism or stroke, and that this time, the words in the letter would make more sense.

Dear Dad,

I know that's it's been a long time since we talked, and I hope that this letter finds you well. I've gone through some hard times recently, stuff that I won't bore you with, but know that some of those hard times were because you weren't around. I used to be angry with you. I used to be angry that you didn't fight harder for me when you and Mom split. But I know now that it took both of you to rip my life apart.

It wasn't easy for me growing up without a father, especially since you were so great when you were there. But I want you to know that I've gotten over it. I've gotten over it all. I'm in a good place now, a happy place.

The reason you're receiving this letter is because my relationship with you, and with Mom, has prevented me from attaining my bliss... and I want that. I want it so bad.

That's why I sent you this letter. I'm not doing it to make you feel bad, and if you do, please don't. Life's too short to feel anger or hurt. I sent you this letter so that I might close the wound of my past, so that I might better be able to enjoy the present.

This may all seem weird to you, but believe me, the weirdest thing out there isn't me... it's the world. I want you to be happy. I believe that a great calamity is coming, a judgment that will change the face of the world as we know it. Only those that have truly enjoyed life will be spared, so please, Dad, if you do one thing for me, live your life to the fullest, and know that I forgive you, and in my heart, I have found the love for you that was hidden for so long.

Yours truly,
Cleo

Matt read the letter again for the fifth time. He set it on the end table and looked at his dingy living room. The parts of the room that he didn't use were covered in a layer of dust. Old newspapers were stacked on the coffee table even though he had cancelled his subscription six months ago when they had streamlined the format. More empty bottles were stashed around the house, and the floor was so dirty that he doubted he could ever get it clean.

It was the living room of an old forgotten man, but he was only 42, still capable of outrunning 90% of the population. He hadn't slowed a bit physically, but in his mind and in his heart, he had been dead ever since the divorce.

The letter... that damned letter. Something was wrong. It sounded nothing like the little girl he knew, and immediately, he blamed Naomi.

His first instinct was to blame his wife, to say, "This is what happens when you raise your child in such a permissive manner." But Naomi had never been the problem. He had always been the problem. His daughter was twenty now, and she was old enough to think for herself. When life had taken off the training wheels, she had careened into something that he didn't particularly care for, and that was his fault, his alone. He knew it. Cleo had said as much in her letter.

Matt picked up the envelope and looked at it. There was no return address, nor did he expect there to be. The postmark read, "Logansport, IN."

He stood up and walked to the bathroom. It was time to shave.

Be Sure to Check out:

The Abbey

By Jacy Morris

Here is a sneak preview:

THE ABBEY

PROLOGUE

He would make him scream. So far they had all screamed, their unused voices quaking and cracking with pain that was made even worse by the fact that they were breaking their vows to their Lord, their sole reason for existence. Shattering their vows was their last act on earth, and then they were gone. Now there was only one left. A lone monk had taken flight into the abbey's lower regions, a labyrinthine winding of corridors and catacombs lined with the boxed up remains of the dead and their trinkets.

Brenley Denman's boots clanked off of the rough-hewn, blue stone as he trounced through the abbey's crypts, following the whiff of smoke from the monk's torch and the echo of his harried footsteps. His men were spread out through the underworks, funneling the monk ahead of them, driving him the way hounds drove a fox. The monk would lead them to his den, and then the prize would be theirs. And then the world.

He held his torch up high, watching the flames glimmer off of golden urns and silver swords, ancient relics of a nobility that had long since gone extinct, their glory only known by faded etchings in marble sarcophagi, the remaining glint of their once-prized possessions, and the spiders who built their webs in the darkness. Once they were done with the monk, they would take anything that glittered, but first they needed the talisman, the fabled bauble that resided at the bottom of the mountain the abbey was built on.

Throughout the land, legends of the talisman had been told for decades around hearthfires and inns throughout the isles. Then the tellers had begun to vanish, until the talisman of Inchorgrath and its stories had all but been forgotten. But Denman knew. He remembered the stories his father had told him while they sat around the fire of their stone house, built less than ten yards from the cemetery. His father's knuckles were cracked and dried from hours in the elements digging graves and rifling pockets when no one was looking. He knew secrets when he saw them. His father had first heard the story from the old Celts, the remains of the land's indigenous population, reduced to poverty and begging in the streets. His father said the old Celts' stories were two-thirds bullshit and one-third truth. They told of a relic, a key to the Celts' uprising and reclamation of the land, buried in the deepest part of the tallest mountain on the Isles. Of course, they spoke of regeneration and the return of Gods among men as well, but the relic... that was the important part. That was the part that was worth money. And now, he was here, with his men, ready to make his fortune.

He heard shouts, but it was impossible to tell where they were coming from. Sound echoed and bounced off of the blue, quartzite stone blocks, warping reality. He chose the corridor to his right, quickening his pace, his long legs eating up the distance. His men knew not to start without him, but you never knew when a monk would lash out, going against their discipline and training and earning a sword through the throat for their duplicity. That would be unacceptable to Denman. The monk must scream before he died.

His breathing quickened along with his pace, and he could feel the warmth of anticipation spread through his limbs as his breath puffed into the cold crypt air. Miles... they had come miles through these crypts, twisting and turning, burrowing into the secret heart of the earth, chasing the last monk who skittered through the hallways like a spider. The other monks had all known the secret of the abbey, the power it harbored, the relic it hid in its bowels. To a man, they had sat on their knees, their robes collecting condensation in the green grass of the morning, refusing to divulge the abbey's mysteries.

They had died, twisted, mangled and beaten. But still, all he could pull from them were the screams, musical expulsions of the throat that he ended with a smile as he dragged the razor-fine edge of his knife across their throats. Their blood had bubbled out, vivid against the morning sun, to splash on the grass.

When there was only one left, they had let him go. The youngest monk in the abbey, grown to manhood, but still soft about the face, his intelligent eyes filled with horror, stood and ran, his robe stained with the pooled blood of the monks that had died to his left and right. He was like one of the homing pigeons they used in the lowlands, leading them to home... to the relic. They had chased him, hooting and hollering the whole way, their voices and taunts driving the monk before them like a fox. The chase would end at his burrow; it always did.

Ahead, he heard laughing, and with that Denman knew that the chase was at an end. He rounded one last corner to see the monk being worked over by his men, savage pieces of stupidity who were good for two things, lifting heavy objects and killing people. Denman waved his hand and they let the suffering monk go. The monk sagged to the ground, his head bent over, his eyes leaking tears. He sobbed in silence.

Denman stood in the secret of the crypt, a room at the heart of the mountain, the place where legends hid. How deep had they gone? At first there had been stairs, but then they had reached a deeper part of the crypt where the corridors twisted and turned, the floor pitched ever downward. Time and distance had lost all meaning in the breast of the world. How long had it taken them to carve this place, the monks working in silence to protect their treasure? Hundreds of years? A thousand?

The room was simple and small, as the order's aesthetics demanded, filled by Denman and the nine men that he had brought to take the abbey's secrets. Wait, one was missing. He looked at his men, brutal pieces of humanity, covered in dirt, mud and blood. The boy wasn't there. Denman shrugged. He would find his way down eventually.

The walls of the room were blue-gray, stone blocks stacked one on top of the other without the benefit of mortar, the weight of the mountain providing the only glue that was needed. The only other features of the room were an alcove with two thick, tallow candles in cheap tin holders and an ancient oak table.

The smoke from his men's torches hung in the air, creating a stinging miasma that stung his eyes. Brenley Denman squatted next to the monk and used his weathered hand to raise the monk's head by his chin. He looked into the monk's eyes, and instead of the fear that he expected to see, there was something else.

"What is this? Defiance?" he asked, amused by the monk's bravado. Denman stood and kicked the monk in the mouth with his boot, a shit-covered piece of leather that was harder than his heart; teeth and blood decorated the stones.

"Where is it?" he asked the monk. There was no answer. Denman had expected none. Say what you will about the Lord's terrestrial servants, but they were loyal... which made everything more difficult... more exhilarating. Denman was a man that loved a challenge.

He handed his torch to one of his men, a broken-faced simpleton whose only gifts were strength and the ability to do what he was told. Denman knew that he would need both hands to make the monk sing his secrets.

400

"Hand me the Tearmaker," he said to another of his men. Radan, built like a rat with stubby arms and powerful legs, reached to his belt and produced a knife, skinny and flexible, designed not so much for murder as it was for removing savory meat from skin and fat. It made excellent work of fish, and it would most likely prove delightfully deft at making a tight-lipped monk break his vows.

As he reached out to take the proffered knife from his man, the monk scrambled to his feet and dove for the alcove. Before they could stop him, the monk grasped both of the candle sticks and yanked on them. The candlesticks rose into the air. Rusted, metal chains were affixed to their bases, and they clanked against the surrounding stone of the alcove as the monk pulled on them.

The distant sound of stones grinding upon stones reverberated throughout the crypt. Somewhere, something was moving. Denman glared at the monk. The robed figure dropped the candlesticks and turned to face them. With his head cast downward, he reached into the folds of his robe and produced a rosary. He folded his hands and began to pray, beads moving through his fingers, his lips moving without making sound.

The crypt shook as an unseen weight clattered through the halls of the crypt. Dust fell from the ceiling, hanging in the air, buoyed upwards by the tumbling smoke of their torches.

"What have you done?" Denman asked.

The monk did not respond. Instead, he reached into the hanging sleeve of one of his robes and produced a small stone thimble, roughly-made and ancient. It was shiny and black, the type of black that seemed to steal the light from the room. The monk put it up to his mouth, hesitated for a second and then swallowed it, grimacing in pain as the object slid down his throat.

In the hallway behind them, the grinding had stopped. The crypt was silent, but for the guttering of the

401

torches and their own breathing. "Go see what happened," he said to the oaf and the rat. The other men followed them, leaving Denman alone with the monk and his unceasing, silent supplications to the Lord above.

Denman forced the monk onto the oak table. He offered little resistance. With Tearmaker in his hand, Denman began to carve the skin lovingly off of the monk's fingers. First, he carved a circle around the man's fingers, then a line. With the edge of his knife, he prodded a corner of the skin up, and then, grasping tightly, he ripped the skin away from the muscle and bone, dropping the wet flesh onto the ground. He did this to each finger, one by one. Sweat stood out on Denman's brow, and the monk had yet to scream. He hadn't so much as gasped or hissed in pain. He was turning out to be more work than he was worth. Except for the blood pulsing from his skinned fingers, he appeared to be asleep, his eyes softly closed.

"Where is it, you bastard?" There was no response but for the bleeding.

Denman pulled the monk's robe up around his waist. It was a quick jump, but he was eager to be done with the man on the table. Usually, he would take his time with a challenge like the monk, savoring the sensation of skin ripping from muscle and bone, but he could feel the weight of the mountain about him, its walls shrinking with every minute. Sweat covered his body, and the monk's calm demeanor was unnerving.

Radan rounded the corner at a run, his body dripping with sweat and panic on his face. He skidded to a stop, his boots grinding dust into the blue stones. "We're sealed in here," he said.

Denman looked at the monk lying on the table. His hand gripped Tearmaker tight. "What have you done?" The monk lay there, his eyes closed, a look of peace on his face. "What have you done!" he screamed, jabbing the knife into the monk's ribs. Then Denman saw the monk's hands.

Where before his index and pointer finger had been reduced to skinless chunks of muscle and bone dripping blood on the table, there was now skin. "Impossible," Denman whispered.

The monk's eyes snapped open, and finally, Denman got the scream that he had been waiting for.

ABOUT THE AUTHOR

Jacy Morris is a Native American author who has brought to life zombies, cults, demons, and spirits. You can learn more about him at the following:

Website: **http://jacymorris.com**

Email: **jacy@jacymorris.com**

Facebook: Do a search for Jacy Morris Author

Twitter: https://twitter.com/Vocabulariast

If you don't feel like connecting, at least do me a solid and leave an honest review. It's the best way to support me in the long run. I'd appreciate it.

Lightning Source UK Ltd.
Milton Keynes UK
UKHW020836151220
375245UK00004B/656